Things happen when you travel...

Gareth Jones

SEMI-DETACHED

ISBN 978-184426-831-3

First published 2010 by

FASTPRINT PUBLISHING

Peterborough, England.

Printed in England by

www.printondemand-worldwide.com

Dedicated to my Mum and Dad

Thanks for your continued support in everything that I do. I told you I would get this book finished; just promise me you won't bloody read it!

Acknowledgements

Firstly I would like to thank my Grandma for making this trip possible and all the weird and wonderful people I met along the way who made it such a memorable journey.

For all his advice and insightful comments a big thanks to Tom Dean whose early encouragement was vital in developing the original diary.

For her continued support I would like to thank Natalie Karim who read many drafts and helped me to keep my focus and kindly let me use her laptop.

Finally a big thank you to Claire Murray and Adam Costello for designing all the artwork and accepting lava lamps as payment, they are in the post...

'A man travels the world in search of what he needs and returns home to find it'

George Moore (1873 – 1958)

Author's foreword

There are no great achievements or self-sacrifices in this diary. It is about friendship, having fun and pushing life's boundaries in an environment of intense freedom.

Introduction

So there I was sat in a Bolivian prison cell being told how the system works by Jacques. He had been an inmate of La Paz's San Pedro prison for five years, arrested at the age of twenty-two for drug smuggling. He was a year older than myself but looked twice his age. I could tell prison life was tough.

Jacques was six foot and scrawny with scruffy blonde hair. He had grown up in the heart of Paris, a place that he could now only see in his dreams. He stood in front of Mark and I wearing dirty blue jeans and a tatty dark green shirt.

Being new to the prison he could see that both of us were nervous and not at all at ease with our new surroundings. Sitting in a Bolivian prison was off the beaten narrative of the trip we had both envisaged when at home in northern England. He motioned for us both to sit down on the bed in his cell before asking if either of us would like a drink;

'Can I get you both a drink? Coca-Cola, Sprite, water? Anything you want,' he offered.

'Sprite please,' I nervously responded.

'Same here,' followed Mark.

Jacques opened the door of his cell and yelled to someone at the bottom of the stairs.

Jacques' cell was situated at the top of a tight staircase in the far left corner of the main court yard that minutes earlier we had come through. He looked at us both with a stern face and said;

'This prison is very dangerous. You need to keep safe, they think you are American Gringo!' he warned us.

'Who are they?' Mark asked.

'The Bolivian prisoners that stared as you came through the gates. They do not like Americans,' explained Jacques.

'What's the problem with Americans?' I was eager to hear his response.

'Because they are bastards!' he barked.

I wanted to ask him why but didn't. Jacques had an unsettling look in his eye and it felt like his mood could change. I just nodded politely and agreed.

The awkward tension in the air broke as someone wrapped a fleshy fist against the heavy wooden cell door,

'Jacques it is me, I have your drinks,' came a soft Spanish voice.

'Come in the door is open,' ordered Jacques.

The door creaked open on its rotten brackets and in walked a small Bolivian woman with black hair in a bob and caramel skin. She smiled warmly at Mark and I as she placed two bottles of ice cold Sprite onto Jacques' small bedside table.

Jacques grabbed hold of the woman, who giggled. He then introduced her,

'This is my wife Maria, she is pregnant with my child.'

Before entering the prison I had expected the worse. I was expecting the conditions to resemble those of the Turkish prison in Oliver Stone's Midnight Express. Thankfully they were not. Jacques' cell was closer in prison terms to the Orient Express; he had everything he could ask for apart from his freedom.

I scanned his cell and was amazed to see that at the bottom of his bed he had a twenty-six inch television. On the far wall was a black shelf full of books and stacks of CDs. Underneath the shelf on the chipped concrete floor sat a CD player and another tower of music discs.

In the right corner he had a small kitchenette consisting of a small gas stove and sink. I sat on his raised bed looking towards a blocked off room by the entrance to his cell. Maria could see that I was inquisitive so told me,

'It is the shower.'

Jacques' cell was small but he had everything he needed, including a wife. He lived in better conditions than we had backpacking through Peru. I was amazed that prison could be so comfortable.

We all know that prison puts the 'ow' into shower. If I had to stay here it was something that I would most certainly ask for, Jacques was lucky.

As I finished my inspection of his cell, Jacques turned his back on us. He faced the book shelf and started to flick through his collection of CDs. I couldn't see what exactly he was doing and started thinking that perhaps he wanted to play some music to break the awkward silences that punctured our conversations. I was wrong.

He turned to face us holding out a rolled up Bolivian bank note and casually asked if we would like a line of cocaine. I sat at the end of his bed in shock;

'It will put you at ease my friends, go on try it's the best!'

I couldn't believe the situation we were both in. Sat inside a cell in Bolivia's most notorious jail with an inmate kindly asking if we would like some cocaine to compliment our bottles of Sprite.

Jacques could see that we were both sceptical so before we answered he took the note and snorted two large lines up his right nostril. He pinched the end of his large nose and asked us again;

'Please my friends I insist,' he said.

As we mulled over his offer Maria helped herself to a small line she had racked up;

'Only a small one Jacques, because I am pregnant,' she explained.

Mark and I looked at each other in sheer bewilderment; this was the most unreal tour of our lives.

Mark and I had arrived earlier that day in a taxi. We had been told to find a man called Kenny who acted as an unofficial tour operator for the prison. He was lurking in the shadows of the main square under one of several large trees.

Kenny was a dirty looking, pony-tailed South African man. His skin was red with sun burn and cracked. His teeth were yellow or black; he looked like a pirate suffering from scurvy.

Kenny was leaning casually against a tree eating an orange. The bright juice dribbled through his grey beard as we approached him. We asked if he was indeed Kenny;

'Are you the man they call Kenny?' Mark enquired.

'Yes that is me, what can I do for you?' he asked in a thick South African accent.

'Is there a possibility of getting into the prison?'

'More than a possibility my friends.'

Kenny explained that the prison was divided into two sections. The first was the International side, that he considered the safer option. If we were brave he could get us into the Bolivian section of the jail but, as he sunk his black teeth into an orange, warned,

'It's full of rapists and murderers. You will be given a security guard but there is a chance you may be stabbed or raped.'

Kenny wore a large green bomber jacket with a pair of light grey cotton jogging pants. His eyes were covered with a pair of light brown aviators. I didn't trust him or feel comfortable with what we were doing.

The San Pedro prison tour was illegal. Nonetheless, hundreds, possibly thousands of tourists have taken the tour. It had become increasingly popular and therefore profitable for the prison after the release of Marching Powder by Rusty Young.

The book tells of life inside the prison from the viewpoint of Thomas McFadden, a British drug smuggler who survived his sentence by offering prison tours to foreign tourists. The author also tells of the illegal activities that occur inside the jail including the manufacturing and sale of cocaine. It was something we had to experience.

We were both hungover after a big night out in La Paz and as a result were more anxious than perhaps we could have been. Mark looked into Kenny's sunglasses and said;

'We will go to the International side. Not in the mood for being stabbed today.'

Within minutes we were by the main gate of the prison as Kenny negotiated with one of the guards to let us into the prison. We were taken into a concrete room with no windows where we were asked to hand over our passports.

I felt uneasy entering through the huge iron gates of the prison. Prisoners hung against walls and leisurely dangled their arms through the bars like monkeys at the zoo, trying to catch a glimpse of us.

We stood looking around a large courtyard as people looked and then continued with what they were doing. My first impression as Jacques explained that he would be our tour guide was that this looked nothing like a prison.

There were children playing, market stalls, restaurants and hairdressers. The main area of the prison had the feel of a small village but I could still not relax as the sun bore down on us, it was still a prison and I knew the mood could quickly change.

The shared courtyard was covered with plastic Coca-Cola tables and chairs. Coca-Cola really do get everywhere. Inmates sat around, seemingly without a care in the world, playing dominos and enjoying the sun.

I scanned the area and noticed a basketball hoop and a concrete football pitch. There were no guards, no uniforms and no metal bars apart from those at the entrance. This was not at all what I expected a Bolivian prison to look like.

We followed Jacques up to his cell and asked him questions about the prison and how it was run.

He told us the prison was run by money with inmates having to pay rent for a cell. It was simple; if you didn't have money, you didn't get a cell.

Jacques had to pay $1500 boliviano a month for his room. He did the tours to make money. Others worked inside the jail, selling groceries and working on the food stalls. Others worked as hairdressers, laundry staff, carpenters, shoe-shine boys, anything to survive and make some money.

If you had money you could have a relatively comfortable stay at the prison. If you didn't it would be a living nightmare, one that in all likelihood you would not live through. The stained cement walls of a dark, cold crowded cell would be the last thing you would see before dying alone.

Jacques confirmed to us that San Pedro was the place where most of the country's cocaine production takes place. According to Jacques it is made after hours in the poorest of the eight sections of the prison when the guards finish their patrols.

The underground laboratories were in the Bolivian side of San Pedro, located in the myriad of underground tunnels. Access to these darker areas of the prison was prohibited, it was considered too dangerous.

Inside the laboratories the prisoners make a product called base. This is a cheaper form of cocaine, and it is more concentrated. Many of the inmates become addicted to this form of drug as it offers them a temporary escape from reality.

Jacques told us that base was evil; he was only interested in cocaine.

'I have never touched that stuff. It is the product of the devil,' he declared.

I guessed that in his eyes cocaine was just a naughty, misguided schoolboy.

Almost all of the international prisoners serving time at San Pedro had been caught drug trafficking. It was a lucrative business if you were able to get away with it.

The irony of them being in a prison that was financially reliant on its manufacture and distribution was not lost on me. The prisoners, Jacques included, were not being reformed, they were selling drugs to survive in an environment where money mattered.

Jacques painted a picture of freedom. Mark and I sat there thinking that it wouldn't be that bad living there. Jacques' tone changed as he began describing to us how alone he felt, how he missed going to discos, going to the shops, doing what every free law abiding citizen took for granted. It was easy to get lost in the distractions but the cold facts were that it was still a prison and it was still dangerous.

Jacques left us in his room after again offering us a CD case with lines of coke available for us to snort. He had been called to a meeting regarding his release date. Before he left the room he introduced us both to Sebastian, a Dutch gentleman tasked with showing us around the prison.

Sebastian looked like a crazy science teacher. He had a vacant glaze over his eyes, which looked like big muffins. He was less intimidating than Jacques and I immediately liked him.

Sebastian explained that he was also in prison for drug trafficking.

'I'm not a donkey, I'm no fucking mule!' he proclaimed.

He talked like a master technician about what he done and without directly blaming anyone, he told us that he had been double crossed, stabbed in the back. He boasted about his life before prison and was philosophical about his sentence;

'It's life, it's what happens, I will be ok once more,' he told us.

Sebastian was one crazy Dutch bastard. It came as no surprise when he pulled out a small re-sealable bag of cocaine. He helped himself to two lines before ushering us out of the room for our tour of the prison.

We were shown a few cells that contrasted sharply with the luxurious room that Jacques paid for. Many of the prisoners essentially lived in caves with nothing. In the corners of the room lay half-eaten foam beds, I guessed taken by rats and mice for insulation. The conditions were insufferable and made for unpleasant viewing.

Sebastian took us to the sections gym. It was a small blue room with only a work bench and a selection of weights. A huge wardrobe of a man was working out. He stopped at what I guessed was his nine hundredth repetition and stared at Mark and I.

The realisation hit that real people actually lived here in the prison and, temporarily at least, it was their home.

We walked around staring into cells and at the inmates like they were animals at a zoo; I felt guilty and wanted to leave at the earliest opportunity.

While walking through the restaurants and shops Sebastian enjoyed telling us a few of his stories about the prison. I wasn't sure whether they were true but it was entertaining. Unlike Jacques he did not have a wife and you could tell he enjoyed our company.

Sebastian spoke how he walked, in a hurried fashion. He told us of his hopes and dreams for the future which extended past watching the world cup on Jacques' cable TV.

He had the belief that when he was freed from the prison he would open up a hostel in La Paz. It was to be funded with his hidden drug money. I asked him where this hidden fund was but he was not giving it away. I doubted its existence, but wanted it to be true for Sebastian's sake.

Jacques had told us earlier that he was writing a book called Oceans. It was going to be similar to Marching Powder, only he would tell the truth. I guessed that in prison more than anywhere else it was important to have goals. Goals offered hope and hope offered survival.

Before we left Sebastian thanked us for visiting and offered us more cocaine. He told us to stay in touch and to visit anytime. I gave him some money before leaving through the front gates we had entered through two hours earlier.

I wondered what it would be like walking out after fifteen years.

ENGLAND

Leeds

I sat staring at the white walls of my rented apartment as for the fourth day in a row my alarm woke me up at 7:00am. Water splashed down my window; outside it was dark and raining once again.

I got up and, for the fourth day in a row, put on my suit. Only one more day till the weekend I thought as I opened my umbrella and left the flat. I walked down the same road, past the same shops, at the same time as I had done for weeks and weeks.

I had settled into an office job working as a recruitment consultant. The job gave me enough money to live in a city centre flat while affording me a more than decent social life. I had a lot of friends and enjoyed the weekends, but I wasn't happy. I had fallen into a routine and needed a change.

Routine, due to its familiarity, has a way of making your life speed by. I was worried that if I didn't change something I would still be in the same job and the same routine in five or ten years. I sat at my desk hoping for a change, dreaming of an adventure.

I booked the trip upon receiving £3000 from my Grandmother after she had reworked her finances. The lease on my flat was coming to an end and the recession was making life at work insufferable. I took the unexpected windfall as a sign. I needed to break my routine.

It is not every day that you are just given money; it came as a total surprise. My Grandmother routinely wrote me a cheque for £5 every birthday with the warning to 'not spend it all at once'.

As with the birthday messages, I ignored this advice. Feeling guilty, I wrote her a letter outlining my proposed adventure;

Dear Gran,

Thank you so much for the card and the cheque, I've decided to go on a South American trek. I'm booked to go at the start of November; it's something I'm sure I'll always remember. It's personally come at a really good time, so instead of a letter, thought I'd write you a rhyme!

At the minute I feel rather perplexed, I'm hoping this trip will help me think what's next? A change in career or something new, I've lots of time to think it through!

I'm flying via Toronto to Mexico City, upon arrival I'll find a welcome committee; I'm meeting up with some old travel mates, who will be in Mexico on similar dates! We plan to travel around Mexico, my bags are packed I can't wait to go!

From there we might fly to a place called Peru, it all depends on what we want to do. From cultural cities to Inca trails, I'm sure I'll have fun and have lots of tales!

It will be really good, feed my curiosity, and all thanks to you and your generosity!

As way of thanks, I'll try to make you a millionaire, whether it wins or not be happy, take care.

Love and thanks

Gaz

Lottery Ticket - 01 09 10 26 29 46

There was no backing out of the trip, it was booked for the 1st November 2008 and I needed to inform my boss that I was leaving.

My head wrestled with the decision of going away. Had I not booked the trip already I may have changed my mind. Fortunately I had and I couldn't.

Did I need to go travelling again or was I just running away from my life? Was it my job or was it me? I wasn't sure.

As these thoughts raced through my mind I realised that I was scared. I was finally breaking my routine and had no idea what lay ahead. I was as nervous as I was excited.

I handed in my notice at work; at long last the decision was made.

The last three years of my life had involved other people's decisions mixed with my indecision. My girlfriend decided that after four happy years together she wanted to break up. She told me that she just didn't see a future for us and that I didn't listen, or something like that, I can't remember.

I didn't deal with this news well. I woke up every morning thinking that it was just a bad dream, only to realise as I dressed for work that it wasn't; my life was a nightmare. I stopped trying at work as I had only worked there to make money. I no longer cared about money because I had no one to spend it on.

I had foolishly thought that I had my life planned out in front of me; five words had changed everything;

'I'm breaking up with you.'

The money that could have been spent on city breaks and gifts was now being channelled into the wrong areas. I started drinking heavily to blot out the reality of the situation I was in. Weekends now began on a Thursday and ended on a Monday. If I wasn't drunk I was sat hungover at my desk living in the past, worrying about the future and not concentrating on the present. I felt trapped.

I worked 8:00am to 6:00pm above a Subway sandwich shop in a tired city centre office block. It was not what I had dreamt about as a child. I could still remember what I wanted to be, it was still mounted on black cartridge paper in my Primary School work book;

'When I grow up I want to be a footballer, like Gazza or Maradona and play for England and be famous and rich with lots of money and a big house and a big family.'

Sadly at the age of twenty-six I had admitted defeat. The nearest I could get to playing football for my country was by creating myself on Football Manager or Pro Evolution Soccer on the computer.

The reality was that my life had become an exercise in wasting as much time as possible in an office, and I was good at it.

I remember one day at work spending about forty minutes in the toilet; I was warned by my boss. I tried explaining to him that, if he had what I had, then he would also have been on the toilet for that amount of time.

'What have you got?' he asked.

'The Daily Star, the Sun and the Guardian.'

When I wasn't on the toilet or making cups of tea, I was sat at my desk. I would regularly call my own phone to increase my outgoing calls whilst emailing friends and co-workers with joke emails.

I emailed Daisy, a cute blonde girl that had just started work in the office and was keen to impress. I told her to call a candidate called Paige Turner urgently about one of her live vacancies and gave her the number of Leeds Library.

Instead of doing my work, I flirted with a girl from the company's head office in Nottingham. After forging a strong connection over email and checking out each other's Facebook profiles, we decided to meet up at a Premier Travel Inn in Sheffield.

I was concerned she was going to be a fifty-year-old paedophile but, as I was twenty-five, that seemed a little farfetched. I was too old to interest a paedophile. At worst she would be a murderer, at least it would be exciting.

It turned out she was great. She was a petit girl with long dark hair and mysterious dark eyes. Rochelle made me feel alive and that anything was possible. She took me away from reality and let my mind go wherever it wanted. I felt happy.

After three months, the dream was over. She called things off and moved to London. She wasn't magical; behind all the far-fetched ideas was a confused young girl that like me sought change. The difference between us was that she had the guts to do something about it. I sat at my desk staring at the grey midweek sky before congratulating her on her colourful future by email.

'I think that today with your actions you should be proud, even if they were prompted by a big grey cloud! You are so much better than Staffline; clearly that dull cloud was a neon sign!

You've got some big decisions in which to choose, I'll help all I can and share my views! I wish you all the best in London town; just you try and stop me coming down. You have nothing to lose, none of this is drastic, you'll do really well coz your simply fantastic!

I think that I am in a similar boat, need to change something not just my coat, A new beginning, a brand new start, the problem is my brain not my heart!

I don't want to fall into that bracket you hate, still living at home when I'm twenty-eight. Maybe you're my human catalyst? Should I stick or should I twist?

Something I'll ponder when on my own, maybe even discuss with you my clone? I know that I'm full of some mad potential, so making a change is fairly essential.

Over time, changes will unravel; perhaps I'll save and commit to travel? I'm getting to another metaphorical crossroad, with so many thoughts my brain could explode!'

My brain thankfully didn't explode but despite the 'good on you' attitude I was devastated. In a bid to cheer me up my Dad came into my room and asked if I wanted to go out for dinner with him and my mother; I politely declined. It was Valentine's Day.

I rang through my friends to see if anyone fancied going for a drink but they were all busy with their girlfriends. I felt alone.

My friend told me that when he started going out with his girlfriend, just after she would go to sleep at night, he would put nicotine patches on her arms. He then removed them just before she woke up. The idea was that if she ever wanted to leave, she would get withdrawal symptoms, think it was love, and come back. I doubted that it worked but they were still together, maybe he was a genius?

Back at work things were far from genius. My boss told me daily that it was important to have a competitive streak; I was clearly devoid of one. I often thought it would be funny to get naked and challenge him to a race around the office, couldn't complain then could he?

I could no longer pass the time emailing Rochelle at head office; she had left for London and a new life. I spent my time at work looking for other jobs at other companies. The problem was that nothing interested me.

I was offered a job working for a stationery company. I didn't take it as I felt that they just weren't going anywhere. Neither was I and it was becoming a problem.

I moved out of my parents' home and into a flat with a colleague from work. Temporarily I fooled myself that I was happy.

I had already travelled before with the aforementioned ex-girlfriend. It had been the best year of my life and the best of ours as a couple. I felt that I had had my time away and I needed to resist the urge to do it again. It wouldn't be the same the second time.

As the months disappeared I couldn't shake the underlying unhappiness. My friend Mark, who I had met in Australia, told me that he was planning a trip to South America and suggested that I should meet him over there. The thought would not leave my mind.

South America was a place without rules, where people did what they wanted and acted on instincts. Latin people were spontaneous, passionate and knew how to have fun. I wanted to experience it. I wanted more colour in my life.

My mother tried her best to stop me from booking the trip. She told me that I needed to settle down, find a girlfriend and start a career; I disagreed. I had had enough of girlfriends and needed a break from the life that I was living.

I viewed office life and the rat race in general as crazy. It came as quite the shock when my friends started thinking that it was me that was mad. They were all settling down, moving in with girlfriends and making plans for the future. I was dreaming about flying off on another adventure, hitting the eject button and escaping normality.

The money from my Gran made these dreams an instant reality.

I sat in the back of my father's black BMW shaking as we pulled into the car park at Heathrow. I was still filled with indecision and wasn't sure that I should go.

Weeks before arriving at Heathrow I had met a girl called Hannah. Since meeting her I had been looking for reasons not to go. As the date got nearer it felt like I was slowly getting to grips with my life. I was worried that travelling would jeopardise everything.

In some ways it seemed unnecessary to seek more confusion in my life. South America was the great unknown; it was undeniably exciting but intimidating in equal measures. I felt overwhelmed, but had made my choice.

Everything would be the same when I returned home. I needed to get out of my comfort zone and see new things. I needed to find out about myself.

After an emotional goodbye with my Dad, I took a deep gulp and checked in before disappearing alone into the airport.

I walked through the airport in a daze. My Dad's last words of 'I love you' echoed in my head as I drifted through security. I stood at the end of the security bay waiting for my hand luggage. I noticed that an orange light was flashing above the scanner. Two security guards made their way over to the machine. I broke into a cold sweat and wondered what was happening.

I had packed my bag the night before leaving after a three-day drinking session around Leeds. I was worried that I had packed something I shouldn't have.

'Is this your belt sir?' quizzed the large black security guard.

'It is indeed Mr Security Man, what seems to be the problem?' I coolly replied.

'You realise there is a weapon represented on this buckle. This is in breach of airport security,' he declared, 'This image could intimidate other passengers on the aircraft'

I looked at my belt. There was nothing unusual about it. The strap was black leather and the metal buckle read 'Velvet Revolver', with an image of a small pistol to the left.

'It's a revolver, it symbolises a band, don't worry it's not loaded. Neither is the magazine in my bag, it's FHM,' I joked.

'This is no laughing matter sir. I'm sorry but you will not be allowed to take this belt onto the plane. You can either check it in or we can arrange for it to be sent to your home address.' he stated

'Just keep it, you lot are mental.'

My head was even more confused as I sat waiting to board the plane. I could not comprehend a passenger being scared of a belt buckle. Heathrow security had gone mad.

I thought it was a good job that I didn't have thalidomide as I'd have been charged under the terrorism act, for trying to take small arms onto the plane.

Gareth Jones

I boarded my flight to Toronto walking like John Wayne in a bid to stop my jeans from falling down. It looked like I had shit myself and mentally I had.

CANADA

Toronto

I arrived into Canada, tired after a seven hour flight. It was the first time I had boarded a plane alone and it felt strange being totally alone for the first time. My first task was to get out of the airport and find a hostel in the centre of Toronto. I approached the immigration gate, where I was greeted by a pleasant woman in a full navy police uniform.

'Welcome to Canada sir, what is the purpose of your visit?' she asked as she scanned my passport and immigration forms.

I wearily replied,

'I'm just here for a few days before going to Mexico. I want to see the waterfall basically.'

She didn't look happy,

'Do you have family in Canada or are you visiting friends?'

'No I don't know anyone as I said just passing through.'

'Where are you planning on staying?'

'Somewhere in town, I have a few ideas. Is there a problem?' I asked.

'Come with me sir.'

I was tired and confused as one of her colleagues walked me across the large arrival halls into a small room against the far wall. His boots echoed off the marble floor and he said nothing.

I sat down as an angry looking policeman asked me a series of questions concerning my trip. He looked at me like I was made of swastikas; I looked at him like he was retarded after he questioned whether or not I could be a terrorist threat.

'Did you pack your own bags? Why are you here? Who do you work for?'

I felt like James Bond. I answered each of his questions, thankful that I was no longer wearing my Velvet Revolver belt.

The officer's mood calmed as I showed him a printout of the hostel I was planning on staying at in town. He made me ring and book a bed before allowing me to collect my bags from the now empty carousel. It was some welcome, 'Bienvenue Canada'.

I checked into the fantastically named Celine Dion dorm at a hostel in downtown Toronto called the Canadiana. Once more I opened the door to the familiar sight of numbered bunk beds and cramped living space.

I walked around the hostel and noticed that all the rooms were named after famous Canadians. The room next to mine was called the 'Bryan Adams dorm' and down the hall was the 'Jim Carrey computer room'. I went online to inform my parents that I had arrived safe and well.

The hostel had a really strange atmosphere. It was a converted house set out over three floors. There were no real communal areas so it was hard to interact with people. In the main social area by reception, people sat by a large oak table on their laptops; no one seemed to be talking. Unsure what to do with myself, I decided to go out.

I walked the streets of Toronto with an empty but expectant feeling in my stomach. I felt isolated and totally alone. It was surreal walking aimlessly in a foreign city. I stared at billboards and into the night sky wondering what would happen in the months ahead.

In theory I could do anything. No one back home would ever know. I drifted past building after building, down street after street. Physically I was in Toronto but my mind was wandering in the sky.

I decided to stop at an Irish bar and have a few beers. Irish bars always had a familiar feel to them and could be relied upon for a good pint; this one did not disappoint.

After a few beers I went back to the hostel and finally to bed. There would be plenty of time to be more adventurous.

The next morning I woke up and thought I was still at home. It came as quite the shock when I realised that I wasn't. I lay on the top bunk of my temporary bed as two people in the room packed ready to leave the hostel.

A young Indian looking man looked at me and introduced himself,

'I am Karthik from Philadelphia.'

'I'm Gaz from England,' I replied.

'Fancy getting some breakfast? I know a cool place around the corner.'

'Yeah why not.'

Karthik was about 5ft 9in and extremely clean cut. I was sure that he was in Toronto to study, as he didn't look like the travelling type. He was harmless and a bit of a geek, but I appreciated him asking if I would like breakfast. It was nice to be in someone's company, as despite only being away for little over twenty-four hours, I felt alone.

I spent the day with Karthik wandering around the city. Toronto is a large urban centre and had a similar feel to New York without the same hustle and bustle. Toronto was a city of high-rise buildings, the tallest being the iconic CN Tower that defined the city's skyline. The rest of the architecture varied in style and age but it all knitted together to make up the city's landscape.

The CN Tower was an impressive structure and the focal point of tourism in the city.

I stood at the bottom of the tower and looked up into the clear blue sky, it really was huge. We decided to go to the viewing tower a few floors from the top.

I didn't cope too well when we reached the top of the tower. The lift opened to a circular room that offered panoramic views of the city and Lake Ontario. The lake was so large that at first I thought it was the Atlantic Ocean as it spanned out of view beyond the horizon for miles.

One floor down from the viewing tower was the famous glass bottom floor. This allowed visitors to stand and look directly at the city below them. As young children jumped up and down on what in my eyes was a glass trap door, I stood tentatively at the edge of the platform sweating and swamped in anxiety. I looked every inch the paedophile as I struggled across the glass floor to the other side of the room wearing an uncomfortable smile.

Despite my fear of heights, the view from the tower was incredible. Toronto was a huge city, home to over 2.5 million residents making it one of the largest urban centres in North America.

Toronto was a clean, well-planned city and thus incredibly easy to navigate. The buildings we passed varied in design and age but I couldn't get excited by the place. By late afternoon I was beginning to get bored.

Karthik went back to the hostel as I toyed with the idea of visiting the Ice Hockey Hall of Fame. I had never watched Ice Hockey. The only knowledge I had of the sport was through Disney film The Mighty Ducks. I was so bored that I considered going in for a good half an hour, whilst eating a hotdog from a vendor on the corner of a busy sidewalk.

I woke early the next morning as I was going to visit Niagara Falls. The Falls had been the main reason why I had chosen to stay in Toronto for a few days. I had grown up watching Superman and had wanted to see Niagara ever since that little boy fell from the railings while showing off to his mother.

Before I knew it, I was once again up a tower. I had never scaled a tower and I had now scaled two in two days. The Skylon Tower overlooks the waterfall that plummets down into plumes of mist and spray into the river below. I got a text on my phone from my dad, which read:

'Glad you arrived safely. Enjoy Viagra Falls. Love Dad.'

The falls Niagara, sadly not Viagra, were remarkable. The whole area rumbled with the sound of water and after a while it became almost peaceful. It was similar to the sound of a running bath. I imagined a lot of people in the area checking their taps constantly, convinced they were running. I bet it got annoying after a while.

I walked down the promenade by the side of the Falls and for the first time felt at ease in my own company. Maybe this journey wasn't such a bad idea after all? Time would tell but for now I was happy.

It was strange being in such spectacular surroundings without anyone to share it with me. Many people proposed at Niagara Falls, being on my own I engaged in a few beers and took photographs with my new camera.

We arrived back at the hostel after a long day. As I was leaving the next day I decided to call it a night and go to bed.

The main talking point during my time in Toronto surrounded the Presidential elections in America. I sat eating breakfast with Karthik in a traditional American diner for the second day running as the results were announced. His eyes were transfixed on the television as mine looked around at all the old photographs that covered the walls of the narrow restaurant.

I didn't give a shit about the outcome of the election but Karthik clearly did. As the news filtered through that Obama had beaten McCain to become President he jumped up from our booth in joy.

I was happy for him but joked that Obama would break a long tradition by being the first black man to enter the White House without a mop and a bucket. He didn't find it funny so I continued in a bid to turn the situation around,

'Seriously though, it's great that America is to have a black President, I bet you can't wait to see the White House on MTV cribs.'

'Ha ha you crack me up,' he laughed.

I congratulated him before then admitting that I knew nothing about politics.

I made my excuses to Karthik so I could spend the morning alone; I liked him but wanted some time to reflect on the start of my trip.

It was a beautifully clear day so I sat in a small park collecting my thoughts about Toronto while thinking about Mexico and its people.

The people I had met in Toronto didn't have the same type of banter as I had so it proved hard to engage with them; they were far too serious.

Most of them just walked around wearing baseball caps backwards and talking about crap sports like baseball that they charged an arm and a leg to see. I'd rather keep my arms and my legs!

I couldn't wait to get to Mexico and be surrounded by easy-going, relaxed people that knew how to party. Anyone that chose to have a nap in the middle of the afternoon was all right by me; I couldn't wait.

Toronto was pleasant; there was nothing bad about it, but nothing apart from the Tower that really blew me away. I had seen it all before and wanted to see something different, something new and exotic.

If Toronto was a woman it would be the girl next door; comfortable and safe but offering no surprises or adventure.

I knew as I boarded the plane to Mexico that the adventure was about to begin.

MEXICO

Mexico City

I negotiated a busy airport without incident for the first time on the trip and before I could draw breath I was pushed into an aging yellow taxi by a small Mexican man. He spoke no English. I was unconvinced he knew where I wanted to go. I had no idea, just an address scrawled roughly onto a piece of paper that read:

Hostel Amigo

Isabel La Catolica 61, Col. Centro

As the taxi tore through the scores of traffic I gazed out of the window. The streets and buildings all seemed to be covered in graffiti. We stopped at a red light as my eyes narrowed on a grubby iron-sheeted taco wagon that straddled the roadside to our immediate right. A few metres on, hoards of scantily clad women tapped their plastic heels against the hard curb as cars slowly pulled in before darting off at speed. It was the human version of Ten Green Bottles and it fascinated me.

The dark night air had a mysterious other worldly feel to it. Everything felt new, foreign and different. I was finally excited. Strip lights lit up torn billboards with instantly recognisable brands - Me Gusta Coca-Cola - as the taxi snaked through the streets of this ever-changing city.

I arrived on the cobbled street outside the aptly named Hostel Amigos at 1:00am. Inside I could hear people at the bar and hoped that Mark and Craig were both there. I hadn't seen either of them for over a year.

We had stayed in touch since meeting in Australia and between them they had convinced me to join them on this trip. The start of my trip had been strange as I wasn't as excited as I should have been. I spent a lot of time in Canada wondering what was going to happen in the coming months and that made me apprehensive. I needed time to relax.

I pressed the buzzer and the iron security gate that covered the entrance to the hostel fizzed open. The muffled conversations emanating from the bar stopped and I heard several footsteps coming towards the door. I pushed my right arm against the heavy wooden door that opened into the reception and bar area. Stood before me were Craig and Mark,

'Come here you northern mug,' Craig bellowed in his typical cockney manner.

'Good to see you mate, here 'av a beer,' announced Mark.

I took a bottle of Corona from his hand and immediately began to loosen up. I knew that the trip was a good idea, now that I was around familiar faces.

Mark and Craig physically looked like the original odd couple. Mark stood over six feet, while Craig was very small. Mark's arms and legs were thin and long while Craig's were short and stocky. They looked different but both acted exactly the same.

Craig was a stereotypical cockney geezer, or at least he tried to be. He made up for his size by being incredibly loud, most of the time he shouted enthusiastically rather than talk. He was an infectious character and good to hang around with.

Mark was more laid-back and liked to quietly get drunk and talk to women. He was from Manchester and had a confidence about him that made him really approachable. I liked them both equally.

Mark introduced me to Gemma, a girl he had grown up with back home in England. She had already been travelling for eight months and had decided to meet up with us in Mexico City. Gemma was a tall girl who looked athletic. She had long dark hair and a distinctive face. I didn't find her attractive as I thought she looked like ex-wrestling superstar Bret 'The Hitman' Hart.

Gemma was really drunk; she stumbled over with a wide grin on her face and began speaking to me in spastic riddles as she knocked over a wooden bar stool,

'I am Gemmargh it's good to (hiccup) meet youwse,'

I couldn't work out whether she was going to be a lot of fun or a complete nightmare. As she jumped up onto the bar and started dancing the jury was still well and truly out.

Hostel Amigo had a colonial feel to it. Running from the main bar were a series of high arched ceilings and stonewalls, predominantly terracotta and cream in colour. It felt like a convent. It was the type of place I had stayed at on school residential.

The bar area was brought to life by an abundance of Mexican memorabilia. Anything stereotypically Mexican was in view including Ponchos, sombreros, cacti and numerous bottles of Tequila. The hostel had a cheery ambience that I immediately liked. I dropped my bags into our shared dormitory before going for a couple of beers at a nearby bar to catch up. Gemma passed out in bed.

We entered the small, smoke-filled bar just past 1:00am. It was busy with an aging clientele. We sat down by a thin marble table and ordered some drinks from the waitress while listening to guitar-led Latin melodies.

My eyes scanned the bar and were disappointed to find no good looking girls for us to chat to. I was tired but fuelled by the excitement of meeting the boys. Mark stumbled back from the toilets with two local women. I couldn't work out which of them was worse? One looked like Mike Tyson while the other smaller girl looked like a tanned Gollum. I was sure they were both prostitutes.

I watched in horror as Mark tried to chat up the female boxer. She hadn't just been beaten with the ugly stick; it looked like she had been gang raped by the entire forest. He didn't seem to mind at all.

Thankfully for Mark communication problems meant that nothing happened. Craig and I arrived back at the hostel gutted.

I woke the next morning and once again momentarily thought I was still in Leeds. I climbed out of bed and walked down the stone hallway to get some breakfast.

Breakfast consisted of refried beans, salsa and cheese on a crusty loaf of bread. There was the option for some fresh chilli but I politely declined. Where were the cornflakes?

The four of us hit the streets of Mexico City for the first time. We didn't have any particular plans other than to walk around and soak in the atmosphere. After ten minutes Craig and Mark decided that their top priority was to find a sex shop,

"Ere Mark we should go for a little peep you know,' suggested Craig.

'That we should my little amigo, that we should,' answered Mark.

It was 11:00am.

We walked for thirty minutes before eventually finding a small sex shop in one of hundreds of small market arcades. Unfortunately they were told by a neighbouring shop owner that the store did not open until 2:30pm, which was three hours away.

For those that don't know 'a little peep', as Craig termed it, is a peep show. It comprises of a series of dark cubicles each with a small glass window set around a circular stage. Women then come out and remove their clothes, revolving around the circular platform as the paying customer hides behind a glass screen doing as they see fit. It was something that didn't interest me at all.

They walked with Gemma and I around what was an incredibly busy city, both preoccupied by thoughts of the peep show. They would have to wait.

At 2.29pm the walking erections arrived back at the store for their much anticipated peep. Gemma and I had left them and caught the subway to another part of the city.

Unfortunately for Mark and Craig they had misunderstood the gentleman's instructions, there would be no peep show until the evening.

Undeterred by this setback and unwilling to wait, they elected to both jerk off in a video cabin. They walked into separate booths with a few sheets of Mexican muck roll and a DVD of their choosing. It was anyone's guess as to what they each watched, I didn't want to know.

Their visit to a sex shop did get me thinking about how I was going to fair on the trip. Hostels were not the ideal environment for masturbation. I likened it to living in a house with fifty parents; you couldn't afford to relax for a second or you would be caught and they would know exactly what was going on.

I didn't like the thought of going in a wank booth as they made me feel awkward. So I began to think about where would be a good spot to spunk when travelling?

Had I gone with the boys into a cabin I am fearful that it would have resulted in me having a crank. A wank over the film I would be watching followed by, or in conjunction with, tears over the location I found myself in. Surely I deserved more lavish quarters; no one should have to jerk off in a private black box.

Back at home I was puzzled as to why I never had a girlfriend; there was no reason for it. People not half as friendly or fun as me had girlfriends, idiots had girlfriends. Maybe I would meet someone on this trip?

I often dreamt of having a Latin wife, my internet history can testify to that. I longed to meet Penelope Cruz, Eva Longoria or Eva Mendez. I wasn't fussy; I would take any of them. It could happen, why not? Ok, maybe not them but I was sure I could find an equally attractive alternative. I didn't have to resort to dark video booths just yet.

It was time to crack on with looking around the city. We sat in the middle of the Zocolo in the historic centre of the city enjoying the sun and taking in the surroundings. It had an earthy feel as the buildings were all built in beiges and browns, draped in the colours of the national flag. This was a proud nation.

Great, unplanned streets threaded neatly through the stunning architecture of the old and the new that blended uniquely with one another. The streets were narrow, providing a cramped, claustrophobic backdrop for thousands of cars and people to go about their daily lives. The atmosphere was incredible, full of colour, noise and life.

The city was knee-deep in nachos; on every street you could find a taco or burrito stand. The city reeked of food and fumes as the countless number of cars and illicit corn snacks fused into one. It was unlike any city I had visited before and I had only seen a part of it.

We walked down street after street just observing the city, it was impossible for my brain to take in all the visual information it was receiving. I battled against the army of short fat squared people that filled the streets. People stood relaxed by the side of narrow roads feeding their stomachs with spicy foods and chatting like they had all the time in the world.

Mexicans did not look how I had expected. In Toronto I dreamt of loin burning Latinos, I could only see tanned uninspiring stumps.

I had always wondered why Mexico didn't have an Olympics team. I could see within my first day why. It was because they were all tiny and fat. I guessed that anyone who could run, jump and swim had already crossed the border into America!

The fact the people were so small was accentuated by the height of the curbs in the city. The sidewalks sat high above the roads. I had to take a giant step to scale them. Craig and some locals literally had to climb; it was like watching a child clamber out of a swimming pool.

Apart from a few people at the hostel, no one seemed to speak any English, making it hard to converse with locals. I thought I had a good understanding of Spanish from going to Ibiza but I was sorely mistaken. I knew how to say 'Hello' and 'Thank you' and that was about it. The problem was that you cannot eat a 'Hello' or drink a 'Thank you,' so I had to resort to pointing.

My dinner was similar to what I had eaten for breakfast. Without going to a restaurant or spending a lot of money the options were slim. I was glad that I enjoyed hot food and cheese as it was here in abundance.

It was no wonder all the people were human squares. Imagine living on a diet of cheese and crisps. As I got ready for our night out I toyed with the idea of Mexico City being the dream capital of the world. Not because of its history or beauty but because of its people's consumption of cheese.

Mark was into his music and had kindly arranged tickets for us to go to a gig in the city to celebrate our first full night together. We were going to see an American band called Band of Horses. I hoped to arrive to the site of Red Rum on drums, Party Politics on percussion and Desert Orchid on lead guitar. Sadly the members of the band were not horses; it was just a name, they were a band of humans.

We caught the underground transit system to the gig that was being held at a university in a suburban area of the city. We sat outside drinking cans of lager before entering the venue drunk and ready to have a good time.

The venue felt and looked the same as any student union I had ever been in. It was dark with low ceilings and the floors were sticky with a week's worth of spilt drink. The stage sat against the far wall a couple of metres off the floor and faced the bar that sat at the opposite end. The bar was long with laser blue lighting. The bar top, like the floor, was incredibly sticky.

I bought a round of drinks before each of us got lost in the crowd of students out to have a good time. There was an abundance of students that could speak English and were far from ugly.

Maybe my early assumptions on the people of Mexico were wrong? Perhaps the ugly people just lived in the historic centre? Or maybe I was just drunk. I stood drinking heavily listening to the band;

'The world is such a wonderful place La di da, La di da, La di da, La di da'

It really was.

I stood at the bar drinking shots of my old Leeds stable mate Jagermeister arm in arm with Craig and Mark, swaying along to the music and enjoying the fact that any worries I had about this trip were gone.

We left the union and flooded onto the streets into a river of drunken students. I found that being drunk helped to bridge the language barrier with the locals. After ten pints I had mastered Spanglish.

Before getting a taxi back to the hostel we decided to get some food from a local diner. Upon ordering food I realised that my voice had changed. I ordered in a Spanish accent,

'Amigo I would like un taco pollo and un taco beef with chilli pepper.'

'Si senor,' replied the confused clerk.

I realised that most English people, including myself, change their voice when on foreign shores. If you can't speak the language, talk slowly with an accent and people will understand what you want. I remembered years of my dad ordering food for the whole family while on holiday using this very technique. How embarrassing.

The next morning I woke up early and ran to the toilet. As I sat there I remembered Mark challenging me to eat a large Jalapeno pepper that was sitting in a basket on the counter of the restaurant. I had eaten four and was now paying the price for my gamesmanship.

I walked into the breakfast room hungover and shaking as Craig kindly made me a cup of coffee. Once again breakfast consisted of bread with refried beans, salsa and cheese, it was no wonder the people looked how they did.

I suggested to Craig that perhaps a lot of the country's problems could be solved by making cheese, like peep shows, illegal till after 2:00pm. Either that or they could introduce some sort of cheese rationing system in a bid to watch the waistlines of its inhabitants?

'Santiago you have five pieces of cheese to last till tomorrow. Don't eat them all at once my son!'

'Too late Mama, I've eaten them all already. I put them on my cereals.'

'Well no more cheese for you my dear boy.'

We left the hostel feeling ill from the night of drinking and agreeing that we needed to sort out some plans for the rest of the trip. We booked a bus pass through the hostel that enabled each of us to travel throughout Mexico and Guatemala. The country was far bigger that we thought and it made sense to see as much of it as possible. I had always wanted to go to Cancun.

We booked to leave the following morning from the main bus station in town.

Happy that our immediate future was resolved we spent the day again just walking around the streets of this huge urban area.

I continued my ever increasing love hate relationship with towers, following the two in Canada with Latin America's tallest building, the Lationoamericana.

I stood at the top of this building in a cage as a cool breeze flowed through my body.

I turned into an anxious mess, amplified by the monstrous hangover I convinced myself that I was going to fall to my death. I clung to the barrier as my knuckles turned white with fear and I began to feel faint.

Thankfully the longer I stood there the better I began to feel. Once I settled I was able to enjoy the views on offer.

Mexico is home to over twenty million people so you couldn't help but be impressed with its scale. I looked out at the endless landscape of seemingly unplanned skyscrapers and housing split by narrow roads and the physical geography of the basin.

The city's atmosphere was thick with smog; a toxic soup that you could see stirring above the city. The horizon clouded with a haze of what looked like smoke. I was told it was pollution.

'Eight out of ten days are declared hazardous to human health in Mexico City. Just breathing is the equivalent of smoking two packs of cigarettes a day,' suggested an American that stood by me taking photographs.

'It's a major problem this city faces, be happy you don't live here,' he stated before shuffling around the corner to take more photos of the city's skyline.

This wasn't good news at all. I was already trying really hard not to start smoking and here I was in a city doing so without even realising.

I had always been against smoking. My Grandma sounded like a sixty-year-old miner and lived in an ashtray. I used to hate going to see her because of it.

Against my better judgement I had started to smoke back home on nights out as with the smoking ban my mates were constantly stood outside bars rather than in them. Most of them wanted to stop but just couldn't. I remember my mate's girlfriend buying him Alan Carr's book 'Easy Way To Stop Smoking'. I thought that it was strange and destined to fail; how was a fag going to help you stop smoking?

I spent the evening worrying that if I stayed in Mexico City much longer I was to become a hardened smoker and die of lung cancer. It was time to make our way out of the city towards the coast, a place where I was more likely to be killed by a giant crab.

Oaxaca

The coast was sixteen hours away so we decided that we would stop inland at the historic city of Oaxaca. The bus took two hours to get out of Mexico City, buildings just went on and on before gradually giving way to the mountainous countryside.

On the outskirts of the city we drove past a medium-sized factory that produced piñatas. There were hundreds of them, ranging from animals to superheroes including Spiderman and The Hulk. I noticed in the far corner behind the wire fence a collection of festive characters that included a four foot Santa Claus.

It was strange seeing Saint Nick stuck behind a wire fence in a Mexican Factory. His bright red clothes stood out against the sandy backdrop of the factory and the surroundings. I wondered if he was even aware of the cruel fate that was awaiting him in little over a month.

My mind drifted to a theoretical Mexican Christmas.

I wake up as an excited seven-year-old Mexican boy and run down the stairs eager to open my presents. I had been a good boy and was sure I was getting lots of cool things. Mother is in the kitchen preparing Turkey and cranberry fajitas.

My father stands by the back door smiling while holding a blindfold. He must have heard me coming down the stairs. After a year I once again catch a glimpse of the big red bastard hanging from the tree outside grinning in my direction. I want to hit him but cannot get to him as my dad blocks my way. I have to wait,

'Hey Niño, come here and put on your blindfold, you have lots of gifts.'

I run over and allow him to blindfold me. He hands me a wooden bat after spinning me several times to make me disorientated. This was not going to be easy, it never was.

'Now go open him up son, he has eaten all you gifts and needs punished.'

I stumble into the garden swinging the bat viciously in the air but connect with nothing. It is only a matter of time.

I loved the idea of children ferociously attacking a mock Santa with a bat. I hoped that it happened. Why else would they have a piñata of Father Christmas?

I wasn't sure where I would be for Christmas but at the next opportunity I was getting a festive piñata. It was a much better idea than a woollen sock over the fireplace.

After hours of winding mountain roads and spectacular desert terrain we dropped into the glowing city of Oaxaca by nightfall. The city had a calm ambience with cobbled streets and soft lighting. It was a world away from Mexico City.

We got into a taxi outside the old bus station and checked into a hostel away from the centre of town. It seemed a charming place.

I woke the next morning and ran straight for the toilets. Since arriving in Mexico everything that I had eaten contained chilli. I remember having travellers' diarrhoea in Thailand where they frequently charged to use the bathroom. I found in the first few weeks that I was spending more money getting rid of food than I was buying it. Thankfully in Mexico you could shit for free.

We decided to go on a tour with the hostel to Hierve el Agua, a natural spring that lay in the mountains surrounding the city of Oaxaca. On the way we stopped at a local market on the way in the small town of Mitla for half an hour.

The village was beautiful, authentically Mexican with simple, single story white washed buildings and constant references to Jesus and the Christian faith. We walked through the colourful market that sold handmade jewellery and woollen goods, to the sound of light chatter and the gentle plucking of guitar strings. I was in another world.

The village was unbelievably peaceful. I half expected a rogue Mariachi to burst from the darkness of a crumbling bar with a guitar case full of guns. I had seen too many movies; I doubted anything like that ever happened in this sleepy town.

The warm springs of Hierve el Agua sat twenty minutes from the village in the surrounding hills and it was stunning. The naturally warm pools ran over the face of the mountain and plummeted into a dramatic cactus strewn valley.

The sun was relentlessly warm, so the cold mountain water could not have looked more inviting. I sat in the pool talking to Mark and enjoying the captivating views on offer. With thoughts of gun-slinging Mexicans fresh in my mind I couldn't help but think I was in the Wild West.

A few hours later our small minibus drove from the mountains back towards Oaxaca. We stopped halfway back at a Mescal distillery that sat seemingly in the middle of nowhere. The distillery was small in size and looked like a traditional cowboy saloon. The entrance compromised of two shutters and opened into one large room, centred round the main bar. Inside were hundreds of stacked bottles of Mescal.

Mescal was very similar to Tequila, but was made in a different region of Mexico. It was the fizzy wine to Tequila's Champagne. It was the same thing but with a different name.

Behind the building lay a series of metal garages where the Mescal was produced. Our guide walked us around the side of the main bar and began to tell us how the drink was made and the history behind it. The process behind the Mescal had not changed for hundreds of years, neither had the equipment.

Too many things in modern society are complex. Why have complicated machines to churn produce when you can just simply whip a donkey? Not enough donkeys got whipped these days.

The tour guide flipped from Spanish to English as he ran through the history of the drink and its role in Mexican society. Mark, Craig, Gemma and I slowly got bored as it increasingly felt like a school trip.

As I began to drift off the guide announced that he had talked enough, a point I agreed on, and now it was time for us to enjoy some free samples.

Each of us began to feel the effects of several harsh shots. Mark goaded me into eating several dried worms from a plate sat at the end of the bar. I ate them like crisps before requesting some more shots.

'I can't believe you just wolfed down those worms you sick bastard. I'd never eat worms, not even if you paid me,' Mark announced.

Rather than salt, the bar girl provided everyone with a shaker full of orange powder. It tasted like salt but obviously wasn't, we guessed it was a mild chilli. It wasn't until we were on our way back to the hostel that out driver announced that it was crushed worms. I looked at Mark and laughed.

Each of us were blind drunk from the Mescal by the time we got back to the hostel. We decided that it would be a good idea to take advantage and make a night of things. Several beers and a bottle of vodka later we spilled onto the streets of Oaxaca for the first time.

We were joined by a number of people from the hostel including a boy called Rob who we had all met but not really got to know in Mexico City. Rob was travelling on his own and had been through Colombia and Central America. His stories made me excited about the months ahead.

All the bars in Oaxaca were small. Nearly all of them were single rooms cut into the aging walls of historic buildings. They were simple and purely functional. I found them charming and, despite it being a Sunday, very social.

I left our group and began trying to interact with the locals. It was clear they were interested in us. I spoke Spanglish to a group of four Mexican men in their late twenties. I had no idea what they were talking about and guessed it was the same case for them. I decided it was best to buy them a drink and leave.

We sat at the other side of the bar around one of several large wooden beer kegs that acted as tables. The bar only served bottles of Mexican beer and Tequila or Mescal and was simple in appearance. I sat intoxicated on a stool listening to the usual travel talk while sipping on bottle after bottle of lager.

I felt a tap on my left shoulder and reacted by spinning around on my chair.

'Amigo we go to another bar!' said one the four Mexicans I had spoken to earlier

I spoke no Spanish but thankfully Michael, a well-travelled Ethiopian that was with us, did. Moments later six of us were clambering into the back of a navy blue pickup truck and heading at speed out of town.

None of us had any idea where we were going as the dusty night air blasted our faces and helped each of us sober up. And as we sobered up, this journey felt like less and less of a good idea.

I convinced myself that this was what travelling was all about, meeting locals, getting out of my comfort zone and living. So they could drive us into the desert and kill each of us in the most inhumane way possible, but equally they could take us to a really good party. It was worth the chance.

I stared to my left through the back window of the cabin as my back pressed against the sides of the truck. One of guys turned round and made a rock 'n' roll gesture with his hands while nodding his head up and down. Moments later the pickup screeched to a halt amid a plume of dust. The hatch at the rear of the truck opened.

'Amigos, come on fiesta!' shouted one of the shadowy figures.

The dust settled as my bleary eyes focused on a bar in front of us. The softly lit saloon was open but was not as busy as we had all hoped. Gemma was just happy that we were not going to be killed, well not yet.

The bar was similar in appearance to the distillery we had visited earlier that day. The walls were cream in colour and full of old farming equipment and pictures of the barren landscape. The floor compromised of grey cement and was cluttered with yellow plastic chairs and tables advertising Sol lager. In the corner sat an old piano.

We sat down and ordered a round of drinks.

The others did not interact with the four men that had brought us here, which I felt was rude. So, to compensate, I spent a lot of time trying to talk with them. At their request I went outside for a harmless smoke.

Rather than roll a joint or offer me a cigarette they each seemed happy to smoke from a small wooden pipe. I couldn't speak Spanish so was unable to ask what they were smoking. I guessed it was just some weed.

We stood about laughing, resorting to pulling faces as communication was difficult. I have rather stretchy skin so was able to keep them entertained; you don't get called foreskin face at school for nothing.

The pipe was passed around for the third time as I muddled through a sparse list of Mexican footballers' names and random nouns.

As I did this the craziest looking of the Mexicans refilled the pipe. He had long black hair that was tied back and tanned skin that was covered in a number of black tattoos. He was the most vocal of the group and when I looked into his eyes I could see that he led a crazy life.

He passed me the pipe and motioned for me to smoke. By this point the weed had got to my brain and I started to feel disorientated. It churned around my brain with all the beer and Mescal and I felt myself begin to slide.

I sucked back lightly on the pipe; it tasted different, unlike what we had been smoking before. I exhaled and began to cough like a weary old dragon. I looked up as the long haired Mexican began laughing.

Within minutes I was overcome with the worst paranoia of my life. I was standing outside a secluded bar in the heart of Mexico with four strangers, convinced one of the men, the quietest of the four, wanted to rape me. He wore a rather suspect black handlebar moustache, and sucked on the pipe while touching my arm and looking at me like I was made out of chocolate. I had to leave. I had to get inside and find my friends.

I fell back into the bar through the wooden shutters riddled with anxiety and looking confused. Mark stood by the jukebox that lay behind the old piano with the rest of the group. I made my way over clutching my forehead between my thumb and my finger, unsure as to what was happening.

Mark looked at me and asked if I was ok.

I couldn't talk as time slowed and everything seemed to flicker in slow motion. Concerned he put his warm arm around me and simply said,

'Banter.'

My mind eased and time at least returned to normal. Music filled the bar and as it did so my hands began to move with the music. I had no control over them; I was playing an air piano, convinced that I was a musical genius, a modern day Mozart. I was in the throes of Piano Paranoia in a foreign land. What had I taken?

Mark and Craig decided that it was best that we leave the bar, so we jumped into a taxi. I sat in the back throwing my arms around.

I woke up at 2:00pm the following day depressed and confused about what had happened to me. I sat in a hammock that hung in the courtyard of the hostel drinking a bottle of water in the hope that it would aid my recovery.

Mark returned from a walk around town and told me that we were all going to leave that evening on a night bus to Porto Escondido on the Pacific Coast. I hadn't seen much of Oaxaca but just nodded in agreement, the beach would be just fine.

Before leaving for the bus we walked around the city. There was a great atmosphere as a local market was taking place in the main square. It was lost on me as I felt vacant. My body and mind were empty. I stared up at the fairy lights that decorated the night sky longing for sleep.

Rather than going to bed I walked with Mark and Craig through a horrible indoor meat market. It looked like someone had just dropped a grenade in a farm, not what the doctor ordered, but then neither was a ten hour bus journey.

Puerto Escondido

We arrived in Puerto Escondido at 6:00am and caught a taxi to a hostel Gemma had found online called Tower Bridge. We walked into the hostel but no one was there to check us in. I collapsed on an old worn sofa, shattered after what had been a horrible bus journey. After a frustrating two hour wait the owner of the hostel finally arrived and we were able to check in.

The owner was an English man called Steve. He was quirky and seemed quite the character. He asked if we had arrived for the World Surf Competition.

'Are you here for that World Surfing Competition you groovy guys?'

'Didn't know there was one Steve, isn't this a fishing village?' I asked.

'Yeah man but it's got some great waves. The beach is famous full of babes.'

Mark's Lonely Planet guide described Puerto Escondido as a traditional fishing village, so if Steve was actually telling the truth it was a welcome surprise.

I wasn't excited about the potential surf competition itself as I didn't know any surfers and I didn't understand the rules. I knew that surfers liked to get up early while I liked to get up late. It was not going to be a marriage made in heaven.

However I was excited about what the competition would bring. The town would be busier than normal and there would be lots of people and parties.

The hostel was really dirty. Gemma had booked it through Hostel World as it had a pool and was cheap. I stood over the pool as Steve chatted away to Mark and Craig. You couldn't argue that it was a pool, but it looked nothing like the images on the website. On the website it was bright blue, clean and new. It now looked like Shrek had bathed in it. It was half expected but that didn't stop me feeling disappointed.

It reminded me of ordering a burger at McDonald's. I would look up at a triumphant glowing picture of a cheese burger and think despite knowing otherwise.

'Wow look at that sandwich, it looks amazing and it's only £0.99. How is this even possible?'

My hope of the burger from the photo never materialised. Time after time I was handed a burger that looked more like a greasy dead vagina. In life you get what you pay for and Tower Bridge Hostel was no different.

We dropped our bags into the dormitory and headed for the beach. I really wanted a McDonald's but as we were in a small town I doubted there was one and settled for some chicken tacos by the sea. I asked about the surf competition and was told that it was to take place over five days a few miles down the coast at Zicatela beach.

I spent the rest of the day laying by the ocean relaxing and catching up on some much needed sleep. It was nice to be by the coast, the secluded bay we had found was beautiful and reminded me of Thailand.

I got up early the next day to catch the start of the surf competition. Mark, Craig, Gemma and I arrived on the beach at 10:00am where a number of large white tents had been erected for the start of the competition.

The tournament was sponsored by Vans; their logo was everywhere you looked. To the right of the judging platform stood two huge inflatable yellow Corona bottles, in the middle was a temporary bar. It was too early for a drink.

We sat on the sand and cast our eyes out to the small figures that bobbed up and down in the water like coconuts. The waves that crashed against the beach were huge. I looked down the beach and noticed that every hundred metres or so a red flag was pitched in the sand. There was obviously a strong undertow making the area unsuitable for swimming.

As we got comfortable the announcement came that the last two surfers were going out to compete. I thought we had got there early but I was wrong. The tournament had started at 6:00am. I sat trying to imagine something worse that floating around in the sea at 6:00am. Surfers were a completely different animal.

I lay on the beach relaxing as the sun broke through the clouds. An hour passed before Craig woke me up, he was restless and complained of being bored,

'Fancy a game of football geez?' he asked.

I didn't reply as I was still waking up.

'Come on mate, Mark will go in goals and I fancy doing you,' he said enthusiastically.

'Ok but only one game. What we playing to?'

'Five,' he shouted as he created the goals with two beach towels.

The sun beat down on us as Mark launched the first of a series of long balls from his goal line. I was glad it only one game as the combination of the sun and the sand meant it was going to be really tiring.

I beat Craig within ten minutes 5-1. He was far from happy. I stood with Mark by one of the goal posts bent over and panting. Craig insinuated that we had both conspired against him.

'You let those goals; there is no way I lost 5-1. I want a rematch!' he demanded.

I couldn't believe how angry he was about losing so decided that it was just best to agree to another game. He stood waiting for Mark to kick the ball back into play.

Fifteen minutes later and the game had ended. Craig ran into the sea as I collapsed on the floor unable to breathe. The score for the second time read 5-1 and he was fuming.

Craig was an extremely competitive person, and a bad loser. The fact we had to play two games in the midday sun was testament to that. It was a bitter pill for him to take. He came back from the sea, sat on his towel and wouldn't speak to anyone.

After twenty minutes of silence he finally spoke,

'I am seriously considering travelling on my own guys. I may even go home,' he announced.

The three of us laughed.

'What are you on about you nipple?' enquired Mark.

Craig did not answer he just shook his head and ran back into the water. I sat in disbelief that someone could get so angry over a friendly game of football. I had never met anyone so competitive in my life.

I often wondered if Craig suffered from 'Napoleon Complex' or, as it's more commonly known, little man syndrome. He definitely displayed all the symptoms.

Craig frequently was over the top. He was an infectious character riddled with the disease of cockney. His outbursts were as entertaining as they were annoying, you couldn't help but enjoy them. He would get upset over trivial things like losing a game of table tennis. Like a captain at sea you had no option but to ride out the storm.

Craig returned and, after I bought him an ice cream, his temper cooled.

The beach at Zicatela was huge; I guessed it was two kilometres in length and about four hundred wide. Behind the beach was a narrow road with a series of bars, restaurants and small boutiques selling surf wear. It was going to be a busy week.

We went back to the hostel by late afternoon to find Steve sitting outside by his desk dressed up as a goalkeeper. I had come to an early conclusion about Steve; he was barking mad. I wasn't sure if he smoked a lot of marijuana or drank an excessive amount of alcohol but it was clear that both oars were not in the water.

Steve was loud and manic resulting in many of the guests feeling uncomfortable around him. I found him an interesting character. I could sense that he was lonely and meant well.

Steve told me that he was from the south coast of England but had lived in Mexico for almost fifteen years, he didn't tell me why. He looked like an ex-army officer; his hair was shaved short and he looked well conditioned. His eyes were dark and sparkled like a child's. He always seemed distant like he was dreaming or plotting something fun to do.

'Hi Steve, why are you dressed up like a goalkeeper?' I asked.

'Got a match, you guys should come and play, it's only training.'

It turned out that Steve played football for a local team in Escondido. He was their unhinged daredevil goalkeeper, an aging alcoholic in gloves and shin pads.

Craig and I were glad to attend. The two of us crammed onto the back of Steve's small scooter and sped dangerously down the road as Mark decided to stay at the hostel and drink with Gemma.

We played on the outskirts of town, away from the beach and close to the surrounding jungle. It was a strange feeling to be away from the typical tourist areas of the town. It was an opportunity to experience and interact with local people.

It was a good feeling to play with them and they welcomed the two of us with open arms. Craig treated the game like he was on trial for Manchester United.

After the match we returned to the hostel in the back of a huge pickup truck. Mark and Gemma were both drunk and wanted to go into the town to get wasted.

Tower Bridge was a great hostel. It was the most social I had stayed in so you could forgive it for being dirty. As you walked in there was a pool table and collection of hand me down sofas. Behind two pillars sat a large television with two more sofas. At the back of this area was a small wooden bridge that looped over the small swimming pool. The rooms sat around the pool between the green jungle vegetation. It was a charming place.

We went into town with several people that were staying at the hostel.

Puerto Escondido had a vibrant feel to it and I was glad that we had stumbled across it. It was an undiscovered fishing town that, unlike the more famous seaside resorts of Acapulco and Cancun, had yet to be overrun by tourism.

We sat on stools at Wipe-out bar in the centre of town looking out onto the street. It was one of three main bars in the town and played a selection of heavy dance music. A group of Americans walked around with a bottle bong challenging people to have a go. We were not interested.

As the drinks flowed the mood between the four of us started to sour. Every time that Mark talked to a girl, Gemma would be stood there. Whenever Craig or I were talking to girls, Gemma would be stood there. It was becoming annoying as we were all convinced she was preventing us from hooking up with anyone. This angered Mark the most.

I began to worry that we would not travel as a four for much longer. We were only ten days into the trip and already there were problems. I got on with Gemma but found her irritating. Craig was besotted with Mark and I could tell he wished it was just the two of them. He didn't like to share. Mark clearly resented asking Gemma to join us and was convinced that she liked him.

Travelling as a four was not as fantastic as Marvel Comics would lead you to believe; our group was fantastically flawed. Something was not working but I chose to just ignore it in the hope that it would go away. I guessed that life wasn't a comic book.

I sat by the bar imagining if we did live in a comic book world. Visual clouds floating over people's heads letting everyone know what they were thinking. I looked at a blonde, long-haired girl who was deep in conversation with a huge American across the bar and wondered what she was thinking. If she had a thought cloud I would know. Maybe she wanted to have sex with me?

Meanwhile, across the room Mark stood talking to an undesirable young woman in a long red dress. I didn't need thought bubbles to know what he was thinking. I watched as he walked out of the bar holding her hand. She was so ugly that I bet she couldn't turn a TV on.

Craig and I laughed but Gemma sat with a face like thunder. Outside it began to rain.

Over the next few days the atmosphere between the four of us soured. Our days were simple; we walked to the beach and lay in the sun. On the nights we drank heavily, disguising the obvious problems between us. It could only last so long.

Sunset bar was my favourite in Puerto Escondido. It sat at the back of Zicatela beach near to the numerous shops and restaurants. The bar was circular with a radius of about ten metres. Around a central pillar sat a range of spirits and bottled beers that cooled in small fridges. The roof was straw and decorated with coloured fairy lights. Our first night had ended there and since then it became our favourite.

The owner Luis gave away free shots of Mescal. So while there was a relaxed atmosphere, it always ended in anarchy before we tottered along the strip to a later venue.

On the third night Mark once again upset Gemma. I lay passed out in the reception of the hostel for the second night running as Mark clumsily slammed the iron-fenced door shut. He wasn't alone. I looked up and saw that he was with the young barmaid from Sunset, Melissa.

Melissa had dark hair and constantly looked like she was on drugs. She was holding onto Mark's arm and was dressed in next to nothing. She looked at me and pointed before screaming,

'You are the Devil!'

I lay confused as her and Mark crashed into the room where I was meant to be sleeping. Five minutes later Melissa came storming out of room shouting but thankfully left with haste.

I never found out why she referred to me as 'El Diablo.' Perhaps it was because I had burnt red skin after a few days in the sun. Perhaps it was that I had a goatee beard, or maybe she just thought that I was one hell of a guy?

The next morning I woke up to find that Gemma had gone to the beach by herself. My worst fears were realised. Gemma and Mark could not be around each other and there was no other option but to split up.

Craig said that he wanted to travel on his own, his mind was made up. Mark just wanted to get away from Gemma, it was as simple as that.

I resented him for asking her to join us on the trip. He admitted that back home he knew that she liked him. It wasn't her fault but she had managed to ruin everything.

I had come on this trip as a multi-purpose accessory, to be part of an outfit. I didn't want to travel on my own. What use was a belt without jeans? I hadn't planned the trip, I had just decided to be part of it and now it seemed I was going to be alone.

I decided to spend some time away them as it felt like I had been tricked.

I had made friends with a girl from Sweden called Gordana. She asked if I would like to spend the evening with her. I hadn't seen Mark, Craig or Gemma all day so I agreed.

We met up with an American couple for dinner in town, then we took a walk along the beach and spotted a small fire gently burning a few hundred metres ahead of us. We decided to walk over.

Sat around the fire were a group of likeable people that were travelling through Mexico. Two of the guys were French-Canadian, two Mexican and one big-haired gentleman from Israel who looked like Sideshow Bob from the Simpsons.

They asked us to join them. We sat around the fire drinking Mescal and talking about life. I sat and listened as they conversed predominantly in Spanish. The beach was dark and peaceful. We were the only people there. The only voices we could hear were distant and coming from the nearby bars.

It was peaceful and exactly what I had been looking for. The light of the fire flickered across each of our faces as the moon lit the now calm ocean. I began to forget about my small troubles and just enjoyed the company of positive, relaxed people.

The following morning I woke up and Mark told me that he had booked to leave Puerto Escondido that evening. I sat in my bunk shaking as I had no idea what I should do.

I had no idea where to go. I had no plans. I couldn't speak Spanish. I didn't know how I was going to get to South America and had no desire to go there on my own. I looked at Mark and disguised my worries,

'Yeah no worries mate, have a good trip.'

I left him packing in the room before asking Gordana if she would like to go for breakfast then the beach.

Gordana could speak Spanish but I chose to order my own food. If I was going to be on my own I had to stop relying on others.

On ordering, another in a long line of communication breakdowns occurred. We sat outside the beach side cafe looking through the menu for something to eat as the waitress came over to take our order,

'Can I have a coke please?' I mumbled at the waitress.

'Si,' she responded.

'To eat, tacos pollo. Gracias,' I replied.

Five minutes later the small Mexican waitress came over with our order. Gordana got what she asked for but I sat looking down at the table in confusion at a bowl of cornflakes, a pot of milk and a full banana. My chicken tacos sat by the side on a different plate.

Gordana started laughing as I wracked my hungover brain for an answer. 'Coke please' had been confused for 'cornflakes'. I was officially useless.

Rather than complain I joked that 'for fuck's sake' would lead to a plate of pancakes. I just decided to eat what was in front of me. I could buy a drink on the beach.

Behind the laughter a big problem had been highlighted. If I couldn't successfully order a breakfast how was I going to cope alone in South America?

At home I had fallen into the trap of being negative. If something was going right I would wait for it to go wrong. I was worried that this trip was going down the same plug hole. I had just begun to settle and feel comfortable and now the rug had been pulled from under me. It was out of my control.

I found the only escape at home was to drink but here that was not the answer. What I needed was to be around positive people. The situation I was in was a test. It was maybe something I needed but it didn't make it any easier.

Gordana and I walked down the steep concrete steps and spent the day on one of the more secluded beaches surrounded by rocks and small fishing boats.

Gordana was twenty years old and from Malmo. She dressed well and had black hair with soft features. She had a beautifully calm nature about her and was the perfect person to be around.

Nothing seemed to faze her which was unique for a girl her age. She was in Escondido after finishing a six week Spanish course at a university in Mexico City. She had come to the coast for a holiday before returning back home.

I liked the simple way she viewed life. She told me to give things a go with the trip and to not take the easy option of going home. She said being scared was not a negative but a positive situation to be in.

Back at the hostel things felt far from positive. Craig and Gemma both told me that they had booked to leave Puerto Escondido with Mark that evening. Craig stuck the dagger in further by telling me,

'You can't come either mate; I checked, the bus is full.'

I had a bad time sleeping that night. I was over thinking and being melodramatic. They were all on the same bus going to the same place. I couldn't help but think it was me that was the problem.

It was best that I stayed at Tower Bridge. I had no other option.

The next day I woke up lying next to Gordana. We spent the day around the hostel enjoying each other's company, she was a great distraction. I booked to leave the hostel the following evening as she was due to go back home to Sweden and I had to begin the next stage of my trip.

I sat on the sofa with Gordana and as evening arrived so did Brian and Gene. They had returned from a few days further down the coast and wanted a big night out to celebrate their return to Tower Bridge.

I told them what had happened with the guys and they reassured me that everything would be fine, something I was still trying to convince myself about.

They had travelled throughout South America so I used the opportunity to pick their brains about where I could go and what I should expect. Mark had taken the Lonely Planet guide so I had no idea. I decided to just see what happened; there was no use worrying about the future.

We all went into town and I got drunk, really drunk.

I stumbled back into the hostel with Gordana at around 3:00am. I couldn't remember much from the night out other than that I was in a good mood. We sat on the sofa talking before we finally kissed.

Brian had somehow unlocked one of the private rooms and looked over at us like a crazy pirate,

'Guys go in there,' he instructed.

We lay on the bed kissing which was good but downstairs I was living the life of a sixty-year-old man with erectile dysfunction. As things between us advanced I knew that I was not going to be able to have sex with her, especially if I had to wear a condom.

I didn't agree with condoms. Imagine if a girl was about to wank you off and you said,

'Don't mind putting this marigold on do you? Just you know, not sure where your fingers have been!'

It kills the moment, and it killed this one.

The next day I woke up in bed with my arm around Gordana who, after more fumbling around, I did sleep with. I wasn't sure what it was but I felt nervous. She had helped me through a tough time and, though I had only known her for four days, I liked her a lot.

We were both leaving Escondido that night and the likelihood was that we would never see each other again. I wondered if I had latched onto her as I didn't want to be on my own. Was it the situation that drew me towards her, or did I have real feelings? Once again I was confused.

My mind was like a rollercoaster driven by a psychotic mad man. I was only two weeks into the trip and I had already experienced giddy highs and terrifying lows. There were sure to be plenty of twists along the way and I had to be ready to face them head on.

Things could be much better travelling on my own, I owed it to myself to find out.

After saying goodbye to Gordana, I left the hostel and walked to the bus stop to board the night bus to a place called San Cristobal. Even I could catch a bus.

I arrived at the bus station twenty minutes before the bus was due to depart. I went to the counter and gave the woman behind the screen my eight digit booking number. She smiled at me as she punched the numbers into the computer. She looked up at me shaking her head,

'No ticket senor, no ticket no boose!' she told me.

'Si, si, senorita I do! The touristico companio sorted it, take this numero,' I replied.

I was unable to understand a thing that she was saying. The bus was due to depart and still I wasn't allowed to board. Maybe I was going to be stuck in Puerto Escondido forever.

Another attendant came out from the back office and requested my passport. I duly obliged.

A few confusing minutes passed before they managed to find my booking. It was my fault for having the wrong booking number.

I was convinced that a name search would have been easier. I didn't think that many people with the name Gareth Jones were travelling around in Mexico, let alone on this bus.

I sat in my seat with seconds to spare and breathed a sigh of relief. Travelling alone was tough.

San Cristobal

Sat in front of me on the bus was a guy called Andy from Liverpool. He had been staying at Tower Bridge but we hadn't really spoken. He had told me about his ear infection; that was as far as our conversation had gone.

Andy looked like a typical English office worker. He was clean shaven with short brown hair that he brushed forward. He wore thin framed glasses and looked like he wouldn't hurt a fly. He was wearing a t-shirt that he had bought in Thailand, it read:

'Phuk Mi.'

I thought the exact same thing about why he would wear such a thing and guessed that if someone actually offered to, he would run a mile. There was nothing exciting about Andy, but he was harmless so I spoke to him as the bus pulled away into the night.

I didn't like Andy at first; he didn't stop talking for the first three hours of the trip. He mostly talked about sex and girls, like a laxative he irritated the shit out of me. I could tell he would want to hang around with me as we were both English and travelling alone.

The bus wound up the mountain roads in pitch darkness at reckless speeds, making it virtually impossible to get any sleep. It was my Mission Impossible and, like Tom Cruise, I decided to give it a go.

1) I contorted my body into different shapes in a bid to sleep, using the window as a pillow

2) I managed to beat the odds and sleep for a short period of time 3) I then flipped out, unaware of my surroundings as the bus swayed viciously to one side

4) I fell asleep again this time across the seats

6) I woke up believing for a short time that I was paralysed

7) The feeling eventually returns to my dead arms as I sat up in my seat

8) I checked the time by pressing the top left button on the side of my Casio watch

9) I looked and realised that only an hour had passed since I last looked

10) Annoyed and with limited options, I decided to revert to step one in the hope of more luck

The process continued until early morning when the sun broke. I opened my eyes and the bright morning sunshine hit me like a slap in the face. I was so tired and confused that I thought that I was dreaming. The bus pulled into the station, we had arrived in San Cristobal.

San Cristobal is a colonial city in the state of Chiapas, resting in the central highlands of Mexico 2100ft above sea level. I wasn't sure what the mountain range was called as I didn't have a Lonely Planet guide and whenever I went on the internet I just got distracted by other more important things; Facebook, music and porn. It was a hard habit to break.

I enjoyed downloading music and porn back home; it had become a lot easier with the introduction of home broadband. I still remembered leaving downloads for a full day only to return and find that nothing had downloaded or the connection had been lost.

Kids nowadays don't realise how lucky they are when it comes to porn on the internet. They can switch on the computer and have vast amounts in seconds. When I was at primary school I used to have a wank when I typed the digits **55318008** into a calculator.

Our generation are obsessed with the internet. Social networking sites like MySpace and Facebook were the ultimate in procrastination. My boss had to ban staff from using them at work because no one was working, we were just farting around.

I remember a colleague at work being asked to make some coffees as he was behind his targets. Before he made them my computer flashed up with a Facebook update:

'Mudassar is pissed off he has to make his boss another coffee.'

The world had gone internet mad. I was going to have to use it as I had no idea what to do or where to go.

Andy predictably suggested that we should check into a hostel together. He had written a few down and seemed to know what he was doing. We jumped into the back of a taxi.

The town's buildings were all low rise, colourful but run down and made of concrete. I noticed that a lot of them were colonial homes with an indigenous flavour. The narrow streets had a real charm and character about them. I liked what I saw.

As I woke up and began to relax, I warmed to Andy. We sat in the main square close to an ornate orange and red pastel church and had a coffee while taking in the atmosphere.

San Cristobal was awash with locals trying to sell things to tourists. The main culprits were small children and old women. The women looked like leather couches with eyes and, like furniture stores, they were having a sale.

The small indigenous children swam around in the sea of tourists trying to sell cigarettes and chewing gum that they carried in small wooden trays attached round their small necks.

After walking around for a few hours I decided to go back to Casa Sol, the hostel we had checked into that morning.

On the way back to the room I bumped into two familiar faces, Mark and Craig were walking down the road in my direction. It was instantly awkward. Our interaction reminded me of bumping into my old girlfriend in the supermarket.

'Hi, long time no see. What are you doing here?' I asked.

'You know just getting some food,' she replied.

'So am I, but then why else would we be here right?'

'Well good to see you, I need to go up here for some chicken.'

I stood in the supermarket watching as she pushed her trolley down the pet food aisle; once a dog always a dog.

Like the supermarket scenario it was inevitable that we would bump into each other, San Cristobal was only a small town. We decided to do the sensible thing and meet up for dinner that evening as both Mark and Craig were leaving the following morning, apparently to different places. I had my doubts.

I met them at a bar called Revolution. It wasn't very Mexican but was full of Mexican people. They were sat around a table with familiar faces from earlier parts of the trip. Brendan, a dreadlocked Australian we had met at Tower Bridge, was sat between Nanna and Mirte, two Danish sisters I had spoken with briefly when we arrived in Oaxaca. Finally there was Inga who had been in Puerto Escondido with us for our first few days. Andy and I sat down.

Conversation flowed as easily as the beer. Everyone liked Andy whose laugh was hilarious, sounding like an un-tuned radio on full blast. He had brought along a small bottle of Mescal and generously shared it with the group.

After dinner Mark and Craig left as they were still recovering from the previous night. Andy and I stayed at the bar with Inga and Nanna to listen to the live music that was about to start.

Inga was from Amsterdam and was a laid-back woman. She had long, matted blonde hair and a white face covered with freckles, looking like a cookie. She dressed for comfort, sitting warmly in traditional Mexican woollen items.

Nanna had beautiful skin and a cute, blemish-free face that was framed with a pretty blonde hair. She was the proud owner of a pair of large firm-looking breasts, a point that Andy repeatedly reminded me of.

The music on offer was strange; I was unable to categorise it into any specific genre. The lead singer wailed into the microphone as if chanting. To his left a small man in a poncho beat a small pair of bongos. To the other side a tall woman played what looked like an accordion.

We decided after four similar sounding songs that things were not going to improve and so we braved the cold that was stirring around the streets outside.

I walked back through the cobbled streets of San Cristobal with Inga. Andy had randomly run off as we left the bar. I assumed that he had stolen something.

Outside it was freezing. The sky was crystal clear, meaning that the temperature dropped considerably. Maybe Andy had just run to keep warm?

Locals huddled up outside the numerous monuments and churches covering their faces with dark ponchos and woolly hats. The soft street lights danced off them, making them look like bags of rubbish against a wall.

Small groups of children presumably orphans slept by the huge church doorways, as passing tourists left bits of change. I toyed with the idea of telling Inga a joke to break the silence,

'Why do orphans go to church? It's the only place they can call someone Father.'

I decided to break the silence with some loose change instead.

On the way to the hostel we walked past a bar that looked lively so we decided to have a couple more drinks before calling it a night.

We walked into a throw-back disco as Cher's hit If I Could Turn Back Time echoed off the cement walls. I sat down and scanned the bar; it looked and sounded like someone had beaten her to it. Green lasers skipped off the black walls as we ordered a couple of strawberry daiquiris from the bar.

It took about five minutes before I realised it was a gay bar. The barmen were all staring at me wearing yellow hard hats and white vests. That was my first clue. The second came when I realised that all the music had been of the camp variety. The case was solved with the third and final clue. I noticed that I was drinking a daiquiri and singing Sisters Sledge's We are Family. I had to leave before I became emasculated. I looked at Inga and spoke like Sherlock Holmes,

'This is all very queer Inga. Hard hats, daiquiris, eighties anthems, men kissing by the toilets, why I deduce that these are the acts of a gay proprietor; we must leave with haste.'

I climbed off my large metal stool, tipped back the rest of my drink and left.

On return to Andy's room I was unable to get in. He had the key and through the clouded glass I could see that he had passed out.

Inga kindly offered to let me sleep with her. I lay with her in bed fully clothed as it was freezing. She had more layers than an onion so there was no chance of anything happening. We were just friends. It was so cold if I had got an erection it would have probably snapped in two.

I woke the next day and decided to go on a canyon tour that was arranged through the tour company I had booked my bus tickets with. It was free and gave a structure to my day.

The Canyon de Sumidero was spectacular. The boat whistled across the narrow river of water that intersected the towering cliffs on either side. The tour guide only spoke Spanish. He was about as useful as an erection in a convent. The initial wonder passed after ten minutes.

I spent the next three hours sat on a boat listening to a middle-aged German lady talk to me about birds and crocodiles. She sat at the edge of the boat snapping away constantly with her camera. The sound was torturous.

The problem with going on trips alone is that you leave yourself in the cruel hands of fate. I had been dealt a bad hand. I had to spend most of my day chatting to a Nazi loner. I hoped that next time it would fall in my favour.

I arrived back in beautiful San Cristobal by late afternoon and decided that I wanted to leave the following day. I had the choice of going into Guatemala or sticking with Mexico and making my way to the Yucatán via Palenque. I chose the second of these options.

San Cristobal was too cold and Guatemala seemed too much of a challenge. I looked forward to waving goodbye to humble sad people in ponchos, and saying hello to happy females in bikinis.

Palenque

I woke up at 6:00am and it was deathly cold. I took off several layers of clothes, feeling like a pass the parcel item before I finally reached the prize of my skin. I attempted to shower down the hall but the water was like ice. I decided to just get changed and pack my bags.

It was my nephew Ben's third birthday so I took out my neglected mobile and gave him a call, safe in the knowledge that by lunch time he would have forgotten about it. It was a pity that my mobile phone provider could not do the same.

It is a real nightmare talking to a three-year-old on the phone; throw a slight phone delay into the mix and it became impossible. I sat on the curb waiting for the minibus, talking like a character from Sesame Street while asking him a series of short questions.

'What have you got for your birthday? What is your cake like? What is it like being three?'

The one that interested me was the last one. At the age of twenty-six I had totally forgotten what is was like to be three years old. I hoped that it was exciting.

The minibus to Palenque arrived an hour late. Rather than be annoyed I was just thankful that it had eventually showed up. I didn't want to stay in San Cristobal.

The driver greeted me enthusiastically. He was a short Mexican gentleman in his forties and wore a cowboy hat. I climbed into the back of the bus and said hello to the fellow passengers. To my delight two Australian girls were sat on the back seat who I had spoken to briefly in San Cristobal. Jackpot!

The driver seemed determined to make back the lost minutes, he accelerated so hard I was surprised his foot hadn't gone through the bottom of the bus. He may have been in his forties but he drove like a ten year old playing a computer game with no regards for our safety. We thundered down the mountains at a frantic pace, he was going so fast that I would not have been surprised if we reached our destination yesterday.

Our first stop was called Agua Azul, a waterfall that joined two of the rivers flowing through the Chiapas region. The waterfall was beautiful but paled in comparison to Niagara Falls that I had seen only three weeks earlier.

As I jumped out of the bus a siege of cute children surrounded me trying to sell cigarettes and fruit. I wanted neither. But, because they were all cute I took a photograph and gave each of them a couple of pesos.

I walked around the waterfall with the feeling that I was being followed. It turned out that I was. Rather than an old man or anyone remotely threatening, I was being followed by a group of female students from a nearby school. They were all about twelve years old.

After a prolonged period of time one of the girls came over and asked if she could have her photograph taken with me. Of course I agreed.

One photograph ended up being ten as each of the girls wanted their picture taken against the backdrop of the beautiful waterfall. Just when I thought my obligations were over the teacher suggested an eleventh and final picture with everyone in it. I felt famous and far from being annoying, I loved it.

The smallest of the girls came over to me, smiling wildly in my direction and asked,

'Nombre?'

I thought that she was asking for my mobile number and didn't know what to do. A picture was fine but giving out contact details to an underage child could land me in serious water. What if her dad was gang affiliated? I wouldn't see out the week.

Not wanting to hurt her feelings I took my phone out of my pocket and was going to tell her that it was broken, I couldn't think of anything else. As I pulled out my phone the group of on-looking girls started laughing. The girl touched my hand laughing and said,

'Non, nombre.'

The ball dropped. My skin started to burn as I smiled,

'Lo syiento amiga. My name is Gareth. Ga-re-th,' I repeated slowly.

Feeling overwhelmed I walked back to the car park and sat on a wooden bench in the sun waiting for the rest of the group to return.

We had dropped from the highlands and were now surrounded by tropical jungle. By late afternoon we arrived in Palenque. We drove through the small, tired-looking town straight up to the entrance of the archaeological site a few miles into the surrounding forest.

Outside the site were a number of street vendors in traditional Mayan costumes. They offered everything from food to handicrafts, hats, ponchos, maps, and jewellery. They also offered guided tours of the ruins. Old wooden shops flanked either side of the entrance; I stood and stared at a small family that rested under a tree. Each of them wore bright white gowns tied across the midriff with old rope. They looked biblical.

The Maya ruins at Palenque were breathtaking. It was such a peaceful, mystical place. There were a lot of people but it was quiet, it felt like the gods were watching my every move. I sat in the grounds relaxing and for the first time was glad to be on my own. Rather than explore too much I sat on the dark green grass by one of the main structures and found peace. It had been an incredible few weeks.

The trip had not given the form of escape that I was after. If anything I was more confused and anxious than I had been at home. I wanted the trip to be simple and fun. I wanted to relax and not worry about anything. Sitting on my own in such spiritual surroundings I realised that this could still be the case. I had to be comfortable in myself and stop relying on other people. The rest would take care of itself.

The site closed at 7:00pm so I ambled back to the coach talking with the two girls from Australia. They had decided they were going to go to Palenque and get a bus straight to Merida overnight. They asked if I wanted to join them. I was tempted but after a long day I just wanted to put my feet up and relax.

I jumped out of the coach a mile down the road at the simply named Palenque Hostel. The hostel sat away from the road leading up to the ruins and resembled a jungle retreat. As there were no dormitories I checked into my own private bungalow.

The hostel centred on a large restaurant near the entrance. From there a host of paths weaved in and out of the trees leading to a series of small bungalows, it was like a small village. As darkness descended I could barely see a thing. I lay on my bed listening to the sound of distant monkeys and the buzzing of mosquitos while reading.

I walked towards the hazy glow of the restaurant, the darkness alleviated for small split seconds by the thousands of fireflies that circled overhead. I was hungry and had arranged to meet some people I had spoken to when checking in.

I sat down on a table of twenty as they went around the table introducing themselves. I felt like a king and decided to stop listening to the deluge of names after storing those closest to me. I could ask them if it was deemed necessary.

I felt a tap on my right shoulder. Before I could turn a long thing arm had wrapped around my neck and was tipping my chair from side to side,

'What are you doing here you nipple?' asked the familiar voice.

He released the grip from my neck. It was Mark.

'Alright mate. Decided I would prefer to party in Cancun than go to Guatemala basically.'

'Same here,' he replied.

'Where is Craig?' I asked.

'He has gone with Inga to Guatemala, meant to be meeting him at some point pre-Peru. Mate I'm gonna jog the booked Machu Picchu trip, just cannot be around Gemma at all,' he said.

'Yeah it was awkward. Who are you with? I'll come over in a bit'

'Come now you berk. Just there with the great Danes and Brendan.'

I looked round and waved at them. Perhaps fate was finally working in my favour. I finished my drink and went over to their table.

The restaurant was open, resembling a huge gazebo. A series of black pillars held up the wooden and straw roof. A series of lights and fans hung on the underside of the roof above all the tables and chairs. The bar and kitchen area sat to the left of the main dining area, the latter housed inside a green building open on one side.

I ended up getting completely smashed sat around the table. Mark was more relaxed than I had seen him the whole trip and I enjoyed his company. He explained his reasons for leaving Puerto Escondido and suggested that if I was going to Cancun we should travel together. I surprisingly wasn't so sure but was willing to see how things would go.

Mark left the restaurant with Mirte, and Brendan had long since gone to bed as Mark and he had got really drunk the previous night. This left me sitting with the beautiful Nanna. I asked if she would like me to walk her back to their room. She liked the idea very much,

'Yes that would be very nice of you, thank you.'

'It is not a problem, the jungle isn't safe at night,' I joked.

We stumbled through the trees in relative darkness. The fireflies from earlier were probably tucked up in bed asleep. The only light came from the moon that struggled to break through the jungle canopy. Nanna knew the way to her room; I had no idea at all where mine was.

As I said good night she grabbed my left arm and said,

'I like you Gaz, you are nice.'

She kissed me before I had chance to agree.

Her room was a lot bigger than mine but similar in appearance. It was simple and split into two main rooms with a bathroom, separated by flimsy wooden shutters. The light in the main room as we entered the apartment was on. Brendan was on one of the beds passed out. Mark and Mirte were in the other room presumably asleep as it was dark. Nanna went to check that her sister was safe as I lay down in the main room, across from Brendan. The bed was covered with ants.

I heard water running in the bathroom. As Nanna got ready for bed I lay on the empty bed optimistic staring in the direction of the bathroom. In a few minutes she would appear in her sexy underwear and jump on me.

She came back into the room wearing a white t-shirt, some comfortable looking navy blue sweat pants, and had toothpaste around her mouth. It wasn't going to be as easy as I thought. She flicked off the single light bulb that lit the room and climbed into bed.

We kissed in the darkness as the sounds of the forest echoed outside. I started to celebrate my home run, moving up and down before the umpire made a controversial late call. Nanna had changed her mind,

'We have to stop. Not with Brendan in the room, it's not right.'

I lay half naked in the darkness staring up at the white ceiling as Nanna rested on my chest. I could feel ants crawling on the sheets, but did not have the energy to move.

I wished that the ants were English and able to understand and obey my orders. Rather than look for crumbs on the bed, I wished for them to get together and carry Brendan out the room. I was willing to make it worth their time.

It was no use, they were Spanish speaking and under strict instructions to collect the broken digestive biscuits from the mattress and floor. Where were English ants when you needed them the most?

The next time I pack my bags for a long trip, I will think more about what I put in there:

- Toothpaste
- Clothes
- Sleeping bag
- Towel
- Torch
- Mosquito net
- Jar of English ants
- Lonely Planet guides

I woke up early the next morning as birds and monkeys whistled and howled respectively. I stumbled into the bathroom holding my fuzzy head in my hands. I looked into the mirror and saw a red mark to the left of my mouth. Concerned, I picked at it with my middle finger nail. It was an ant that had been crushed and subsequently murdered by my face. I peeled it off and quickly flushed the evidence down the toilet.

Everyone was still asleep so I left quietly and now that it was light, I was able to easily find my room.

I spent the morning sat in the restaurant reading and talking to people that I had apparently told my life story to the previous evening. I had no knowledge of speaking to half of them.

Mark and Brendan both joined me as the two Danish girls decided that they were going on a supervised trek through the jungle to some waterfalls.

After lunch Brendan and I had a few beers. We decided that we should try to catch one of the Howler Monkeys that live in the surrounding jungle and could be heard with every breathing second.

Mark decided to stay at the hostel, offering to book the night bus to Merida, which was to be our next destination.

Brendan and I were an advert for what not to do in the jungle. We set off with no medical supplies, no compass, no water and no idea. Drunk and unfazed by an overgrown garden we walked away from the main road into dense vegetation, in shorts wearing open sandals. Brendan was determined to catch a monkey.

I followed close behind with the voice of BBC presenter Michael Burke ringing in my ears. Growing up he had hosted a programme that reconstructed rescue attempts for those in trouble, called 999. I didn't know the emergency numbers for Mexico, even if I did it was no use as neither of us had taken our phones.

As we disappeared into the jungle Michael's voice would not disappear. I was acting out a live reconstruction and was waiting for something to go wrong,

'Hello and welcome to tonight's episode of 999, I'm Michael Burke. We start tonight's very special episode in the heart of central Mexico in the state of Chiapas as two inexperienced backpackers make the mistake of entering the jungle without an experienced guide.'

'The two men have set off without water and are ill-equipped for the challenges that lay ahead of them. They set off with four bottles of Corona in humid 30c temperatures.'

'The average human body looses two litres of water per hour. In a state of intoxication these numbers are doubled as alcohol accelerates the process of dehydration. Without water both of these young men will be in serious trouble.'

'Unaware of the risks the jungle poses they skip into its depths pretending to be monkeys howling up into the trees, alerting dangerous animals to their presence. In the space of few hours they could be lost forever. After the break we will show you what happened. I'm Michael Burke.'

Brendan returned from the jungle annoyed. He was enthusiastic about nature, a Steve Irwin with dreadlocks and was disappointed that we had not managed to even catch a glimpse of the area's monkey population,

'There aren't any fuckers out there. It is all a fantasy for tourists. I bet they have bloody speakers in the trees. Pissed off.'

'We saw some monkeys,' shouted Mirte excitedly.

'I bet your even more pissed now Brendan,' joked Mark.

I ordered two bottles of water from the bar and threw one over to an inconsolable Brendan.

The Danish girls decided that they were going to join us in Merida. Brendan decided that he was going to go to Guatemala so we said our goodbyes.

Before leaving Mark managed to convince me to down a shot of red hot sauce. The label depicted a man in pain breathing fire as a happy looking chilli stood next to him wearing a sombrero.

After drinking the sauce I collapsed on the concrete floor sweating and unable to breathe. It felt like I had just swallowed the sun, I awaited the flames and hoped to see the happy chilli make an appearance; least then the pain would be worth it.

Merida and Chichen Itze

Merida is the capital and largest city within the Yucatan state of Mexico. It is known as the 'White City', not because it was created for white people or inhabited solely by whites, but because of the large amount of limestone used in the town's architecture. It looked like a beautiful city.

The night bus left the four of us drained. Mark had taken a host of items from the girls to try and help him sleep including:

- Two sleeping pills

- A blow up pillow

- Pyjama bottoms

- A pink sleeping bag

It looked like a six foot glow worm was catching the night bus; he looked an idiot, not to mention a major fire hazard. Apparently none of the items had helped him. As we pulled into the station the giant glow worm looked at me,

'I've had no fucking sleep again, not even an hour.'

'Rubbish mate I saw you sleeping,' I countered.

'Just closing my eyes mate, closing my eyes.'

I stumbled off the bus irritated and tired as we paced through the busy terminal. My annoyance was alleviated briefly when I spotted a short fat Mexican in a red Manchester United shirt. He leant against an iron pillar chatting casually on his mobile phone by the entrance to the station. I approached him like a Spanish conquistador and demanded a photograph.

'Manchester United. Bueno. Photo senor?" I asked.

'Si,' he beamed.

He wore shades and his hair was black but receding. He looked like a Mexican David Guest. The man smiled like a Cheshire cat towards the camera as I pulled a disgusted face directed at the shirt. I hated Manchester United, as did Mark.

The first thing I noticed as I walked through Merida was not the architecture, but the town's obsession with hammocks and Panama hats. Every second shop sold hammocks and every one between, Panama hats.

I didn't want a hat or a hammock, we needed a hostel. I walked in the sunshine sweating like a pregnant nun, exhausted and needing to sleep.

We found a hostel near to the main square in the city centre. Mark and I went straight to bed while the Danish duo decided to go for a walk around the town.

I woke up and had a look around the hostel we had checked into. It was similar to the one we had stayed at in Oaxaca. The hostel was a single story property with simple high ceiling rooms built around a main courtyard. The cement walls and arches were all terracotta giving the place a colonial feel similar to the place in Mexico City.

I noticed a lot of signs attached to the walls, on further inspection I realised that they were rules. One read:

'No noise after 11:00pm. If you disturb the peace you will be asked to leave.'

Someone had gone on a PowerPoint power trip. There was no way we would be sticking to half the instructions they had put up. Despite sleeping I was sure Mark had already broken some of them.

The reception sat by the entrance to the hostel in a light blue room. There was a main desk with a number of books and leaflets outlining potential activities in the surrounding area. There was also another printed sign with the warning, 'Beware, do not pay too much for your hammock'.

I couldn't help but laugh. What was it with this place and hammocks? Was it really necessary to beware of being ripped off for a hammock?

I'm sure worse things happened to people when travelling. They should have mentioned other things on laminated paper as well, 'Beware of men, they could rape you'. Or, 'Beware of people with knives'.

Hammocks were the least of my worries. I was more concerned with breaking the hostel rules. I must be quiet after 11:00pm repeated over and over in my head.

'Why do you laugh my friend?' asked an unrecognised voice.

I peered over the tall counter and saw a short man sitting down behind the reception desk watching what looked like a Mexican soap opera on a small portable television.

'The obsession with hammocks mainly my man.'

The receptionist's name was Pablo. He felt the need to tell me about his experiences with hammocks,

'My friend, I used to have a single hammock, but as I got older and had a family the hammock got bigger. Now at home my whole family sleep in one hammock.'

'How many are in your family?' I asked.

'There are six of us. If I am to have more children I will buy a bigger hammock. When my children are old enough they will get their own hammock and I may downsize mine. I will have to discuss this with my wife.'

'What is wrong with a bed Pablo?'

'Nothing, we just prefer hammocks. They are made here and are good for your back.'

I didn't want to challenge his belief system too much, it was clear that he loved hammocks so it was easier to just agree,

'I love hammocks Pablo; if I had one everyday would feel like a holiday! You are a lucky man.'

I woke Mark up. The girls had not returned so we had the evening to ourselves. Mark was convinced that when we returned we would sleep with the two of them that night,

'Mate, imagine the two of us having sex with them at the same time. Two Danish sisters in the same room being reduced. It will happen,' he announced.

Being more pragmatic I was not so sure. It was the sort of situation I dreamed about being in back home so didn't want to get my hopes up. Mark's were already soaring. To him it was simple and it was going to happen.

Before heading into town Mark left a note on the small wooden desk in our shared room,

'Hello Girls, gone for scran in town. We will be back to reduce you later.'

Mark thought writing a note in slang would completely throw the two of them and he was right. After some uninspiring food and a walk around the town we returned to the hostel.

The girls were lying in bed reading. Mirte glanced at the letter we had left and questions arose immediately,

'Mark what is scran?'

(Pause)

'What does reduce mean?' she asked.

'Scran just means food. Reduce just means to meet you. Gone for food back to meet you later on,' he explained.

'Oh ok, that's what we both thought,' she then satisfactorily replied.

'It's just a northern thing, don't worry about it,' he assured.

I remained silent during this brief exchange, looking at Mark's surly grin and trying my best not to laugh.

'You guys are just crazy,' Nanna said.

'Are we?' Mark jokingly concluded.

We sat in the dorm room winding down and chatting with one another. The room was nothing special; it comprised of two large bunk beds, a white desk and a set of four lockers.

As the night drew to its conclusion I was joined in bed by Nanna as Mark had cheekily got in with Mirte. Maybe his earlier prediction was going to come true? I began to get excited.

I lay in the dark with Nanna listening to the two of them kissing. It made Nanna feel awkward. No one wanted to hear their older sister having sex; she was no different.

The best course of action was to put on some music and kiss ourselves, that way she wouldn't hear anything. It was the perfect solution. I put on Jose Gonzales, whose lyrics strangely mirrored the situation we were in.

'To lead me past, their sly disguise, my moves are slow but soon they'll know, behind the scenes they grow their schemes, hiding intentions, revealing only fractions.'

My moves went from slow to non-existent within a few minutes. The situation felt forced. I liked Nanna but her mind was preoccupied with the events on the other bed. I decided to stop. She looked over at the outline of shadows moving on the adjacent bunk as I just stared at the wall, a prisoner on my own bed.

I turned the music up hoping that it could lead to my expulsion from the hostel. It was worth the risk as it beat listening to Mark procreating a few metres away.

I sat in the court yard having breakfast the following morning. Mark told me that despite the noises nothing had happened with Mirte because her baby sister was in the room. They had cancelled each other out, we had both failed.

Mark and I decided to leave Merida and take the short ride by mini bus to Chichen Itze which was the most well known archaeological site in Mexico. I had seen pictures of it on the internet, clearly it was symbolic of the nation and I looked forward to seeing it up close.

Chichen Itze was only a few hours away, halfway between Merida and the tourist resort of Cancun. We parked up at the site and could not have been blamed for thinking it was Disney World.

The car park was huge and full of coaches. The entrance was large with theatrical letters cut into a cliff face, the queues were endless. I mused there were probably rides and characters inside to mollify the mass of American tourists; it was so different to Palenque.

As we waited in line to enter the site gone were indigenous locals selling handicrafts, jewellery and cheap food. Instead there were restaurants with steak subs and jumbo hot dogs, payable in pesos or dollars.

I was disgusted by what I saw and was not holding much hope for the site. As we entered through the futuristic turnstiles I momentarily thought I was entering space camp.

The elaborate entrance opened after a few hundred yards into a large grass field. In the middle sat the main part of the ruins, a large stepped pyramid that felt familiar. The sun beat off its aging white rock and it looked incredible, far larger than I had anticipated. In each corner of the field were a series of paths that led to other parts of the site.

I was pleased that the ruins were authentic. They were well preserved and unlike Palenque you were not allowed to climb on them.

Fortunately there was no Mayan Mouse or the Chichen Itze chicken, but there were thousands of American day trippers from Cancun. They were loud and annoying which totally spoilt the site's spirituality. For the first time in weeks we were caught in a tourist trap and, with Cancun being the next destination, it was only going to get worse. We had no choice but to just go with it.

We were distracted by the mass of tourists. Rather than enjoy the wonder of the site and its ruins we played spot the ridiculous American. There were quite a few to choose from.

I spotted one gentleman across the field leaning against a tree standing like a teapot. He was wearing inconceivably short shorts and a huge t-shirt with the slogan 'Sun Cream Inspector' across it. He looked like a registered sex offender.

Mark spotted a teenager wearing a beer hat. It was made of yellow plastic and had two black can holders at either side with a large straw coming from each. In the holders he had two paper cups full of juice.

He walked behind his parents sucking on the straw, staring down at his feet bored. I remembered my parents taking me on tours when I was younger, how could parents be so selfish. The novelty hat had at least softened the blow.

The ruins were spectacular, but they didn't have the charm or personal effect that I experienced days earlier in Palenque. I wondered whether it was because I wasn't on my own and Mark distracted me or more that my enjoyment was stifled by the sheer volume of people.

We spent a few hours lying around in the sun. It was hotter than two rats fucking in a wool sock so we took the opportunity to sunbathe.

Chichen Itze town was small and there was nothing there apart from a few overpriced hotels. It only existed to service people visiting the ruins and was boring. We were both tired but decided it best to get on the bus to Cancun. The weekend was approaching and after all the cultural stimulation it was time for the both of us to party.

Unaware of the time, we missed the first class bus along the coast to Cancun. So rather than an hour drive we had no choice but to get the local bus that took six. The bus was old and battered. As night fell we sat in complete darkness as the bus stopped in every town and at every stop. We were both freezing cold.

Cancun

Six hours of dimly lit towns and darkness gradually subsided as we approached Cancun. I glared through the rain soaked window of the bus and winced at a trail of neon signs that straddled the road like cheap prostitutes.

My eyes adjusted to the light as I awoke from my half sleep. I was momentarily confused as we passed a Dominos Pizza and a large Kentucky Fried Chicken. Had we been drugged and flown to Florida, I couldn't believe this was still Mexico.

I woke Mark, who was again not sleeping as we drove by a Blockbuster Video store and the first of several McDonald's. It was so far removed from the places I had visited in Mexico.

We sat in amazement, shocked by the clear exploitation on this patch of paradise. Ahead we could see the faint outline of huge towering hotel developments that blocked the night sky. There was a clear difference between travelling and going on holiday. It was clear Cancun would highlight this to the extreme.

I started to doubt the point in visiting a place like this. Why would people want to eat the same food they could get at home, or go to similar bars? I guessed we were creatures of comfort and some people just liked the safe, the familiar.

I could sense I wasn't going to like the place; my opinions had shifted. Places like this used to excite me, I now found them boring. Everything about Cancun was geared towards taking my money and it didn't hide that fact.

As we walked out through the station, I spotted a big shopping arcade with a huge TGI Friday to the left of its glass entrance. I overheard a fat America woman sat on her huge suitcase that lay on the pavement,

'Hey man, frigging awesome they got a TGI Fridays. I'm like, so eating there tomorrow.'

I bet Mark that she would more than likely eat there within ten minutes such was her excitement. We got into a taxi and headed towards a hostel that Mark picked out of the budget section of his Lonely Planet guide.

The hostel was situated in a residential area of downtown. A dirty refuge for local people to live away from the glitz and glamour of high class hotels that parked up and down the coastline.

The hostel made me feel anxious as it was a converted house. We approached the front door like we were about to ask a stranger if we could possibly pay to stay with them for a few nights. I always found bed and breakfasts at home a strange concept.

The homeowner was a tall blonde woman called Monica, she was extremely pleasant. After showing us around her home she made us a couple of Margaritas. We sat in the garden with her and a few other guests having a cordial chat. Monica had blatantly had cosmetic surgery; she was in her forties but had the breasts of a teenager and a permanent smile.

Monica liked the two of us which made conversation less awkward than it could have been. She told us that as well as running the hostel she was a dance instructor, often putting on shows in the local area. She bought her performers from Cuba.

As she continued it was apparent that she was actually running a theatrical slave trade. She paid off the government to allow these people into Mexico, where they became her responsibility. Sometimes they tried to escape,

'Last year six of my best dancers stole my choreography and vanished. They tried to put on the show in other towns before attempting to dance across the border into America. They were caught and deported back to Cuba. They should not have left me,' she said.

I was in total shock and preferred to just nod in agreement.

I wondered whether she had Cubans working for her in other areas away from the theatre. I asked if she had made the mistake of hiring a Cuban accountant, apparently they always fideled the books. With thoughts of her disobedient Cuban army in my head I decided to call it a night. It had been a long day and she was beginning to scare me.

I lay in bed unable to sleep, concerned that the Margaritas I had drank had been spiked. Mark and I would wake up the next morning in cages as part of Maniac Monica's travelling Circus.

I woke refreshed and unharmed the following morning and went with Mark to the beach, a short bus ride from downtown Cancun on the hotel strip.

Cancun is home to more than a hundred hotels and has around four million visitors per year. As I walked down to the beach I found my eyes being constantly diverted by large billboards promoting parties and upcoming events. A series of bars drenched the main street with free bar promotions and attention grabbing signs. It felt a lot like Las Vegas, it was artificial but fun.

We cut down a narrow path between two large hotels and onto the beach. We settled outside the Hard Rock Café by some hard rocks. The beach, while narrow, was beautiful. The sand was almost perfectly white, inviting turquoise water lapped gently onto the beach.

Behind us the Café had a huge black sign with a bent fork saying 'we will, we will feed you,' a clever reworking of 'we will rock you'. It contrasted sharply to the light natural beauty of the beach, one of the two felt totally out of place.

I wished I had visited Cancun before the explosion of international tourism. It was a good looking girl that wore too much make up and dressed like a slag.

I started speaking to some Scandinavian girls on the beach hoping that they were slags. It was ok for humans to be slags. The girls were all from Malmo, the same city as Gordana, who I had met in Puerto Escondido. It made conversation pretty easy as I knew quite a bit about Malmo as a result of my time with Gordana.

I asked if they were excited by the construction of the new Malmo metro line for example,

'I believe it will be completed by 2012, got to be handy that hasn't it?'

I didn't get the enthusiastic reply I was looking for and guessed that they just thought I was weird. In retrospect talking about transport links in the company of five topless girls on the beach was a mistake. I attempted to redeem myself with a topical joke,

'Did you hear about the Swedish thief?' I asked.

'No,'

'He tried to take Stockholm.'

Half of them laughed including the two I considered the best looking. I sat down on the sand. The girls were all at the end of their trip and were having ten days in Cancun to round things off before heading back to Sweden. Mark eventually came over and we sat with them for an hour talking about our travels.

They planned on going to a club called Daddy O's that night and suggested that we meet them there,

'We will see, not sure what we are doing to be honest,' I replied.

They knew as well as we did that we would both be there no matter what. We said our goodbyes and made our way back to Monica's after a long day in the sun.

After eating at a local food market we bought some beers and sat on the roof terrace of Monica's house with a real pick 'n' mix of guests.

Firstly there was a fifty-five-year-old toothless Irish man called Paul, who lived in America and was in Cancun on holiday. Then there was a student called John from Sheffield whose voice was that stale that he could have put a glass eye to sleep. He was due to be studying volcanic activity in Guatemala for the next few months and had just arrived.

Two Korean students sat with us smoking cigarettes and listening to all of our stupid stories from back home and earlier in the trip.

Finally there was Malcolm. Malcolm was originally from Malta but had lived in London for many years. He was taking time out of work to travel and had just returned from a short trip to Cuba. He had a bad experience there and could not stop talking about the place.

He sat in the beret made famous by Che Guevara and after a few joints wanted to start a revolution of his own. Paradoxically the more he smoked the less motivated he became. His ideas would have to wait; he was all talk and no action.

Just as we were about to leave the hostel and go into town three new people showed up at Monica's; two Australian girls and an English man they had met at the airport. One of the girls, Mimi, decided to dump her bags and come out with us. I liked her carefree attitude and was happy for her to come along. Malcolm stayed at the hostel stoned and unable to move.

The streets of Cancun resembled that of any bar street across the world. Promoters desperately clawed at us and demanded that we drink at their establishments. Each of them tried to offer something different but in reality they were all offering the same thing. It was extremely loud and hostile on the strip with neon lights and fast music dominating the atmosphere. Places that by day looked like nothing more than half built stages were now heaving with people dancing around and having fun.

We ignored the majority of the promoters on the street until one offered us cheap tickets to Daddy O's. All of the bars on the strip charged an upfront fee for entry. Once in you were then entitled to drink as much alcohol as you could. Mark and I were excited, putting the two of us in a free bar was like letting Michael Douglas loose in a strip club, neither of us had any self control.

Daddy O's was a really big place split over several large rooms. Lasers flashed off the towering black walls as music spilled out of huge speaker systems onto the larger dance floor. It was almost impossible to hear each other speak so we didn't, we just drank and drank.

As I began to drown my body in alcohol I started talking to anyone that showed an interest. We found out that it was Thanksgiving, which went someway to explaining the number of Americans that we met.

In one of the quieter rooms I started to talk to a big American man called Geoff. He was chubby, with a grizzly beard and dry, mid-length hair. He looked like either a wrestler or an oil tycoon, I couldn't decide which. I found that Geoff laughed at almost anything that I said. He looked at me and asked if I would wait where I was while he got his wife.

'You just stay there boy, my wife has got to meet you. She will love you, just you wait, she has to meet you,' he cackled.

I decided to obey his order, who was I to quash a precious moment in his over-enthused life? As the minutes passed I increasingly felt like this was going to be a bad idea. I stood by the side of the room drinking vodka and orange, wondering what to expect.

Geoff had run off into another room like a child on a scavenger hunt, I convinced myself that he was not going to return. However, as I was about to leave my post, he reappeared with an aging but still attractive woman in a black dress. Geoff did not introduce her to me, preferring to shout like a hyperactive child into her ear,

'See I told you, doesn't he look like that English guy from that movie? What was it? My god I can't think! You know the English guy?" he stood expectantly.

'Forgetting Sarah Marshall?' she replied almost instantly. 'Not really, I guess he has long hair and is English but that's about it!'

Geoff looked mortified and clearly didn't agree,

'You know jack all.'

He was clearly disappointed and offered to buy me what felt like a consolation drink. After another short interchange there wasn't too much else to be said so I made my excuses and decided to just get on with the rest of my life.

I found Mark at the bar with Mimi ordering six double vodka cokes, he wasn't sure where the others had gone and didn't really seem to care. I grabbed a couple of the vodkas and made my way onto one of the several dance floors.

The elusive Swedes from the beach finally reared their heads hours after I had forgotten they were the reason we had gone there. It was better than expected as three of them stood at the front of the dance floor on stage about to compete in the club's Bikini Battle.

Two of them managed to get to the final, predictably losing out to a Mexican woman, but they did get a bottle of champagne which I gladly helped them drink in a booth away from the main area of the club.

I lost the group I was with including Mark, and ended up with the five girls from Sweden. Time seemed to pass quickly as no sooner were we all drinking Champagne, we were sat on a bus going back towards downtown. Rather than talk about transport I was now trying to woo each of them on it. My drunken mind created a game whereby you could only talk through the advent of song; 'Public Bus - The Musical' was born.

'Did you have a good night, good night?'

'Yes I did, lots of rum of coke, from that American bloke, yes I did.'

'He thought that I was Russell Brand, tried to hold my hand, maybe gay?'

'Sounding slightly gay, what did the big man say, did he call you pretty?'

"Not pretty just witty, move to mine in New York City, he would say.'

'Ok not joking, end of song he was gay!'

Back at the girl's hostel we messed around in the pool. One of them gave me a kiss but then vanished to bed. Before I knew it I was in the pool alone with an orange basketball. I walked back to Monica's house that conveniently was round the corner from their hostel. I was soaked and without a key. Luckily a guest let me in before I passed out on my bed in my wet boxers.

The free bar didn't come without a cost. The next day both Mark and I were in pieces. As Cancun was expensive we spent the day on the beach, deciding that the next morning we would catch a short ferry to Isla Mujeres, the Island of Women.

Isla Mujeres

It took thirty minutes to reach Isla Mujeres by ferry. We arrived at midday in glorious sunshine accompanied by Mimi, her best friend Tahlia, and Dan, who they had met on the way to Cancun.

Mimi was a bubbly girl with a lot of confidence. She had short blonde hair and a pretty face but had too big a figure for me to consider her attractive. She reminded me of my friend's mother back home.

Tahlia was less vocal than Mimi and I wasn't sure whether she liked us. She had an undeniably beautiful figure and long brown hair but beyond her looks I couldn't see anything else. She was the type of girl I would go for but something was missing. I wanted to find out what that was.

Isla Mujeres translated to Island of Women. As we left the ferry I didn't see much evidence of their presence, what I did see was the island's beauty. Despite only being thirty minutes from Cancun it was a different world. We had left the overcrowded theme park and found the park. I stood by the road as several golf carts drove past. My mouth made the shape of an O as my left arm pointed straight at them.

We got into a taxi and made our way across the Island to a hostel. Mark and I were both concerned that the Island of Women would more accurately be the beach of boys. Rather than be surrounded by women we would invariably be swimming in the deep end with dudes.

The thought of the Island of Women sounded too good to be true. We expected disappointment, but hoped we would be proved wrong. The name of the island alone was the standout reason for our visit.

When given the option Mark and I always checked into mixed bedrooms. With the booking came hope, the hope that you check into a room with five or six sex starved girls in their underwear. Booking into an all male dorm and ruling out this possibility for yourself was therefore considered gay.

Not visiting the Island of Women would have been gay. We checked into a mixed room at the hostel. In our room were the five of us and two men. Maybe we would be lucky with our next booking?

The hostel strangely made all its guests wear fluorescent wristbands as a security measure. I went for a walk around the island and was able to spot the people who were staying at the hostel. They all wore the same fluorescent yellow bands which read 'Pocna Hostel Guest', followed by a specific number, mine was 8065.

It was the holiday edition of the Holocaust. Rather than sad, pale, hungry Jews tagged with yellow stars this island had young, happy, tanned travellers with yellow wristbands walking the streets. The tags, like stars, clearly marked us out as foreign, but that was the rule so we had to wear them.

Isla Mujeres reminded me a lot of the southern islands of Thailand.

The streets were all narrow and flanked either side by colourful low rise concrete buildings, each typically a gift shop or restaurant. The owners of the restaurants constantly clamoured for my attention trying to get me to sit down at their tables. The Island was simple, there were no tricks. I was instantly charmed.

I walked away from the light hustle of the town a few miles around the beach, enjoying the sun and soaking up the beautiful surroundings. The laid-back atmosphere was ideal and I felt at home almost straight away.

Different parts of the beach offered different things. If you wanted to be active there were volleyball nets and small football goals. If you just wanted to relax there were bars and sun loungers. Whatever people were doing it was stress free, it was paradise.

I met Mark and the girls on the beach closest to the hostel, but couldn't settle as everyone was so relaxed and quiet. I had nothing to read and nothing to lie on, so decided in my state of peaceful boredom to make what ended up a DJ out of a coconut.

I used the coconut as the head and put a snorkel on it to mark out the eyes. I put seaweed in Mark's cap and balanced it on top of the coconut to represent his hair. I then used branches for his limbs before propping him up against a sandbag. On the sandbag I put my iPod and speakers. Coconut Mike was born and his first DJ set began on the beach in Isla Mujeres to a mixed review.

Our first night on the Island was messy as we drank a lot of alcohol. I still remembered the good old days when binge drinking was known as getting pissed. Mark and I sat on some plastic chairs in town by a dirty food stall with a bottle of Bacardi and some beers. We were joined by Mimi and Tahlia.

The woman at the food stall sold what looked like burnt brown leather shoes on sticks. She assured us that it was meat but I decided against making a purchase. Her stall sat at the end of the main strip of restaurants under a sheet of corrugated iron where she had placed a few plastic tables and chairs. She was happy for us to sit down and drink.

We sat there for hours managing to drink two bottles of rum and several beers between the four of us. We staggered to our feet and left the stall around midnight, deciding to go to the beach bar attached to our hostel. As the alcohol slopped around in my stomach my mind went blank, leaving the shores of Isla Mujeres.

When I woke up the next morning with Tahlia it was a pleasant surprise. I couldn't remember the two of us actually talking; most conversations were dominated by Mimi. I lay there trying to piece together what had happened after the food stall. Tahlia was fast asleep.

All I could remember was meeting some lad in a Tottenham Hotspur shirt who had curly hair like a clown and wore a trilby. I had a vague thought of going to a club in town but nothing concrete to work with. I did remember being back in the room.

I was unable to climb onto my bunk as ladders and lagers just don't mix. I had no choice but to grab the white sheets off my top bunk and try to get into someone's bottom bunk. I cringed and laughed in equal measures as I remembered staggering around the room with my sheet wrapped around my head, proclaiming in my finest Indian voice I was 'Mohammered.'

The room contained six bunk beds, lying opposite each other in banks of three. I passed out in the middle on the hard wood floor, using someone's backpack as a pillow. From that point my memory once again went black.

I guessed at some point I must have got up and crawled like a wounded soldier into Tahlia's bed. I wasn't sure if she even knew I was there, the last thing I wanted was for her screaming so I tried to shuffle away from her. As I did she grabbed onto my arm and pulled it over her like a thick duvet. She clearly did not mind and neither did I.

One person who did mind was Dan. He stormed out of the room leaving his toys all over the floor. He clearly had his eye on Tahlia and it seemed that I had somehow ruined everything.

As the room emptied Tahlia and I got closer. We were both half naked in bed and after prolonged periods of touching we finally had sex. We had to keep stopping as people came in and out of the room; it was a new experience for me and a strange one.

We were interrupted several times by the same person, an American in our room called Justin. He was a laid-back musician from Texas with mousy brown hair who always seemed happy. I was convinced by the third time that he was also a pervert,

'Sorry guys I forgot my beach towel,' he shouted as he walked into the room.

Two minutes passed before he once again made an appearance.

'My god it's hot out there. When you get up don't forget your lotion guys.'

Tahlia and I begin to relax as the room was once again empty.

'You know what I think I'm going to go snorkelling,' Jason shouts as the door bangs open for the third time.'

We both stopped and looked over as he slowly looked through his backpack. I was certain that there was no snorkel in his bag.

'You know what I changed my mind. I will leave you guys to it.'

On the way out I caught him trying to look up the thin white sheets we had covered our bodies in. Finally he was gone.

'I can never look at that guy again, he saw everything,' she said.

I laughed at her before finishing what we had started. I went down to the beach to find Mark and collapse on the sand. Mark wanted to know everything; he was clearly impressed with my work.

We sat on the same patch of sand as the first day enjoying the sun and nursing our respective hangovers. I looked over to the palm tree where I had left coconut Mike. He had not lasted the night and by the looks of things had been brutally murdered on the beach. I found his head several metres down the beach pressed down in the sand. It was a tragic loss.

In a bid to cheer me up, Mark set me one of his challenges. Out on the horizon there was an implausibly fat American paddling around in the turquoise waters. The bet was simply to swim out to this stranger and give him an affectionate cuddle. Despite the loss of Coconut Mike, I was in a good mood so I accepted the challenge.

I waded out into the water towards my target, much to the amusement of Mark. He was further out than I had thought and as I got nearer I realised how big he actually was. The man was so fat that I thought the horse on his polo shirt was real. I wasn't entirely sure what it was I was going to do.

I drifted up behind him and decided to wrap my arms around his back like a Koala on the trunk of a tree,

'What the hell are you doing man!' he shouted in a lazy American tone.

I had to think fast,

'I told you last night I wanted a hug!'

'I think you have the wrong person,' he stated in a matter of fact fashion.

'You are Mike right?' I questioned.

'No sir, I am Tom from Alabama in the US of A,' he answered proudly.

I could faintly hear Mark laughing by the shore. I glanced back at the Island to see him stood up pointing in our direction. He was joined by Mimi and Tahlia who must have made their way to the beach.

Tom was a kind man who was on holiday with his family. He was well over six foot and must have weighed twice as much as me. He wore a black baseball cap that covered his big bald head, a blue Ralph Lauren shirt, dark in places with water and sweat, and a pair of long red swimming shorts. He was a genuine man who worked hard to provide for his loved ones.

I spoke with him for several minutes about the island and my trip before heading back to the beach feeling slightly guilty about the dare.

In the evening Mark and I went to a small seafood restaurant in the town. It had been recommended by a South African called Derek as the food and beer was cheap. We invited anyone that wanted to come to join us.

We sat down as staff hurried around, pulling the small metal tables together to form one long table at the front of the restaurant on the street. We managed to entice twelve people, the table resembled a UN conference such was the spread of nationalities, but that was where the similarities ended.

The restaurant sat in the middle of the main part of the town. As night fell we sat under a canopy taking advantage of the cheap beer and enjoying the atmosphere around us. Couples walked past looking for somewhere to eat, waiters shouted at people to eat at their restaurants, and the sounds and smell of food were everywhere.

Local children paced up and down the narrow street trying to sell people bracelets while Mariachis plucked their guitar strings and serenaded tables for a few pesos.

The group of travellers at our table were all really vocal apart from Tahlia and Dan who sat next to each other barely talking. Two French-Canadians that I recognised were sat on our table, but I couldn't place them. I had to ask,

'I know you guys don't I?'

'Yes man I was thinking the same thing. You were in Escondido right?' one of them replied.

'That's it, you were on the beach with the fire. Small world!'

'You got us so much free Mescal at that bar,' he laughed.

The two lads were called Alias and David. I introduced both to Mark. Several beers later Mark told me that he wanted to go to a strip club. He had been told by a lad at the hostel called Joe that there was one on the Island.

Joe was the curly-haired Tottenham supporter that we met hazily on the first night. He had been on the Island for a week and seemed to know absolutely everyone at the hostel. He was a petit man with curly hair that he covered up with a trilby hat. He had a nice aura about him and good energy so you could not help but like him.

Joe had told Mark that he slept with a girl from the strip club so after an hour of badgering I finally gave in and agreed to catch a cab to this club called Casa Blanca. David decided that he would join us.

Casa Blanca was not like the strip clubs back in England. The club sat on the outskirts of the town hidden behind a neglected billboard with a faded advertisement across it. Rather than a club it felt more like an old Spanish home.

The walls were a dirty white and the roof was made up of terracotta tiles. There was no door into the house, just an opening in the wall. The room was dark. The host came over and escorted us to a plastic table that was covered with a dirty red cloth. We ordered beers from the uncared for bar.

The three of us sat down near the back of the room close to the wall. I wasn't sure where to look at first. Mark in comparison looked right at home, David fell somewhere in the middle.

David had a shaved head and a piercing look about him which made me feel uncomfortable. His English wasn't great but he knew enough so that conversation was not too awkward. He leant over to the middle of the table to grab a handful of the peanuts that were sat on a small paper plate. I winced as he ate each of the nuts, wondering whose hands had been on them and rumouring that they were probably a lot saltier than they should be. David didn't seem to care, he was French and they eat snails and horses.

Being in Mexico I couldn't help but draw comparisons to the club on From Dusk Till Dawn.

Girls straddled old men while others leered at the main stage as cheap coloured lights flashed off numerous naked bodies. It was a strange place to be in and I found it impossible to relax. Mark's eyes fixed on the girls on stage, David ate peanuts as I played with the dirty red table cloth and daydreamed.

I half expected the manager to come over with more beers and tempt us into a private room with the enthusiastic proposal put forward in the film,

'Alright, pussy, pussy, pussy! Come on in pussy lovers! Here at Casa Blanca we're slashing pussy in half! Give us an offer on our vast selection of pussy, this is a pussy blow out! Alright, we got white pussy, black pussy, Spanish pussy, yellow pussy, we got hot pussy, cold pussy, and we got wet pussy. If we don't got it, you don't want it! Come on in, pussy lovers!'

He would trick us and then predictably turn into a Vampire and kill each of us without anyone knowing. We ordered more beers and I sat waiting for this unfortunate event to unravel.

He came over and lazily slammed the beers down onto the table before walking off. There was no sales pitch, no half price pussy, and thankfully no Vampires.

A few women approached us but left soon after when they realised that none of us had much money. Mark tried to cut himself a deal but failed; they simply wanted too much money. After becoming frustrated we finally left and got into a taxi back to the hostel.

Our group from earlier sat around a plastic table outside our dorm room away from the bar with a three litre bottle of rum. I could hear Mimi's voice a mile off, she had an insatiable appetite for rum and was once again hammered.

An hour later we were all marching around the hostel like drunken Pirates intoxicated with rum. I sat on a log by the simple beach bar drinking cold cocktails until my body could take no more.

I ended up in the toilets by our room with Tahlia. Unable to find the light we fumbled around in the dark and tried to have sex on what must have been the toilet seat.

Due to the amount of booze I had consumed not much happened as I went down like a weary battle ship. Rather than give him and go admirably I chose to stand in the middle of the dorm room pointing at my jelly sword and asking the question, 'What is wrong with it?' A more pertinent question as I stood half naked in a room of strangers would have been, 'What is wrong with me?'

The next day I stumbled out of the dormitory down the concrete stairs to the bar, leaning onto the white stone wall for support. As I walked through the bar I could feel people's eyes burning holes in my back. I was glad I was not wearing my favourite top.

I didn't have a clue why people were looking at me but assumed it would be related to my actions the previous night. At times memory loss was a blessing. I walked through the bar and down onto the beach past the row of palm trees. I spent the day falling in and out of consciousness on the beach, twitching and sweating like an epileptic at a rave. I looked at Mark and told him,

'Mate I am not drinking for a few days, this place is just too much.'

'I agree sir, but what else is there to do?' he warned.

I drifted off into an uncomfortable sleep trying to think of an answer.

My personal drinking ban managed to last all of six hours. I was set on staying in until Tahlia and Mimi announced,

'We are leaving tomorrow so you have to come out and celebrate with us.'

This was one of the perils of travelling; there was always an excuse to drink if you wanted one. It could be someone leaving, it could be a new arrival that you just met, it could be because it's the weekend, because it's a weekday or because you can't do it once you get home because that would class as being an alcoholic. The list of excuses is endless.

Mark held strong. He was having problems with his on/off girlfriend back home and, after three days of drinking, was depressed. I went out as it was their last night.

Mimi bought a month's supply of rum from the supermarket that we managed to drink within the space of a few hours. I sat around a plastic table with a large group of people talking while my head spun and distorted the images being processed by my eyes.

I had been on the island for a few days and had managed to meet a whole host of people from different backgrounds and walks of life. It was the main thing I liked about travelling, everyone in this world has more in common that they think. At Pocna we had developed into a community, each bound by our fluorescent yellow wristbands.

I loved listening to people talk about where they were from and why they had decided to travel. Sat outside by the bar was the ideal setting.

Kfir, who looked like a homeless Tobey Maguire, had just completed three years' service as a navigational officer on a naval ship in the Israeli army. He came away to experience freedom and another way of life that was far removed from home. Sat around this table meant a lot to Kfir, he finally had the chance to do what he wanted do, even if that was something simple like doing nothing.

During the day I had spoke to two outgoing lads from South Africa that had served for the British Army in the Falklands. They had your usual war horror stories that they chose not to elaborate on, but then also a few that you just couldn't make up. Doug explained enthusiastically as we bobbed up and down in calm waters off the beach,

'At night soldiers used to watch penguins waddle about parts of the island, many of which were littered with land mines. We would then each pick a penguin and take bets on which one would blow up first!'

His words painted a vivid scenario in my mind which I played out,

'Alright see that little cuddly twat in the fur tuxedo; yeah my money is on that fucker!'

'I bet you £20 that it's that black one over there with the huge beak!'

'You got yourself a bet there, let's do this.'

Five minutes would pass before one of the penguins flew into the air and scattered like microwave popcorn.

'Ha, I told you that prom suit-wearing penguin's days were numbered! P-p-p-p-p-pick up your purse, I win.'

'I'll get you tomorrow night, let's get back to base!'

(Bang)

'Whoa there goes your little fella! Never mind, I'll buy you a consolation beer. What is it now seven to two in my favour?'

Doug and Jared were now out of the army and just travelling the world before planning on settling down to life back home. I couldn't imagine the real horror of war, thinking about exploding penguins was far easier for my mind to take.

Everyone around the table had their own experiences and own reasons for travelling. As I drank more and more the numbers at the table seemed to increase. The table of ten now looked like a table of one hundred as my mind began to play tricks on me. I should have stayed in with Mark.

As it was Tahlia's last night we must have decided to go for a walk away from the crowd on the beach. We had been told repeatedly that the beach was dangerous at night, but as we were drunk we thought nothing of it. By this point I was only loosely aware that it was beach.

We stumbled about in the dark to the soundtrack of crashing waves and distant voices before deciding to climb up an old wooden watch tower that sat several metres from the surf. The wind swirled overhead and the tower looked alluring.

The tower was notorious around the hostel as a hot bed for sex. Rather than saving lives it was more likely to create unwanted new ones. We managed to climb up the narrow wooden ladder and fell on the uneven decking laughing in a drunken stupor at each other.

Within a few minutes the laughter died down and we were fumbling around each other's bodies staring up at the night sky. The air blew through the wooden slats of the tower and began to go to my ailing head. I kept zoning out as we kissed, unaware of my surroundings and who it was I was kissing. I tried to snap out of it and focus on Tahlia who now had two heads.

Rather than feeling like a threesome with gorgeous twins it felt like I was kissing a pair of Siamese twins. There was two heads but only one body, I closed my eyes hoping that the next time I opened them things would have returned to normal.

I opted kissing the one on the left as she looked the better of the two heads I found confronting me. It was the wrong choice as I kissed the air and hit my head into the wooden decking; I covered up well by kissing her neck.

My vision improved and as things between us began to heat up I felt a long hard pole run down my back. I turned my head convinced it was nothing. I was wrong. I jumped back as a large imposing shadow bore down on both of us. As there was no light apart from the glow of the moon I couldn't work out who it was. Justin had left the Island so it couldn't have been him. Mark had stayed in so I knew it wasn't him. Who was it? I was scared.

I lay on the decking with Tahlia, disorientated and shuffled back into my shorts, not knowing what to do. Then the shadow spoke.

'Parada! Usted está en apuro,' came the authoritative tone.

I nervously replied,

'I don't speak Spanish mate, can you leave us alone?'

'Policia,' was the response as he pointed a baton at my face.

My stomach dropped and I sobered up in seconds as the adrenalin ran through my body. We were both in a lot of trouble and it wasn't going to be easy to get out of it.

Tahlia went deathly silent as I pleaded with the officer,

'Lo syiento mi amigo, tranqulio amigo.'

It fell on deaf ears as he insisted over and over that we go to the 'estación'.

We came down from the tower, which was a lot harder than climbing up it. I was clearly still inebriated as my head spun with a vicious cocktail of booze and fear. I was shaken and stirred but there was no way I was going to the police station.

The thought then came to me that this guy was probably just a local in fancy dress. I didn't see a police car so perhaps he was just a pervert after some money. It was worth a shot and if I was wrong it wouldn't make much difference.

The officer agreed to let Tahlia go, motioning her away with his baton that he held firm in his right hand. She ran off back towards the light of the hostel, leaving me to deal with things. I decided to offer him a bribe. I had $100 pesos in my pocket so I reluctantly offered him the lot. He snatched the money from my hands,

'Si amigo.'

Just after this transaction Tahlia returned with the security guard from the hostel. As he approached the policeman backed away and, after a few stiff words in Spanish, he ran off down the beach. I was understandably relieved.

I excitedly bounced around the beach bar with Joe telling people about the near escape on the beach. The beach bar offered two for one on all its cocktails meaning that more often than not I had several too many.

The bar sat in front of the hostel and was constructed entirely of branches and pieces of wood. The seating, if you could call it that, was just a variety of tree trucks thrown on the beach in an ad hoc manner. They decorated the area with fairy lights, which created a chilled atmosphere for guests to frolic and do as they pleased. Everyone including myself loved the place.

I left Joe passed out on the beach in the arms of a Canadian woman and decided to call it a night, knowing full well the next day was going to be a complete wash out.

The next morning Mimi and Tahlia left the hostel and, after three days of solid drinking, I spent the whole day between bed and the beach trying to resolve a range of issues going on in my head.

I was worried that my trip was gradually sliding into the same pattern as the one that I was trying to get away from back home. This Island had become Leeds. The hostel had become Call Lane.

I didn't want my trip to pass me by; jumping from one hangover to another. I wanted to use it to discover more about myself. I wanted to see different ways of living and decide upon the life I wanted for myself. I resolved that the first thing I needed to do was not drink. That evening I stayed in the dorm and weathered the storm of alcohol deprivation.

I actually think I felt worse staying in than I would have getting drunk. The room was unbearably hot and the solitary fan, that barely blew any air, sounded like a lawn mower. I lay half asleep with one eye open, convinced I was about to be attacked by a psychotic landscape gardener.

I was woken at 4:00am to the cries of Mark saying,

'Is it really that wrong?'

What followed was an unfortunate series of events culminating in attempted rape. Mark had drunkenly got into my bed and was imposing himself on me,

'Yes mate it really is that wrong,' I tiredly shouted as his penis touched my leg.

I pushed him off my bed onto the floor. He just lay on the hard wooden floor sprawled out like I had delivered a knock-out blow. He passed out naked on the floor. I covered him with a white towel and once again began to worry about the gardener hanging from the ceiling.

Isla Mujeres was only 7km in length so it would not take long for us to cover. Transportation on the Island consisted solely of taxis, golf carts and scooters. It was strange seeing golf carts driving up and down the high street but we had become accustomed to it.

The next morning I was tired but had no hangover, the same could not be said for Mark. After breakfast we discussed the possibility of getting either a golf cart or scooter as we were eager to see the rest of the island. Every day all we had done was go to the beach, it was time to do something else.

Still drunk, Mark took the driving responsibilities. I was not confident of handling a scooter with a drunk thirteen stone baby clung to my back, so it made sense. We picked the scooter as it could go twice the speed of the golf carts that we feared would be boring.

We left the small rental office in town on our navy blue scooter, both wearing plastic white cycle helmets that clipped under our chins. Mark weaved in and out of traffic, beeping the bike's rather pathetic horn. I clung onto the back of the scooter with my left hand as my right arm waved at locals like it was an inaugural ceremony.

The road opened up as we got away from the port and Mark turned the throttle to full speed. We sped around, overtaking numerous golf carts and shouting at people as we whizzed past them. Mark and I were developing a tight bond. I was glad that we were travelling together. The troubles in Puerto Escondido seemed like a lifetime ago.

We reached the far end of the Island within twenty minutes and it was beautiful. We stopped at the edge of a cliff face that plummeted into the inviting ocean beneath. Waves played against the rocks as the water glistened in the midday sun. By the cliff sat a simple wooden shack with a tropical sign that read, 'Coco Frios'.

A small man sat at the other side of the window hatch in the shade. He was selling cold coconuts. The hut clung to the headland, it felt like we were both in the Caribbean. It was idyllic.

Unbeknownst to both of us, something far from idyllic was waiting for us a few miles back towards town. We raced off from the headland in search of a beach. The sun by this point was baking so we wanted to have a rest.

As we picked up speed we noticed a red scooter coming in the opposite direction. From a distance it looked like a woman was driving as we could both see her bright, neon pink top. Mark began to beep our horn and as they drew nearer we started shouting,

'Buenos tardes amigos.'

As our scooters advanced closer and closer both of us slowed down. Both our engines purred as we stopped side by side in the road. I decided to ask them,

'Dónde está playa?'

The reply that came shocked both of us.

'Are you gay?'

'No we are not,' I replied unsure as to what it was I was talking to.

'Argh Inglaterra, I show you the playa,' she replied in the most obscure manner.

Mark and I both smiled as she insisted that we follow her on her red scooter. The voice had thrown both of us. She sounded like a gay Spanish witch. I couldn't make any sense of it at all.

We turned around and set off in tandem down the gravel road that straddled the coast both knowing that this was more than likely going to end badly. As we followed her and her younger looking partner we started to notice things that had evaded us initially.

We had noticed she had huge breasts that we knew had been cosmetically enhanced as they looked hard and firm like bags of sand. We also observed that this woman had an equally large head. What we had missed was her legs. Mark spotted them and nearly lost control of our scooter. He pointed at them and shouted as the wind whizzed past my face,

'Look at her legs, look at her legs!'

I looked and couldn't decide whether to laugh or throw up. We both studied this creature in more detail as she glanced at us, licking her lips and staring deep into our souls with her piercing green eyes. She had everything that a man could ever want; big muscles, hairy legs, and a big moustache. I reached for my camera.

Its scooter began to slow down as we approached a hedged area by the side of the road, we decided that we were not going to follow suit. As it began to pull in Mark hit the accelerator and we both playfully screamed,

'See you later.'

As we edged away I began to feel strange as I played out what could have happened on the beach. I wondered if she still had a penis. I had seen lady boys in Thailand and had not found them threatening. A friend of mine actually knows a transvestite that lives in London. He is a fat, alcoholic. All he does is eat, drink and be Mary!

This Mexican creation was a sexual predator; a strong man that tried to trick people by having large boobs. We were not stupid, we knew the truth.

That night was to be our last on Isla Mujeres so we inevitably got drunk. We met some guys, Andreas and Kasper that told us they were in a Danish hip hop band called Suspekt. They introduced us to a new drink that they called fist.

'Fist' was a concoction of vodka and water. Sober it tasted like vodka and water and made me feel sick. But once I was drunk it began to taste more like water. Andreas told me that you don't get a hangover,

'The water it hydrates you.'

I believed him and me and Mark got absolutely steaming.

I met a girl from the Netherlands called Mirtte who had just arrived on the Island. I wasn't sure I was ready yet as Tahlia had just left the Island but she just jumped on me by the bar. I didn't complain at all as she was stunning. She had long dark brown hair and big inviting eyes.

Mark once again looked on wondering what was going on. He had been unsuccessful on the Island and moaned to me that his confidence was low,

'Why can't I convert any women mate?' he asked.

'It's because you are a deeply ugly human being,' I replied.

After a few more hours drinking outside the beach bar I ended up in bed with Mirtte. Isla Mujeres had delivered what it had promised to do. It really was the Island of Women.

The next morning we left reluctantly left the island with Joe and Kfir, who decided to join the two of us in Playa Del Carmen.

We got to the docks and boarded a ferry at midday. I cast my eye back towards the shore as the golf carts and scooters strolled down the narrow roads beeping their horns, trying to get where they needed to go.

Playa Del Carmen

Isla Mujeres was the first place on the trip that was difficult to leave. It was a good feeling to have. I was happy to have visited the Island but at the same time excited to finally move on.

On the way to Playa Del Carmen the large silver tour bus drove past a series of exclusive holiday resorts. Each of the resorts had grand, over-the-top entrances like Jurassic Park. Behind each lay a theme park of staged authenticity and luxury accommodation. Each of the guests at these resorts probably spent more in two weeks that I had for five months. I found it crazy.

Travelling on a budget has an effect on a person and I was no different. Before my year around Asia I would have looked at these resorts and dreamt of staying in them. I cast my mind back four years. I was sat on my bed with my then girlfriend on a cold November evening flicking through a Thomas Cook travel brochure, looking for the perfect holiday.

Rather than look at the country's culture the first thing we both checked was the average temperature followed by the average precipitation rates for that time of year. Far from budding weather enthusiasts we were concerned with one thing, getting a tan.

Still unconcerned about location, the next thing to consider was the price. The winner of this game was the one that could find the biggest pool, at the lowest cost. Extra points were awarded for pool shape.

After covering the bases it was then time to book a holiday and lavish the country, not just the hotel and its pool with superlatives. The countdown at work began.

'In two weeks we go on holiday to Turkey. It is so cheap and looks amazing. The pool is the shape of a dolphin; it's fantastic. It has a bar in the water and a Jacuzzi which will be heaven. And it is hot, blazing sunshine every day,' I purred to my colleague.

Two weeks later we were both sat by the dolphin shaped pool that was more like a diseased kidney, at a half constructed all-inclusive resort in

Turkey. She had diarrhoea and moaned that it was too hot to sit out in the sun.

On returning home we both agreed that, despite not leaving the resort, Turkey was a country that you should avoid at all costs.

After travelling I could never see myself sat by the pool of an all inclusive hotel. I would find it boring, I needed excitement.

Holidays should be about exploration, eating local food, learning about the country's culture and mixing with the local people. At these luxury resorts we drove past, the only thing Mexican encountered would be the people serving you. That wasn't visiting Mexico. It was a false reality.

Mark and I left Joe and Kfir as our tour operator had arranged a free home stay on our behalf. It gave us a chance to stay for two nights with a local Mexican family in the suburbs of Playa Del Carmen. It was an area most people would not see and we were looking forward to it.

Mark and I walked down a residential street on the outskirts of town looking sweaty and confused. The area resembled those in inner city, coming of age films like Boys in the Hood. The houses were all cheap and made of wood, each having its own identical square yard. Dogs barked from behind the low wooden fences as residents clawed at their curtains, looking suspiciously from their front windows to see what the dogs were barking at.

After circling the block several times we finally found the house. It was an old detached building that had been attacked by an army of vegetation. In a few more years I was convinced that the vegetation would win the war against the bricks, making the house a bush with windows.

Inside the bush there were ornaments everywhere. Her home was an Aladdin's cave of crap; my eyes didn't know where to look. The wallpaper in the house was a stale green colour and there was no natural light because of all the greenery. The lady was in her late sixties and looked like a tanned Mrs. Doubtfire. She spoke no English. She pointed towards a wooden door at the far side of the long corridor, instructing us to follow her.

The room was horrible. The worn dressing table was home to several dolls that stared at us with their horrible porcelain eyes. They were letting me know that this was their room and that we should leave.

There was only one single bed that sat in the corner of the room opposite the dolls. It was brown and covered in yellow stains. Hanging from the off-white ceiling was a loose cable that attached to a single light bulb. There was no fan and the room was stuffy. Mark and I looked at each other trying not to laugh,

'Amiga solo bed?' Mark quizzed.

'Como?' replied a confused Mrs. Doubtfire.

'Solo bed?' this time he swung his arms and pointed at the mattress that looked like a soggy piece of toast.

'Si senor,' was the response.

'Amiga Sin homosexual. Non bueno solo bed. Non suck cock,' Mark motioned with his hand.

She looked at him with a confused face. I couldn't hold back the laughter. We decided it was in our best interests to leave. After wasting two hours of our time we now needed to find something else. It was dark and funnily enough both of us wished we could just stay in a really nice hotel with a pool.

We got a taxi into town and checked into a cheap hostel.

The room that we booked into had enough room in it for three bunk beds. The manager had crammed in five, it was dreadful. We stood by the entrance of the room looking for the free beds in the landfill of clothes thrown across the room. We heard a careless whisper from one of the bunks; someone was lying down on the corner bed.

The man looked like George Michael. He lay there in the darkness beaten up and groaning. It looked like he had submerged half his face in Ribena. I felt sorry for him.

There was nothing we could do to heal the pain but I told him that he should give Playa one more try. I suggested to him that he should try to go outside. I had been beaten up last Christmas and knew from experience that some fast love would sort him out. He refused to leave the room and warned us that Playa was a bad place.

He made it sound like some sort of barbaric land, far removed from the upmarket holiday town we had been told about by others. Rather than find a bed we decided to return to reception and asked for a private room that was worth the extra cost.

Mark finally picked up on my use of George Michael song titles when I told him that I was going to have a short nap,

'Mate wake me up before you go go?' I asked.

He laughed before replying.

'You've gotta have faith.'

I woke up at 10:00pm after Mark had showered and changed. We decided to go for a wander around town and had no real plans for the evening apart from trying to find Joe and Kfir.

We dropped onto the main strip that ran adjacent to the beach in Playa Del Carmen called Avenida Five. The street was busy and lined with all kinds of shops, art and craft galleries, cafes, restaurants and bars that sat away from the road in lovely pristine white buildings. The street was modern and luxurious and not what I had expected at all.

Playa had a strong Spanish feel to it, you could smell the money in the air. It felt similar to affluent holiday areas in Europe like Marbella. I took a step back and just looked at what people were wearing and how they were walking.

Everyone was strolling along, relaxed and as happy as can be. It immediately felt like a holiday and we feared that meant expensive. Fairy lights flanked the pristine cobbled streets as elegantly dressed holiday makers sat eating and drinking in a catalogue of ambient restaurants.

Mark and I got some tacos for the equivalent of 10p each and waited for Kfir and Joe who we had loosely arranged to meet outside the nearby McDonald's. We looked like your typical backpackers.

They arrived and, after battling against the wave of street vendors trying to sell us drugs and hookers, we ended up sitting at a shiesha bar; we were with an Israeli so it was an obvious choice. After inspecting the menu we chose not to order any drinks as everything on it was too expensive.

We walked away from the main strip as the drink prices were too high for our budgets. As we got away from the fairy lit main street shop keepers still pestered us selling drugs and one did his best to sell Mark a hooker,

'Any type of woman you like my friend,' he shouted.

We bought some alcohol from a local supermarket and sat across from a small bar in a softly lit pedestrian area of the town. We all started drinking. Soon the beers were replaced with a two litre bottle of rum and a cheap bottle of vodka.

The vodka was so cheap that we offered cups of it to passers by, some decided to join us. We got extremely pissed and like any good bacteria we multiplied and spread. We had started our very own street party. All we needed now was music.

Our numbers grew to an impressive twelve, we were now a strong vociferous group. We decided on Gabriel's recommendation to take our merriment to a bar called Mezcalina. He was a Mexican and was dressed like something from a comic. He was a friendly guy, about twenty years of age and we all liked him.

On Joe's recommendation we made our way down to the bar in a conga line singing Ricky Martin's Livin' La Vida Loca. We indeed were.

We bounced back onto Avienda Five. The fairy lights now looked like those pictures people take of traffic at night. The light from them just smeared across the sky, like someone had given a child an aluminous marker pen and left them unattended.

I had Gabriel shouting in my ear, proclaiming that his lips were devil red and his skin the colour mocha. It was disorientating but lots of fun, drunken stupors always were. We danced down the cobbled hill towards the neon signs of the bars laughing and creating a lot of noise.

I decided to climb into a shopping trolley full of empty Corona bottles that sat to the left of the bar entrance. Joe kindly offered to be my driver. Rather than go towards the street he grabbed the trolley and pushed me straight through the bar at speed, the wheels rattling loudly against the concrete floor. Staff and patrons looked on in horror as we careered like an old mining cart past the bar, before crashing against the base of the dance floor and falling like wounded soldiers to the ground. We both lay staring at the cracked red painted ceiling in fits of drunken laughter.

We apologised, returned the trolley outside to the left of the bar and ordered some drinks. The bartender looked at us like a child picking up his first book. Although he was clearly confused he just decided after several awkward seconds to laugh and pour all of us some shots of Mescal on the house.

I had worked at a bar back in Leeds to save some extra money for my travels. One of the most annoying things was when you asked a customer what they want and they replied,

'Surprise me.'

I often thought how good would it be to show them a naked picture of their wife or daughter and watch their response.

Mezcalina was a really relaxed bar with a great ambience. The aluminium tables outside were full of young holiday makers with steal wine coolers full of ice and cold beer bottles.

Inside the walls were all predominantly painted blood red. A statue of the devil sat in the corner with the slogan,

'Fumar es causa de cancer.'

I rested a lit cigarette in its mouth and took a picture. The back of the bar was silver in colour and home to the raised black dance floor.

The DJ spun out immediately forgettable tunes as everyone just danced how they liked, fuelled by Tequila rather than music.

It felt like I was dancing inside a giant coke can, as the ceiling arched towards the rear of the room. I loved the place and it seemed that we could get away with anything. Sadly I was wrong.

Twenty minutes later we all stood on the street staring back into the bar that we had just been thrown out of. It had all started with Mark casually hitting the top of my beer bottle with his. This made the beer spill from the bottle and froth up so I responded by pouring my beer over his head. Things escalated quickly, within seconds Mark, Joe and our new friends ran around the bar spraying drinks like we had won the World Cup. We were politely asked to leave.

We took our Mexican contingent with us to a club in the corner of the cul-de-sac we were in called Coco Maya. The cul-de-sac was filled with bars and clubs, jostling with each other for attention. It reminded me of Ibiza.

Entry to the club was free but the drinks were not. A double vodka cost more than the two litre bottle of rum we had bought earlier at the supermarket. Rather than be deterred by this Joe and I decided it was a great idea to dance up to tables and drink the remains of other people's drinks.

The bar was dark and there were glasses and bottles everywhere, they couldn't all be full and it was fun to find out.

We minced around the bar dancing to cheesy nineties' music with dirty baselines scanning everywhere, not just for girls but for unattended booze. Billy Joel's River of Dreams started blaring out of the music booth as we started what was our fifth sweep of the dance floor.

'In the middle of the night
The price of drinks is too steep
From the bar of the club
they ain't all that cheap
So I go lookin' for something
Something that isn't gonna cost
other people's old drink
so they can't be cross
Just in case we have a think
I walk down, grab a beer for free and I score
I look at Joe, smile and wink
Then I finally drink what I'm not paying for.'

It turned out that this fifth run would be our last. As I picked up a full beer and smiled triumphantly at Joe, I was confronted by a topless Mexican. The smiled disappeared. This man was either wearing a realistic muscle suit or he went to the gym. My luck was out, not only did this man go the gym but he was a boxer, muscular and compact like corned beef. He looked angry.

He stood aggressively half a metre from my face wearing a black cap with a red motif and a pair of cut-off jeans. He stared into my eyes, had I been sober I would have physically shit myself. Joe and I just stood by the series of couches at the back of the room hammered, waiting to see what would happen next.

I had a glass of red wine in my right hand and his unopened beer in my left. Joe had what we guessed was a vodka-based cocktail, which he held by his right side.

The bloke looked at me and spoke some unrecognisable Spanish. Sensing I was confused, he reverted to English,

'What are you doing with my beer, boy?' he sneered.

'Nothing, just wanted the ice bucket,' I replied, impressed by my quick thinking.

'That better be what you were doing, I thought you wanted my beer.'

'I will if you don't want it?' The joke completely diffused the situation.

He was a really nice bloke and by that time spoke better English than either Joe or me. He let us have the beer and sat down on one of several leather couches. It was clear that he wanted to talk with us. He told us that he wanted to be part of the Mexican Olympic Boxing team; but was kicked out for street fighting. It was clear that he had a temper on him.

Before leaving he suggested we meet up the following evening as Oscar Del la Hoya was fighting Manny Pacquiao on ESPN. We agreed that we would. A minute after he shook our hands and left we had both forgotten where it was he wanted to meet. We were too busy nursing our crushed hands.

Mark had been left unattended in the Club with a few of the Mexicans and had bought some cocaine. I decided against getting involved and stumbled back up the hill away from the bars to our private room alone.

I was woken up at 11:00am by the manager of the hostel. He told me that we had to leave as he had booked out our room. It would have been nice of him to ask if we had wanted to stay but he didn't. I looked over at Mark passed out on his bed, dead to the world; there was no waking him. I was convinced that he had done something to upset the management as he had only stumbled in an hour earlier and looked a mess.

I managed to sort out a new room across the road at a place called the Happy Gecko without any trouble at all. It was a good job as it felt like a pig had shit in my head.

On the coach to Playa Mark had joked that on the first night he was going to get drunk, buy a kebab and go to Pleasure Palace - a renowned high class brothel. As he woke it turned out that the joke had become a reality and it had cost him $200. I dragged him across the road to our new home.

The new room was better than the one we had left, but the same price. We had our own kitchen, bathroom and cable TV. The room had white walls decorated with two framed watercolours of the beach. The floor was tiled white, creating the feeling of space. Behind a light brown wooden shield lay two large double beds. We had hit the jackpot.

We spent the day in the room watching TV before having an early night, allowing our bodies, and in Mark's case his wallet, time to recover. It was much needed.

The next morning the sun was shining down on Playa Del Carmen. Joe, who was staying in a grim twenty-bed room at a hostel in town, moved in with us at the Happy Gecko. After fourteen hours of sleep Mark and I felt refreshed and ready for the beach.

We set up on the beach not far from the ferry that took people to Cozumel. We lay down in front of a beautiful white chapel. It was the widest area of the beach and therefore the busiest. The beach itself narrowed as it stretched northward past the numerous beach bars, restaurants and dive shops. I lay there drinking large bottles of Sol lager, sweating like an alter-boy at church. Mark, as normal, lay half asleep with his iPod plugged firmly into his ears. Joe and I sat talking and instigating conversation with anyone who walked past.

I got talking to some girls from France called Maria and Barbara who laughed at everything I had to say. Maria was beautiful; she looked like she was from a perfume commercial. Mark clearly fancied her as he stopped listening to his iPod and started drinking.

By late afternoon Joe and I were drunk and Mark was trying to catch us up. We decided to get some booze from the supermarket and drink back at the hostel. To our horror we entered a nearby shop to find that all the fridges were bolted shut with chains and locks. At the counter there was a cardboard sign that read, 'Ningún alcohol en venta después de 5.'

We guessed that it meant that no alcohol was for sale after 5.00pm. I looked down at my watch, it told me that the time was 5.05pm.

It reminded me of the Whammy burger scene in Falling Down. Michael Douglas is stood at 11.05am trying to order a breakfast meal only told that the breakfast menu stops at 11:00am. I was now living the scene in my mind,

'Hey Marquez cerveza parra mi?' I asked politely.

'Yo no soy permitido. es la ley,' he replied.

I could have blown up like in the film and replied,

'Why am I calling you by your first name? I don't even know you. I still call my boss 'Mister' and I've been working for him for five years, but all of a sudden I walk in here and I'm calling you Marquez and Juan like we're in some kind of AA meeting... I don't want to be your buddy, Marquez. I just want some Bacardi.'

I then pull out a shot gun and fire two rounds into the store ceiling.

Fortunately, unlike Michael Douglas' character, I am not psychotic and even if I was I didn't have a gun so I simply replied,

'Gracias mi amigo, Buenos tardes.' It wasn't his fault but that didn't stop me being annoyed.

As a result of Sunday's prohibition we all sobered up considerably and decided to take a walk around Playa before going back to the hostel.

While essentially a town built for tourism, Playa did feel Mexican. My opinion was that it struck a nice balance between catering for tourists and keeping its traditional ties. It was clearly an affluent place. One for holiday makers rather than budget travellers but I couldn't help but enjoy being in such a place. Like Isla Mujeres, I knew that we would be staying here longer than a few days.

Mark and I desperately needed to sort out our flights to South America. We didn't have the time or money to travel through Central America so flying was the only option. We had an Inca trail booked to Machu Picchu on the 7th December so had to get to Peru around that date. We were almost certainly going to miss it.

We checked for flights on the Internet. All of them were around £600 which I could not afford. I had only come away with £800 in my bank and a credit card. I had made the mistake of thinking internal flights would be cheap and I was very wrong. I feared that I may have to cut my trip short and was devastated. There had to be other options. We went out on the night to forget about things and have fun.

The supermarkets had all closed as it was Sunday so we started drinking at a local sports bar, which essentially looked like a Mexican working men's club. The bar was square in shape and pretty uninspiring. It was carved into a two-story cement block, the high ceilings made it feel cold. At the centre of the large room sat a square bar that was about the size of a boxing ring. Scattered out from the bar were numerous wooden stools and benches full of depressed-looking Mexicans arching their necks and staring up at the TV screens that hung off the decaying chip cement walls.

After several bottles of Corona I went over to the computerised jukebox in the corner of the room. I dropped in enough money that I could pick four songs. I scanned the room trying to think of an appropriate song, one that would lift the gloom and put a smile on all the weary faces in the bar. I made my choice.

I walked back over to Mark and Joe with a huge smile across my face. Before Mark asked what I smiling for I said to them both,

'We should probably get going.'

We drank up as the jukebox finished spinning the end of the last song and began to play mine. The beat kicked in and everyone in the bar looked up.

'In the navy
Yes, you can sail the seven seas
In the navy
Yes, you can put your mind at ease
In the navy
Come on now, people, make a stand
In the navy, in the navy
Can't you see we need a hand
In the navy
Come on, protect the motherland
In the navy
Come on and join your fellow man
In the navy.'

We walked along the street laughing as the music fell away into the distance. Mark turned and asked me,

'What have you put on next you idiot?'

'The same song four times, I don't think that bar will want me as a new recruit,' I joked.

We ended up at a club called the Blue Parrot that sat in the opposite corner to Coco Maya, where we had gone on the first night. It had the same basic layout but the music was louder and harder. Rather than Billy Joel, the music was funky house and dance. The bar was an epileptic's nightmare as strobe lights rebounded off the walls and the large white cloth that hung from the ceiling and across the dance floor. It was a war zone.

I stood at the bar waiting patiently to order some drinks. Mark and Joe sat a few metres away on a couch talking to some girls. Stood next to me at the bar was a heavily set American who began talking to me to pass the time. He wore a black Hawaiian shirt with huge blue dolphins on it that splashed in pools of water. He bore a striking resemblance to porn star Ron Jeremy as he had long black hair and a moustache.

The man had a rotund face and tiny eyes like that of a crab. He announced,

'I'm a pirate. Do you want to be a pirate? You can if you want?'

I thought about it for a few moments before deciding to sail with this idea,

'Funny you should ask, I have always wanted to be a pirate.'

In truth since travelling I wasn't sure whether I was a pirate or a pyromaniac as I couldn't stop burning DVDs. I waited intently for Ron Jeremy's response. It came,

'I thought so. You look the type. My boat is over there,' he pointed into the darkness.

All I could see beyond the dance floor were a pile of sun loungers stacked up and about four plastic pedal boats.

'So you want me to get on your boat with you. How does that make me a pirate?'

This man was clearly mental but I was intrigued and wanted to see where the conversation was going. He continued,

'We shall steal the tills from the bar and set sail via the beach with the loot.'

'On one of those pedal boats?'

'On my vessel young man.'

I couldn't help but think that his 'vessel' was his penis and rather than a pirate he was just a confused, mentally ill homosexual. I finally ordered three drinks from the bar and wished him well with his skulduggery.

I was fatigued after drinking in the daytime so I sat down and tried my best to get drunk.

Joe went off dancing on the stage, managing to attract the attention of two beautiful Israeli girls. I watched them dancing in the rain and fantasised about joining in.

Mark was busy talking to two Danish girls, trying to decide which of them would be the easiest to sleep with. Tired, I decided that it was best to go back to the hostel.

Late at night Playa Del Carmen was awash with prostitutes looking to make money from drunken holiday makers. I was wary of these women as I had heard stories of people being beaten up and robbed.

I sauntered back to the hostel drunk and on my own, making me a prime target for the toe-tapping tarts that patrolled the dark streets. I walked down a dimly lit road close to the hostel when I heard someone whisper from the shadow of a doorway,

'Comme estas?'

I was drunk and stopped walking. Confused I stared into the dark corner. That momentary pause was all the encouragement that was needed. Within seconds this lady approached me wearing very little in the way of clothes. Without saying a word she grabbed my shirt and pulled me towards her. Her hand wandered between my legs and she began to feel me up. She spoke in a gritty but feminine Spanish tone,

'You want to fuck me?' she asked.

'Not really. I am just on my way home, to my (pause) mi casa,' I quivered as she rubbed at my groin.

'Chico I give you good price,' she assured me.

It was not a good price, I calculated that she wanted £150.

'Non mucho de niro chica, I'm not interested,' came my nervous reply.

She pulled me into the doorway was away from the dim street lighting and in seconds had her right hand around my now growing member.

'You have condom and I will fuck you for free,' she dirtily whispered into my innocent ear.

'Can't you just jerk me off gratis?'

'How much you have?' she replied, obviously thinking about it.

I rooted around in my empty pockets and found six pesos. I offered them to her.

'Non, hand relief $20 pesos.'

I pulled away finally realizing what was happening. I became conscious of how drunk I was and where she had taken me. I was three metres from the main street and could have easily been attacked without anyone seeing.

'Non gracias chica, hasta luego!' I said firmly as I did up the fly of my trousers and left.

I stumbled back onto the street declining her services but was left intrigued by the whole ordeal. Someone really needed to teach her how to barter; to go from £150 to nothing was crazy. A small portion of me regretted turning her down.

Had I fucked her without money changing hands would it still have classed as prostitution? Or would it have just been a socially acceptable one night stand? I decided that I would ask Mark in the morning.

Back at the room I found Mark asleep in bed with an old looking Mexican with short hair. The Danish girls must have blown him off and he had chosen an easier target.

I told Mark and Joe about my experience with the prostitute. I laughed at the irony of her referring to wanking me off as 'hand relief'.

She was willing to stand half naked on a freezing street selling her body to an endless succession of strangers, night after night, in order to fuel a lethal drug habit. But she wouldn't lower herself to use the word 'wank'.

I asked Mark about the Mexican, who must have left the room before we all got up,

'What was that about then, she looked disgusting,' I said.

'She was disgusting sir.'

'You didn't have sex with her did you? She looked like a leather cube with hair.'

'She wouldn't let me.'

'Would you have wanted in her leathery lobster pot?'

'Lobster pot?'

'Her vagina.'

'Probably.'

The weather in Playa for the second day was grey. Being a beach resort meant that most activities were reliant on the weather being good. It was a beautiful town but without the sun it just wasn't the same. It was like eating your favourite cereal without milk.

As the day had been dull, Mark decided that on the night we should find a strip club. We drank on the roof of the hostel with the staff and several guests for a few hours as they had kindly arranged a barbeque. The barbeque was an old rusting oil drum that had been sawn in half and was in keeping with the half finished lazy décor on the roof. The environment was relaxing and I liked it.

At 10:00pm Mark began harassing Joe and I about going to a club. Half an hour passed before we yielded and left the hostel. Mark flagged down a taxi and climbed into the front seat. Joe and I sat in the back and left him to sort everything out,

'Where is strippy strip? Where is club la chicas?' he asked.

The driver looked at him like he was insulted. Mark, unsure that he was being understood, began rubbing his hands over his own body imitating a stripper, pretending he had breasts. The driver smiled and seemingly understanding his request, sped off down the road and out of town.

We pulled up outside an old grey tower block to the side of the busy highway. On the ground floor was a dark façade with flashing pink lights that read:

'The Neon Cactus.'

Two huge doormen stared at us as we paid the driver and got out of his cab. They were both dressed like they were in the FBI.

I was now a lot more comfortable with the idea of strip clubs. Mark was at home in them which made things a lot less awkward. He told me on the roof of the hostel that,

'Strip clubs will become one of the core themes of our trip sir.'

So far they had.

We once again sat at a plastic table with complimentary peanuts as the centre piece. At first I thought we had walked into a Muslim strip club, as all this place seemed to feature was full on facial nudity. The girls on the stage were fully clothed and looked miserable. We sat bored with a bottle of beer each. I almost reached for the peanuts.

I scanned the uninspiring, dark listless bar looking at the girls, at the customers and the staff and felt so far from aroused it was untrue. I thought arousal was the whole point of these places.

Our chairs sat in the middle of the room facing the stage. I turned and looked over my left shoulder to see what Mark was doing as he had been far too quiet. All that I could see was the top of his bald head as he was buried in one of the girl's breasts. He looked like a giant baby getting his feed. It made for uncomfortable viewing.

I turned back towards the stage where a huge Dominican woman was peeling off her bikini, I wasn't sure where to look.

Mark was again left frustrated at the club's high prices so, as had happened in Isla Mujeres, we left soon after. We walked back into town along the freeway as the taxi had only taken a couple of minutes on the way there.

The walk took much longer than we had anticipated. By midnight we had got back onto Avienda Five.

As with every night in Playa, the street was alive and bustling with people. We sparred with several of the street merchants, promising each day that we would buy wrestling masks tomorrow.

We sat on the street drinking a bottle of rum by Starbucks. On the way down to Mezcalina, we decided to buy some cocaine from one of shop owners. He had offered us drugs on numerous other occasions and was always sticking his business in other people's noses. That night we decided why not?

We went down a quiet side street away from the crowd and sat on the curb behind an old rusty green Mini Cooper. None of us admitted it but there was a nervous mood in the air. I stood leaning casually against the back of the car making sure no one could see us.

Mark lined up the powder on the back of our plastic room card and we all had a bump. I was far from a cocaine connoisseur, but started to worry that whatever it was that I had just snorted up my right nostril was not cocaine. My nose burned and I began to sweat like Lee Evans doing stand up.

We all sheepishly appeared from behind the car wide-eyed and walked casually down the cobbled hill to the cul-de-sac and Mezcalina. I felt short of breath and anxious as I entered the bar, so I elected to sit down on an aluminium chair by the entrance and asked Joe to get some beers.

I still didn't feel myself twenty minutes later so left the bar for a few moments to get some air from the street. I stood by the side of the bar looking out at the expanse of people, and that is when I saw her.

Across the road stood the Spanish witch from Isla Mujeres, the mutant woman on the motorbike with the cold eyes. She was dressed to impress in a tight black dress and was walking up and down the strip. I still didn't know her name but Mark and I referred to her as 'Transvestbike,' in honour of our chance meeting on scooters. I found the very sight of her remarkable.

She was displeasing to the eye, having a face that looked like a dropped meat pie. She exhibited such confidence for someone so ugly. You had to respect her for that. It takes balls to be a transvestite. Her large hippo-like head was bobbing up and down harassing intoxicated men with dirty talk. I walked closer as she grabbed a white-shirted American.

'Argh pretty American, I souk yar dick,' she cackled as both her huge breasts pressed into his unsuspecting face.

The air worked and I began to feel normal again. I stood looking at Transvestbike trying to imagine being drunk enough that she would look attractive. It was impossible. Put some tits on Stephen Hawking and I would probably be tempted but not her. The image of Stephen Hawking with fake tits masturbating flashed through my drug-fuelled mind. Now that was a stroke of genius.

I went back into the bar, the music that had sounded far away and distant filtered into my ears as my mind was now clear. The powder I had snorted had either taken hold or worn off and my nose was no longer stinging.

After several beers in a noisy and packed Mezcalina I asked Mark where Joe had gone. He had not been seen for about twenty minutes. Mark had no idea so I decided that I would look around the bar for him. He wasn't there. Rather than worry I went out on to the street for a cigarette, he had probably gone back to the hostel.

I looked down to the bottom of the cul-de-sac where the two clubs, the Blue Parrot and Coco Maya, were situated. As it was getting late there were now a number of prostitutes patrolling the area including Transvestbike, who stuck out like a sore thumb.

To my amazement she was chewing the face off some poor unsuspecting bloke in a trilby who had his back to me. He was a lot smaller than her and I would not have been surprised if she stood on her heels and swallowed him whole like an anaconda.

They were talking and kissing and it looked as if she was trying to take the poor little bloke off for some action as she pointed past me up the hill.

She grabbed at his left arm and he turned ninety degrees, allowing me to finally see his face. It was a face I recognised. It was my friend. It was Joe. Rather than go over to help him I turned and ran back into the bar like a gazelle,

'Mark, come quickly you have to see this,' I bellowed across the bar.

Mark was sat trying to chat up to some girls. He looked up and sluggishly replied,

'What is it?'

'Probably the funniest thing you are ever likely to see,' was my excited response.

Mark got out of his seat and waded against the sea of people and onto the street.

'Quick, look,' I said pointing straight at Joe.

Mark's face was one of sheer shock as his mouth made the shape of an O. Joe was once again kissing the lady beast. We stood staring at them. Mark then said,

'I wonder if they both have erections.'

Once we had a laugh we went over to save poor Joe. I grabbed his right arm with my eyes still streaming with laughter. He was punch drunk, and didn't have a clue what was going on. After several protests Transvestbike let go of his other arm and scuttled off down the road to pray on another unsuspecting soul.

We sat down outside a shiesha bar that lay opposite to Mezcalina and began the inquest into what Joe was thinking. He could barely speak and mumbled that he wanted to go to Blue Parrot.

Joe went missing again within ten minutes. Mark and I decided to call it a night as we were both fucked up. We stumbled back to the hostel like two old alcoholics, not bothering to look for Joe for the second time. He knew where the hostel was and would be fine.

I stopped at King Kebab while Mark went back to the hostel.

I sat in the small restaurant eating as Mark gently slid his room card into the door of our room. He then flicked on the light. His eyes narrowed as they adjusted to the harsh light of the room. He heard voices from behind the wooden shutter.

Mark looked on in horror as Joe was lying on top on a woman sucking on her erect nipples. Mark looked up and then saw that familiar large face, the one that looked like a bucket of smashed crabs. It was Transvestbike! He didn't know whether to laugh or cry.

Joe was rattled by the light and stopped chewing on her fraudulent chest. He began screaming at the body beneath him,

'Get out, you have a penis. You have a willy. Get out please!'

She sat up on the bed giggling, dishevelled with her tits hanging out.

Mark grabbed her by the arm and told her to get out. She left as Joe lay on the bed shaking with his face buried into one of several soft pillows.

Transvestbike fell onto the street staggering around with her tits still hanging out the top of her black dress. It was at this point that I saw her myself. The very sight made me choke on my kebab. I walked back to the room eager to hear what had happened.

Mark came out onto the street laughing and filled me in with the androgynous antics that had happened in the room. He told me that she had offered to suck his dick,

'Gaz would it really have been that wrong?' he asked.

He didn't need an answer and I hoped that he was joking. I sat with Mark on a stone bench outside the hostel. He had been nagging me all day about the prostitute that offered to have sex with me for free and wanted to know where she was,

'Tell me,' he asked.

'It was just up the road there, by the kebab house,' I pointed in the general direction.

I left Mark on the bench as I was tired and wanted to sleep. I passed Joe in the corridor, he looked like he had just witnessed a war crime. The reality was probably worse.

The next morning I felt the best way to deal with what happened the night before was to make light of it. Joe conveniently could not remember anything of the night which was probably a good thing. I looked over the breakfast table at him and asked,

'What was the best thing about shagging a transvestite?'

'I didn't shag her you twat,' came the curt response.

'I heard that when you reach round, it feels like it's gone all the way through.'

'I don't remember.'

'So you did shag her then?' I asked again.

Joe then realised that he had to make a joke of the situation and decided to start telling everyone at the hostel.

As the weather was terrible we decided to have a session on the Internet. Mark and I finally booked our flights to South America after weeks of trying. We had to fly via Fort Lauderdale in America, and it was expensive at £400, but we had no other choice. In a week we would be touching down at Lima airport, the capital of Peru. I was excited.

After dinner Mark told me that after I had gone to bed he found the prostitute by the Kebab house and had paid $20 pesos to have sex with her. Joe then admitted that he too had sex with her but had only paid $50 pesos. Both of them were crazy.

We decided that we had had enough of Playa Del Carmen and booked a bus to Tulum that was due to leave the following evening.

On our last night we went to the bar we had visited most nights, called Pura Vida. It was a small Argentinean surf bar and the staff there loved us. It was located away from Avienda Five opposite where we had drank on the street the first night.

Joe and I challenged the barmen to a penalty shoot-out competition using the iron shutter of the pizza parlour next door as a goal. The age-old rivalry of England vs. Argentina was re-ignited.

After what was a close affair, England came out on top and we were rewarded with a full bottle of vodka.

As we sat outside the bar on large stools drinking the vodka we saw Maria and Barbara who we had met on the beach a few days previous. We coaxed them into joining us on our small table.

The night for me slid into an intoxicated blur that took me down to Mezcalina and to a club close to the hostel. I had no recollection of getting home or going to bed.

The next morning I woke up having drooled all over my pillow. Mark was full of life, I wondered why he was so happy. Before I could ask he told me that he had kissed Maria on the way home and that he had feelings for her. I started to laugh but then stopped when I realised that he was not joking.

Before leaving for Tulum I walked around the market stalls with him so that he could buy a gift for her to remember him by. I had never seen Mark like this but it was nice to see as it looked like he was finally getting over his girlfriend back home.

Tulum

Mark took his gift of a bracelet to Maria before we then got on a minibus to Tulum. Joe and I wanted to take a break from drinking and find some better weather; Mark wanted to stay in Playa.

I had really enjoyed Playa Del Carmen but the time had come to leave. Mark and I had three nights left in Mexico and had heard that the beach and ruins of Tulum were something that we had to see. Since arriving in Cancun we had been on holiday. There was no denying that it had been fun but I wanted my trip to be more than just drinking.

I enjoyed getting drunk and making friends, but I wanted to get back to taking photographs and indulging in a bit of history. My body really needed a break as the three of us together had been acting like a rock band on tour. Our bodies were quite simply falling apart.

I slept for the majority of the two hour drive down the coast to Tulum. I woke a few times as the bus dropped workers off at the gates of the huge resorts that dotted the coastline.

Mark woke me up as we arrived outside a hostel that was situated on the side of the motorway. We decided to get a private room as we all needed the rest and collectively it worked out a similar price to the dorms.

The hostel was small, falling under the no frills bracket. We got our bags and checked into our room on the first of two floors. The room resembled a rundown honeymoon suite. We looked in through the door and saw two four poster beds complete with white laced drapes. At the foot of each bed was a dressing table with a vase full of plastic flowers. I remembered when I was fourteen years old and I saw two men kissing outside a shopping centre. It was the gayest thing that I had ever seen until I saw this room. We felt uncomfortable.

Mark took the bed against the far wall, leaving Joe and me with no option but to share the other. Mark and Joe jumped onto their respective beds and had a rest while I decided to have a shower.

As the room was small I got changed and went down to the main living space to meet some of the guests and ask about Tulum. There were a number of people sat around a long dining table, some of the faces looked familiar.

The German who I had the misfortune of being stuck on a boat with in San Cristobal was sat at one end of the table playing with her camera. I sat at the other next to the two Israeli girls that I had spoken with briefly as they danced in the rain at Blue Parrot.

I sat down rather embarrassed and started to chat with Tal, who I had tried to kiss in Playa, and her friend Gal. The reason that I was embarrassed was not because she had rejected my advances but because I had emailed her still half drunk the next day on Facebook. I posted a short message on her wall that read:

'Hope to see you in Tulum, fancy a bum?'

Not the greatest rhyme I had ever come up with, I sat wondering if she had read it.

Everyone at the hostel planned on going to the beach after they had eaten. They planned to drink some beers and relax and asked if I would like to go. I wasn't sure as I just wanted to sleep. Undecided I sat on an orange sofa watching the news on TV as they grabbed a push bike each from a wooden shed and left. I hadn't watched the news for nearly two months.

When you travel you completely lose touch with what is going on in the world. You have so much to see and do that you simply forget about home and just live each day for what it is. This was something I liked about travelling, just living in the present without any real worries.

I sat in the now empty hostel watching the news. It said that Barack Obama was enjoying what they termed a 'honeymoon period' with the American people. My mind began to race as it stuck on the words 'honeymoon period'. What man would enjoy that? It would ruin the whole trip.

I had completely forgotten that Obama was the American President. It seemed a long time ago that I was sat in a Canadian diner worrying about what to expect on this trip.

I started to reminisce about my time in Mexico and let my mind speculate about Peru and South America. It was only a few days away. I sat both excited and apprehensive as it was the great unknown.

After all these thoughts about travelling I decided that I wanted to go down to the beach. There was no reason not to. I coaxed Joe into coming with me but Mark was too tired and was happy lying in his fancy bed listening to his iPod.

Joe got changed and met me by the big table where everyone had been sitting. We walked to the back of the small garden and pulled two push bikes out of the shed. Unsure where the beach was we woke the receptionist who sat slumped at the main desk. She pointed us in the right direction.

We snaked down the hard shoulder of the motorway without lights and in near darkness. Cars and trucks blew past, throwing dust into our tired faces. We turned right away from the dangerous highway and onto a dark and dusty side road that we hoped went down to the beach.

Both of our bikes were demented. My back wheel was buckled and pressed against the metal frame of the bike. It had chipped away all of the paint and meant that each push of the pedals was met with a slight resistance. I was shattered.

For twenty minutes we cycled down a dark jungle road on broken bikes while mosquitos attacked both of us. I wished that we had stayed at the hostel, no beach was worth this effort.

The jungle began to clear and we could hear the calming sound of waves lapping ahead. Through the trees lay the beach and it was breathtaking. The moon lit up the white sands underfoot. The water sparkled like diamonds as it gently stroked the coastline. It was a peaceful, spectacular setting. We looked at each other struggling to pull our bikes through the sand and agreed to just dump them.

We found the group sat on large pieces of driftwood around a campfire. They were all drinking apart from Julio who sat in the middle of the circle by the fire plucking his guitar. It felt like we were part of a hippy retreat. I laid down, stared up at the clear night sky and couldn't help but think I led a charmed life.

Joe and I flirted with the two Israeli girls and talking about Playa Del Carmen. It certainly was more fun that being sat in our gay room listening to The Smiths on Mark's iPod. He was missing out; I was glad I had made the effort.

Tal and Gal asked Joe and I if we wanted to go for a swim. They stripped to their underwear and ran off into the waves.

They bobbed up and down in the water, both of them looked amazing as the water soaked their bodies. They shone in the moonlight like giant slugs, we decided to join them.

As Joe and I got into the water the girls decided to get out. It reminded me of a swimming class when I was seven years old at Primary School. We had gone swimming to our local baths when a girl in my class called Becky accidently released a brown shark into the clean water. Within seconds everyone had got out of the water and was screaming. While neither Tal nor Gal had screamed they had got out of the water quickly, leaving Joe and myself both feeling like shit.

We stayed in the water for five minutes before collecting our clothes and deciding to go back to the hostel. We didn't have any beers and both felt rejected.

The next morning we had breakfast sat around the huge communal table on the ground floor of the small hostel, before making our way on broken bikes down to the ruins. The ruins were down the same track that Joe and I had rode the previous night. Being midday, it was a lot harder as temperatures soared into the late twenties.

The ruins of Tulum were a spectacular site. If truth be told I was more in love with the setting on the beach. It was a place to declare heaven. The dazzling turquoise waters, the white sands and the bold black cliffs joined to create an awe-inspiring picture.

We spent a few hours on the beach before the weather started to cloud over. Mark asked if we could go back to Playa Del Carmen,

'We only have two nights left in Mexico and Pura Vida is having its first year anniversary on Friday.'

'I'm sure it has nothing to do with Maria,' I countered.

'Mate, seriously it doesn't.'

Joe and I didn't believe him but agreed that we would have a lot more fun back in Playa. Tulum was the sort of place to relax in when you had a lot of time; we didn't.

Playa Del Carmen

We arrived back in Playa Del Carmen early Thursday evening and checked back into the Happy Gecko. The staff looked confused but at the same time happy we had returned.

On the night we went to Pura Vida to see what they had planned for their party the next night. We spent the night at the bar listening to music and having a few beers. Rather predictably we were joined by Barbara and Maria, the French girl that Mark was besotted with.

After weeks of playing hide and seek, the sun finally reared its head on Friday and we could go back on the beach. We pitched up in our usual spot to the left of the beautiful white church that looked, like the beach, much prettier in the sun.

The beach was packed with holiday-makers, many of whom looked Mexican. I had noticed that Mexicans tended to have a lot of religious tattoos on their bodies. I turned to Mark as yet another heavily tattooed local walked past us and said,

'What's the difference between Jesus and Mexicans?'

'I don't know you nipple.'

'Jesus doesn't have Mexicans tattooed all over him.'

'He might have done, who knows?'

'Fuck off,' I said as we both laughed.

Sat behind us on coloured deckchairs were a group of lads that couldn't have looked more English if they had tried. I imagined them two weeks from now sat in an English pub telling their mates about the trip,

'Well right, the beach was full of lazy Mexicans sitting under palm trees high on drugs. The hotel was full of fat Americans who would trample on kids just to get to the buffet. We were keen not to be stereotyped like them, so we just say by the bar for two weeks totally pissed, wearing our England football tops.'

My assumption was right, they were from London. I decided I was going to speak to them. After a brief chat we decided to have a game of football by the church. There was a pitch and for once it was not being used.

I had watched people play football on the beach and they were terrible. They were constantly falling over and misplacing passes, it reminded me of watching Manchester City under Alan Ball.

After playing on the sandy surface I realised that I had been harsh. It was like playing in a bowl of cake mixture with a ball of toffee. After ten minutes the scores were stuck at one all. Half the people that started the game had now given up. I crouched over with my hands on my knees unable to breathe as the sun beat down on my back. We decided to blow for full time.

After football I walked around the beach telling people about the party at Pura Vida that evening. Mark and Joe suggested telling more girls than boys about the party. I decided to go a step further and just tell girls,

'Hey girls what are you all doing tonight?

(Pause)

'There is a one year anniversary at my friend's bar. Free drinks all night, you should come!'

As the first group of girls started to talk about the night, a group of men overheard and called me over,

'What was that about a free bar dude?' one of them arrogantly asked.

'It's not free really, just trying to get them to come down so keep quiet,' I replied with a wink.

'Nice work my man, nice work,' complimented the unnamed gentleman.

We left the beach at 4:00pm as it once again began to cloud over. Mark and I went for some food at our favourite taco wagon next to the bus terminal, Taco Lite. Playa was full of small vendors selling food, Taco Lite was in our opinion was the best.

It resembled an American hotdog cart and served a variety of easy-to-eat food. He offered three types of taco; Beef, Chicken and Chorizo. You could then choose from a series of sauces and sundries. It was quick and cheap so we ate there most days.

The owner of Taco Lite was a charming character that was full of life. You could hear him screaming proudly from half a mile away,

'Rico's amigos, tacos e tortas amigos!'

He was so loud and cheerful that you couldn't help but like him. Even if I was not hungry I was still drawn to his wagon. As we were regular customers he was always very kind to us, addressing us as his 'English Amigos'.

He always wore the same white overalls and white cap. Mark and I wondered if he just ate from his cart as it looked like he had a space hopper hidden in his overalls. He was so fat his cereal bowl probably had a lifeguard. The amount of money he made, there was no doubting he could afford one.

After filling our faces with tacos we walked back to the hostel and had a nap, it was going to be a long night.

We arrived at Pura Vida for 10:00pm after having a couple of beers at the hostel. Mark, Joe and I walked into the bar like The Beach Boys,

'Round?'
'Round?'
'Get a round'
'I get a round?'
'Get a round...'

Carlos told us to stop arguing, the drinks were all free so it didn't matter who got them. I told him that I had been promoting the bar all day on the beach. It was a slight exaggeration but it won each of us a high five and a free round of Tequila shots. Tonight, our penultimate in Mexico, was according to Carlos, going to be, 'Fun Fun Fun'.

The bar ran the whole length of the small room. They had filled coolers full of ice and bottles of beer and had these placed on the street to cope with what would be a busy night. The place looked like a surf shack with surf murals on the walls and a broken board hanging above the toilets. The bar had a relaxed vibe to it; the people in it knew how to have a good time.

The DJ got behind the booth by the left of the bar and started to spin some tunes. As the bar was small the sound echoed off the walls. I could barely hear myself think as the beat from the speakers flowed through my sneakers. The bar was filled with good vibrations.

I went outside for some rest bite as the bar was loud and becoming increasingly warm. I sat with Mark and Joe on an elevated table on the pavement. The breeze from the nearby beach came as a welcome relief.

After an hour people began to arrive and the bar was buzzing with people spilling out onto the streets. It turned in the space of half an hour into a big street party and we were right in the middle of it.

It reminded me of the Bacardi adverts on television back home. No one gave a shit, there were no rules, no cash was needed and the atmosphere was one of hedonistic celebration.

In the scrum of people two ladies from America grabbed hold of me. They were California girls on holiday. After the usual pleasantries I found that their topics of conversation became more lewd. I had met two real life desperate housewives. They were nowhere near as good as looking as their TV counterparts, so despite them asking,

'Wouldn't it be nice to come back to our room?'

I replied,

'I would far rather stay here drinking.'

Both of these women were divorced and in their late forties, they seemed disappointed that I had turned them down. In truth I was scared of them. As I walked off it felt like a missed opportunity. I knew that Mark would not have passed it up.

I had to escape more unwanted sexual attention moments later as I stood by the entrance of the bar with a glass of vodka lemonade in my hand. A man grabbed by arm and introduced himself,

'I am Victor,' he said.

'Hi, I'm Gareth how are you?'

'Good thank you,' he smiled.

He asked what the middle-aged women had said to me. I told him and said that I just wasn't interested in them. He responded by saying,

'It is ok Gareth, I understand. I will look after you!'

As he said this I noticed that he was rubbing my right arm. His facial features went soft and welcoming looking like a dog that wanted a walk. He lent against the wall of the bar and asked,

'Gareth, can I buy you a drink? Anything you want!'

I looked at him puzzled as he gripped onto my arm,

'Victor that is very nice of you but I am fine. It's a free bar so I am sorted for drinks, but if you could loosen your grip on my arm that would be just super, thanks!'

I looked out of the corner of my eye and saw that the two American ladies were walking hand in hand down the road and into the night with what looked like an Albino and a tall bloke with long dark hair. I was glad of the missed opportunity.

Victor let go of my arm. I went back over to the table on the pavement where Mark and Joe were still sat. They were joined by Maria and Barbara.

The bar was heaving with people trying to get drinks. It reminded me of the Hillsborough disaster where Liverpool fans were crushed to death pushing forward into the ground.

No one at this bar was calm. The flow of people was suffocating, it was crazy. People were crowd-surfing from the bar out on to the street as the bar tenders flung Tequila around their heads, filling any open mouths. I gave up trying to get served, it wasn't worth risking my life.

On the street a guy with bongos arrived and started beating some fast rhythmic beats which got the ever growing crowd excited. People created a tight circle around the bongo player as others were pushed into the middle to dance to the sounds of the bongo and chorus of sweaty palms. I looked up into the sky, watching the energy radiate from the bar and was thankful to be where I was.

The night spiralled into random chats and a pool of free booze as my mind began to fade; the party was out of control and I loved every minute of it.

I stumbled back to the room with the help of Cecilla, a girl I met outside Pura Vida an hour or so earlier. She was a Mexican girl from Monterrey in the north and was in Playa on Holiday. She had caramel skin, dark chocolate eyes and long dark hair that curled. She told me that she was a model. I was too drunk to decide whether or not I believed her.

Mark had told me in Merida of a personal challenge he had set himself at the start of the trip. He planned to sleep with a girl from each of the countries that he was going to visit. I laughed at the thought of him sleeping with a Bolivian as, from what I had seen on television, they looked like leather hamsters. I knew that he didn't care. Mark had already slept with a Mexican so he was on course to achieve his goal.

I was not interested in such challenges. Back home I had gone over a year without having sex and it was something that did not really bother me. That said, as I staggered into the room, thoughts of sleeping with a Mexican on my last night would not leave my head. Maybe a juvenile challenge was what I needed?

I fell at the first hurdle as it was that time of the month for Cecilla, meaning that we did not have sex. She did give me a blow job in the bathroom though so I woke the next morning proud of my night's work. Mark looked at me like a proud father,

'Well done mate she looked alright. The Mexican times.'

We got up and both said our goodbyes to Joe who was returning to England. In a few days we would be in South America while he would be home in England slap bang in the middle of winter. It didn't seem fair and I felt sorry for him.

Mark and I got our bags together and made sure we were all set for our flight from Mexico to America. We were meant to get a coach to Cancun to be near to the airport but had woken up late and missed it. Feeling like death we decided to stay in Playa Del Carmen and go directly to the airport early the following morning.

This worked out well for Mark as it meant he could spend more time with Maria who he had still not managed to sleep with. They talked about the possibility of her meeting up with us in Buenos Aires as they walked hand in hand down Aveinda Five for the last time. I walked several metres behind in silence with Barbara, who was one of those annoying French people that refused to speak English as she hated the people.

I went home soon after as we had to be up early the next morning and could ill afford to miss the flight. I left the love birds to it.

My last meal in Mexico was a McDonald's breakfast at the airport that was covered with cheese and chilli. I laughed as I peeled back the grease proof paper but would not have wanted it any other way.

USA

Fort Lauderdale

We arrived in Fort Lauderdale after a short flight from Cancun. I spent the two hour flight deep in conversation with an American man who introduced himself as Mike from Miami, Florida. He had been in Cancun for the weekend.

Mike looked like a pumped up Dr. Evil. His cleanly shaved head looked like another muscle, only it wore black sunglasses. Sat next to Mike was his number two – Peter, a black man from Key West.

They were equally obsessed with what they termed, 'My massive adventure.'

They wanted to know everything about my adventure. I found it strange how materialistic they both were. They both freely admitted that they would rather have a big car than a big adventure but respected people like me who dared to do it. Neither of them had any adventure in them. Other countries seemed to scare them, they were governed by fear.

Dr Evil wanted to live vicariously through me. He requested my email address and my Facebook details so he could look through my pictures. I'm not sure whose pictures he got to look at as I gave him fake details.

We booked into an Econo-Lodge a few miles from the airport after deciding that Miami was just that bit too far and would be too expensive for just one night.

The Econo-Lodge was your stereotypical American movie-style roadside motel. The motel was set over two floors and hooked like a horse shoe around a small rectangular swimming pool. The walls outside were all pebbled grey with red beams separating the roof and door entrances. It had a seventies feel to it, and reminded me of Vice City in Grand Theft Auto.

My mind raced at a frightening pace as I began to think about all the drug deals, prostitutes and shootings that no doubt went on at this motel, if indeed this was Vice City.

The door to our room swung open and it was huge. Two queen-sized beds took up the majority of the carpeted floor space. I had not seen a carpet since leaving England two months earlier. At the foot of the beds there was an oak cabinet that housed a large TV. Our plan was to lie down, eat junk food and watch cable TV. It was important to absorb the culture of the country we were visiting.

I lay half asleep drowning on my huge bed, watching a horrendous horror film about a lawless mutant alligator eating scantily clad women. Mark sat up against his headboard snapping though the local phone book for scantily clad women.

At first I thought that he was just being curious but as I fell in and out of consciousness I distantly heard him on the phone calling one number after another. Like the alligator he was on the hunt.

He rang and spoke in such a relaxed manner it was like he was ringing for a pizza. I woke up and started to listen to the words that came out of his mouth. He wasn't just calling strip clubs, he was ringing escorts and asking the person down the phone to run through what was on offer,

'So what have you got on offer?'

(Pause as the gentleman on the phone answered)

'Hmmm…… what are the brunettes like that you have, any with big tits?' he asked.

(Another pause)

'Nice tits? How much roughly are we talking for nice tits?'

(Pause)

'Ok I'll get back to you, thanks!' as the numbers calculated in his brain.

Mark told me that it was about $150 - $200 dollars for an escort to visit the room. I looked at him in disbelief and told him to stop being stupid. He argued that it was America and therefore she would probably be the best looking girl he could ever get with,

'Haven't you seen the movies? Women in Miami are phenomenal.'

He went on to suggest that I get one too,

'It would be good for you. You shouldn't take sex so seriously.'

'No thanks,' I responded.

We left our room and walked down a busy road into the nearby town of Hollywood as it began to get dark. The area didn't have a warm feel to it. The people kept themselves to themselves and didn't even acknowledge that we were there. It was quiet but then it was Sunday.

We drank a couple of beers on a sidewalk as a couple of neon signs flicked on, letting people know their establishments were open. Other shops sat in darkness clearly closed.

Mark wanted to go to a strip club, we only had one night in America and as he had said, 'a theme of the trip'. We got into a taxi and pulled up outside a club off the freeway called Starlets. The club had a huge neon sign that buzzed overhead as he passed the two imposing bouncers on the door.

We walked up to the counter as waves of 1980s' rock wafted out the main doors and waitresses emerged with empty drinks. I was excited about this place as it looked a lot better than the clubs I had been dragged to in Mexico. I felt comfortable about entering this club.

Unfortunately I would have to wait as Mark was refused entry. He had forgotten to bring out his ID. Having recently shaved, his face looked like an eleven-year-old potato with eyes so he couldn't really complain. He did anyway, but to no avail.

Without his ID we were not getting in anywhere so we reluctantly returned back to the Econo-Lodge to watch some films and eat junk food as originally planned.

I turned on the TV and began to flick through the hundred or so channels on offer. Mark sat on his bed frustrated by what had happened at the strip club. He once again started to flick through the phone directory as I sat and laughed at him.

'What are you laughing for? I'm really pissed off,' he said.

'Mate you are not going to book one, just accept that it's not meant to be,' I joked.

'Fuck you, I'm doing that ring,' he answered defiantly.

He picked up the phone and made the call. From what I could make out he booked a brunette that would be at the motel to see him within half an hour. I couldn't believe he had done it. He had booked for a complete stranger to come to our room. It could be anyone, they could just come in and rob all our stuff and what was I going to do, wait in the bathroom?

Five minutes later he asked me in the nicest of voices,

'Mate come on please; just go in like twenty minutes. I don't want her arriving and there being two of us here, she could get scared.'

I liked that he was thinking about the girl's welfare and so, like any good mate, eventually told him that I would leave the room. I didn't want a scared prostitute on my conscience.

So rather than walk aimlessly into town I sat on a plastic sun lounger outside the room. It was past midnight and it was cold. I stared into the uninspiring dimly lit pool waiting for his mystery woman to appear. I didn't have to wait long.

Headlights shined into my face as a large black car pulled into the car park. My eyes narrowed as the dark silhouette of a woman elegantly opened the rear door and stepped out onto the road. The engine still purred so I guessed that she had been chauffeur driven by her pimp. I couldn't see any of her features as the beams of light from the car shone straight into my eyes.

The figure approached slowly and the anticipation of seeing her was like the opening of a concert. She opened the white metal, low swing gate by the side of the grey reception office, and as it slammed shut the lights of the car dimmed and faded into a hue. Random spots of light flickered in front of me as my eyes once more adjusted to the darkness.

She walked a few metres in front of me but her eyes were fixed on three gold numbers glued to a white door. The three numbers Mark had spoken down the phone,

'It is Room 118 mate.'

Mark's order had arrived on time but I knew that he has going to be disappointed. I arched my head gently like a detective on a stakeout to catch a glimpse of him ushering her sheepishly into the room.

I thought about the times I had ordered food only for the wrong thing to come. It is really annoying when that happens but at least you can ring up again and ask for what you wanted. I wondered if you could do the same with humans, how awkward would that be? Humans, unlike food, have feelings.

The phone rings.

'Hi this is Prostitute Pizzas, you're talking to Drew Peacock, how can I help you?'

'Yes hello, I just err ordered one of your humans from the specials menu. I asked for the medium brunette with brown eyes in a C cup bra.'

'Yeah I remember, what seems to be the problem?'

'Well she has just been delivered to my door while her pimp waits in the car and to be honest, looks nothing like she does on the menu.'

'The menu was designed a few years ago, just go with the flow man,' he reassures.

'Listen I want to send her back, she's thin and crispy, and I don't want to stuff her crust.'

'I understand sir, we don't want to lose your business so this one is on us.'

'Ok,' comes the reluctant reply.

The phone goes dead.

I was glad that Mark had asked for me to sit outside but I was interested on what he was going to do about the situation he was in. Would he just eat what had arrived or was he going to back out and asked for a refund?

The girl arrived at Room 118 looking like she had been fucked like an animal all night; half a gram of Ketamine will do that to a person. Her skin was translucent grey and paper thin. Her hair was dry, thin and curly - looking like a bonfire that had never actually burned, she was in bad condition. He had asked for a swimming pool and got a puddle.

I walked across the three-lane road to the glowing 7-Eleven and bought myself a chilli dog from a vending machine. I sat on a wooden bench looking over the road at the big black vehicle that still sat in the car park.

Mark's hour session lasted about ten minutes. I saw the thin figure of the girl walk back to the big black car and as the engine rumbled and lights flicked on they were gone.

I wondered if he had asked her to leave. I hoped that given the awkward nature of the situation he had broken the news to her through song. Lenny Kravitz would have been my choice;

'American woman, I said get away
American woman, listen what I say
Don't come hanging around my door
Don't want to see your face no more
I don't need your war machines
I don't need your ghetto scenes
Coloured lights can hypnotize
Sparkle someone else's eyes
Now woman, get away.'

Mark walked across the three lanes of the road and sat next to me with a shocked expression on his face outside the Mini-mart. I finished my hotdog as he broke the silence,

'She was quite honestly disgusting, a smack head riddled with poison,' he summarised.

Inevitably I had to ask,

'Did you do it?'

'You're joking aren't you no way mate. I told her that I had a girlfriend and had changed my mind.'

Clever thinking I thought.

'Did she charge you then?'

'No, not in the end though I gave her $20 for petrol. Let's not talk about it, can we go get some food and watch a film?'

'That has been the plan all night,' I replied.

'Why do I do these things?' Mark smirked.

Unsure as to whether his question was rhetorical I replied,

'Because you are a horrible man.'

The following morning we sat around the hotel waiting to go to the airport. South America was finally a few hours away, I couldn't wait. North America was too similar to home. It offered nothing different and it posed no challenges. I knew that South America would.

The first challenge came sooner than either of us predicted as the lady at the check-in desk was suspicious about the two of us. We did not have flights booked out of Peru so according to her, without an onward journey we were not allowed out of the country.

We each had proof of flights home from Brazil in March as we planned to bus around South America to save money and see more of the country. The woman did not believe us.

We were subjected to a number of high security searches that included them rooting through our bags. Thankfully a full cavity search was not necessary.

I was asked by airport security if I'd left my suitcase unattended at any time. Growing more and more frustrated by the delays I replied,

'Yes, it's been in the fucking loft for the last ten months.'

'Calm down sir, it's airport procedure, I don't want to have to detain you,' the guard replied.

'Why? For swearing?'

'Aggressive behaviour,' he answered.

What was it with me and airports? Perhaps it was my ongoing theme? Mark had his, this could be mine. First I was stopped for wearing an intimidating belt buckle. Then I was stopped for travelling alone without accommodation and now in America it was a visa violation and random bag searches. I stood thinking what next.

We got onto the plane with minutes to spare despite arriving a full three hours before departure. I was glad to be leaving America. In six hours we would be landing on a new continent, one I had dreamed of visiting but never thought I would.

America, like Britain, was a materialistic society that had lost sight of the sheer joy of being alive and replaced it with dreams of cars and big houses. I couldn't see any purpose in it. Maybe I would find my purpose and direction somewhere in South America.

PERU

Lima

Mark and I arrived in Lima and had no problems getting through airport security as suggested by the woman in America. Six hours of in-flight worry had been for nothing.

Minutes later Mark shit himself at the arrivals hall. The airport was jam packed with people so we decided to get away from the crowd of people and have a beer before leaving the airport.

We were having a drink in the airport bar celebrating getting into the country when a Middle-Eastern gentleman rushed by us screaming,

'Allah, Allah, Allah, Allah, Allah... alava coke and bag of nuts please.'

'Did you just hear that stuttering bastard?' I asked.

Mark's reaction was genius. He was off his seat ready to bomb towards the exit. His worried expression faded and we sat until we finished off our drinks,

'You thought he was a terrorist didn't you?' I teased.

'No,' he replied, really meaning yes.

We ignored the huge queues of people waiting for an official airport taxi and elected to follow what I guessed was a crazy local to the car park.

He had approached us as we left the bar; clearly he had been watching us. I felt it was worth the risk as he was small and Mark was tall. He couldn't hurt us.

The man offered to take us into town for $40 pesos. We agreed and creaked away from the airport in his aging motor vehicle. The driver looked like a fat mafia boss; he was tanned and wore a black suit. He told us that the hostel we requested was full, and offered somewhere that he said was 'far superior'.

We decided to ignore his words of bullshit and got dropped at Loki Hostel in Mira Flores. We had been told by countless travellers that the Loki hostels were the best in South America. Known for being safe and full of backpackers, it was the ideal location to start our South American adventure.

The taxi driver was correct, as the receptionist told Mark that the hostel was full. Our South American adventure started with the two of us walking the streets of Lima at midnight looking for somewhere to stay.

We ended up in a squalid bed and breakfast hidden on a dirty back street in the middle of Mila Flores. Mila Flores was, we had been told, the affluent area of Lima. I didn't hold out much hope for the place if this was indeed the case.

We dumped our bags by the rotting door of our unremarkable room and decided to get some sleep on our antique wooden beds. I lay under my single sheet excited about the coming days and months.

Like Mexico City, Lima was busy and unplanned. After the weeks of partying in the Yucatan peninsula it was once again time to experience real travel. We'd had our holiday.

Lima was founded by Spanish conquistadors as the 'The City of Kings' and was made the capital of the Republic of Peru. From my early experience I hadn't seen a place less deserving of the title 'King' since flame grilled whoppers entered my life.

Mark and I decided in the morning to leave the bed and breakfast and check into the Loki hostel across the square. We spent the day walking around Lima, taking in its atmosphere.

The sun was out but struggled to break through a grey mist that engulfed the city's skyline. The haze was similar to the one in Mexico City and I wasn't sure whether it was pollution or just clouds.

Noises from people, cars, shops, restaurants and markets filtered into my ears from all directions. I was looking forward to seeing what this city had to offer. It was alive with noise and colour.

Lima, like any capital city, was busy. The roads were jammed with cars, buses and scooters sounding their horns as everyone went about their daily business. It was a nice change to the resort areas of Mexico. You could just take a step back and view everyday life.

The first thing that Mark noticed when he stepped back was not the colonial architecture or glass skyscrapers; it was the women. We had expected Peruvians to be an unattractive race of people.

The only Peruvian I had ever seen was the famous footballer Nolberto Solano. He looked like Count von Count from Sesame Street so the omens were not good. Therefore it came as a shock to see scores of good looking women.

We walked around the affluent area of Mila Flores and Lancomar, a newly developed shopping centre hanging from a cliff, before hailing a taxi and asking the driver to take us downtown to Lima's historical centre.

The taxi driver was sat in what looked like a makeshift wire dog kennel. We assumed it was for safety but it looked ridiculous. It reminded me of the stunt car from Death Proof, in the movie the car is only death proof for the driver.

The film involves a stuntman picking up girls in his reinforced car before subjecting them to terrifying and deadly ordeals. The taxi driver did not look like a psychotic stuntman, but I wasn't convinced.

His driving led to some terrifying but not deadly trials as he weaved in and out of the scores of traffic and towards the downtown area of this huge city.

I looked out the window up at large billboards of recognisable global brands that reached towards the sky. I then looked down at the dirty markets and people sat shivering in doorways by closed shops. It seemed wrong that multi-billion pound companies advertised their products above a backdrop of extreme poverty and despair.

It was almost 4:00pm so we got some food at a local restaurant, lured in by the neon sign that flashed outside. Mark probably thought it was a strip club.

It was here that I tried Inca Cola for the first time. I was concerned to start with, as it looked like a bottle of fizzy piss given its bright yellow appearance. The cola was exclusive to Peru and tasted like bubblegum.

The centre of Lima showed signs of aging. This once golden city of trade was now a shadow of its former glories. We walked randomly around the streets with no real purpose. We both just enjoying taking in the relaxed historic nature of the downtown area of the city.

The atmosphere changed from sluggish to spirited with the turning of a corner. We cut down a street to the left and ended up in the middle of a protest. We had no idea what it was about but it was hostile.

A policeman came over spotting our confusion and told us in clear English,

'The protest is to do with our country's unemployment rates, do not worry.'

The recession was clearly affecting everywhere. It was the first time I had even thought about it since being away; I wondered if any of my friends had lost their jobs?

I looked round the now heaving street and thought that there was around 200 riot police flanking each side of the square. The protest had achieved something as there were more police on patrol than normal.

The police wore full riot gear, including batons and shields embroiled with the slogan 'Polizia'. At the bottom of the street to the left of what looked an important building, sat three green tanks that made me uneasy.

'This protest could flip into a riot at any time.

'We best get moving,' I sensibly suggested.

'Go ask that policeman for a photo, I dare you!' Mark responded.

'What the one that just spoke with us?'

'That's the one, sure. It would make a good photo.'

So despite being scared about the situation I walked tentatively over to the policeman and asked,

'Amigo possible photo parra me?'

'Si,' was the one worded response.

I was slightly surprised given the situation. I joined him and the police force by the curb, unsure that he had understood my attempts at Spanish. Mark took the first photo as I stood in line with ten officers smiling.

I decided to push my luck, and asked Arthur if I could wear his helmet or carry his plastic shield. He gave me both without question. I felt like I had when I was five years old and the local fire station came to visit.

The kindness of Arthur the policeman diffused any uneasiness we may have felt towards the swarms of people swinging blood red flags in the evening sky. They were directing the jeers and taunts at the government not at two white backpackers from England. We were most definitely safe.

We continued our exploration of downtown Lima. As in Mexico City, Mark was looking for a sex shop and he found one.

I followed him up a dark stairwell adjacent to a well lit respectable looking sports shop. At the top of stairway hung a green light that fizzed in the stale air. Under the light sat an old man hunched on a wooden chair fast asleep. Mark looked at the graffiti adorning the walls and saw the sign,

'Sex Shop -------->'

We walked through the hard wooden door and I couldn't believe my eyes. I stood scanning the area in disbelief, before the disbelief turned to laughter. We found ourselves stood in the middle of an office. At an oak desk in the corner sat an old Peruvian man dressed smartly in a navy blue suit. He was examining a stack of papers on his desk, I noticed that his right hand was moving under the table. Surely he wasn't was he?

The man looked up at us briefly before once again burying his head into his papers. His hand had stopped moving. I always thought the most sensitive part of your body when wanking was your ears; his were clearly blocked.

I started laughing as he looked like a paedophilic version of Penfold from Danger Mouse, his glasses had slightly steamed and he looked flustered. Rather than explain himself he just raised his head from his papers and stared at the two of us.

As if that was not enough of a visual fare for my eyes to digest, I noticed his desk was surrounded by an impressive arsenal of dildos. It was a rubber cock shop and he had an impressive collection. They ranged in colour from your real life skin beiges, to phantom blacks, through to your futuristic neon pinks.

The dildos brought a bit of colour to the otherwise dreary beech wood office. We turned round and left without saying anything. We didn't want to buy any of his multicoloured manhood toys and there was no pornography or live sex shows unless you enjoyed watching a man in his fifties relieve himself behind a desk. We didn't.

As night began to fall we got a cab from the main square back to the hostel. After a quick turnaround in our cheap but comfortable private room I walked through the hostel to meet Mark at the bar.

As I walked into the bar I noticed two pretty girls looking at me; they were sat to the left on a small wooden table.

'Nine,' I heard one whisper as I passed.

Feeling pretty pleased with myself I swaggered over to Mark and told him a girl had just rated me as nine out of ten. I was showered, clean and obviously looking good.

'I don't want to ruin it for you,' he said. 'But when I walked in they were speaking German.'

I grabbed a beer from the barman and, rather than feel stupid, refused to believe what Mark had said was true.

The hostel was a real travellers' hangout and had something for everyone. I was delighted to discover that the checkout time was 1:00pm. This was favourable as we planned to go out and then leave Lima the following morning. No one needs to be up at 10:00am with a hangover.

A white board at the bar suggested activities for the coming week. Tonight's suggestion was scrawled in blue marker, it told people go to Bartini Bar's ladies night in Lancomar. It was our one night in Lima so I took a mental note of the bar before we headed into town for some dinner.

As my food digested Mark was negotiating entry to a local strip club with a man on the street. He shepherded me into a cab and, before I knew what was happening, we were on our way through the city to a place called Eclipse.

I was concerned during the twenty minute drive to the club as I was nowhere near drunk enough to feel comfortable. Mark reassured me,

'Mate, relax it's going to be banter.'

As part of the tickets Mark had bought we got vouchers for two free drinks and a pisco sour, a local Peruvian spirit. I went over to the bar and ordered all three.

The women in Eclipse had a feral quality and were stunning. Unlike the Mexican joints we had frequented this one was of good quality, offering debauched exoticism. The girls danced to classic rock songs as Mark and I sat transfixed on the stage, attracted like moths to a light.

Being on a budget I couldn't afford a private dance but nor was I drunk enough to feel comfortable enough to get one. Mark was in his element as he had decided to have a separate account for affairs of the penis. He walked off to a private room to blow his money.

I sat on a red sofa a few metres from the front of the stage. I sat pretending to drink from my now empty bottle of lager, staring at the empty stage, feeling rather empty myself. Several girls approached asking if I would like a dance or if I would like to buy them a drink. I was tempted to say yes but said no to them all.

Mark came back over from the far right of the club and was furious about wasting money on what was only a dance; he had been looking for more. He decided that it was time to for us to leave. I suggested that we go to Bartini.

We met up with some lads from the hostel and went down to the bar. Bartini was an upmarket bar located in the modern Lancomar shopping centre, next to the Peruvian Hooters.

On entering the bar I was hit with a wall of loud music the bar was heaving. I looked around the dark floor space and saw that the bar was full of intoxicated men each sweating like a dyslexic on Countdown. I stood by the bar and ordered some drinks while looking around for girls. It was then that I was grabbed by the arm. I turned around to see a thin, good looking blonde smiling at me. As I was drunk I just turned and kissed her. Her name was Mariella and she lived in Lima.

Mark wanted to leave the bar as it was too busy but he did not want to go home. The gentleman that sent us to Eclipse had firstly tried to get us to go to a club called Emmanuelle's. We chose the former as it was the cheaper of the two but as he was now drunk, Mark no longer cared. He had a separate account for affairs of the penis and said he would pay for the both of us.

I said goodbye to Mariella who told me she would be in Cusco for Christmas. Mark and I planned to be in Cusco as it was a major tourist stop off. It acted as a base for trips to Machu Picchu, a trip that we now had to rebook after missing our original date.

The cab we climbed into was tiny, resembling a child's go-kart. Mark's 6ft plus frame meant we looked hilarious travelling through town in a toy car. As the cab pulled up to the club I decided to climb onto its roof, pretending I was urban surfing. It was 3:00am and I was smashed.

The club was full of hot women that all sat around the main lounge looking worn out from a night of dance erotica. It was like we had walked in moments after the end of an orgy. The air was thick with body odour and the wall-to-wall mirrors were noticeably cloudy with sweat. We had missed the battle but there would be several more before the war was won.

We both got chatting to separate girls that sat by the bar swinging their bare legs playfully. It was implied that this club had now, as the night ended, turned into a brothel. Both of us were propositioned by more than one of the girls, not for a private dance but for sex.

I was as drunk as a fiddler's bitch but I still felt awkward with the idea of paying for sex. It was something that I just didn't agree with and just had to accept. I stood from the bar stool I was sat on and stumbled onto the empty stage. If I danced on the stage maybe the girls would stop approaching me, it was worth a try.

While I removed my top dancing to Shakira, Mark was being handed a phone number on a piece of toilet paper from one of the girls. She wanted to meet him outside the club.

This piece of paper instantly became Mark's sole focus. The club closed and after standing around for thirty minutes we got a taxi back to the hostel. I went to bed as he walked to some nearby payphones to call the eleven-digit number on the toilet tissue.

I woke up at 11:00am as Mark clattered into the room like a caveman. I looked at him and knew that we would not be leaving Lima as planned.

I went for breakfast at the bar and chatted to some travellers before relaxing on the roof terrace reading for a few hours.

Mark came up about 1:00pm and told me what had happened after I had gone to bed,

'The number on the paper didn't work mate, got no answer did I so I flagged down a taxi and went on a hunt round town.'

'A hunt for what?' I asked, half knowing the answer.

'A brothel mate, I had to, was well frustrated that the number didn't work, she was well up for it,' he lamented.

'So what happened?' I sat my book down on the floor.

'I got a newspaper and looked up whores, the taxi driver helped but it was all to no avail,' he signed.

I sat there in disbelief.

He then asked if we could stay in Lima for one more night,

'Mate I have to get hold of the girl on this paper, can we just leave tomorrow when we feel less fucked up?'

'Ok mate, not a problem with me.'

We went out into town to see a bit more of Lima. It turned out we did not get too far as for nearly an hour I stood by the side of a plastic phone box as Mark rang the number again and again. Finally he got an answer and it was one of the most uncomfortable calls I have ever heard,

'Ring, ring, ring, ring.'

'Err alright love it's Mark from last night, sorry ola.'

(Pause for response)

'Emmanuelle's, last night, paper, sex, me, you, meet, si?'

(Pause)

'Err McDonalds 3:00pm? Tres, tardes, mucho gusto,'

There was obviously some confusion as Mark attempted Spanish words.

'Chica Linda, si ciao.'

He hung up the phone convinced she would show up in a few hours. We hung around like school children by McDonald's for over two hours before she arrived.

She strutted along the road wearing a dark jacket; a low cut white top, tight blue jeans and cowboy boots. She had long dark hair and what looked like firm breasts. Her face was average and while not disappointed, I could sense that Mark felt short changed.

They kissed each other on the cheek, the way that strangers do and held an awkward conversation that did not advance past, 'How are you?'

The three of us walked back to the hostel. Mark openly joked in front of her that I should have a go on her as well. The way he spoke was like she was ride at the fare. I replied,

'I would rather drink a diarrhoea milkshake mate.'

So as the tale of the toilet paper finally reached its conclusion in our room, I went for the sexually safe option and had a wank in the hostel showers.

I sat on the roof terrace waiting for Mark and talking to other travellers. A heavily bearded man with long hair sat with me and we talked about Peruvian women. He warned me to be careful,

'I have heard stories man. One was that Peruvian women are desperate to join the pudding club with western men,' he said.

'The pudding club?' I asked.

'They want to get pregnant man. In order to get pregnant I was told that some get your used condom (if you wear one) and stick them right into their butcher's dustbins.'

I thought about asking what a 'butcher's dustbin' was but managed to work that out for myself. I feared for Mark but it was too late, he had already finished.

After the completion of his mission Mark and I had a quiet last night in Lima catching up on some much needed sleep. The following day we got on a local bus down the coast to a town called Ica.

Ica

I had no preconceptions about Peru as it was a place I never thought I would visit. It was going to be an adventure and in my mind that was a good thing. I was like Christopher Columbus, discovering new lands, but probably had more in common with Dora the Explorer.

I stared out of the bus window as we drove across the bleak monotonous coastline. Continuous stretches of grey sand were broken only by the occasional sparsely populated settlement.

The difference since leaving Lima was beyond comparison. On one hand you had an aging world city and on the other a desolate coast bereft of any money or amenities. It was purely survival out here.

One third of the country's population live in the metropolitan area of Lima and already I could see why. It was obvious that Lima held all of Peru's money and with that its jobs and opportunities.

The bus stopped by a small port as people left the bus to visit a collection of islands only accessible by boat. They were referred to by backpackers as the poor man's Galapagos. In real terms they were called Isla Ballestas. I wanted to visit the islands, but being on a budget I decided it would be best to just stay on the bus and head to Ica.

We arrived in the town by the evening. Ica looked like something from an Indiana Jones movie and the first meal I was served held a similar culinary surprise to the Monkey brain soup in Temple of Doom.

Ica is home to around 200,000 people, and as we left the bus station it appeared that they all worked as taxi or tuc tuc drivers. The insane amount of traffic looked out of place in an otherwise peaceful, eerie desert city.

We walked away from the bus station and took refuge in an extremely bare restaurant that was cut into the cement wall that flanked either side of the main road. The place was effectively a square cave. The owner had painted his square cave yellow and decided to serve food. The one next to him had painted his white and was selling electronics.

We sat down on some red plastic furniture and ordered an unknown meal deal that was scrawled with a red marker on a whiteboard outside. We both sat at the table smiling, no one else in the restaurant was.

The mystery of the meal began with some chicken soup. We both slurped away, fairly pleased with what had arrived. As I stirred up the now shallow broth my spoon touched against something hard at the bottom of the bowl. My smile soured. To my horror a chicken's foot floated up like an old corpse in a grotty canal.

I looked around the disgusting restaurant and wondered why I had agreed to eat in such a place. I looked outside at the dusty landscape and realised that my notions of what South America was like would be far from the mark.

Most people's perceptions of places are governed by what they see on TV. I was no different. I expected to see smiling salsa dancers, mystical jungle life, beautiful sunny beaches and carefree happy people.

Ica had none of these. I felt like I had reached the toilet at the end of the rainbow. There were to be no golden moments, at least not for a while. Ica felt a million miles away from Lima, geographically it was only a few hundred.

We jumped into a tuc tuc and went five miles down the road to the neighbouring village of Huacachina where the majority of hostels had been built. We had been advised to stay there as it was considered safer than the city of Ica.

Huacachina was a small settlement of around one hundred people and was a desert oasis. Buildings had been built around its main lake.

We booked into a hostel around midnight. The small town was completely dead and, with limited street lighting, we could barely see a thing. We decided to go straight to bed.

I woke the next morning and went outside to get some air. I was surprised to see a large pool with sun loungers. I looked up at the sky, shocked to see sand dunes everywhere. I rubbed my eyes to check that I was not dreaming.

The weather was hot and dry so I woke Mark and we spent the day by the pool talking to other travellers and sunbathing. Christmas was around the corner so what better place to work on a Christmas tan than in the desert.

I was sweating on my lounger, opening my eyes occasionally to remove the beads of water in my sockets. It was baking hot. Each time I opened my eyes I still looked in sheer disbelief at the surrounding sand dunes. They towered over the place like huge brown skyscrapers.

Foolishly I had not applied any sun cream so by 3:00pm my skin was suffering, my face felt like a jacket potato. I was fortunate that Claire, a girl we had previously spoken to, had noticed and told me to get into the shade. It looked like I had been sunbathing on a George Foreman grill. I was a lean mean burning sweat machine.

Claire was also from England and was travelling with her boyfriend. This was a shame as both Mark and I thought she was cute. We each thought that she fancied the other.

Late afternoon I tore Mark away from his lounger and we met a group of people who wanted to go sand boarding. Sand boarding was the main reason for our stop in Huacachina.

The opportunity to board in the desert without a scarf, gloves or snow intrigued me no end. I was ready to see what the dunes had to offer.

We hopped into a sand buggy that would not have looked out of place on Mario Kart. It had eight red seats protected by a lime green steel cage and huge black wheels. We strapped ourselves in as the engine began to roar and set off towards the desert.

The driver beeped his horn, turned his head and stared in our direction; he looked like a total psychopath.

One look at the driver's evil grin should have set alarm bells ringing, not to mention the fact that he insisted we wear our seatbelts. We climbed up the first dune before the driver checked for the second time that we were all strapped in. What was he planning?

The next thirty minutes passed in a blur of turns, skids and swerves while the driver cackled maniacally to himself while throwing the buggy up and down the steep dunes. It was like being on a never ending rollercoaster that threw sand constantly into your face.

We screeched to a halt in the middle of the desert with the engine ringing in our ears and about to overheat. Everyone was ashen-faced, it felt like we had just stood by a wood chipper for half an hour. My face was in pain.

I got out of the buggy and the realisation hit that we were in the middle of the desert. It was beautiful as the sun began to set.

The boarding involved flying down dunes on waxed boards, letting gravity take its course and clinging on for dear life. On Mark's second run he completely lost control. Approaching speeds of forty miles an hour, his board flipped as he tumbled into the air and down the dune of his back. As he groggily got to his feet covered in sand he looked like Imhotep from the Mummy.

The sun set as we sat on top of one of the highest dunes in the area. All that could be seen was desert that stretched for miles. Numerous couples sat in each other's arms, enjoying the beautiful colours that made up the sky. I stood with a moaning shaven-headed Englishman covered in sand complaining,

'Mate I need the hospital, my back has completely gone.'

Back at the hostel we decided to get really drunk and see what Huacachina and Ica had to offer. After several beers we managed to rope in a number of people. After drinking Pisco from a ten litre glass bottle we went out.

We were told to leave our valuables at home by the owner of the hostel. He also advised us not to go into town,

'Being western, it is more than a possibility you could be robbed and perhaps stabbed.'

We ignored his warning; I was convinced it was because he wanted us to spend money at the hostel. I convinced the others this was the case and we got taxis to The Who, a club in the centre of Ica.

The only thing that got robbed on the dance floor of The Who club was my memory, and the only thing stabbing when I woke the next morning was my head.

I sat up in bed piecing the night back together but found it an impossible puzzle to complete as too many pieces were missing. Mark was fast asleep in someone else's bed which confused me still further. With all these unanswered questions floating around my head I drifted off back to sleep for an hour.

I remembered precious little from the night, thus in a way making the night a waste of time and money. Mark awoke and was worried that he had tried to kiss Claire, who we remembered had fallen out with her overly possessive boyfriend John. It didn't surprise me that Mark had done this. After a few pints he would try it on with his best mate's mother, no matter what she looked liked.

We got up at midday. Mark was predictably questioning why he wasn't in his own bed and was annoyed that I didn't have the answer. We concluded that he was unable to climb the 4ft ladder to his bed and had got into the neighbouring bottom bunk as it was free. It seemed the most plausible scenario but neither of us was convinced.

We went down to the pool and just as we sat down on some loungers, the mystery began to unravel.

Walking towards us looking far from pleased was a middle-aged moustached Frenchman. While annoyed he also looked hilarious as he wore tight black swimming trunks with big walking boots. His moustache curled at the ends making him look like a 1920s' boxer. I expected him to challenge us both to a duel.

He stood over Mark and said,

'If you are to stay in the dorm this night then do not get into bed with my son.'

Mark was speechless and sat in total shock before stuttering a response,

'I'm I'm I'm so so so sor-sor-sorry. I can't remember anything, what have I done?'

This was one of the greatest and most awkward human interactions I had ever seen. A smile stuck in my head like a pop song for the rest of the day. Mark looked like he had just been sentenced to ten years behind bars as he learned what had happened.

Mark had come in from the night in Ica and got into bed with this man's eight-year-old boy. They had checked into our room an hour or so before we had gone on our night out. I remembered thinking it was strange that a family had checked into a shared room.

While his father should not have had his family in a shared room, this was not acceptable and Mark knew it. I joked about it by the pool.

'Can you imagine the horror on the boy's face as a tall skinhead jumped into his bed, pulling at the sheets and groaning like a giant bear?' I giggled.

'Shut up mate, I didn't do that,' Mark defended.

'You did mate. I remember you asking for a cuddle and asking 'is it really that wrong?''

'You don't.'

'He yelped sir. It woke me,' I said.

'Fuck off, it's done now. How awkward is tonight going to be?'

'For you, very!'

I joked with Mark that perhaps he was acting on instinct. Maybe he was a secret paedophile and it took a few drinks for this disease to rise to the surface. I loved Mark but he was a fucking immature arsehole. I was unable to let the subject drop,

'Has it ever occurred to you that maybe you are a paedophile, but you just haven't met the right child yet?'

'Yes' was his one word response.

Feeling suitably uncomfortable around the pool and the French family, Mark asked if I fancied going for a walk around Ica. I didn't as I had begun to feel hungover but felt it was for the best. I didn't need him in a swimming pool with young children, not today.

Ica was a run down but charming desert city. As we walked around still half pissed from the night out we could really feel what this town was all about. It was very real and nothing was staged. There were no travellers and no western people, it was so far removed from home.

We bounced up and down the decaying streets taking photographs of rotten food, rotten buildings and rotten-looking people. One gentleman stood by a half eaten cart of watermelons. I tried to get a picture of him but he quickly pulled a melon in front of his face. I flicked to the picture on my camera and laughed as the man stood in grey pants with a yellow Arsenal football top and a big green watermelon for a head.

Imagine on Crimewatch if instead of blurred faces they used big bits of fruit to hide identities. It would far more entertaining to see a banana attacking a pineapple down a dark alley in London than a blurred face. If this had happened I would have had a lot less nightmares as a child.

The local people were intrigued by us meaning that we were famous for the day. One group of girls asked if they could film us. Unsure what to do, we had a mock fight outside a historic church in the centre of the city's main square.

Walking around Ica was a great experience. Behind our male bravado we both felt uncomfortable as it didn't feel safe and we stuck out like sore thumbs. It was the feeling of uneasiness that made it such a good thing to do. Travelling was all about pushing your boundaries and stepping out of the familiar. This was the first time in a while that we had really done that and it left us wanting more.

After a quiet and obviously awkward night with our French roommates we spent the next day by the pool, before catching an overnight bus to Cusco.

Cusco promised great things and it was only five days till Christmas. We both agreed that the party hats were going on for the next week, if they were not on already.

Cusco

At first the bus to Cusco seemed luxurious and comfortable. An hour into the journey we were served dinner by a stewardess, it was like being on a plane. I looked down at the culinary abortion on my lap and from that point, as the bus climbed the mountains to Cusco, the journey nose-dived.

The bus slid down the class scale from comfort to being trapped inside a black coffin with wheels. We wound around the snake-like roads of the Andes for nineteen torturous hours in total darkness breathing in increasingly thin air.

We arrived bleary-eyed and out of breath in Cusco at 1:00pm the following day. I felt like I had been punched in the stomach. I had heard the altitude in Cusco caused breathing difficulties but was not prepared for it being so bad. My head was spinning.

I cast an eye over the city as the bus terminal sat up on the side of the valley. In the distance I saw a sign scorched into one of the several mountains, it read,

'VIVA
EL PERU
GLORIOSO
BEM 9
CUSCO'

The city of Cusco lies at an altitude of 3300 metres. We quickly learned that feeling out of breath was something we would have to get used to until our bodies adapted to the conditions. We jumped into a cab and made our way to Pirwa hostel which sat on the corner of one of the town's colonial squares.

The first thing we did after checking in was to find the Loki hostel and check if Craig was still in Cusco. We had planned to do the Inca Trail with Craig and Gemma as it had been arranged and paid for before we left England. Mark and I had missed this trip by nine days. We had not heard from him in weeks.

He wasn't at the hostel but we did see his name on the large white board that hung in the reception area. There were three Craigs, one of them had to be him. We left the hostel and scaled a steep cobbled road to get an overall view of the city. I looked down at all the terracotta roof tops and what looked like unplanned housing. The city sprawled over the natural landscape, covering it like an unsupervised child with a pot of paint.

My first impression walking through Cusco was favourable. The town had clearly grown and thrived as a place of tourism. There were a lot of travellers and a lot of European-style restaurants and bars to cater for them. I noticed hundreds of travel agents offering tours to the nearby site of Machu Picchu and beyond.

While provisions for travellers were aplenty it was clear that the city was also home to poverty and struggle. As I walked I was constantly bothered for money by small children trying to sell things that I didn't want or need. Toothless old ladies in local attire demanded money for mug shots.

Being harassed by people was something I could deal with and had become accustomed to travelling. However, I wasn't used to the altitude. I was constantly short of breath, it was like being a fat asthmatic.

Mark and I were puffing and panting our way down yet another cobbled street when we heard an instantly familiar voice booming from the other side of the road. It was Craig. He hobbled across the street and embraced us like lost children. On Craig's insistence I went with him for a beer but Mark was shattered and went back to the hostel to sleep.

We went to Paddy's, Irish bar that proclaimed to be the 'Highest Irish Pub in the World'. While Mark and I had a fantastic time in Mexico, it was clear that Craig hadn't had a good couple of months. While Mark and I were partying in Cancun he was alone in a hut deep in Guatemala. While we were lying on a beach on Isla Mujeres surrounded by girls, he was sat in the rain with some boys in Belize. I could sense by his excitement in seeing us that he felt lonely.

I wasn't sure whose experience was more valuable or more preferable. All I knew was that my personal adventure was all that I could have wished for. I doubted he felt the same. We finished our beers and agreed to meet up the following day.

The first priority on our first full day in Cusco was to arrange a hike up the hills to Machu Picchu. I hadn't read too much about the place but had seen the odd image on the TV back home as it was one of the symbols of this huge continent.

Machu Picchu was and still remains my Dad's dream. It was something that we had planned to do together for his sixtieth birthday so I felt a bit guilty. It was his dream not mine, and I was going to book it three years ahead of schedule without him.

After dawdling around like idiots and almost arranging nothing we finally got the trip booked for the 27th December. This was sensible as we planned on drinking our weight in beer over Christmas. While there we also booked a white water rafting trip for Christmas Eve. Mark thought it was a good idea as it would prevent us from spending the whole day drinking. I reluctantly agreed.

We didn't want to miss New Year so we booked a two-day, one-night expedition to the site. On the 28th December Mark and I would be arriving at one of the Seven Wonders of the World by car, while others would undergo a gruelling four-day hike. I couldn't work out who was more stupid, them or us.

On the night Mark and I met up with Craig and the two Australian girls from Isla Mujeres, Tahlia and Mimi. We caught up over a meal at a Japanese restaurant. It was only two days till Christmas and it seemed like everyone that was travelling in South America was in Cusco. We all agreed that this Christmas would live long in the memory.

Back at the hostel I had a couple of beers. At the bar I had the pleasure of meeting Roger. He was sat on a stool by the main bar wearing an England football top and shorts. He was heavily set and looked like a cross between your stereotypical hooligan and a dead frog. I stood by the bar and asked the barman for a beer.

As I turned to go sit by the television Roger turned his lumbering head around and said,

'Oi you cant, whure bouts in England r ya from?'

Why I responded to being called a 'cunt' I don't know but I did,

'Leeds mate, London I take it.'

'No mate, Essex.' was his slurred response.

I instantly knew that Roger was obnoxious but he would be entertaining to talk to over a beer. I dragged a stool across the bar and sat down.

It turned out that Roger was an ex-ice cream salesman who had given up on his life back home and come travelling. He was so far removed from your average traveller it was unbelievable. Roger was, it turned out, a racist England fanatic with some fundamentally wrong views.

He held the belief that the poverty experienced in much of South America could be solved by one simple solution. The solution was this,

'All South Americans should be sterilised.'

I imagined scores of Latin men at the vets getting their bollocks removed and couldn't help but laugh. I soon realised however that he was not joking as he went on,

'It may seem a bit extreme right, but I'd sort the fuckers out. Having kids when they can't afford to feed them the daft cants, look at all the shit houses; wouldn't need 'em if they just wore condoms or got sterilised. I'm not joking, it's simple maths.'

I wasn't sure how to respond. There was no point in arguing as he was swimming in a sea of stupidity and I didn't want to rock the boat and upset him. I decided to tentatively nod my head in agreement. He bought me a beer and I knew I had made the right decision, sometimes it was best to just agree with people.

I woke up early on Christmas Eve to the sound of rain beating against the dorm window. I drew back the curtains and looked outside in horror. We were going white water rafting in an hour. It took Mark one minute to announce that he was not going. It took me a minute to realise that we had woken up an hour late and would now be late getting our train tickets for Machu Picchu.

After the aggravation at the station Mark went back to bed as he was still struggling to get to terms with the altitude. He was complaining about not being able to sleep. It felt like that was all he was doing.

I met up with Craig and we went to the most popular restaurant in Cusco, Jacks. The weather had improved by lunchtime but it was still wet underfoot. Water gathered in the crevices of the cobbled streets as everyone hopped around in an attempt to keep their feet dry.

Despite the cold weather there was a warm atmosphere in the town. Christmas markets had all set up in the main square and there was a real sense of community. I didn't enjoy Christmas that much back home. Whoever invented it should be nailed to a cross. For me, like many things back home, it had lost its meaning. In Cusco it felt very different.

Small children sat huddled by the large Cathedral in their brightly coloured traditional clothes. Babies lay in cotton sacks hanging from the backs of their mothers. Fathers sat chewing on coca leaves and smoking. Some families were accompanied by pet Llamas that looked like small woolly camels.

Volunteers walked up and down the rows of people handing out small gifts and parcels of food; it was a humbling experience. To see people so grateful for what was next to nothing really hit a nerve with me. It was like they had all received petrol soaked moustaches the way their faces lit up.

I remembered as a child getting upset if I didn't get the bike that I wanted or the game I had asked for. It was clear that these families were thankful for anything they received; this is how it should be. As Cusco pulled together to help each other, Craig and I went to the Irish bar and had the bartender pull us a couple of pints.

As night fell we went up the hill to Loki where practically every other backpacker, traveller, explorer, call them what you will, were staying. Mark and I signed in as guests and made our way up to the large bar area that overlooked a huge courtyard. The building was a huge converted house and looked over the city of Cusco. It was crawling with people.

At the bar I bumped into countless people that I recognised from other parts of my trip. Those I didn't know became new friends. Ben, who Mark and I had met in Lima, introduced us to Hanna and Simon. Hanna and Simon had been going out for a year and were travelling as a couple around South America. After talking with them for a good hour they invited me to their room.

Hanna, originally from Sweden, was a really good looking girl with long brown hair and a subtle tan. Simon from London was very much in awe of his girlfriend and was a nice enough lad. We all settled down in their room as Simon brought out some cocaine. He looked up at the two of us and began to rack up a few lines.

I didn't want to have too much but did want to try some. It was Christmas Eve and my first big night in Cusco. I rolled up a bank note that I pulled from my wallet and snorted the first line.

Within seconds my nose was burning but not in an unpleasant way. I took a sip of my beer and felt the coke drip down the back of my throat, almost making me throw it back up. Moments later after they had their lines we sat on the bed chatting. I felt really confident, it was like Simon and Hanna had been my friends for life not just a few hours.

I left the room and made my way up the old wooden stairway in the courtyard back to the main bar to find Mark. Strangely the bar had gone quiet and Mark was nowhere to be seen. It was then that I noticed that everyone had gone to different dorms, I wondered if the owner of the hostel had sent everyone to bed for being too loud.

I stood for a moment to collect my thoughts as people spilled out of dorm entrances and onto the narrow corridors of the hostel with eyes like bin lids. Like me, it was obvious they had all had been taking drugs. It was unofficially coke-a-clock.

I stood in the corridor looking on in sheer bewilderment, as people smiled all the way back to the bar. As I was about to follow, three Australians came up to me and asked,

'Hey man, we just got some coke, can you help us out as we ain't sure what to do with it. Back home it's way too expensive, like $300 Aussie dollars.'

Feeling confident and ready to take on the world I coolly responded,

'Yeah no problem lads, where's your room at?'

I pulled out a wooden locker from underneath one of several bunks in the room. Using my driving license and credit card I cut seven large lines, two for each of them and one for myself.

On adverts back home they say that 'there is a darker side to coke'. I had always just assumed they were talking about the dealer. I could for the first time in my life feel myself wanting more. I was lucky that I was born without an addictive personality as this Peruvian stuff was really good. The cocaine was so good that for the next three days I couldn't really justify my actions nor have any real sense of time. It was just day and then it was night.

After the escapades in the room I went back to the bar and found Mark. We got a cab into town with Harry and Sam; two Australians that had made friends with Craig and. Harry and Sam were from Sydney and had that typical Australian confidence about them, confidence that is commonly mistaken for arrogance. I immediately liked both of them.

The central area of Cusco is home to a number of bars that mostly all sit in the top left corner of the main square. Being the new kids in town we just went where we were told, which was Uptown Bar.

The bar itself was really simplistic, predominantly dark in colour but lit cleverly by a series of spot lights. It felt like being back at home as everywhere I looked I saw European faces. It was clear this bar was popular with gringos.

I ordered several rum and cokes and sat down on a low backless leather stool. The others assembled around a low-lying glass table. As I sat down Sam came back from the toilets with a piece of card folded up like a tiny envelope. He carefully opened it up to reveal what I instantly recognised as cocaine. I sat in total shock as we were in a bar, a public place in view of everyone and, despite being drunk, I was worried.

'Sam mate, you can't do that here,' I nervously warned.

'It's ok mate, don't worry, they don't care. We've been doing it a lot here,' he reassured.

'Stop being a pussy Gaz,' yelled Harry in his over exuberant voice.

'Where did you get it? Have they got a dispenser in the toilet or something, a condom and coke machine?' I asked.

'That would be good but no. You see that guy over there with the dreadlocks?'

I looked over and saw a Newton Faulkner look-a-like lurking by the entrance to the toilets. It couldn't have looked more obvious.

'Yeah well he is here every night and sorts everyone out.'

'Cool,' I concluded, unsure what to really say.

After several drinks and lines at Uptown Bar we walked up the road to a place called Mythology. We then ended the night next door at Mama Africa, the most popular night club in Cusco. By this point my mind had gone extremely sketchy. The heavy techno beats being spun by the DJ were not helping my cause. Unlike Uptown bar, Mama Africa had a mixed crowd of locals and foreigners.

The bar itself was intimate and clung to the back wall behind the main dance floor. I walked around chatting nonsense to anyone that would listen before drinking so much that my memory deserted me.

I woke up on Christmas morning in my bunk with a girl nestled rather uncomfortably under my arm. I gently squeezed her side in an attempt to wake her up. I wasn't sure whether she was a Christmas present or a Christmas nightmare. The anticipation was killing me.

She rolled over and murmured at me before angling her head and saying,

'Good morning.'

I looked and instantly recognised the face, but had no idea how she had ended up in my bed. It was Tahlia from Isla Mujeres.

Being Christmas I decided to open the present, forgetting that Mark was asleep in the bunk next to mine. I only realised when I caught him looking over in my direction with a wry smile on his face. To my surprise I saw that he was not alone. A girl was hidden against the wall behind his large frame. It was Melissa, an instantly forgettable girl that we had both spoken to on the nauseating bus journey from Ica to Cusco.

It was a strange morning listening to Mark having sex while nursing a hangover. I lay with Tahlia waiting for the inevitable comedown to kick in. Things got worse for Mark when after a series of muffled conversations from his bunk I heard Melissa say,

'Yay Christmas baby.'

I came to the logical conclusion that he hadn't worn a condom and she was not on the pill. I had to laugh but Mark was far from happy. His mood worsened when I came back from reception with the news that we had to leave the hostel as we had only booked for three nights. We had just assumed that it would be ok to extend our stay but we were wrong, the hostel was full. The girls both left agreeing to meet up with us later that day or evening at Loki. Mark and I then realised that we were homeless on Christmas day.

We staggered around the streets of Cusco looking for a new hostel and found one on our third attempt. We checked into a private room on the main square of Cusco just down from Mama Africa so the location was ideal. What wasn't ideal was sharing a hostel with a gang of Peruvian scouts. The uniforms, complete with green tunic and toggles, did little to help our now ailing minds. I was petrified of them. Adults in scout outfits had to equal paedophilic opportunists; it was simple math. I stayed in the room.

Luckily I had had the foresight to call my parents on Christmas Eve in order to wish them a Merry Christmas. So while Mark braved the outside world to call home I lay in bed in our new windowless room watching Men in Black on TV.

At the end of the film Will Smith's character started stamping on cockroaches in an attempt to distract an evil alien cockroach returning to his home planet.

'Whoops, was that your Auntie? That must mean this is your Uncle! I'm sorry, all y'all look the same!' he says mockingly, as he kills them.

I lay there in bed imagining the outrage this would cause if the roles were reversed?

Once again it's one rule for intergalactic, extraterrestrial space cockroaches, and another for black people.

Thoughts of discrimination and racist mutants ran through my tired head as I tried to get some sleep. Travelling was opening my mind in more ways than one.

I woke up at 8:00pm and in turn woke Mark. I had been sweating profusely, a by-product of the night's excesses. I felt disgusting but at least somewhat human again. Mark and I had not arranged to have Christmas dinner anywhere. So while everyone else in the town had turkey and all the trimmings, we settled for tasteless tacos from a fast food chain in the square called Bembos. It had been the worst Christmas day I had ever experienced.

Not learning our lesson from the previous night we got in a taxi and went back up to the old converted house on the hill, Loki. We had the night to turn things around.

Christmas night followed the same routine as the one before it. Before I knew it we were once again in Uptown Bar negotiating with the spider haired dealer for cocaine and washing it down with bottle after bottle of rum.

As I staggered down the steep stairway back onto the street the cold air hit the back of my throat and I felt more awake than I had all day. I stood wide-eyed as the mix of drugs and alcohol began to take hold.

Bright orange snakes flashed across the sky as the street lights lit up and blurred the now black sky. Strange people grabbed onto me, wishing me a Merry Christmas then dancing off to the next bar before my brain processed what they had said. My senses felt heightened and every sound was amplified.

My response time to everything seemed slower. It was probably only seconds out but it felt like minutes. I knew what to say and how to say it but the words wouldn't come.

Mark shouted from the entrance of the next bar for me to hurry up. He was waving some bits of coloured paper that were free drink coupons.

Unlike Uptown Bar, we couldn't get a table in Mythology, so rather than stand against a wall and drink we took to the dance floor to spank the planks. Being overly confident and wired there was no other option, so we all happily danced around in drunken delirium to forgotten songs from the late nineties.

The DJ threw on the classic Shania Twain hit Man I Feel Like a Woman, and I danced like one. I stood in the middle of the dance floor spinning around and singing my own version of what, for that moment, was my favourite song,

I'm going out tonight - I'm high as a kite
Gonna let it all hang out
Going to do a turn, look at you and gurn
Yeah you know you want it no doubt
Sod local traditions - make no conditions
Get me another line
I ain't gonna act politically correct
I only wanna have a good time!

The best thing about being a piss head
Is the prerogative to have a little fun (fun fun)

As I neared the end of what in my dilated eyes was a successful X-Factor audition, my right leg stuck to the floor as I performed the last of my out of control pirouettes. My knee stood still and clicked as my body twisted.

I dropped to the floor like I'd been shot. It was 'Murder on the Dance floor'.

Thankfully I hadn't been murdered but, given the pain in my knee, had definitely killed the groove. I hobbled off the dance floor to scores of laughter, man I looked like a dickhead.

Harry, Sam and Mark had no idea what I had done. It's hard enough getting sympathy from your mates sober, but impossible when they are all bent on alcohol and drugs. I limped without assistance to Mama Africa but, after an insurmountable amount of time on my feet, the injury worsened. I gave up and went back to the hostel feeling strangely sober.

On arriving back at my nearby hostel I was greeted in the reception by Tahlia. I hadn't seen her out and wondered why she was there waiting for me. It was strange but I was too battered to question her.

I awkwardly made my way up the narrow staircase and along the corridor into my room as Tahlia followed. I was not sure if she was after sex, if she was she would be disappointed as it had been removed from the menu and replaced with the pain of knee and a side of insanity.

I climbed under my sheets and into bed. My leg began to throb so I immediately removed the covers. I sat up staring at my knee for what felt like an hour; gently prodding the swollen skin to determine where it hurt and how I could fix it.

Tahlia was in the bathroom throwing up what sounded like a lifetime of booze. I put on some music in a bid to bring a bit of sunshine into both our lives. It was Christmas and I had never felt so low.

Things seemingly could not have got any worse, but low and behold I was wrong. Mark arrived back to the room just as I had finally managed to get to sleep. He was once again accompanied by Melissa. I assumed that she was his last resort after numerous failed advances on other girls in Mama Africa.

I lay there trying to sleep listening to Jose Gonzales once again featuring Mark and his slow moves.

I woke the next day about 11:00am. It felt like I had been in a boxing match. Tahlia was lying next to me. After a morning fumble with her and a shower she left along with Melissa.

I looked across the room at Mark and said,

'We need to cool our boots sir. We better have a quiet day and stay off the ale!'

'Sure,' came his groggy response.

'Shit I've just remembered, we are going to Machu Picchu tomorrow.'

'So?' quizzed Mark.

'Look at my knee, I'm gonna be fucked!'

'Could get you a wheelchair sir, skip the queues.'

'You raise a valid point. Let's go get some lunch.'

We left the dark cave-like room in search of some fresh air. Our room had a depressing air about it, there was no natural light and no sparkle whatsoever, making it feel like a squat. I hobbled onto the streets of Cusco glad to leave the room and, unlike the previous day, the weather was clear, helping to alleviate the gloom in my head.

The cobbled streets proved difficult for my right knee to take so I decided to go into a pharmacy and get some pain killers. Either they had no oral pain killers in store or what I had requested had been lost in translation.

Moments after entering the store I was lying down half naked in a back room of the shop with my face buried into a white pillow. The pharmacist was a Peruvian lady who wore a white coat. She stood over me laughing with a long needle in her hand that looked like a fencing sword. I wasn't sure she was even a doctor. She sensed that I was uneasy,

'Tranquillo Amigo!' she assured.

She sank the needle into my left bum cheek and administered whatever drug it was into my blood stream. Twenty seconds later my arse felt numb and started to contract uncontrollably, my arse was having a heart attack. Rather than show concern Mark grabbed my camera and began taking pictures and laughing.

The lady came over with a large blue knee support and warning about trying to walk to Machu Picchu. I thanked her for her time and left the chemist looking like a cast-off from the TV show Gladiators.

There are moments in everyone's life where a small decision over something simple can have a knock-on effect that can change their lives. Our next decision was one of these rare moments; our very own sliding door.

Rather than eat at Jacks as we had most of the week in Cusco, we decided we would eat at 'the world's highest Irish pub' as they were showing the Boxing Day clash between Aston Villa and Arsenal. A pie and piece of Premiership football was just what the doctor ordered.

We sat on uncomfortable wooden stools drinking glasses of water around an elevated circular table, craning our necks to watch the screen that hung from the ceiling. It was strange to see images of home.

Thousands of ghost-white people were wrapped up in team scarves and hats shouting and screaming at the players on the pitch. The pictures felt foreign, from a culture and place that I was not part of. I was outside the window looking in and it somehow felt different. My own country was a place that I had forgotten about without even realising. It was familiar but unfamiliar, travelling does that.

I had become accustomed to my new surroundings, making those at home strange. Outside on the streets of Cusco was an army of four foot tall caramel-skinned Peruvians all dressed in multi-coloured traditionally Quenca attire. They walked the streets with pet Llama and Alpaca, begging for money and chewing on coca leaves. Inside the bar I was sat transfixed with images of an English football game, laughing at the state of a working class Villa fan eating a chicken balti pie.

Sitting in front of us were two Australian lads, one that was clearly supporting Arsenal. He kept swearing at the screen and at a middle-aged couple that sat behind us in a comfortable looking booth. The Arsenal fan turned his head and barked at us,

'What the fuck are you drinking?'

'Just water mate, it has been a heavy Christmas,' I replied.

'I ain't been to bed for three days. I don't even know what day it is, who gives a fuck. You're not drinking water, I'll tell you that for nothing.'

The bar maid brought over two vodka oranges. I shouted over to the Australians,

"I'd have preferred a non alcoholic cider but thanks.'

'What the fuck is non alcoholic cider?'

'Apple juice,' I said.

'You stupid fucker,' he laughed.

After drinking the vodkas we felt it necessary to buy them one back. They thanked us before leaving the bar and joining our table. By the end of the game I was wasted again.

The two lads introduced themselves,

'I'm Kash and this cunt here is Nash.'

Kash wore a bowler hat, jeans and a white top with the slogan 'Franz Fucking Ferdinand' in black font. Nash, who we decided looked like John Terry, wore shorts and a black top. Kash and Nash were the sort of people you only met once in your life and never forgot.

We sat round our small circular table laughing and talking like we had been friends for longer than a few minutes. Our food arrived and Nash was pumped and up for taking on some challenges. It was clear that he was wanted to make an impression on us so we gave him the platform to do so.

'I'm Nash and I'm Australian, I will pretty much do anything so long as it's funny!' he boasted.

Mark put a dollop of his mash potato on the table covered it with Tabasco sauce and said,

'Go on then Nash, snort that, I will film you,' as he drew his camera from his left pocket.

Mark turned on his camera and clicked record. After laughing for a few seconds Nash reached into his glass and bit into the straw he was drinking from. He then lowered his head to the table and put the shortened straw into his right nostril while covering the left. After bracing himself he snorted violently, and as the potato disappeared from the table he began to gag. He raised his head and his eyes were blood red but he was smiling,

'That hurt, fucking oath!' he exclaimed in triumph.

The Peruvian bartender looked over in sheer bewilderment and he wasn't the only one. An elderly looking Irish gentleman at the corner of the bar looked on in confusion. We assumed that he must have been Paddy the owner. Paddy had been stood at the bar getting pissed longer than we had. I joked that he was probably trying to work out why he's only got three brothers when his sister has four.

Mark and I were in hysterics and couldn't believe what Nash had just done. There was no complaint or big song and dance; he just did it. It was clear that Kash felt left out, he was jealous. Not to be outdone by his friend he grabbed the Tabasco bottle and said in a vicious tone,

'Watch this then.'

He pulled at the waist of his jeans and poured Tabasco all over the tip of his penis before falling to the floor and writhing around in agony. Seconds later Nash followed suit,

'Fuck you mate, that is easy,' he roared.

As the two of them rolled around on the deck of the bar Mark and I looked at each other in disbelief before busting into streams of laughter. These two Australian lads had to be the stupidest people I had ever met and I loved them. The owner of Paddy's did not love them and instructed the barman to refuse us alcohol before politely asking the four of us to leave.

Mark and I had promised each other we wouldn't drink. In the back of our minds we knew that we had to be up early for Machu Picchu. However, it was only 2:00pm and our new found friends were not going to let us go home and we didn't want to.
As the sun was out we all took off our tops, ignoring the fact that it was bitterly cold. I was walking the streets of Cusco on Boxing Day wearing ridiculously small 1980s' blue and white football shorts and my newly acquired leg support.

It was clear that not wearing a top in Cusco was frowned upon, it may have been illegal; we didn't know and we didn't care. We walked through the main square by the cathedral shouting at each other and play fighting. I could feel myself losing control.

Kash, in a bid for further attention, decided to climb onto the top of a tour bus and stand like Leonardo Di Caprio in Titanic; we all felt on top of the world. I looked to the left as Nash foolishly flipped into a flower bed in the middle of the square. Mark and I just looked on and laughed.

Nash's dive into the flower bed alerted the attention of the police who I had caught conspiring in the corner of my eye. As he argued with them under a stone archway, Kash mistakenly elbowed a passing baby in the head as he put his t-shirt back on.

The timing could not have been worse. This small Peruvian woman screamed into his face like a drill sergeant before pleading with the police to arrest him. I backed away from the situation as it spiralled way out of control.

Luckily the police took no action. They requested that we calm down and go somewhere else. We took sanctuary around the corner in an English Pub called the Real McCoy. Inside numerous travellers were tucking into festive lunches while watching repeats of the football from earlier in the day. We tucked into shots of Tequila and pints of beer.

By late afternoon we were being really loud and disrespectful to others. The manager at the Real McCoy asked us to calm down but instead we asked him to join us. Kash bought a round of Jagerbombs for all the staff.

Within half an hour we had cleared the bar and strangely enough the manager didn't seem to mind. He was having as good a time as we were.

The four of us together were lethal mix and there was far too much aggressive chemistry for people to deal with. It was as rare and beautiful as it was destructive, and it showed no signs of abating.

I was so drunk and twisted; it was like watching a movie of myself. I knew what I was doing and what I was saying but it felt like someone else was in control. This someone wanted to push me to the edge and surrounded me with people that would not hesitate in helping me over it.

Mark, who had toyed with the idea of getting a tattoo all trip, suggested that we all get the initials 'J.T' permanently etched onto our arses in honour of Nash's likeness to the England and Chelsea captain. We all agreed it was a good idea.

We left the bar in search of a tattooist. I suggested that instead of 'J.T' on the arse we get Vinnie Jones on our dicks. That way they would look hard even when they weren't. It never happened and neither did the 'J.T' idea as we were told by a heavily inked tattooist that we were too drunk.

I had no idea what time it was but it was still light. We were all absolutely hammered, most notably Nash who had mysteriously disappeared. This did not deter the three of us from buying a bottle of rum and going to our hostel in the hope that we could drink ourselves sober.

After trashing our room we found ourselves back on the streets of Cusco. A local Peruvian sheepishly approached us and asked,

'Want Charlie? Want cocaine?'

We were in the mood to take or do anything. We followed him like lost sheep up a narrow cobbled alley to a small restaurant that sold local food. He assured us that he would not be long,

'Cinqo minutes,' he said.

Ten minutes passed before I was hit with a huge wave of paranoia. I couldn't work out if it was the alcohol and days of excess or if we really were in danger. I tried in broken Spanish to ask the rotund lady running the restaurant what was happening but it was to no avail.

Five more minutes went by and there was still no sign of the gentleman, no sign of the cocaine and no sign of anything happening at all. My mind was made up, he was setting a trap, an elaborate sting and we had walked right into the middle of it. They had probably been tracking us all day since Paddy's; we had to get out of there as quickly and inconspicuously as possible.

We make an immediate and quick exit out of the restaurant, scurrying like rats off a boat down the street and into the first bar we came to. We were thankfully safe.

We drank a couple of beers slowly before getting a taxi back to the safe house that was Loki. At the time I had no idea where I was or where we were going; it felt like a dream.

My last memory of the night was Nash reappearing at the bar of Loki to show off his new tattoo. He had left us earlier that day on the street adamant that he was getting a tattoo. He found someone that had no problem in doing it and it had taken six hours to complete.

Rather than get the agreed 'J.T' on his arse he had got an Inca tribal war mask that covered his upper leg and hip. We all agreed that it was horrible.

I woke the next morning back in our room fully clothed and covered in mustard. I had a thousand questions in my mind that I wanted answered. I remembered nothing of the night with my last memory being Nash and his tattoo. I was concerned. This concern turned to distress as Mark awoke with the words,

'Shit. Machu Picchu.'

I had completely forgotten what day it was. We had missed our trip. I looked at my watch, it wasn't even morning, it was 1:00pm and we had no chance of getting there. We both sat in bed mortified.

I looked around the room and saw that it was trashed. The lightly coloured walls were now dashed with slashes of cheap rum and coke. The bed side lamp was smashed. Glass covered the tiled floor of the bathroom. We had to get out of there.

I felt absolutely awful and had completely lost control. We had missed what promised to be one of the highlights of our trip for the second time and had a room that resembled a crack den.

We aimlessly walked the streets for over an hour before going back to the room exhausted and embarrassed by our actions. The day was a write-off; I slept and watched TV in a room that reeked of rum and was strewn with smashed glass and broken minds. My brain was in absolute tatters.

I awoke from a twitchy sleep to what sounded like someone peeling a banana in the room. I looked up and saw Mark standing by the TV shaking. The TV was on a stand in the top right hand corner of the room. It took me a few seconds to realise what he was doing.

He was stood watching the Home Shopping Channel while having a wank into a plastic bag. I couldn't deny the female presenter was attractive but I was appalled. I should have been on the way to one of the Seven Wonders of the World, instead I was in a dark room that stank of alcohol listening to Mark jerking off into a bag. It was a new low.

The following day we came to terms with what had happened and booked Machu Picchu for the third and final time. That evening I changed the broken light bulb. A bit later on, I crossed the road and walked into a bar. I realised that my life was becoming a big joke.

Machu Picchu

I woke up at 6:00am as a Peruvian plumber tapped away at our door. The bathroom was leaking into the room beneath ours and he needed to fix it. Somehow Mark managed to stay asleep but I sat up and listened to my iPod.

I woke Mark at 7:00am giving him half an hour to get ready for Machu Picchu. We arranged to leave our backpacks at the hostel as there was no need to take everything with us for a few days.

With little more than our wallets and a change of clothes we got into the small people carrier and left Cusco by 8:00am. I had experienced a range of emotions in Cusco, a series of terrific highs and terrifying lows and was in need of a break. The cycle had to be broken and a stress-free excursion to something as magnificent as Machu Picchu was just what the doctor ordered.

On the way we picked up a group of Brazilian men who were all friends. Only one of the eight spoke any English. Once again the dream of a group of girls had eluded us, we looked at each other and without saying anything knew what the other was thinking.

A few hours into the drive we stopped at a small settlement that clung to the side of the steep Andean mountains. The town was called Ollantaytambo and it was unreal. It was the northern gateway to the Sacred Valley of the Incas.

The houses were a pale sand colour and the roads cobbled. The town had an undeniable old world feel to it; the gateway to a lost civilisation. The people had a weathered humility about them and despite all the tourists they just went about their everyday business farming the land. I had noticed that as we got further into the Andes the people became more and more indigenous. The difference in appearance from the Peruvians in Lima to Cusco, and now Ollantaytambo, was nothing short of incredible.

We used a restaurant toilet and purchased a few essential provisions. For me this was:

- A tube of Pringles

- Two bottles of blue flavoured Powerade

- A packet of sour Skittles

- A Snickers

We were told by the English speaking Brazilian that this would be the only stop till we reached Agua Calientes, four hours away at the base of Machu Picchu.

We left the town and the mini bus climbed gradually into the sky through a network of winding roads. Within an hour we were surrounded by what I thought was fog, but then realised was cloud.

My mum often accused me of having my head in the clouds and for once she was right. I thought about getting out of the bus and building a shack by the side of the road, cementing her long held belief that I also lived in the clouds.

The sun had disappeared and the landscape around us was wet and unforgiving. We drove passed many small dispersed dwellings that were people's homes, passed local farmers who lived simple subsistence lives and their obvious struggle scared the life out of me. How and why did people live here? I couldn't understand.

We stopped for a break at a widening in the road that I guessed was the highest point we would climb to. Outside a gale was blowing, it was freezing cold and incredibly hard to breathe.

At the stop stood a concrete grey house strewn with red and blue graffiti, none of which I could make any sense of. As we got out of the small bus to stretch our long legs two small children ran out from the back of the house and began playing metres away from us.

They each had old plastic coke bottles that had been converted into cars by attaching four plastic wheels. They were connected with what looked like straws. The cars then had string attached to the bottle necks. They looked extremely happy pulling their makeshift toys along the cold gritty mountain terrain.

I wondered if they had been Christmas presents. I then wondered what a child in England would have made of such a present; it really was a different world. I felt a degree of guilt for all the things I had and how much I took them for granted, the world was not a fair place.

We got back into the now cold mini bus and began our descent to Machu Picchu. I gazed out of the window still thinking about the two little boys, thinking about how unfair the world really was.

As we descended the mountain the weather gradually improved and it was sunny once more. The landscape turned from marshy highland to a large lush valley. The road became an increasing concern to me as it narrowed and narrowed until it clung to the cliff like a piece of string.

I sat in the back of the bus looking out of the left hand window and all I could see were 100ft drops. One small error of judgement by our driver and we were dead. I asked him through our Brazilian interpreter to slow down. He was hurtling around the cliffs like we were on a Formula 1 circuit and I grew increasingly scared.

The road was no more than three metres wide and we were going about sixty miles an hour. We splashed through small tributaries of water that intersected the road and bounced furiously up and down in our seats. I felt sick and wanted to get out of the van as soon as possible.

I lost count of the number of blind hairpins we negotiated. I noticed that each turn had a small selection of stones by them. It wasn't until further down the road I realised that people had died and that these were graves. I closed my eyes and, though not a religious person, I prayed.

The bus approached yet another turn at speed and as we veered left on the road towards a sheer sixty foot drop, a car appeared from nowhere coming in the opposite direction. It must have lasted for about two seconds but it felt like it had lasted ten minutes. Time slowed like it had never done before in my life.

Our driver clutched his hands around the steering wheel and pulled us back to the comfort of the cliff face on our right. The other car whisked past brushing our wing mirror, we had narrowly avoided what would have been a fatal head-on crash. My heart attempted to escape the confines of my chest as Mark finally lost his patience,

'Slow down you massive prick.'

It was useless as he had no understanding of English. Luckily there was no more drama and, four hours after leaving Ollanyantambo, we arrived for lunch in the small town of Santa Teresa. Santa Teresa was a small settlement linked by train to Agua Calientes and Machu Picchu. We were safe.

We sat in silence eating, both wishing that we had opted to do the trek as most people visiting Peru would do. What made matters worse was we knew that we were only halfway. Tomorrow, after visiting Machu Picchu, we had to get back to Cusco.

I toyed with the idea of settling down in Santa Teresa. Yes there was nothing there and I would be bored but at least I would be safe. I didn't want anything to do with that road ever again.

We arrived at the base town of Agua Calientes late in the afternoon by train. The town sat in a deep valley and there were no roads. The high street sat either side of the train track which comprised of restaurants and shops geared towards tourists.

I had never seen a town like this in my life. The surrounding mountains dominated the skyline; they were so steep and powerful, dwarfing the town and blotting out the sky. The town crammed into the valley by what looked like was a powerful river. It was a claustrophobic place.

We walked away from the main street and up a narrow road on a steep gradient to the Pirwa hostel. It was our accommodation for the evening. The road ran up to the famous hot pools from which the town got its name. By the time we reached the hostel we were both shattered and decided against going.

On the evening I had a walk around the town, it had a busy oriental feel to it coupled with an exciting atmosphere. People were looking forward to Machu Picchu, while others were returning after treks and relaxing in the comfortable restaurants with new found friends.

After dinner and an explanation of what was to happen the next morning, Mark and I had an early night as we had to be up at 4:00am and we were worried about sleeping in.

We thankfully woke up on time at 4:00am. I had reservations about my ability to walk up what was an imposing mountain. My knee was clearly going to be a problem. I felt that I owed it to myself to try. I thought by walking and struggling up to the summit I would have a greater appreciation of what I was going to see.

Outside the hostel it was dark and cold. A cool mist whizzed through the town like someone nearby had just opened a large freezer door. Scores of travellers trekked out of a wealth of hostels in total silence towards the high street and what felt like an unofficial starting line.

It was like the living dead had come to life. Scores of zombie backpackers meeting in the town centre in the dead of night, preparing to attack an unsuspecting and unprepared neighbouring town. They would surely still be asleep and thus easy prey.

The group let out an occasional groan as we began our accent up to the lost civilisation of the Incas. It as it promised to be one of the highlights of our trip.

I bought a cup of coca leaf tea from a small indigenous woman at the base of the mountain. Coca leaves were known to give you energy and combat altitude sickness; they were also the raw material used in cocaine production. I needed all the help I could get and was thankful that I still had one bottle of blue Powerade.

We began our climb and there was an air of excitement helped by the mist that engulfed the whole valley. I felt like Bear Grylls; I was to triumph against the odds, this was my adventure.

The excitement was short lived when it became apparent that this famous hike was just an energy-sapping walk up a never ending staircase of rocks.

An hour and a half later Mark and I reached the entrance to Machu Picchu, the two of us were sweating like kids with a weekend invite to Neverland and felt uncomfortable.

There was a queue to enter the site, the hike had brought us to the very same entrance as the coaches. Any feeling of accomplishment or deeper appreciation of the site evaporated in an instant. I was tired and my knee was throbbing. We were both pissed off.

We entered the site in time for sunrise at about 6:00am. Unfortunately, due to the low-lying cloud, we failed to see this but the sight was still breathtaking. The cloud's gradually cleared before disappearing and giving way to a beautifully clear morning. I was taken aback by what I saw. How had this site been constructed and why was it here? These were all questions our guide had heard thousands of times and had no trouble answering.

I thought about my Dad and how much I would have loved for him to have been with me. Though I was undeniably impressed with the site, I also felt empty and unfulfilled. Was this it? What was it I expected? What was I looking for?

As a person I find it hard emotionally to show or feel extremes towards things. To many people Machu Picchu is amazing, for my Dad it is his dream. I felt pressured to feel the same. I searched inside myself and all I could come up with was that it was 'pretty good' or 'alright'.

This was the same feeling I experienced when I visited the Grand Canyon or went scuba diving on the Great Barrier Reef. The initial wonder and amazement gradually gave way on each occasion to,

'Ok seen it, bored, let's go somewhere else.'

It felt like I had a long list in my brain of things I wanted to see and tick off. They were not lifetime ambitions, religious pilgrimages or personal goals; it was just a list for the sake of having a list. I had hoped it would make my happier but slowly began to realise that it wouldn't.

I stood overlooking the site waiting for Mark to take a photo on my camera, he was taking ages. Mark was prone to being thick at times but even he could work a simple point and click digital camera,

'I can't work it mate, the front bit won't open,' he shouted.

'It was fine on the way up mate, stop being a tool.'

'Mate it's not working.'

I walked over slightly pissed off and grabbed the camera from the Neanderthal.

'You just press the .... Shit!'

I stared down at my silver camera and realised instantly that the battery had gone. One of the picture card moments of the trip and my camera had died. Mark looked at me and laughed.

We walked around the site with our designated group as the guide talked about the polished dry stone walls, how the site was built and why it was considered a sacred place.

The biggest question I had upon leaving Machu Picchu is why I felt it necessary to sneak away from our guide and have Mark take a picture of me pulling my pants down while staring longingly at the horizon like a ship captain.

Like a reality TV wrong 'un I was facing the prospect of being ejected from the Machu Picchu house,

'Who goes? Eduardo decides.'

As I exposed my bottom I heard a loud whistle from far away. It didn't sound like an impressed girl calling me, it sounded more like an angry referee. Facing the prospect of a red card I darted into a nearby cove, taking off my hat and putting on a jumper. The disguise, though lacking in originality, gave me a chance.

I casually walked out as if nothing had happened, thinking that I had gotten away it. I walked back to join the group flustered but relieved, thinking to myself that what I had just done, even for me, was stupid.

Just as I started to tell Mark about my great escape I was grabbed aggressively by my left shoulder. It was one of the guides, I had been caught.

Speaking no Spanish I just kept saying,

'Tranquilo Eduardo!'

I had got his name from the name tag on the right of his right chest. My plea was not working and as people looked on I faced the indignity of being kicked out.

'Tranquilo Eduardo, mucho de niro!' I said.

Eduardo stopped and walked me over to a high stone wall away from the crowd of people. He put out his hand and urgently requested money. I reached into my pocket and pulled out $20 soles, about £4.

He took the money and left in an instant. I felt a degree of shame for what I had done but it served as a reminder of the financial hardship of these people. With money I was convinced that anyone could get away with anything.

Back in Agua Calientes we sat waiting for the train in one of the numerous pizzerias that lined the main street as it began to rain heavily. The train arrived an hour later than scheduled and was rammed with disgruntled tourists that were soaking wet and looking for answers.

I noticed that the local people did not complain. They sat happily as if nothing was wrong and there had been no inconvenience. I wondered, given the simple nature of their lives, if time meant as much to them as it did to us. Time was a man made construct and maybe to them it bore no real significance, and so an hour here or an hour there really made little difference.

The train took another hour to leave the station as the conductor believed that a number of people had not paid for tickets. I slumped to the floor, turned on my iPod and mentally switched off.

The journey back to Santa Teresa took three hours. This was odd as it had only taken thirty minutes on the way in. When we eventually got back to our mini bus it was late afternoon and the rain was still relentlessly falling.

My thoughts shifted to the road ahead. I was scared on the way to Machu Picchu when it was sunny. Now with it getting dark and storms brewing overhead I was inconsolable, knowing the next four hours were going to be horrible.

Ignoring the conditions our driver found it necessary to drive equally as fast and as dangerously as he had on the way here. We hurdled around the saturated hills at high speed hanging on for dear life.

The driver began talking to the Brazilians, something that he had not done before and it sounded serious. Mark and I were in the dark as to what it was all about. Our translator could not express in English what was wrong, he said something about low-lying cloud and the road could possibly be closed. We had the option to continue or to go back to Santa Teresa for the night; we chose the first of the two options.

We continued along the road more cautiously than had been up the side of the Andean mountains towards Cusco. We came to one of the tributaries on the way to Santa Teresa that gently ran over the road. It was now flowing aggressively, creating a ford across the narrow road. The water shot over the edge creating a temporary waterfall. Our van stopped.

The road was now a surface of crumbling wet mud and grit. It was no more than four metres wide with an unstable sheer rock face to its left and impending death to the right.

I thought the driver was going to turn around and take us back to the sanctuary of Santa Teresa but I was wrong. He reached to the rear view mirror and kissed the hanging symbol of Jesus before marking an invisible cross in the air. Before anyone could say anything his foot hit the accelerator and we sped towards the flowing water. The driver had made the call that it was passable, our lives rested in his hands.

We hit the water at speed and slid badly to the left before the van snaked across to the right. The front wheels churned through the mud and water struggling for grip. I didn't scream as the back wheels teetered towards the brink of disaster nor did the others. I was unable to breathe and, in that moment, felt detached from both myself and the situation. I was watching a film or tragedy unfold from afar as time stood still. I felt nothing.

The back wheels gripped to the edge of the road as our driver pulled it back onto the narrow road and we thankfully had got across the water. I felt more alive than I had ever felt as my heart once more tried escaping from my chest.

The rain didn't relent as we tip-toed around unforgiving mountains on the dental floss of a road. I worried about what was lurking around every bend as we still had a long way to go and it was now pitch black.

Cars going in the opposite direction flashed their headlights and beeped their horns at us. I had no idea what was going on, assuming it was to do with the low-lying cloud. A few miles on we found out what the real problem was.

The road was blocked and hundreds of cars were sat by the edge of the road parked up. We were not going to be moving anytime fast. The cliff face had become saturated due to the rain and large chunks of rock had fallen and blocked the road. There had been a landslide on the one and only route back to Cusco and we were stuck.

There was an untold amount of debris on the road. It was impassable, meaning we faced the implausible reality of a night on the road. The mini bus was designed for six people, including the driver we had nine; it was going to be a nightmare.

I sat, squirmed and squatted trying to do whatever I could to get comfortable. I looked at my watch to find it was only 9:00pm, four hours had passed. I gave up on comfort and accepted that it was best to accept that it was awful. I worried that more debris was going to fall which made me feel helpless. My life was no longer in my own hands, it was at the mercy of nature.

I sat lamenting the fact we had got so drunk on Boxing Day and missed our original trip. If we had gone as planned we would have been fine. If we had not gone to Paddy's for lunch and met Kash and Nash none of this would have happened.

If I'd had signal on my phone I would have changed my Facebook status to 'Suicidal – standing on the edge of a cliff', in the hope someone would poke me. Behind the laughter we were both terrified.

Before travelling to South America I thought that it would provide excitement and the feeling of being out of control, but this was not what I had envisaged.

With so much going on in my head I took Mark up on his offer of some sleeping pills. I began to feel drowsy and uncomfortably fell in and out of consciousness.

Ten hours passed before night gave way to day. I woke to the distant sound of a JCB digger beginning its mechanical assault at the mountain of rubble. I looked at my watch, it was New Year's Eve.

I looked out the back of our van and saw that the relatively small queue from last night now stretched back for miles. Lines of cars stuck to the side of the mountain road.

The digger made little progress. As it shovelled a mass of rocks, more fell to replace those that had been cleared. It was apparent this operation was going to take time and the atmosphere in the camp was tense. Much like on the train, locals seemed unconcerned by time. They just wanted the road to be cleared as safely as possible.

The longer it took, the more and more people arrived. By 9:00am it had developed into something resembling a refugee camp as locals from the surrounding villages crept over the hills selling food and drink. Some people in the camp openly shit on the road and wiped their arses in full view of those that looked. The road looked like Times Square on New Year with all the decorated paper.

Mark sat in the van like a tranquilised ape moaning that he needed a shit. He informed me he couldn't go,

'It would be far too messy mate. My stomach has gone.'

'Well just go mate, people are shitting on the street, it's mental,' I told him.

'It's not happening mate.'

Mark was more worried that we would be seeing in the New Year sober, stuck on a cliff with a host of people we had nothing in common with. This was a thought that I shared,

'I'm sure they will clear the road soon we will get back.'

'I bet they don't,' Mark glumly replied.

It was now 1:00pm, twenty-four hours since we had left Agua Calientes. Like Mark I needed the toilet, but unlike him I had to go. This posed a question,

'Where do you shit when you're stuck in a van surrounded by thousands of motorists?'

I had a problem with going to the toilet in public. I remembered an incident at work where there were two cubicles in the toilet. I went in desperate for a shit only for the first door to be locked. So I went into the other one, closed the door, dropped my trousers and sat down.

A voice came from the cubicle next to me,

'Hello there mate how are you doing?'

Although I thought that it was a bit strange, I didn't want to be rude and so replied,

'Not too bad, thanks.'

After a short pause I heard the voice again,

'So, what are you up to?'

Again I answered, somewhat reluctantly,

'Just having a quick shit, how about you?'

The next thing I heard him say was,

'Sorry mate, I'll have to call you back. I've got some cunt in the cubicle next to me answering everything I say.'

Going to the toilet to me was a private thing; so there was no way I was going to go on the side of the road in front of thousands of people. There had to be somewhere I could go so I went to look.

I walked down the road staring at the wet cliff face looking for a small ledge or bush to hide behind. I spotted a woman squatting behind a bush on a raised crevice a few hundred metres down the road. Seeing a woman having a shit was not the most pleasant thing I had seen in my life but I was thankful that I had spotted her. She had found the ideal place.

It proved a difficult climb due to the pain in my knee, which had worsened after the hours of sitting in the van. I was rewarded at the summit of the climb by the sight of about 200 stools, varying in appearance. It was an overpopulated poop graveyard and it smelt disgusting. It was clear the woman I saw had not been the first to discover the spot. I pinched my nose with my fingers and tip-toed through the long grass, looking for a clearing and avoiding the human mines.

I got back to the van as the JCB still diced with death, clearing the road piece by piece. I had no choice but to sit in our metal prison cell hoping that no one died as the rocks fell from the cliff edge down into the deep valley. It started to rain and my mood dampened. One question rattled through my head and wouldn't go away. I turned to Mark and asked him,

'Do you think Machu Picchu was worth this?'

Cusco

Mark never answered my question but the relief on his face as the road cleared spoke a thousand words. The rocks had stopped falling and the diggers had slowly made the road passable. In my experience Peruvian people rarely showed emotion, the Indigenous people of the Andes had hard lives and it showed through their stone faces.

As the road was finally declared clear a wave of euphoria swept through the crowd of traffic like wildfire, forlorn faces turned to ones of relief and joy. Regardless of culture, wealth, or religion we all shared a special moment, one I had never felt in my life. It was something simple, something very real, the strength of the human spirit.

Strangers smiled at each other and embraced like they were family as the sound of thousands of car horns filled the air like an army of German yodellers; the sound as beautiful as it was deafening. I felt a rush of adrenalin curse through my veins as the engine of the van began to rumble. People danced up and down the road like we had won something, it felt like we had. Our mini bus slowly made its way across the landslide and each of us breathed a huge sigh of relief.

Our attentions turned immediately to the time and what we were going to do for New Year.

We glided through the Andes and swooped back into Cusco for 5:00pm, over a day later than scheduled. We got back to the hostel where we had left our bags, looking forward to having a shower and getting changed. It had been a remarkable few days.

The owner of the hostel looked at and said,

'I have booked out your room.'

'Why have you done that?' I asked.

'Because you were due back yesterday.'

He had not kept us a room. Despite our protests about the landslide we found ourselves homeless for the second time. I was so tired that I wanted to cry.

Mark found a hostel on the outskirts of town and checked us into a ten bed dorm. It didn't really matter to us as we were not going to be staying there too long.

We both got a shower and began to discuss the night ahead over a meal and some beer. I couldn't hold anything down and started to feel weak. I ordered an espresso thinking that I was just tired but within seconds I was running to the bathroom.

I sat on the toilet as muddy water shot out of me like a water pistol. I began to shake uncontrollably and knew that something was wrong. I broke into a cold sweat as panic set in.

I had made it back from the terror of the mountains in one piece, but now sat in the warm bosom of a restaurant in Cusco, I was falling to pieces. I had bought noodles from a Peruvian peasant in the Andes and was convinced that I had food poisoning.

Any other night I would have gone to bed but it was New Year, so I tried to fight against it. I went with Mark to Loki hostel.

Going to the hostel proved to be a really bad idea as I couldn't hold down any anything. I spent the first half an hour on the toilet.

The other half an hour I had people laughing about my performance on Christmas day. Highlights saw me rolling around on the pool table naked before pouring Tabasco on my genitals. I looked at Kash and Nash, convinced that the later was their idea.

Before I knew it I was once again locked inside the toilet.

Rather than go back to our ten man dorm and spending the turn of the New Year alone I stayed in a private room at Loki that belonged to some friends. Mark promised to wake me up just before midnight.

I lay in the room hallucinating. Images of the landslide and the feeling of falling would not escape my mind. I kept waking covered in thick sweat to the very real feeling that people were in the room all around me laughing. These strange images were interspersed by constant trips to the toilet as my stomach twisted into knots.

Mark and Nash came to check on me at 10:30pm. Nash looked at me and said,

'Mate stop being a pussy, get the fuck up and have a big line of coke with me and Mark. You are not even ill, I'm a fucking flying doctor.'

'Mate honestly, I feel like I could die,' I replied.

I wanted to get up and enjoy myself but I just couldn't. I watched as they both snorted lines by my bedside and left. I drifted back to sleep, back to the nightmares.

I cowered in the corner of the bar like a scared kitten. At 11:58pm, as people shouted and grabbed hold of each other, I saw that Mark, Nash and Kash were at the front of the bar by the stage kissing girls and messing around. I didn't have the energy to let them know I was there and in truth I wasn't.

The clock struck midnight and the crowd of travellers went berserk, throwing drinks in the air and hugging anyone in reach. I reached the lads and told them that I had to leave. I slid out of the back door and onto the streets above Cusco. Outside it had begun to rain heavily. I stood waiting for a taxi saturated by the cold mountain rain, I felt awful.

As I stood like a beaten soldier against the wall of the hostel, the security guard threw a firework in my direction. It fizzed at my feet like a live wire as I jumped up and down to avoid it. Seconds later it went off and a deafening bang thundered through my ears. The security guard stood with a wry smile laughing. I was furious, he was clearly retarded and unaware that what he had done was dangerous. The wheel was turning but the gerbil was dead.

I got into a taxi as the driver assured me he knew the hostel I was staying at. I only had a vague idea as we had only been there for thirty minutes early that evening.

He dropped me close but not outside so I spent the next ten minutes running around in the rain looking for the place. The rain by this point was torrential and the cobbled streets turned to rivers. I was glad I wasn't still stuck on the mountain but this was still a nightmare.

I eventually found the hostel and broke free of my sodden clothes. After several trips to the toilet I lay in my bed shivering cold and sweating. As I closed my eyes I said to myself,

'Happy New Year.'

I didn't get out of bed for two days. I just lay in the dorm falling in and out of consciousness. Mark did his best to look after me, but it was clear that he was becoming restless,

'We have to leave Cusco mate, it's breaking us,' he said.

'I agree mate, just book a bus with a toilet and we can go.'

The next morning we finally left Cusco. It had been quite a place.

Puno

I sat on the bus to Puno, our last stop before entering Bolivia, with mixed thoughts about my time in Cusco. I left with a range of memories both good and bad but something inside of me felt different.

The experience on the return from Machu Picchu was traumatic, but as bad as it seemed I had come through it unscathed. A renewed confidence washed over me as I felt I would be ready for whatever this continent had to throw at me.

As the coach shifted through baron countryside I sat looking out of the window. I saw people working the land and walking to small adobe huts that were their homes. I thought about the two small boys in the Andes and could in my mind map out the story of their lives. The lack of opportunities and options that were available to them scared me.

Poverty stared me in the face wherever I looked. There was no escaping the fact that the world that we all live in was unfair and there was nothing that could be done to change that. It wasn't my fault or a result of anything I had done but I still felt guilty.

We changed buses in an impoverished little town high in the Andean mountains. It made Rochdale look like Rome. Half built buildings crumbled in the rain, roads were falling apart and the people looked miserable. The town looked like a neglected child's sand pit. I could not imagine what it was like living there.

Rain slapped against the windows of the increasingly damp coach as we pulled away from this town and on towards Puno. I was convinced that the sun never shined in this town, it just rained. If the rain ever stopped then it probably snowed faeces.

Puno sits in a shallow valley on the shores of Lake Titicaca. The city is 3500m above sea level and it was freezing. In Peruvian and Inca folklore it is believed that Lake Titicaca gave birth to the sun. It is therefore a historically important and sacred place. It was for this reason that we stopped in Puno.

I didn't buy into the idea that something as incomprehensible in size as the sun could have been born in a random Peruvian lake but I liked it. It was like accepting that ants could give birth to elephants. Religious beliefs made no sense to me at all.

To me religion was like following a football team that never played and had no players. Rather than go to war and kill each over personal beliefs there should be a religion World Cup. Imagine Christianity vs. Islam at Wembley.

Mark and I checked into a cheap Bed and Breakfast with two Ecuadorian girls that had talked to us on the bus into Puno.

Mark decided that we should all go out for dinner so we did, settling on a Pizzeria near to the hostel. It was my first meal since the disastrous lunch at the landslide and I was therefore nervous, wanting to pick something small and plain.

I went for what the menu described as a Pig Meat Pizza. The translation of the menu was pure comedy gold. Mark started off with diet chicken soup before feeling adventurous and ordering the Peruvian delicacy, guinea pig.

I looked over at the clay pizza oven and saw four huge guinea pigs roasting away in the flames. They had clearly led devious lives and had been sent to hell. Mark grinned and hilariously came out with,

'It's my last chance to try one before we leave Peru. You know me, I'll try anything.'

I knew otherwise. He ordered it to impress the Ecuadorian girls, who were sisters. I sat and laughed at his logic. I could see the wheel in his head beginning to turn. By eating a member of the rat family, he would in turn, hopefully see hers. He hadn't been with an Ecuadorian and as he said, Mark would 'try anything'.

His meal came out and his face dropped. On the plate sat a burnt guinea pig. Its legs were stretched out, looking like it was performing a star jump onto a soft bed of lettuce. Mark prodded it with his fork before turning it over. The guinea pig still had its head and you could see two dirty yellow front teeth,

'There is a girl in Puno that misses her pet, I'm sure I saw that one on a missing poster outside. You best eat it quickly,' I joked.

'Look, it still has hair on it,' complained Mark.

'And nails and teeth, and I would guess organs.'

'Just peel back this skin. It is nice,' said one of girls.

I laughed as Mark pulled the pig apart and began hiding parts of it all over his plate. He sat playing with his food and flirting with his chosen target. The girl that held Mark's interest was a lawyer in Quito, the capital of Ecuador. She spoke well and had a fantastic grasp of English. Her sister, who was my responsibility, did not speak a word of English as she had grown up in the jungle. Hence I have put her in my book, she was a jungle VIP.

Mark tried and failed to seduce the lawyer. We walked back across the road to the hostel where he just openly asked her,

'Why don't you and I just get a room?'

She laughed it off unsure whether or not he was being serious; he assured her that he was. Feeling tired I went to bed early, as the next day we planned to visit the lake where the sun was born.

We woke up at 9:00am in the middle of a storm. Rather than go out onto the lake we decided to pack our bags and leave Puno. The town offered little other than the lake and we decided that it was something we could live without seeing.

Many homes in Puno and the surrounding cities in the region were half finished. I was told by a shop keeper that this was done so that the inhabitants do not have to pay taxes. This explained the building site of a town we had passed through the previous day.

Maybe the same rule applied back home? If it did then I planned to return to England with a sledgehammer. Before renting somewhere all I would need to do was smash up the kitchen with my sledgehammer. Being a single man I never cooked and the tax incentive would be worth it.

Puno is a border town lying close to Bolivia. The city's economy relies heavily on the black market. It is a place fuelled by the cheap goods that are smuggled in from Bolivia. We decided to cross the border the other way and go to the capital, La Paz.

We walked awkwardly to the bus station avoiding the huge puddles that now sprawled across the main street running through Puno. To the delight of locals I slipped and went head over heels. I hung suspended in the air for what felt like a lifetime before smashing down onto the concrete floor right into the middle of a puddle. I picked myself up and theatrically bowed to the people that looked on, they in turn clapped their hands and laughed at what they most likely thought was a stupid gringo.

We boarded the bus and were both excited. Peru for us was now complete and we now faced the unknown entity of Bolivia, a landlocked country in the heart of the Andes.

I sat on the bus reading The Motorcycle Diaries and realised how easy my trip across South America would be in comparison to Che Guevara's. Whilst he struggled on a cheap motorbike, I sat comfortably on an air-conditioned bus. I wondered if the ease of travel affected my views and the impact of the places that I visited. People took more things for granted these days and I was no exception.

There wasn't much freedom in getting a bus from place to place. I half wished Mark and I were on a motorbike with only a loose plan, seeing where we ended up.

I reflected on Peru as we drove through deprived settlements and more and more inhospitable farm land. I had been there a little over three weeks but it had felt like longer.

The struggle the native people of this country went through made me seem lazy and ungrateful. I sat with my iPod in my hand knowing that it cost more than what the average farmer made in a year.

This journey was opening my eyes to the hardships people faced on a daily basis. It made me realise how easy I had things and how I had never really done anything the hard way. I was coasting along in a world of opportunities and taking none of them, while they worked hard in a world with none.

The people in the fields worked long hours just to provide food for their families. I realised I did not work hard at anything.

I gazed out the window and let my mind drift away. We were driving through the set of Mel Gibson's Braveheart. Disgruntled gingers warriors running around in skirts with swords were replaced by peaceful groups of women washing clothes by a stream. The houses were the same.

One hundred metres down the road a large rusting billboard with 'Coca-Cola' ruined my dreamy notion of being in the past. We reached the border as I sat still thinking about the haves and the have nots. Mark removed his headphones and tapped me with his orange fingers,

'I could have shagged that lawyer you know.'

His hand then delved back into the large packet of cheesy crisps he had bought for the journey.

BOLIVIA

La Paz

We crossed the border into Bolivia without incident; it was welcome given my previous trips across imaginary lines. We changed buses in the small border town of Copacabana where we had time to pick up some supplies. I had lost confidence in local cuisine so my shopping list contained: boiled sweets, a bottle of coke and a bag of tortilla chips.

Buses were usually filled with backpackers but this one was full of indigenous people travelling to La Paz in search of work. I walked down the bus aisle to my seat holding my large bag of crisps and sweets. After settling down I looked across the aisle to a couple sitting on my immediate left; by appearance it seemed like they had nothing. I felt compelled to offer them some of my sweets.

A small child curiously looked over his seat and into my eyes before burying his head into his mother's chest. I shook the bag of sweets in my left hand and gestured to his mother with my right. She tentatively reached into the bag clutching a handful of sweets before nodding and softly smiling at me.

It felt good so seconds later I decided to walk up and down the bus offering sweets to everyone on board. I returned to my seat with an empty bag. Mark looked at me and laughed,

'Look at you, you twat. Walking up and down the bus like Jesus. You know they probably don't have toothpaste don't you?'

'I prefer to think of myself as a shopping centre Santa Claus my friend. Have you tasted them? No flavour at all, it's like eating a stained glass window.'

'You are a nob, just stay sat down.'

Two hours passed before the bus grinded to a halt in pitch darkness by a large black lake. Everyone got off the bus and started walking towards the water so Mark and I followed. Outside it was raining heavily and was bitterly cold, and as neither of us had jackets.

It took an hour to get back to our seats on the bus as we had to cross the lake on a small motorised fishing boat. Mark and I stood shivering and moaning about the weather as the local people just kept their heads down and accepted there was nothing they could do.

We arrived in to La Paz at 10:00pm still damp and really tired. We got straight into a taxi to the Loki hostel as for once we had booked ahead.

The hostel was converted from an old hotel and looked impressive. After throwing our bags into, what was by travelling standards a luxurious double room, we went for a walk around the city.

La Paz scared me at first. While there was nothing threatening going on, the city had a sinister atmosphere. I had heard about the drugs, I had heard about the police and had heard that it was a dangerous city. Walking aimlessly at 11:00pm on a dark Saturday night was ill advised, I felt threatened but unmistakably alive.

The next morning, after one of the best sleeps of the trip, Mark and I went down to the main bar for some breakfast. Sitting at the bar was an intense Australian who introduced himself as James.

James talked at a thousand miles an hour. I sat in amazement as he went four minutes without taking a breath. He decided that today he would act as our official guide. We had no choice but to accept.

James' eyes and arms darted around the bar faster than the end of his sentences. He was a paranoid maniac with bright white skin and fire red hair. There was something unsettling about James, Mark instantly disliked him.

We left the hostel by late morning and naturally our guide James followed. All James talked about was drugs. When he wasn't talking about drugs, he was taking them. Mark and I waited outside a bar in the centre of La Paz as James told us that he needed the toilet. He came back from the toilet full of energy, looking like a mad professor and it wasn't even lunch time.

I had never in my life met someone so consumed by drugs and it was deeply off putting. He was the poster child for the reasons not to take drugs. It was more powerful than the government adverts I had seen back home. James was a real person, he wasn't acting and it was sad to see.

La Paz felt different to any city I had visited. We were in a landlocked country high in the Andean mountains in a city that sits inside a large crater 3500m above sea level, making it the highest capital city in the world. Buildings scaled the sides of the valley, it was a huge urban fishbowl and it was breathtaking.

As James was so animated, booking any sort of trip or excursion was impossible so we went back to Loki. At the reception there were posters that read:

'Lucho Libre – every Sunday'

Below was a cartoon depicting two women in a ring fighting. We were both intrigued and enquired as to what it was.

An hour later we were climbing away from the city into the suburbs to watch the weekly sporting spectacular of Bolivian Wrestling. The bus stopped at the top of the city some 4000m above sea level. The views of the city from the top of the basin were incredible. It was something we had missed coming into La Paz as it had been dark.

Outside an aging school gym temporary market stalls sold sweets and all manner of strange meat products. I felt like I was in the third world and with the crowds it was chaotic. The wrestling arena was a crumbling sports hall with a tattered ring at its centre. Surrounding the ring stood some flimsy iron fencing, behind which stood a series of plastic seats. We sat on the plastic ringside seats as locals took theirs in the temporary stands against the four walls of the gym. The locals were clearly excited, making the atmosphere electric.

The first of several matches saw Mr Atlas, a balding old man, take on a slightly younger pensioner that was dressed as a Vampire. The wrestling was terrible but went down well with the partisan crowd who whistled and jeered at the appropriate moments.

At the match neared its conclusion the aging Vampire picked up a patrolling Alsatian that circled the ring. He launched the dog at Mr Atlas who fell to the deck, before the dog shook himself free. I sat bewildered with other tourists as the crowd went into raptures. The referee hit the canvas and counted,

'One. Two. Three.'

(Ding Ding)

The referee confirmed the outcome over the crackling sound system; the Vampire was victorious. This announcement led to a chorus of boos from the crowd who started throwing bananas and bottles towards the ring. Sitting in the front row, we had to take cover. Mark was hit by a plastic coke bottle and went down like he had been shot.

I wouldn't have been surprised if it had been aimed at him. The locals were short and probably couldn't see past his head. We all sat in what was our first and probably last wrestling experience with the best seats in the house.

As the matches went on they became more and more farcical. In one match a Teenage Mutant Ninja Turtle rubbed a bright red sanitary towel into his opponent's face. Quite what a used sanitary towel was doing under the ring I had no idea. I said to Mark,

'They are probably always there as an ultra way to excite the crowd.'

The locals loved it.

On our first night out in La Paz we went to the much talked about Route 36. It was high on any young traveller's 'things to do' list but was not found in many travel guides. We had heard about the bar from other travellers and wanted to see it for ourselves.

Rumour was that you could go up to the bar and openly ask for cocaine. The only question that the bar staff would ask was 'How many bags?'

I had heard that the owners of Route 36 paid the police to turn a blind eye. Bolivia by reputation was an extremely corrupt country where money was king.

After drinking at the large hostel bar we walked into La Paz with several other travellers looking for this infamous hangout. James, who hadn't been invited, sat at the bar in Loki smirking before turning around in a cocky fashion and saying,

'Good luck finding it!'

We were out of luck. We asked locals,

'Ruta 36?'

We asked cab drivers,

'Ruta 36?'

We asked locals,

'Ruta 36?'

Either no one knew about it or they were not going to tell us. We went back to the hostel an hour later and got James who was still sat at the bar smirking,

'I told you that it was hard to find. Come with me guys,' he instructed.

We did.

Route 36 was not a place you could easily find. We had walked past it without knowing on several occasions. There was no flashing neon sign, no music or drink promotions, no indication that it even existed. The front door was an old rusting metal iron shutter. To the man on the street it was nothing, it matched countless other rundown buildings in the area.

With all the fresh air I was no longer drunk, so on entering the bar I was apprehensive and unsure about what we were all doing. I had heard stories about police raids and stings on travellers that resulted in huge fines or in serious cases, prison. The government pressured the police to make arrests. This was a potential move, making it look like the drug problem was being tackled when in fact it wasn't.

We descended down a shallow staircase entering the bar's main room. Soft lighting bounced off the aging blood red walls. The walls were filled with a legion of flags from around the world, all covered in messages written in black marker pen. By the looks of it Route 36 was a popular destination for the modern traveller.

I had expected the bar to look far more dog-eared than it actually did. However, despite the comfortable surroundings I still felt uneasy; it was still just a crack den. I kept thinking to myself what if the police showed up, what would we do then? They knew what this place was and they would know that we did too. I didn't want to go to jail and could ill afford a huge fine.

I walked up to the bar awkwardly and asked in a clumsy way for,

'Two bottles of beers and coke.'

'Si senor,' was the response.

The woman came back and placed two bottles of beer and one bottle of Coca-Cola on the counter. Rather than say anything I went back to the table and sat down with the others. I insisted that I was thirsty as Mark insinuated that I had tried to buy some drugs.

'You are useless,' he announced.

'I told you, I was just thirsty.'

James came back to the table and put three small black plastic bags on the table. They resembled tiny bin bags and were the ideal size for Lego men. Each back was sealed shut by lightly burnt plastic.

James opened one of the bags and inside it was a mass of pure white powder. It sparkled against the slight ultraviolet lighting overhead. He racked up several lines that looked more like glistening albino slugs. As one shot up his nose he looked up from the glass table and told each of us,

'Enjoy,' before consuming his second victim.

I went next.

I leant over the table with a short blue straw up my left nostril. I put my finger against my right before sucking back ferociously. I only managed half of the slug in front of me so switched nostrils and finished the rest.

I fell back into the warm sofa still sniffing and pinching my nose. I could feel the anxiety I had escaping from my body and evaporating into nothingness. A wave of euphoria then raced through my body as if I had just won something. It was unlike anything I had experienced before.

I felt confident and awake and couldn't sit still. I looked around the empty, laid-back blood red room wishing we were somewhere more upbeat with girls and music. I wanted to dance. I wanted to flirt. I wanted to do everything. I ended up playing Jenga with James.

A period of time passed before I decided, under duress from Mark, to get some more cocaine from the bar.

The woman behind the counter had an old face and looked like a school dinner lady. I had an appetite but not for food. This time there was no confusion as she placed on the bar two Lego man bin bags, a CD case and a couple of transparent blue straws.

We sat around talking with the others about travelling, about where we were from and what our plans were for the future. My strains of conversation began to go off track. I talked to James about a world where food got you drunk and drink filled you up. The conversation would go something like this:

'No I'm not having a burger, too strong. I'm on fish fingers tonight.'

The next day you wake up covered in ketchup feeling like death and say,

'Fuck me what did we eat last night?'

'Do you not remember ordering that huge curry?'

'I didn't but I do now. My head is all over the place, I need some whiskey.'

James stared at me blankly, I realised that I'd had enough coke and as I did the anxiety and fear began to creep back into my mind.

I got a bottle of water from the bar and asked Mark if we could leave. He did not reply. He was too busy removing a wooden block from the Jenga stack. Mark hadn't blinked for about twenty minutes and was the picture of concentration and self-belief. I decided to leave the bar alone as more and more people from the hostel began to arrive. I was becoming timid and sought the sanctuary of my bed.

I left the bar through the narrow corridor where a security guard lifted an iron bar and motioned for me to get out quickly. As my feet touched the pavement the shutter had long since slammed shut. I had appeared as if from nowhere. My eyes narrowed as the light hit my eyes and to my horror I glanced at my watch to find that it was 7:30am.

I slept till 2:00pm the following afternoon, surprisingly feeling ok. I felt empty and alone but thankfully human. Mark was in pieces. His night finished as my day started. I found him sat with Gemma at the bar looking and sounding like the living dead. He was pale and his skin looked thin and lifeless. I told him to go to bed. After a short conversation with Gemma, who I had not seen since Mexico, I went out.

As Mark slept I walked around La Paz on my own. I sat in one of the main squares by some government buildings thinking about what it was I was here to do. A number of questions played in my mind:

- Was I travelling hoping to learn something?

- Had I learnt anything so far?

- If I had then what was it?

I didn't have the answers and was not in the frame of mind to find out, but it was important to sit and take stock of my situation.

Bolivian people looked and dressed completely different to their Andean cousins. The women, who were mostly short and fat, wore tall hats. The men looked like 1970s' porn stars. The thing both sexes had is common was the complexion of their skin. I wasn't sure whether it was to do with the altitude or whether it was through poor diets but everyone had tough leather skin; they looked like tanned dinosaurs. I couldn't wait to see what the one Mark would try and sleep with would look like.

I got back to the room by late afternoon. Mark was lying in despair listening to the Smiths through our portable iPod speakers. It reminded me of a scene from Irvine Welsh's Trainspotting,

'Don't leave me, seriously don't leave me, I'll pay you,' he groaned.

'It's just a comedown mate, don't worry you are going to be fine,' I assured.

Mark's depression began to affect my state of mind. I bought him a few bottles of Sprite and sat as Morrissey slowly turned me into the Boy With a Thorn in His Side.

Mark drifted off to sleep so I left the room and went to the bar to socialise for the evening.

There are certain books that are popular among travellers. In South America, at the top of the list, had to be Rusty Young's Marching Powder. The book tells the story of a charming English drug trafficker who is caught and thrown into a Bolivian prison. This prison, called San Pedro, is located in La Paz and if you were willing to pay, unofficially you could visit.

Visits to the prison had become so popular that it was mentioned in travel guides as something not to be missed when in La Paz.

It was something that we desperately wanted to experience. I could not believe that you could enter a South American prison and be shown around by an inmate. We had heard from people at the hostel that you could buy and snort cocaine in there. It sounded unreal.

Many things in South America made little if any sense. Taking drugs with criminals in a prison had to be top of the list. It was top of ours so we went the following afternoon.

The prison was an incredible experience and served to highlight my thoughts about money corrupting one of the poorest countries in the Americas. Fraudulent politicians were living a life of relative luxury inside, while others who had committed lesser crimes died of pneumonia in the prison's shadows.

Somewhat shaken by what we had seen in the prison we then went to the Mercado de Brujas, also known as the Witches Market.

The market ran up a series of steep cobbled roads away from the wide high street running through the heart of La Paz. Shops sold a range of woollen items; hats, ponchos, gloves, scarves, masks, you name it and it was probably there. All the stalls sold dried out Alpaca foetuses. They hung from wire-like traitors serving as a reminder not to cross the King. The Alpacas were considered by locals as a sign of good luck. Ireland has its four leaved clovers, Bolivia has dead baby animals.

That night we booked a mountain bike excursion down what is called the Road of Death. The road is a notoriously dangerous stretch of road in Coroico. Its official name is the Unduavi-Yolosa Highway and it claims an average of one hundred lives each year.

We got back to the hostel and sat in the bar having a few beers with friends. Ben, Rhyss, Hanna and Simon sat with us around a large wooden table. We finally caught each other up after what had been a crazy Christmas in Cusco.

Loki was a great hostel for meeting up with other travellers. In South America it was the easy choice, acting as a magnet for everyone, particularly Australians.

As we sat at our table seven good looking girls walked into the bar and sat next to us. Mark challenged me to speak with them so I did. The first girl that I spoke to was called Lauren. She told me,

'Tomorrow we girls were all planning to go to Route 36. Have you been?'

'Yeah it's good I think we are going as well. We should all go together,' I suggested.

'Sweet.'

I couldn't think of anywhere I would rather not go but they were all stunning. I would have hung cooked bacon from my balls and run through a pit of hungry Africans to get with one of them so if I had to go back there it was a small price to pay.

It had been a while since Mark or I had seen a beautiful woman. We guessed that they were all lying on the beaches of Argentina and Brazil. Mark told me that girls are drawn to the sun and the sea, so seeing these seven girls was a welcome surprise.

I fell ill overnight and decided not to go on the mountain biking trip. I gave my ticket to Chris, a mental bloke from Blackpool that seemed to be out drinking every night that we stayed in. It had been one of those nights and I was sure that I had just signed his death warrant.

I had been in La Paz for four days and came to the realisation that I hadn't really achieved anything or had that much fun. I found the place fascinating but on the same hand depressing. People visited La Paz because of the cheap cocaine and, because it was cheap, they had a lot of it.

James, the pale skinned Australian with fiery red hair, personified La Paz. He had been there for three months seemingly unable to leave and entirely consumed by drugs. He was stuck and didn't have the power to leave, he was a lost soul. The day we met him he clung to some postcards he had been meaning to send home for four weeks. I doubted if he knew where home was anymore. I thought his postcards had been written by a child as he had used a series of thick colouring crayons. One of his cards read:

'Yo guys, having a top time out here. The picture on the front is where I am now, it's called La Paz and it is frigging awesome. I have a job and think I will stay for a bit. Increase the peace love James xxx'

After the first night I didn't see James again. He had been thrown out of the hostel for not paying his bill and moved to Cactus Hostel close to the Witches Market. James later got in trouble for climbing onto the roof, convinced he was a monkey and refused to come down for hours until the police arrived.

Drugs in La Paz were not glamorous. They were not for high society parties. They were readily available to anyone and it felt wrong.

Local people had nothing. They received nothing from the government and had to do what they could to survive the cold mountain climate. Women and children of prisoners have to live with their husbands behind bars as there are no other options. Men committed crimes and got into dealing drugs most likely out of desperation, it was a necessity and worth the risk.

Against this struggle tourists come to the town and walk around taking photos and buying drugs, before moving to the next stop on their trip. They are oblivious to the harm that it was causing and the worst thing was that I was no different. La Paz expected you to take drugs so you did. 'When in Rome, do as the Romans do' and leave without any guilt.

I sat alone at bar in Loki knowing what I wanted to get out of my time in La Paz. I wanted to get to a beach and I wanted the seven Australian girls to come with me.

Day turned to night as Mark arrived back from the Road of Death unscathed and in jubilant mood. We got absolutely smashed at the hostel and somehow won the weekly pub quiz. We were rewarded for our efforts with a bottle of Jack Daniels.

I awoke the next morning rewarded with memory loss and a massive hangover. I remembered nothing of the night out but I did recall being stood at 9:00am in the hostel bar wearing a pair of knickers and a bra, asking for some orange juice and a croissant. It was apparently the last in a long line of silly acts before I passed out back in our private room. I was happy that the rest of the night out was a lost memory.

Mark and I agreed that the following day we would leave La Paz so we booked a night bus to Potosi that was fourteen hours south of the country's capital. My actions on the night out meant I was now a well-known figure at the hostel. The Australian girls thought I was mental and to be honest I wasn't ruling that possibility out.

We said bye to friends old and new the next afternoon and went for a curry at the Star of India, the only Indian restaurant in the Andes.

At the Indian the waiter had a really strange voice, he came over halfway through what was a decent meal and said,

'Curry okay?'

I replied,

'Karaoke? Go on then, just one song,'

The joke was lost on everyone but me. We settled the bill and got a taxi to the nearby bus station.

Potosi

We arrived at the city's bus station just after 6:00am. It was so cold getting off the bus that I had to stick my finger up my arse just to poke my willy out.

The air was bitterly cold as Potosi sat 4000m above sea level, making it officially the highest city in the world. The reason this settlement had grown to this size was that the surrounding mountains were known to be 'made of' silver ore. The city was historically important as a supplier of silver to the Spanish Empire.

Mark and I were looking forward to checking into the hostel, safe in the knowledge that we had booked ahead online. We arrived at the hostel at 6:30am both shattered.

The hostel was a low-lying adobe building off one of the main squares in Potosi. The rooms sat around a large courtyard with the reception to the immediate left. We walked into the reception to check in.

We were told by the man on reception that they had no rooms and would not have any until 11:00am. True to form we once again fucked up. We were still both freezing cold and shattered. To compound our bad moods we were then told that we would have to book the mining trip for later that day. If we didn't we would have to wait until Monday. The mines were closed on Sunday as in the heart of Bolivia it was still considered a day of rest. We had little choice but to book the outing for that morning as it was the sole reason for us visiting the city.

The bus for the mines arrived to pick us up at 11:00am, just as our room became available. With no chance of a rest we threw our bags into the room and jumped into an old rusty white van with several other travellers. We then made our way towards the huge mountains that dominated the local landscape.

I was tired and apprehensive about visiting the mines and so was Mark. Both of us had a fear of tight spaces. I sat worrying about cave-ins and underground cannibals as I stared blankly out the window at the red landscape, and the old mines. It reminded me of Zorro.

We stopped at a small town at the base of Cerra Rico, the rich mountain. We sat in a forgotten locker room waiting for our equipment as our guide Julio gave us an overview of the mine's history. He told us that most of the silver had long since been extracted from the mountain,

'Think of the silver like a tree. The trunk has gone, the branches have been stripped away and now only the roots remain.'

Due to a lack of silver the mines were now mainly used to extract tin, leading to gradual economic decline. This was clear to see all around us in the buildings and in people's faces.

We sat in this dark, damp locker room as Julio handed each person their mining gear that consisted of:

-Yellow or green overalls

-Wellington boots

-Hard hat

-Light and battery pack

Now fully suited, we were officially miners for a few hours. On the walk to the mine we stopped at a small shop to pick up provisions. The store was filthy and crammed with items that I struggled to identify. Sat on an old rocking chair was an old Bolivian lady. Julio walked over to speak with her for a moment. He then suggested what he thought we should all buy. I didn't want to buy anything, but I did. I bought:

-2 litres orange soda

-1 carton cigarettes

-1 litre pure alcohol

-2 cans lager

-1 bag coca leaves

-2 sticks dynamite

With an inventory to impress Indiana Jones or Lara Croft I was ready to take on the mines. We arrived at the main entrance just before lunch. To my horror the main entrance into the mine looked incredibly small and unsafe, only supported by three wooden beams. Worried about the mines, I started to mess about outside with an old mining cart.

Julio shouted for us to be careful. He told us about a gold miner that had lost his leg in a terrible carting accident.

'Who is going to want a one-legged gold digger?' he moaned.

I was tempted to suggest Paul McCartney but was convinced the joke would be lost on him.

Tired workers sat high on the red soil above the small dark entrance to the mine eating sandwiches. They were clearly interested by our visit. Julio reassured everyone in broken English,

'The first thing you will notice is the conditions; they are horrible. Not to worry, the main shaft is very safe. Wooden beams very secure. You are not in any danger.'

Julio turned on the lamp on his helmet and guided us through the entrance and into the mine. I looked for one last time at the bright crystal blue sky before descending into darkness. The main shaft was even tighter than I had expected. It was fine for a four foot Bolivian but for tall Europeans it was a real problem. We trudged across the thick wet floor of the mine bent at the knees; my head constantly crashing against the low-lying beams and pipes. The plastic helmets were already proving invaluable.

We stopped at a small clearing for a much needed rest. We had walked non-stop for ten minutes and were now well into the mountain. I had developed a thick sweat as the temperature had risen several degrees and the air was thick and clouded with dirt and dust.

Julio convinced himself that I was either a woman with a beard or a homosexual because of my long hair. He had not let it drop all morning and I was happy to amuse him. He joked that if there was to be a cave-in I would be well looked after.

He informed us as we once again began walking down the tight mine shafts that we would be meeting some real miners that were working deep in the mountain. The items I had picked up from 'Mines 'R' us' were mostly gifts for the miners, a way of thanking them for allowing us into their place of work.

Julio explained the nature of the working conditions inside the mine. As he did his jovial nature gave way to a more serious tone, one of suffering and hardship,

'Due to poor worker conditions, the miners still to this day have a short life expectancy. Most of them will contract silicosis and die by forty years of age. It is estimated that, in the past years of indigenous labour, roughly eight million Indians died, "eaten" by the Rich Hill.'

We walked further into the belly of the mountain. As the tunnels became narrower and even lower I could feel myself beginning to panic. Hot thick air entered my lungs as quickly as it escaped; I was suffocating and wanted to get out.

A few minutes passed before we came to another clearing, sat against the rocky walls were several miners telling each other stories and laughing. Julio knew who they were and spent the next ten minutes catching up and laughing with friends. The six in our group stood there awkwardly in silence. It was like going to a friend's house party and not being introduced to the people that lived there. I noticed a couple of the miners looking past Julio and straight at us.

The miners were all filthy and looked tired and old. It came as a shock when we found out that two of them were still teenagers, I felt saddened. I thought working at a call centre was bad. This was a different world, a living hell.

The conversation between Julio and the miners stopped and we were asked to hand over our gifts. Julio invited us to ask questions and he would translate them for us. We were holding our very own press conference several miles underground in a dark mine shaft filled with asbestos and known for regular cave-ins.

The miners worked long and hard for little reward. Their motivation to work was to keep their children away from the mines and provide them with a good education. In reality this only happened for a few. Their inescapable destiny was to work and be a part of the mines.

As we sat around asking questions the miners and our guide Julio began drinking the alcohol we had provided. Thirty minutes later the miners were all blind drunk and, to my horror, so was Julio. I began to feel really anxious and just hoped that he knew the way out.

While the conditions and lives of the workers scared me, at that moment I didn't care. I cared about my life and wanted to taste and breathe clean air again. The conditions of the mines and the lives of those that worked in them were horrible. I couldn't believe that they were still open as they were clearly not safe.

On the way back through the mine we stopped by a huge wooden statue called Tio, meaning the Devil. The devout Catholic miners believed that Tio controlled the mine and all those that entered it. Upon entering the mine you severed your ties with God and were at the hands of the Devil. I wished that Julio had told us.

This makeshift symbol of the Devil was surrounded by offerings made by the miners. Unopened bags of crisps, cartons of drink and packets of cigarettes lay at its base; it was a really strange sight. I noticed that between Tio's wooden red legs stood a huge erect wooden penis with confetti for pubes. I asked Julio if it was really necessary,

'Julio, what is with the massive cock?' I pointed towards its wooden groin.

'It is a sign of strength and manhood,' he chuckled like a village drunk.

We escaped the clutches of Tio and the mine only three hours after we had entered through the small main entrance. I was happy that I would never have to set foot in the mines again. Three hours had been enough; I didn't know how the miners could cope, working day after day in the hands of the Devil, in the heart of a mountain. I guess that they had little choice but to work in the mines. They needed the money to provide for their families and to survive. It was another example of the haves and the have nots and I felt sick.

We arrived back at the hostel and went straight to bed exhausted. That evening we booked a bus from Potosi to Uyuni, the home of the salt flats and Atacama Desert.

We walked the streets of this mountain city, both thankful that we didn't live there. After dinner Mark looked at me holding his belly,

'Ohh, I fancy an ice cream, but it's a bit cold,' he said.

'Well, that's ice cream for you mate,' I replied.

Thick cunt...

Uyuni and the Salt Flats

We arrived in Uyuni late afternoon the following day. The town serves as a gateway to the Salt Flats, which are known to the local people as Salar de Uyuni. The first thing I noticed was that the town was riddled with backpackers. As in Agua Calientes, there was an atmosphere of excitement and expectation.

Our first act on arriving was to book our trip to the Salt Flats for the following day. We didn't want to hang around in Uyuni as there was nothing in the town apart from pizzerias and gift shops. I bet Mark that there were more pizza restaurants here than in the whole of Milan, it was that ridiculous. This town clearly just catered for tourists visiting the Flats.

We spent the night drinking red wine with some guys we had met in La Paz. Kate, an Australian girl that Mark had slept with, introduced us to Nick and Kath who were going to be on our tour for the next three days. They were both also from Australia.

We left Uyuni hungover at 8:00am the next morning. I had bought some shades from a local store as we had been warned that when the sun was out the light reflecting off the white salt planes was blinding. Mark had ignored this suggestion, preferring to buy some sour cream and chive Pringles that he sat eating with his eyes half closed.

Three miles from the town we stopped at a graveyard; not one for people but for trains. I hadn't ever heard of a graveyard for trains and wondered what other objects may have graveyards. Perhaps somewhere on earth there was crypt full of kettles or a tomb of tea bags. The world was full of all kinds of secrets.

The dirty trains sat against a pristine white backdrop looked incredible. Large rusting machine, a symbol of the decline of the country's silver trade, had now long since been discarded and left to rot in the salty clouds like neglected toys.

Our jeep bounced onto the salt plains and my eyes narrowed as the light hit the back of eyes; it was nothing short of incredible. The jeep glided across the salt and for miles there was seemingly nothing, we were driving in the clouds and it felt weightless.

The first place that we stopped was called Fish Island. It was a rocky outcrop in the middle of this endless white expanse. Our driver prepared lunch on a small metal BARBECUE as we took the opportunity to walk on the Salt Plains for the first time and take some photographs. It was a place I didn't know existed and it had to be seen to be believed.

As more and more jeeps arrived in convoy the atmosphere among us grew. Before lunch a football match broke out on the Flats. The teams were easily arranged, it was South America vs. The Rest of the World. Despite the trouble with my knee I couldn't resist playing. It was a once in a lifetime chance to play football in the clouds and I wasn't going to pass it up.

The pitch looked like compacted snow but rather than slip, my feet gripped to the surface like concrete. The sun shone on the Plain, blinding like floodlights and making it near impossible to focus on the cloud white leather ball that was being passed around. I could make out the odd pass and moan around our goalmouth fifty metres away, before the ball trickled through the makeshift goalposts of two backpacks making the score 1-0 to South America.

The game ended in a 2-2 draw as our drivers shouted over indicating that lunch was ready. Bragging rights were shared as we all jogged off the field to eat.

Due to a lack of horizon and the flat landscape there is no perspective on the Salts, meaning it is possible to take some crazy photographs simply by placing things several metres in front of you. A can of coke could look the same size as a six foot man. Mark and I were terrible at this. While others took pictures of themselves climbing into tubes of Pringles or sitting on a desert spoon, Mark and I took off our clothes and did star jumps. I wanted a new profile picture on Facebook and after an hour of trying it was the best either of us could muster.

After a lunch of chicken and rice our journey continued along the Plain. The driver allowed us to take it in turns to sit up on the roof of the jeep on top of our bags. He warned us to hold on as there was no denying that to fall from the roof onto the hard salt floor would result in death. It was worth the risk.

I sat as an icy cold onslaught of wind blew relentlessly against my face as the car climbed to 70mph. All around me there was nothing except the wide expanse of salt. It really felt like I was flying. It was another world.

The experience gave me a strange sense of freedom and with that came a feeling of insignificance. I didn't know this place existed and there I was sat on the roof of a jeep experiencing it. I wondered which other places existed that I knew nothing about? I felt an overwhelming urge to find out, to travel.

St. Augustine wrote, 'The world is a book and those who do not travel read only a page.'

In my eyes he was most definitely right. I wanted to read as many pages as I could, I had been stuck on the same page for far too long.

I reflected on my troubles back home and realised that perhaps they didn't matter as much as I had let them. It was up to me where I wanted my life to go. I thought about my Dad and how in that instant I wished that he was sitting on the roof of this jeep with me. I knew that one day he would.

I finished another beer as we sped across the sparkling salt. As another vehicle passed to our left I stood and pulled my pants down. Out of the window gestured a group of French lads that I had being playing football with.

Come early evening we had reached the end of the seemingly endless salt tracks and had driven onto earthy brown soil once more. We spent the night in a hotel just off the white expanse constructed entirely from blocks of salt. The rooms were cold and peppered with faults. I knew it was going to be a long night as we heard that temperatures on the Salt Flats drop well below zero once the sun went down.

Thankfully between our group and the French guys we had picked up a lot booze; A_C_H_L sometimes alcohol is the answer. We sat on a raised plateau up a rocky slope with a group of people from around the world drinking while watching the sun set over the Flats.

I woke up at 6:00am the next morning and not for the first time I remembered nothing. It was so bad that at first I had no idea where I was. It looked like I was trapped inside a dirty square igloo. It was up to two of the French guys, Charles and Mathieu, to remind me.

'Gareth, my friend you are a crazy bitch. You remember last night?' quizzed Charles in his lazy accent.

'I don't even know who you are my friend,' I replied half joking.

'You were so funny, you collapsed in our room after talking to a calendar for twenty minutes about not having a girlfriend,' he continued.

'Probably just after a date.'

'Ha ha you stupid English man, I love it!'

Mathieu entered the room, cuddled me and said,

'You remember drinking that big cup of rum, then taking off your pants?'

'Let's talk about this later; it's going to be a long day.' I had heard enough.

I grabbed my still unopened backpack and climbed into the Jeep, slumping into the back seat like a dog and feeling like death. I went back to sleep for most of the morning.

We spent the whole day sat in the Jeep travelling across the nothingness of the desert. It felt like we were travelling on Mars, it was not Earth as I had knew it. For hours there was no sign of civilisation or life and I wasn't sure what to think.

We stopped overnight by a large lagoon, which was home to a large number of pink Flamingos. It was not something I had expected to see in the middle of the desert, I was puzzled by their presence but failed to ask anyone how they had got there.

I was woken up the next morning at 4:00am. It was cold and black in the shared room. After the initial wonder of the white Salt Flats this trip now felt like being on an army boot camp and I'd had enough. I climbed into the Jeep excited that this was to be the last day.

We arrived two hours later at 6:00am by the famous hot pools that lay close to the border with Chile. The hot pools were not an inviting proposition at this time in the morning. The outside temperature was no more than a couple of degrees above freezing and we were all wrapped up in coats and scarves. Mark challenged me to go into the water naked.

I walked from behind the concrete yellow changing rooms wearing just my white bobble hat. I cupped my ever shrinking manhood with both hands. I began laughing as the crowd of people who were wrapped like Christmas presents stared at me in disbelief. I belly-flopped into the calm warm water with an almighty splash.

My hat floated on the surface of the water as I came up for air. Mark and the French guys were stood on the side in hysterics but not everyone found my act funny. Looking at several faces it was like I had just farted into a space suit. They and their disgruntled faces couldn't get out of the water fast enough which only added to the humour. The numbers in the pool went from about twenty to just a handful. I beckoned for the lads to join me but they refused, it was too cold.

We ended the tour at Lago Verde, a huge green lagoon that reflected the surrounding mountains like a crystal clear mirror. After saying goodbye to the Australians and French, Mark and I took a short ride to the Chilean border.

I was happy to be leaving Bolivia. It had been an experience and opened my eyes to the struggle of many people's lives. In once sense I think that my time in Bolivia would help to put my own life into perspective, but I was also glad to be leaving. I could almost taste the steaks of Argentina and was ready to move on.

CHILE

San Pedro

We crossed the desert border into Chile and I noticed a major difference straight away; the roads were laid with tarmac. It was a mere detail but one people take for granted. We had left Bolivia and were still in the heart of the desert but I could tell things were going to be far more civilised.

We stood in line outside a government office that straddled the roadside for thirty minutes, while a Bassett Hound decided if he liked us enough to allow us into his country. Maybe it was a good way to do things.

'If the dog likes you then you can stay,' barked an official.

The dog sniffed through people's bags and turned his nose up at everything. He walked with a purposeful arrogance, pulling a policewoman along by the lead.

The dog walked back into the wooden building without saying anything, he was clearly too important. The dog must have got inside and told the police that we could all enter the country, as within a few minutes of him leaving we were back in our van and on our way into San Pedro.

'They all smell fine, so please proceed and leave me to my bone,' he woofed.

We arrived in the dusty desert town of San Pedro by the afternoon. Mark passed me the Lonely Planet guide and moaned for me to pick the hotel as he was hungover and had rendered himself useless.

'Mate, I had no sleep, please just sort it out, I feel like a smack head,' he groaned.

'Ok mate, no worries just you relax,' I replied sarcastically.

He fell out the bus and took my lead as we walked through the streets of San Pedro. I decided to book a room at the first hotel we passed. I had no idea what the exchange rate was and didn't know how much we were spending. The room cost $35,000 Chilean that I was later told equalled about £35. The room had cost seven times as much as the last one we had booked in Bolivia and was only slightly better.

The town of San Pedro was beautiful. The streets were flanked by single story adobe buildings, all brown in colour. The centre of the town was home to a brilliant white church; its simplicity and colour shone in the desert sun.

The people bore no resemblance to their Bolivian counterparts, with many looking like they were from mainland Spain. Restaurants offered a wide variety of food and drinks at a range of prices. I could not believe the difference a border and ten miles could make. San Pedro had everything while Bolivia had next to nothing.

It was Wednesday and I found out that no buses were running into Argentina until the following week. Given the price of the accommodation in San Pedro, this was not a viable option. I searched the town for alternatives as Mark lay in bed dribbling onto his pillow. The only alternative I could fine was a private bus that cost $100 US per person. I went back to the hotel to ask Mark,

'Mate we can get out of here tomorrow but it is going to cost $100 American Dollars. What do you think?'

'I think that you are gay,' was his unhelpful response.

I decided to bite the bullet and booked for the two of us to leave the following afternoon.

ARGENTINA

Salta

The journey to Salta took us down the slopes of the Andean mountains and away from the Atacama Desert. The landscape outside changed dramatically with every mile, dry red soils and stretches of salt plains gave way to striking multi-coloured rock faces and lush green forest.

We travelled in a maroon people carrier with two Australian girls; I recognised one of them but could not remember from where.

Rhani had met me briefly at the Loki hostel in La Paz on the night that I failed to remember. She was apparently sat eating breakfast and reading her Lonely Planet while I stood at the bar in women's underwear requesting juice.

'You were stood there in pants and a bra and then you came and sat next to me. You were off your face and I just thought that you were weird,' she said.

'I'm not though am I?' I asked.

'I'm not sure as yet, give me a few hours.'

Going into Argentina my confidence with women had hit a real low. Mark had a few successes during our Andean adventure but I'd had very few. I hoped that a change in country would lead to a change in fortunes as rumour was that Argentinean women were the best looking in all of South America.

After ten hours Rhani gave up and conceded that I wasn't weird. She could see I was a nice guy but she still didn't fancy me. The drought looked likely to continue for a while longer.

We arrived in Salta under a blanket of rain. The city sits at the foothills of the Andes and sprawls across a wide green valley. It was strange driving through what looked a typical European city. There were well known restaurants, takeaway chains and shops that sold recognisable brands like Nike and Nivea.

We drove past two modern petrol stations with more than one pump. They had large forecourts and minimarts, I hadn't seen a big petrol station for over two months and they looked strange.

I couldn't decide if I was happy about what I saw. It was obvious Argentina was going to be more like home. In some ways it was nice to be back in more structured surroundings and in others it wasn't. Salta lacked the buzz and excitement of La Paz or Lima as it felt familiar, thus lacking any sense of adventure. Maybe we had left Bolivia too soon?

We dumped our bags in a pale no frills hostel that hung above one of several sports stores in the centre of town. Mark and I both wanted food as neither of us could remember the last time we had eaten a good meal. The last night on the Salt Flats I had eaten twenty-five biscuits for dinner making it one of the better meals I had eaten in Bolivia.

On the recommendation of the likeable receptionist we caught a taxi to a steakhouse a few miles across town. The receptionist looked European with dark eyes and hair, set against light olive skin. She told us that this restaurant was the best in town. I sat in the back of the leather-seated taxi licking my lips in anticipation.

We arrived at 9:00pm and were the only customers in a restaurant that could sit over one hundred guests. As we were about to leave one of the waiters walked over to greet us. We decided to just give it a go.

We had heard great things about the steaks in Argentina and our first experience did not disappoint. Before the meal we ate basket after basket of bread accompanied by a selection of sauces, beans and dip. By the time the steaks arrived we were both already full.

The steaks were both the size of small children, lying in front of us cooked to perfection. We looked at each other and laughed.

'They looked like flame-grilled black babies,' Mark joked.

'It's bigger than your head sir. It's a slice of genius.'

We sat for two hours eating. I looked around and saw that the restaurant was now full as everyone sat around the marble tables eating steak and drinking red wine. I looked at my watch and saw it was close to midnight. Why was everyone eating so late, maybe Argentina would have a few tricks up its sleeve after all?

Full to the point of being sick we went back to hostel and had an early night. We had plenty of time to explore the city the following day and needed the rest.

I sat reading on the roof terrace at the back of the hostel enjoying the morning sun. It was nice to experience warm weather once again. I spoke with an elderly man called John from Southampton. We each talked about our experiences in South America and I was startled at how mundane his had been in comparison to mine. His accounts could have put a glass eye to sleep and made mine seem crazy. I was glad to be travelling with someone fun like Mark.

Mark got up at midday complaining that he had got no sleep. We walked through the streets of Salta looking at the old colonial architecture and enjoying the atmosphere of what is a beautiful city. We went for lunch in a busy run down market as Mark was worried that he was spending too much money.

'Mate we need to eat with the real people,' he told me.

So we did. We both ordered steak from a fat chef that stood behind a steel counter sweating in a cloud of cooked meat. The market was full of noise, colour and life as food stalls jostled with each other for customers.

We sat eating, trying to decide where we wanted to go next. We had to choose between Cordoba and Mendoza, one rumoured to be full of wine, the other full of students.

We decided to book a bus to Mendoza as Mark had found out that the students were all on summer holiday. We booked a night bus for the following day.

We both were concerned that time was working against us. It was the middle of January and we planned to be in Northern Brazil for Carnival in little over four weeks. Salvador was thousands of miles away and there was so much in between. As it was Friday we decided to go out for what would be our one and only night out in Salta.

After changing back at the hostel I was keen to go out and drink. I sat out on the terrace with a cold bottle of beer waiting a good half an hour for Mark. It puzzled me how he took so long to get ready as unlike me he had no hair - all he had to do was shower and put some clothes on. It was a short task for most men but for Mark it was always a protracted affair.

He came out onto the terrace in just a blue towel. I looked at him and knew by his face that something was on his mind.

'What is it mate, why are you taking so long?' I questioned.

'Look at it, look at it,' he replied in anguish.

'At what?' I looked, seeing nothing obvious.

'Stop messing about, my head you nipple,' he replied as he stuck the top of his head close to mine.

'Honestly mate, you have lost me,' I said, backing away slightly.

'Lost you? My head is two different colours, you're just saying it is ok so I come out,' he shouted.

'Ha ha you're not coming out because your head has peeled slightly in the sun?'

'No I'm not mate. I look like a tit so there is no point.'

'You're acting like one,' I concluded as he stormed back inside.

Underneath all his male bravado Mark was an insecure person, particularly about how he looked. I loved to wind him up but on this occasion I chose to be nice. I didn't want to go out by myself even if his head did look like a jacket potato.

Half an hour later Mark reappeared and after constant reassurances that the marks on his head were not visible we walked into Salta. His head looked like a melted caramel ice cream, whatever he had done had made it worse.

'How did you get rid of those bits of skin? You can hardly tell now,' I said.

'I did that scrub sir. I knew that it looked bad earlier.'

We went to another steak restaurant, washing down our food with a couple of bottles of cheap wine. As on our first night we ate earlier than anyone else in the city.

Slightly drunk we wandered out of the restaurant and back onto the streets of Salta. We sat out on the street drinking a cheap bottle of rum a few hundred metres from the main strip of bars and restaurants. By 11:00pm the restaurants filled up and the bars began to make more noise.

As we sat drinking by the road a horde of vociferous football fans came charging towards us chanting all manner of unrecognisable songs. We found out that two local football sides had played each other in a pre-season friendly. For the fans it was anything but friendly. The group marching past us were all fans of Central Norte from the third tier of Argentinean football.

A Central Norte fan broke from the group and asked Mark for some rum. He was caked in blood from what looked like bullet wounds on his arms and legs. The boy was only seventeen years of age and slight in appearance. He had been shot several times with rubber bullets by the police but was unconcerned by the injuries. Mark had a keen interest in football hooliganism, so while they spoke to each other in broken English I sat drinking.

We stumbled onto what I had termed 'bar street' just before midnight. The street was swarming with girls and we were both officially on the prowl. Unable to hold a decent conversation in Spanish, chatting to girls proved difficult. We were both relying on looks and given the litre of rum and Mark's patchy skin, we were destined to fail.

We saw three Argentineans who we recognised from the hostel in one of the bars. There were two girls and one boy so we decided to join them at their table. One of the girls called Maria had some weed and asked if we would like a smoke.

'That would be great yeah why not, gracias,' I said, forgetting for a moment that they were Spanish.

We left the bar soon after and had a joint together outside by an old church just away from the main strip of bars. We stood for a while trying to talk with one another before giving up and just laughing. The weed brought us closer together. We decided to go to a quieter venue opposite the dark box with lasers.

On the way to this new bar Mark vanished. We looked around for what felt like hours but in reality must have been no more than a few minutes. I looked in sheer disbelief at the three stoned Argentineans; I had no idea what could have happened to him.

I gathered my thoughts as they stood puzzled laughing and decided to take one last look in a live music bar across the street. A band was playing and like a fresh pie by a kitchen window it had drawn Mark in.

Mark was stood by the main stage facing the crowd with his arms folded. If it wasn't for his bright blue shirt he would have looked like security. His face was expressionless and he clearly had no idea where he was. Statue-like, he didn't move as I waved over our new friends to take a look. We shouted from the main door,

'Mark, Mark over here.'

He didn't hear us as if hypnotised by the soft sounding guitar of the lead singer. I broke the spell by pulling on his right arm,

'What is up with you mate, are you even here?'

Mark looked at me like I was a complete stranger before coming around and saying,

'Fucked mate.'

We all left still laughing as Mark shook his head,

'What was in that joint Carlos?'

The Argentineans had not booked any accommodation and planned to spend the night sleeping on the streets. I told them not to be silly, they could stay at ours. I had been at the hostel for only one night and already thought of it as my own.

At the hostel the night porter refused to let us stay up and demanded that we go to bed. He didn't check our keys so I set some beds up on the floor of the dormitory. The effects of the weed had worn off and Mark was angry at being told we had to go to sleep despite it being 4:00am.

'It's our one night out mate let's get back into town. We will go to bed when we want to, not when some jobs worth tells us,' he screamed.

He had a point, it was our only night in Salta and it had only just got going before that joint ended it prematurely. Against my better judgement Mark and I left the Argentineans to sleep and arrived back onto bar street at 5:00am.

Mark told me he wanted another beer but within ten minutes of being out we were in a taxi heading towards a brothel called Barbies. I hoped that they had beers, otherwise he had lied to me. Mark was almost incomprehensible as he slurred from the front seat of the taxi,

'It's going to be amazing mate. Argentinean women are amazing. Wait and see.'

I was so drunk that the act of seeing was going to be my main problem. I could feel my body begin to shut down as the cab pulled up at the side of the road.

We entered the small bar and ordered some beers from a young girl scantily clad in pink underwear who escorted us to some seats at the back of the main room. I sat down and could not fight the feeling of tiredness anymore. I took one sip of my beer and then it went dark.

I woke up some time later with the same girl in pink underwear tapping me across the face with the back of her left hand. I had no idea where I was and flinched violently, knocking several glass bottles of beer from the table. The girl told me they were closing. I looked around and had no idea where Mark had gone so I refused to leave.

I had passed out shortly after entering the bar. I vaguely remembered Mark telling me he was going to get a girl so assumed he was in another room. I demanded to know where he was but none of the staff could understand what I was talking about.

I passed out again as the staff decided it was best to just leave me alone. I woke up at 9:00am to someone shouting in my ear,

'Get up you nipple.'

It was Mark and he was safe.

On the drunken walk back to the hostel Mark told me that he had been whisked across town in a taxi to some sort of slutty motel. I couldn't believe what I was hearing and wondered where had he got the energy from? I felt like the living dead.

After sleeping all day we checked out of the hostel five hours late at 6:00pm. After one last walk around the city we collected our things and headed to the bus station.

Mendoza

The bus to Mendoza took sixteen hours. I was finally becoming accustomed to the long journeys so it wasn't too uncomfortable, it was to be expected. Many people believe that travelling by bus is better than flying as you get to see more of the country. That is true when the sun is up, but the reality is the majority of buses travel at night meaning you see precious little of anything.

In an ideal world we would have flown to each destination, avoiding tedious motorways and speed restrictions while saving a lot of time. I sat in my aisle seat next to Mark folding a piece of white paper that I pulled from my bag into an aeroplane. I dreamt about setting up Origami Airways, the inexpensive way to travel. All you would need were huge pieces of card and some sort of catapult system to fire people in the right direction.

We checked into Winca's Hostel in the heart of downtown Mendoza by late afternoon and had an uneventful first night in the city.

We decided to visit Mendoza as we had been told that the winery tours were incredible. We had heard a rumour that a man in the city allowed people drink as much wine as they could handle, free of charge. We walked the streets trying to find him. His name was Mr Hugo and only one person we asked had heard of him. He said,

'Fuck that Mr Hugo.'

The signs were not good, so we decided to call it a night and start again in the morning.

I woke to what sounded like a punctured football but was in fact a wheezing Argentinean. Resisting the urge to kick him out of the large open window onto the street below I got up and went for a shower.

Mark and I decided to take a chance. Rather than book a wine tour through the hostel we got on a local bus to Mipai that, according to our Lonely Planet guide, was the nearest place to the vineyards. Mr Hugo had to be there and we were intent on finding him.

We jumped off the bus in Mipai thirty minutes after leaving Mendoza. Within seconds of touching the ground we were surrounded by a circle of enthusiastic boys armed with fliers for different tours. Amongst all the shouting we heard the name we were after.

Our gamble had for once paid off. The small boy walked us half a mile down the wide straight road that intersected the small town. He told us that Mr Hugo was his father and that we could expect to drink lots of wine. He pointed across the road towards a small house.

'It is there, say that Javier sent you,' he said as he passed us two marked fliers.

'Cheers little man, sees you later,' I shouted as he ran back to the bus stop.

We looked across the road. Between two trees stood a modest home with a large red sign to the right of it that read:

'BOOK HERE owned by MR HUGO family run MENDOZA BIKES.'

Mark and I walked up the drive sweating like two dogs in Chinatown. The weather was incredibly hot and there was not a cloud in the sky. We both loved the sun so the weather was ideal.

Mr Hugo had a presence about him; it was like meeting a girlfriend's dad for the first time. He stood tall and proud like a statue as he introduced himself,

'I am Mr Hugo, would you like some bicycles and wine?'

'That we would Mr Hugo, you come highly recommended' Mark replied.

After telling us about the route, he armed us with a map before waving us off on some suspect mountain bikes to the first of several wineries marked out.

The first winery was heaving with people from different tours. After ten minutes we both looked at each other and admitted we were bored. It reminded me of the vineyards in France I had visited with my parents.

There were no pretty girls and no open bottles of wine in sight, just a team of middle-aged people being told firstly in Spanish and then English about the processes behind good wine making. Mark looked at me and I knew what he was going to say,

'Let's jog this place on.'

So we did.

We cycled through the countryside and could have easily been biking through the south of France as vineyards dotted the landscape as far as the eye could see. It was a beautiful day and a beautiful place.

At the next winery we opted out of the tour, buying a bottle of red wine from the shop instead. We found a couple of yellow bean bags and sat by the front of the shop drinking and enjoying the summer sun.

The peace was short-lived as within minutes the owner of the winery stormed out of his house and demanded that we move around the back of the building to the vineyard. It was clear he was unhappy as his face looked like a grape.

The site of two topless Englishmen sweating on bean bags was not the image that the winery wished to portray so we moved without argument. I argued with Mark that it was because of his shaved head,

'There is no escaping that you look like a menacing man-child.'

'Least I don't look like a girl with a beard,' he countered.

'Jesus,' I sighed.

After finishing the bottle of wine in a garden surrounded by grapes we decided not to continue with the tour. We thought it would be best to return to Mr Hugo's as we could sit in his garden and drink free wine while enjoying the sun, without having to move or worry about cycling. The bikes had already become an unwanted accessory and paying for wine seemed daft when we could get it for free.

After arriving back at Mr Hugo's house earlier than planned, Mark and I made our way through eight bottles of wine in four hours. Mr Hugo played classic 1990s' music from his large CD player. Ace of Base's I Saw the Sign played while we drank all his wine without paying a penny.

We met some friendly people in his garden that slowly filtered back from the tour out of breath and sweating. We made friends with two Spanish men from Madrid called Hendrick and Ramon who caught a bus back to Mendoza with us.

Back at our hostel Mark and I got changed before heading over to meet our new friends at Hostel Independiencia, considered the best hostel in Mendoza. We arrived to find that neither Ramon nor Hedrick had returned from the tour and were both puzzled.

An hour passed before they stumbled through the gate laughing. They had both passed out in the main square a matter of minutes from the hostel and had only just woken up.

'My friends, I am sorry we fell asleep in the park. Mr Hugo is number one,' shouted Ramon.

Already drunk from a day on the wine, we went for an all-out assault on the town. Matt, an Argentinean who worked at the hostel, decided to join us. It was going to be an interesting night.

We went to an Irish bar that was about as Irish as a Kenyan marathon runner. Mark made a shock early exit after a shot of Jager got the better of him. Rather than go home to act as his personal maid, I decided to stay out with the rest of the group. The group now included two German girls that I had spoken to on the wine tour.

One of the girls called Greta, nicknamed Gretamine due to her drug habit, took a shine to me. Unfortunately for her I was not attracted to girls with nicknames based on their drug of choice, hers being the horse tranquiliser, ketamine. Her advance fell at the first hurdle as I looked her in the eyes and simply said,

'Greta, neigh.'

I stayed out with Ramon and Hedrick as we chatted to local girls outside the Irish bar. With their help I was doing a lot better than usual and was surprised how much my Spanish had improved. Matt came over and suggested that we go to a club, telling us,

'Wednesdays are quiet, it is the best place in town and the only place open till 4am. Come on guys it's round the corner and full of local girls.' He had us convinced.

'Fuck it why not, I'm in,' I bellowed back with drunken enthusiasm.

We entered the club and the first things I noticed were the lack of travellers and the frightening amount of women. Matt had delivered us to a heavenly place. I hugged and thanked him.

The club was extremely dark, bright lasers stroked against the contours of clubber's faces as smoke filtered through the air. I was absolutely smashed and it felt like I was watching someone else in action. It was someone else dancing on the podium and someone else that was approached by a sexy local girl with long, bright blonde hair.

This mysterious lady walked over and made an advance on me instantly. The music was loud making conversation between us impossible. I wondered as she grabbed hold of me if she thought I was Argentinean and would be upset to hear that I was in fact English.

She had a great face, a great body, and an aggressive kissing technique. When she was done kissing me she walked off without saying a word back to her group of friends stood across the dance floor. One of her friends came over and questioned me,

'Where are you from? Are you gay? Do you like her?'

I wasn't sure where to start as my head was spinning. As my eyes came back into focus it suddenly dawned on me that that girl I had kissed had an eight inch clitoris.

I stood in shock as the realisation of kissing a man raced through my poisoned mind. It wasn't my fault I told myself, man she looked like a woman. It wasn't like I had been approached by a fat butch woman, with one of those fancy designer handbags with the words ' GUESS ' on the side. If that had been the case I'd have said,

'About 22 stone and you're a man?'

This girl had tricked me and I blamed Mr Hugo. I was just a spectator as I wasn't there in that club in any real sense. My mind had been left at Mr Hugo's that afternoon.

I began to panic. Spotting my state of confusion Ramon asked,

'Gaz are you ok, what is wrong you look like you have seen a ghost?'

I stood in silence and for several minutes wondered if kissing a man made me a homosexual. I diverted my attention firstly to alcohol and then to a girl called Laura.

Laura was a good looking brunette that lived in Mendoza. Her and her friend had met us in the Irish bar earlier that night. As they spoke little English I hadn't interacted with them up to this point. Ramon clearly liked her friend Eva so it made sense that I talked to Laura. She was pretty and I had to prove to myself that I wasn't gay.

I woke up alone with a sore head in a flat somewhere in Argentina, I had no clue as to where I was. I could hear people in the kitchen but rather than get up and investigate I stayed in bed staring at the white ceiling. I heard someone walking down the hall towards the room and hoped that it was Laura. The door opened and thankfully it was.

I had gone back to her friend's flat with Ramon. He was in the other room, so I relaxed on the bed and breathed a sigh of relief.

Laura climbed back into bed and began touching me. I reached down to check that she didn't have a penis before letting things progress. You couldn't be too careful in these parts, as I regrettably knew.

Ramon called me from the other room soon after and we caught a cab back into town. I found Mark in Independiencia square sunning his body on a patch of grass. He was lying alone in the middle of a park and looked hilarious.

'It's not a beach you fanny,' I shouted.

He was genuinely pleased to see me as he couldn't remember anything past leaving Mr Hugo's garden and was worried that I had left him.

I told him that I had slept with a thirty-year-old Argentinean that I had met in a club full of transsexuals. His face dropped in disbelief. It was like I'd just told him that I had kissed a bloke or something. Mark was gobsmacked.

Rosario

My friend from home sent me an email suggesting we should stay at a hostel in Rosario called Cool Raul. Mark and I rolled into a town without arranging anywhere so it seemed was the logical choice.

It was beginning to feel like Mark and I were just going on a series of city breaks. Not having a car and the freedom to go where you want was annoying. The buses began to feel more and more restricting and the cities all started to look the same.

Cool Raul sat at the end of a five-story terraced block in the heart of downtown Rosario. Inside it was ramshackle at best. We checked into a damp eight-bed dorm room that thankfully was empty. We were assisted by the inconvenienced manager, Omar. Omar was European but looked like a stoned surfer from Malibu. He gazed at us with his tired red eyes and boasted,

'Sorry dudes, I've been up partying all night. Sometimes I forget I'm not travelling like you guys. I need to stop going out as my liver just can't take the damage. It's just I love to party and get wild.'

'Nice one,' was my uninterested response.

Omar clearly thought he was cool, we thought otherwise. He was an aging twat that needed to learn some manners.

He slumped back onto the sofa without bothering to take any of our details. Pulling his curly blonde hair back over his eyes he nodded off back to sleep. He was surrounded in the TV room by what looked like a group of half-baked Israelis hanging off the furniture.

I was still exhausted from the night out in Mendoza and the subsequent bus journey so had to take a nap. We had a choice of eight beds and each was equally unappealing. I felt like Goldilocks.

'This bed is too damp. This one is too high and this one too low. This one is just right,' I joked with Mark.

I took the bottom bunk away from the room door. The pillows on the bed were covered in yellow sweat marks and there were no sheets, regardless I dropped off to sleep.

We agreed to stay in Rosario for one night. Buenos Aires was only 300km away and we had arranged to meet up with Harry and Sam from Cusco. We reluctantly woke up at 11:00am.

Mendoza produced fine wines and Rosario had a reputation for producing fine women. So after a quick shower and making ourselves look presentable we walked out of the hostel and onto the busy road beneath.

Being on a budget there wasn't too much we could do during the day in cities. Typically we walked around, took photographs and soaked up the atmosphere of a place. Rosario was no different.

However, what was different in Rosario was the amount of good looking women, they were everywhere including behind the counter of McDonald's. We both stared at the alarming numbers of attractive females in the city that slid worryingly from women to girls in their early teens.

I felt like a pervert and said to Mark as yet another gorgeous girl walked past,

'Rosario must have a high level of sex crime.'

I got thinking about what the biggest cause of paedophilia in this city could be and came to the conclusion it was probably sexy kids.

'This is ridiculous, look at her over there, she is mint,' Mark pointed out.

'She is also about thirteen you kiddie fiddler,' I responded.

'Fit though!'

'That she is my friend, that she is,' I concluded.

It was a beautiful summer's day and while we did very little, it was a lot of fun. Mark and I had built up a strong relationship on this trip and were now both at total ease with one another. If he was acting in a certain way, I would know why and if he wanted to do something I could tell.

On the evening we had a few beers over dinner. I suggested that we should open our own restaurant in Argentina called Fork-Lands that would be English owned. He laughed as he chewed on his steak. After eating we walked through the streets of Rosario towards the hostel on what was a warm night. We had agreed on an early night but I could tell Mark's mind was wandering.

'You want to stay out don't you mate?' I asked.

'No mate, can't be arsed drinking and you know how messy BA is going to be.'

'Yeah I know can't wait. It's going to be epic,' I replied.

'Fancy going to a strip club sir?' he asked out of the blue.

'Not really mate, I'm tired and can't afford it. They will cost loads here.'

'Sure,' he concluded before wrapping his long arm over my shoulder.

Ten minutes later I was sat in the back of a taxi watching Mark's sexual charades. He kept repeating 'Club la chicas' while pretending to take off his clothes. The driver looked at me in his back mirror and smiled. We sped through the narrow softly lit streets of Rosario before coming to a stop on the corner of San Lorenzo.

'Club chicas amigos, very good, ha ha,' he cackled.

'Mucho gracias senior. You want to come? Didn't think so, see you later,' Mark shrilled.

The street appeared residential, looking similar to the countless others we had walked or driven through that day. We turned the corner and our eyes were hit with the harsh glow of neon light; two legs flashed playfully up and down in front of us.

On this street sat three different clubs. We chose the first, called Lucille Bar. It cost $20 pesos to enter that Mark covered as he knew that he'd dragged me there.

Flat screen TVs dotted the purple painted walls. Had they not been showing hardcore interracial pornography it would have easily passed as a sports bar.

The bar straddled the length of the room clinging to the back wall and built-in rich mahogany. We sat on two large wooden stools by the bar and ordered two beers. The bartender was caked in make-up and had the appearance of a retired stripper. Mark took a shine to her and her huge breasts.

My eyes scanned the room; it was practically empty at this point, housing only about ten people. The elevated stage sat opposite the bar a few metres from the floor and was vacant. We had arrived too early.

Half an hour passed as we sat watching three black gentlemen spoil the hopes and dreams of someone's daughter on screen. As the act reached its explosive conclusion the lights in the bar dimmed and our eyes diverted to the stage.

Appearing from behind a heavy velvet curtain stood one of the most beautiful women I had ever laid my eyes on. She was wearing a latex police outfit, but not for long.

I sat transfixed as this olive-skinned piece of perfection peeled off her clothes while seductively snaking around a silver pole.

The crowd stared open-mouthed in her direction; she owned the room and everyone in it. She lay on the dark floor of the stage thrusting up and down into the air as the lights flickered off her skin. She started to play with herself and it was at that point that I wanted to marry her. She danced to Paradise City and I wondered if Rosario was the place they were singing about.

Mark and I returned to our spot at the bar and ordered two more beers. The bar was filling up with people but the atmosphere remained surprisingly comfortable. Girls now patrolled the floor talking to guests and asking if they would like 'anything'.

Mark was adamant that he had to have the first girl on stage. Without speaking Spanish it was going to be difficult to get her over. He pointed out all the girls he found attractive and wanted my opinion on which of them he could get instead.

The calm, matter-of-fact way in which he spoke amazed me. I knew what a nice person Mark was but when it came to girls it was business. Instead of asking my opinion on what flip-flops he should buy (as he had done earlier) he was asking about girls; he talked about both in the same manner.

I came back from the toilets to find Mark deep in conversation with a large woman who wore lacy black underwear. She had striking pitch black hair that emphasised an already pale complexion. She told him that all the girls fuck for a price. It was like all his Christmases had come at once.

I sat awkwardly talking in Spanish to a young girl that was new to the club. She wore a sparkling white dress and was gorgeous. She had light brown hair, dark chocolate eyes and perfect olive skin. I liked that she was shy and it made me want to take her home but she clung to the arm of the experienced woman in lacy black underwear.

Mark tried to convince me to go with her but I was far too nervous. While my mind had been opened on this trip, I still felt that paying for sex was wrong. I wanted this girl to like me but knew that was impossible, she just wanted my money.

I sat alone with my legs dangling from the tall bar stool watching as Mark walked out the bar with both of the girls. I couldn't help but feel betrayed. It was like my best friend at school kissing the girl he knew I liked just because he could. I was annoyed that I had not taken my chance,

'Soy un perdedor I'm a loser baby so why don't you kill me?'

I sat staring at the stage as two lesbians performed oral on each other while lying in a coffin and the pain slowly subsided. I was very much alive.

I saw that the young stripper I had been talking with had returned to the bar without her guardian and wondered what Mark was up to. I tried to ask her but she did not understand and timidly made her way backstage. I was concerned for Mark but felt it was best to sit by the bar and wait for him to surface.

The next show on stage was more light-hearted and involved some audience participation. I had no idea what was going on and was thankful not to be picked. The willing volunteer sat on a cream sofa that had been brought onto the stage. He laughed as the affable barmaid told a series of jokes to the audience.

Dramatic music began rumbling from the two large speakers either side of the stage and the crowd whistled in anticipation. The velvet curtain parted as a spotlight centred on the middle of the stage. Out came a large whore that had somehow been cruelly trapped in a child's school uniform. Without so much as an introduction she began sucking up and down on this man's cock. Everyone began to laugh as her mouth motored over his member.

Mark returned a few minutes later with a wry smile on his face. He sat down and told me what had happened. The threesome had only lasted a matter of minutes as he was unable to control himself. He couldn't afford to keep both of them for round two so he went with experience. The dark haired woman had stayed.

Any bitterness on my behalf was buried with the lesbians on stage. I was happy Mark had experienced his first threesome. The nearest I would ever come to one would be if I wanked with both hands. Mark was satisfied so we finished our now warm beers and returned to the hostel for 3:00am.

I didn't know what was happening in this town. You had school children dressing like whores and whores dressing like school children. It was a nightmare – I didn't know whether to carry sweets or money.

I lay in my dirty bunk bed back at Cool Raul wondering what it would be like paying for sex and wishing I had the balls to find out.

Buenos Aires

We woke up early and left Cool Raul without paying. Omar was once again passed out on the sofa; not paying was the only cool thing about the place.

Five hours later we arrived in Buenos Aires and checked into the Millhouse hostel. We had to fight our way through a huge protest on the main street running through the city. People carried a score of banners reading 'Free Palestine'. I turned to Mark in all the bedlam and suggested,

'It was giving it away in the first place that got them into all this mess!'

'Shut up you tit,' he replied.

The hostel occupied a stunning, five-storey nineteenth-century house. It was built around a charming, colonial-style atrium and was modern in appearance, more a hotel than a hostel. It had a reputation in Buenos Aires as the main party hostel and that is what we planned to do.

As we walked up the marble staircase to Room 108 we bumped into Harry. Harry had decided to shave his hair and was now the proud owner of a Mohawk. He had a crazed look in his eyes that resembled the look of Robert De Niro's character in Taxi Driver,

'Alright Travis Bickle, how's it going?' I asked as we shared a warm embrace.

'Yeah, yeah, good mate, fucking great seeing you guys,' was his peculiar response.

I looked into his glazed eyes and realised that he was on drugs.

'You're fucked aren't you mate?' I asked.

'Pretty much, I haven't slept for two days,' he admitted.

'Ha ha you crazy little bastard.'

We agreed to meet Harry in his room in an hour as both Mark and I were starving and needed some food. So we dropped our bags and did exactly that.

We entered their room two hours later as a collection of nervous looking travellers stared at us from the floor. We both hugged Sam and asked how he was before meeting the rest of the group.

It was 3:00pm and they were all getting money together to buy some cocaine from a local dealer known to guests at the hostel, coincidentally, as Omar. How everyone had his phone number I had no idea. He must have made an absolute fortune from backpackers, collectively they bought twenty grams.

Unlike Harry and Sam's room, ours had a balcony so we grabbed some beers from a local supermarket and drank in there. Drinking in the rooms was not allowed at the hostel but I guessed neither was the consumption of cocaine.

The hostel hosted its nightly happy hour from 7:00pm. By this point we were all really drunk. I had befriended a curly-haired Irish gentleman called Podric and we laughed and joked like we had known each other for years.

Being ever competitive we took on Harry and Sam in our very own version of the Ashes. Instead of holding cricket bats we held pool cues, but the result was the same - Podric and I got hammered.

We left the hostel around 11:00pm in a fleet of taxis to an area of the city called Palermo. The lads had already been on several occasions and told us it was home to the best bars the city had to offer. The first that we went to was called Limbo.

I sat out of my mind around a table full of people in a similar state for over an hour as a beautiful waitress served us drinks. Before leaving I tried to chat to this girl in my own affable way. I wasn't sure how it had gone as I had no idea what was happening.

We left the bar soon after as Harry suggested a nearby club. The toxic mix of drugs and alcohol finally took hold and got the better of me as my mind went into its own limbo.

I woke the next morning at 11:00am to Mark violently shaking me.

'Fuck off you twat, stop shaking me!' I shouted.

'I can't sleep, fancy coming shopping?' he whispered.

I couldn't think of anything I would rather not do.

'No chance mate, I'd rather go rowing without arms,' I grumbled.

Luckily the room had thick purple velvet curtains so despite the time it was pitch black. I drifted back off to sleep as the weighted door slammed shut.

Mark returned at 2:00pm and woke me up for the second time. He was stood with a recognisable grin etched across his face clutching onto an ocean blue bottle of Gatorade.

'Give us a drink of that mate?' I asked as my hand waved in the air.

He passed me the drink and I sat up asking him where he had gone. As I drank he retold the story of his morning,

'I got the underground to Palermo; it was right hot and agitating. I got there and all that were there was a big shopping centre. I started feeling ill so sacked it off. On the way back here some bloke gave me a blue card.'

He reached into his pocket and passed me the card. I looked and saw a picture of a naked woman in black print. He continued,

'So anyway, I asked him where the place was and it turned out it was just round the corner. I went into this house and sat in a bedroom. Girls started coming in and then I had to pick which one I wanted, it was mint mate.'

I sat, not for the first time in sheer disbelief.

'You went in like that and had sex with a prostitute?' I asked knowing the answer.

'Basically,' he responded.

Mark jumped on me repeatedly screaming over and over,

'Banter.'

I laughed and decided it really was time that I got out of my bed.

I couldn't remember anything about the end of the night. I stared at my hand and noticed a huge black stamp below my knuckles that read 'Club 69'.

I was confused. I then went into my pockets and pulled out a screwed up piece of paper with the number 134 across the top of it in red print. It was an order slip and it read:

'Priscilla 049424847112 princesspri89@yahoo.com'

I washed my face at the sink and stared into the mirror; amnesia really was a bitch.

We went down to the bar and got some food. As Mark sobered up he tried to convince himself that the house he had visited was 'high class', as was the woman he had fucked. He wasn't happy so I told him not to worry,

'Don't worry mate, rather than crabs the bitch has probably given you lobsters.'

'It isn't funny mate, what if I have got something?' he moaned.

Harry, Sam and Juliet, a girl they were travelling with and knew from home, joined us for dinner. We went to a steakhouse in town. We sat around in relative silence piecing together the night before while making plans for the night ahead. It was Friday so we had to go out.

On the way back to the hostel I was bullied into a strip club that hid off the main street behind a large sports store. I had no idea what had happened. One minute I was stood on a busy street waiting for Mark as he looked at football shirts and the next I was sat on a red sofa in relative darkness on my own.

A bedraggled whore sat with me explaining in confusing English the 'Rules of the House'. She kindly got me a warm wine glass full of Pepsi that I had not asked for but felt obliged to drink. She then asked,

'What is it you would like to see?'

I answered in a cowardly voice,

'My friends.'

It was not what she had expected and she seemed far from happy. I looked at her and tried to make an excuse,

'It is early I will come back later, thank you for making me aware of the place.'

The truth was I had no intention of returning to this neon nightmare. The woman who wore a dark silk dressing gown explained in no uncertain terms that I owed her $40 pesos. As I flatly refused to pay her a penny Harry and Mark bundled through the door laughing. They had been collared by the same gentleman that had brought me here.

'Gaz, there you are!' yelled Harry 'What the fuck is this place?'

I shrugged my shoulders as they sat down on a sofa behind mine.

More prostitutes appeared and it became apparent that we were all in trouble. I looked at Mark and motioned with my head that we should aim for the door.

I got up and dashed towards the exit. After some resistance from the small man that had got us into this mess I was once again outside on the street and my head was spinning.

I then realised that Mark and Harry had not followed me; they were still behind the iron door and very much inside. I tried to get back in but couldn't so I had no option but to wait.

Fifteen minutes later they both appeared from behind the door. Mark was seething and shouted back into the darkness,

'Your parents must be thrilled with your line of work you dirty cunts!'

He looked at me and smiled before muttering,

'We better run mate, I think they are calling the police.'

Mark, Harry and I arrived back at the hostel out of breath and laughing as the adrenaline of the chase ran through our bodies. After a short shower back in the room we were once again sat enjoying the hostel's happy hour.

The barman had taken a shine to me from my antics the previous night and therefore plied us all with free Tequila, his name was John. John suggested that the best place to go on a Friday night was a bar called Sugar in Palermo.

I had already been told I looked slightly Argentinean but John told me that I was the double for the Argentinean Big Brother winner Bam Ban. I felt it in my best interests to pretend from that point that I was him.

We went up to Room 108 for a small party. Everyone deserted the bar and ending up in our room, within minutes it had gone wild. We were breaking every rule in the hostel handbook and didn't care. Unfortunately after a while security did and eventually asked everyone to leave.

Sugar had a cool vibe. The walls were all red brick, making it feel like a loft space. Arches separated the different rooms from the bar and the arches were lit with a sharp red hue. We found some seats in the back room near a spiral staircase.

I found looking like a celebrity made talking to local girls a lot easier. I had learnt a few phrases that stripped away the cat and mouse conversations I tended to have back home. It was direct and to the point.

'Guappa! Me guappo?' I would ask.

If the answer was,

'Si,' accompanied by a smile I would then respond, 'Besos?'

We would then hopefully share a kiss. I occasionally deviated from the script and obviously not everyone said yes, but it was at least a start.

It worked well in Sugar. I kissed a beautiful Argentinean at the bar that had said 'Si' and smiled so I offered to buy her a drink. I stood at the bar thinking that my luck was most definitely in only to return minutes later to the sight of her and John down each other's throats.

John apologised a hundred times. I didn't care as much as he thought, so all his constant apologies did was make me like him less and less. I didn't acknowledge the girl or give her the beer I had just bought for her, that was now mine.

Mark came over and told me we were leaving as Harry had been thrown out for dancing on a table. On the way out I pulled the Argentinean's best friend in a petty act of revenge. I felt I could do whatever I wanted, I had just won Big Brother after all.

I stumbled back into my room at 7:00am once again suffering from extreme memory loss. Harry, Sam and Jules were relentless in their mission to get as fucked as they possibly could and I liked going along for the ride.

I lay in my bed unable to sleep as a fat Australian in our room was the world record holder at snoring. I sat in utter frustration throwing objects at him across the room, but it was to no avail, his pig bullets were unrelenting.

That morning Craig arrived at the Millhouse. I could hear him shouting in reception around 10:00am. He bounded into the room in high spirits as Mark and I sluggishly welcomed him. We were joined moments later by Maria.

Maria was here to see Mark. They had met in Playa Del Carmen and she had flown from France to see him for a week. I couldn't believe she was actually standing there, I lay in total shock.

Mark was in two minds about her coming out. He really liked her, but a lot of time had passed since Playa Del Carmen, and he worried if he would still feel the same. We were in one of the big party cities and there were lots of girls so I knew he was going to find it hard to behave.

Another day was wasted tossing and turning in bed. I had been in Buenos Aires for three days and had seen nothing of the city during the day. It all hid behind a heavy purple curtain and I was determined that I would see it.

That evening I promised myself I would stay in. I had arranged a date for the following day with Priscilla, the barmaid from Limbo. I had messaged Priscilla on Facebook asking if she would like to go shopping and she had agreed. I needed to rest.

Mark had told me about an email Craig had sent him explaining that he didn't want to travel with me, it read:

Alright Mark

Any chance the two of us doing a spot of travelling together? Imagine the banter. I like Gaz but I just don't like travelling with him. I like him a lot but at times he is too much. Realise I am putting you in an awkward spot but do that think, and get back to me.

See you both in Buenos for copious amounts of banter!

Love you

Craig

It wasn't something you could really take back and I felt awkward around him as a result. He begged for me to come out that night; Mark was staying in with Maria and all I wanted to do was sleep. I didn't want to go out but felt it was a good opportunity to speak with Craig about the email.

Craig and I jostled for attention as we began drinking yet another bottle of whiskey in one of the rooms. Once again we were with the Australians that now included three girls: Nikki, Claire and Louise.

Craig sat and told us a story about a woman he had met in Belize. He told it the only way that Craig could tell anything, enthusiastically and loud.

'I met this fifty-year-old woman in Belize who told me that she tossed off her autistic son. She told me it was necessary because he couldn't do it himself, nothing to do with abuse.' He paused before boisterously concluding, 'Imagine being wanked off by your mum, by your mum!'

We sat drinking and laughing and in the back of our minds I think we were all imagining being wanked off by our mothers.

As the night wore on Craig and I became more comfortable in each other's company, and with that thoughts about the email went into the recycle bin. I wasn't the type of person to hold a grudge and it was up to him whether or not he wished to travel with me.

The next morning I rang the number off the torn bit of paper to check that my date with Priscilla was still going ahead. I didn't want to go shopping but was intrigued to meet this girl.

I sat outside a furniture store waiting for her at lunch time. It was the first time I had seen any of Buenos Aires in the day and it looked a beautiful city. There was clearly a heavy European influence and it reminded me of Barcelona.

I began to sober up as I waited outside the shop so I began to question what I was doing. I didn't struggle with dates back home as there was always something to talk about but this was going to be different. We were from different parts of the world, spoke different languages and knew nothing about each other. Just as I hoped she was not going to show up, she did.

Neither of us could make a decision about where to go so we ended up in McDonald's. I thought this was a bad idea but after ten minutes she was 'Lovin' it'. We ate and talked really slowly as she was keen to find out about my trip but struggled to understand what I was saying.

Priscilla was studying Dentistry at University and I could tell she was a smart girl. Her grasp of English was good for someone that rarely spoke it and far better than my Spanish, so we managed to muddle through the afternoon.

After a beer at a local cafe we went to the park as it was a sunny afternoon. Being summer it was busy and full of families enjoying each other's company.

Priscilla was a beautiful girl. She was typically Latin with dark features and long flowing, chocolate-coloured hair. I wanted to kiss her and had no option but to try the direct approach, which thankfully worked.

We sat in the park kissing for a few hours before she had to go home and get ready for work. We agreed to meet up again the following day. I caught a cab from Palermo back to the hostel wondering if I had I found my South American sweetheart. I wasn't sure but I really liked her.

Back at the hostel most people were having a quiet night. The next day was Australia day, and as over half of the people in the hostel were Australian it was considered a big occasion.

The seven Australian girls had arrived and told me that they were going to a water park called Central Norte to celebrate Australia day. They suggested that we should join them and it proved a good suggestion.

After passing a medical exam that consisted of raising our arms and showing the bottom of our feet to a man in a white coat, we got our stamps and were allowed into the park. Craig was made up, it was the first time in a while he had passed anything.

We met up with the girls and got settled by the side of the pool. I fancied one of the girls called Mel so was disappointed to learn that she had a boyfriend back home. Mel, like most Australian girls, had a great body. What set her apart was her nature. She was an open book and there was no arrogance about her; a rare commodity in a good looking person.

My first act of the day was to almost kill myself. I ran towards the pool at speed preparing a lavish dive to entertain the troops. The sight of a three-year-old child shoulder deep in the water was a clear indication that this was not a good idea. I realised at the last second that the pool was shallow and tried to slow down but it was too late.

I slipped on the edge of the pool and flipped up into the air backwards. I came crashing down into the water and yelped as my arse slammed onto the cemented base of the pool. It was agony but everyone found it hilarious.

The rest of the afternoon we enjoyed drinking in the sun and being in the company of good friends. Mark sat behind us with Maria; they looked like a married couple. She sat reading a French novel while his eyes darted around the park at other girls. I could see his mind racing and couldn't work out if he was happy or not, it was comical.

We decided against going clubbing that night and once more sat drinking in one of the rooms. Mark and Maria joined us after two days in the wilderness; it was good to have him back.

We left the hostel at 4:00am off our faces from a day of drinking and an evening of cocaine. Earlier that day at the park we had beaten a group of locals at football thanks to Mark's late winner. His two-yard tap-in had now transformed into a twenty-yard wonder goal.

Not happy with just football, it now seemed we were intent on beating Argentineans at a new game called 'Who can go out the latest', and I think we succeeded.

We found one of the few open bars in Palermo and sat drinking around an outside table for hours. Mark was falling around the bar insisting that he was a horrible person and not worthy of Maria's attention,

'You're a real woman and I, well I am a horrible person - a rotten man.'

She had no clue what he was talking about and sat on her chair embarrassed as he fell around the bar. The rest of us sat and laughed at him and he knocked over anything that wasn't screwed or bolted to the floor.

The bar advertised it was open twenty-four hours a day, so why it had locks on the doors I had no idea. I left with Harry and Sam as it began to get light around 7:00am. We had spotted Craig sloping off with a black Canadian girl from the hostel and each wondered what he was up to.

I stumbled back up to the dorm room and caught a glimpse of Craig scurrying out of Room 108 and through a fire exit. I was too tired to follow him and had no doubt he would tell me tomorrow.

I collapsed on my bed exhausted as two Australian girls who must have arrived that day sat up drinking wine and talking. It looked like they'd been taking drugs but who wasn't in this place. I ignored them and drifted off to sleep.

I was half woken from my slumber by one of the girls who whispered that her name was Sara. She pulled on my leg from her neighbouring bunk and said,

'I can't sleep, can I get in bed with you?'

I mumbled back at her unable to conjure up any words. I wasn't sure if this was real or just a dream. I pressed my face back into my pillow and forgot about it.

I heard a gentle shuffle by the side of my bed and woke as Sara climbed into my bed and under my single sheet wearing just her underwear. Unsure what to do I just let her join me as I was too tired to protest. Sara didn't want me going back to sleep. She looked at me and asked,

'Do you fancy a root?'

I wasn't sure what 'root' meant but jumped to the obvious assumption she meant sex. I groggily replied,

'I can't, I don't have any condoms, sorry,'

I turned away from her and faced the white wall of the room, closing my eyes for the second time. I felt her shuffling around behind me on the floor making it impossible to get back to sleep. I was so tired that I was unable to fully wake up. I turned round to see what she was doing. Sara held a condom in her hand like it was a medal and said,

'I've got one so no excuses, take off your pants.'

She tugged at my underwear as she removed her own. I was trapped in my bunk and wasn't sure what to do. I half expected to wake up laughing at what was a very real drug induced dream. I didn't wake up because I wasn't asleep, it was happening.

I accepted my fate and like a submissive kitten agreed that I should be raped. I removed my boxer shorts as Sara slid on the gold medal and climbed on top of me. As she impaled herself on my half erect penis she looked into my tired eyes and winced,

'Be careful it hurts. I've had too much sex recently.'

Her words made the experience all the more unpleasant. I was glad she had used a condom, at least my life wasn't in danger and it would all be over soon. Thankfully I was right, the ordeal only lasted a few minutes.

Sara wanted to try again and I wanted to kill myself. We met halfway and settled for a hug before I finally drifted back to sleep.

I woke up a few hours later with two dead arms and feeling of immense shame. It took ten minutes to regain enough feeling in my arms in order to turn myself over and get up. I left the room and went down to the bar where Craig was sat having breakfast on his own.

Before I could ask he was telling me what had happened with the Canadian. He'd had sex with her in the TV room on the bottom floor and, despite saying it was wrong, he found delight in telling me about it in detail. I found no delight in telling him about the details of my rape but I needed to tell someone. He thought it really funny and decided to point at me shouting over and over,

'You got raped!'

On reflection I did think it was pretty funny. Touching, hilarious and unforgettable; like being raped by a clown. I decided that rather than mope around the hostel I would ring Priscilla and meet up with her in Palermo again. She was pleased to hear from me.

We continued where we had left off the other day, lying in the park kissing and chatting about life. I was at total ease with her and felt so relaxed.

I found it strange that Priscilla and I got on so well. While physically I was attracted to her it felt like something more, we shared a connection. I was happy to have met her but knew it was not going to go anywhere. I put these thoughts to the back of my mind and enjoyed the present, without thinking about the future.

The next morning was my last in Buenos Aires; I spent it with Priscilla who acted as my personal tour guide. I finally made it to La Boca and Recoletta. We walked the narrow colourful streets as tourists revelled at tango dancers that danced up and down the streets.

Corrugated iron houses painted red and yellow flanked the paths and there was graffiti everywhere. Shops all sold football tops and celebrated the area's favourite football team: Boca Juniors. Market stalls sold jewellery, tea towels, clay pots and figures. The streets seemed to move and sway to the rhythm of salsa in a wash of colour, noise and atmosphere.

We walked around the Boca Juniors stadium as Priscilla took pictures of me pulling faces at the countless murals celebrating their country's favourite sporting son, Diego Maradona.

I let Priscilla order food and drinks at a small cafe in her perfect Spanish accent. I was experiencing the true nature of the city and loved it. After lunch we went back to the park and spent the afternoon lying once more on the grass.

With only two hours left until my coach left for Iguassu falls I walked Priscilla home for the first and last time. She hoped that her parents would not be home and told me how much she wanted to make love. I wasn't sure it would be making love but regardless, after all the titillation, I couldn't wait to get to her house.

She kissed me passionately at the door and smiled before gently letting herself in. I heard her talking and with that my stomach sunk. Her mother was in and she wanted to meet me. Instead of having sex as planned I found myself sat in Priscilla's kitchen as her mother poured me a large glass of coke. Her mother spoke no English so her conversation was difficult to follow. I found myself just agreeing with everything she asked, one question must have been,

'Would you like a tour of the house?'

And that is exactly what we did. I saw Priscilla's room but not in the way I had expected. Her mother acted as an estate agent and all I could do was laugh.

I kissed her goodbye and dangled the olive branch that I could perhaps return after Carnival.

I guess it just wasn't to be.

Iguassu Falls

The bus pulled away from Buenos Aires and I reflected on what a great time I'd had there. I had become close friends with Harry and Sam, been on dates with a local girl and made up with Craig. We had arranged to meet with Harry, Sam and Jules in Iguassu the following day.

The bus had an amazing cast. Craig and I sat laughing at the male bus attendant as he patrolled up and down the aisle of the bus. We ordered several small bottles of wine as Craig shouted,

'Oi trolley dolly, come over here.'

Mark sat in front of us listening to his iPod, oblivious to Maria who sat next to him. Something had happened between them but Mark wouldn't tell either of us what it was other than to say,

'It's something sexual.'

Craig and I sat for hours creating a list of possible outcomes. The list looked like this:

1. Strap on
2. Rape
3. Tied up and blindfolded
4. Gagged
5. Golden shower
6. Arse to mouth
7. Shaved each other
8. Enforced shit
9. Use of anal beads
10. Outside party involved
11. Mark drank cum from cup
12. Filmed the sordid affair
13. Use of foreign objects e.g. a baguette
14. Discovery of a small penis

We arrived in Iguassu around 1:00pm the following day after a comfortable fourteen-hour bus journey. We sat in large green leather seats that reclined to the point of almost being flat; it was transport heaven.

The hostel we wanted to stay at was predictably full so we had to come up with another option. We ended up in a hotel room that accommodated four people on the outskirts of town. The hotel was called Raices and it had a pool.

I could tell that things between Mark and Maria had turned sour. I suggested to Craig that we should give them both some space and go for a look around the small town. On the walk down into town we noticed that everywhere seemed to have a pool. It was hot and the blue water looked inviting.

Iguassu town was a humble laid-back place. All of the houses were low rise and simple in design, made mostly of wood and cement. It was a green town with plenty of trees and parks, the type of place where nobody got out of second gear. The contrast from Buenos Aires was immeasurable, we were in the country.

Craig was extremely competitive by nature and constantly looked for a challenge. If you were eating he wanted an eating competition. If you were tired he wanted a sleep off. It was as endearing as it was annoying, depending on what mood you were in.

I was in a good mood so over lunch we decided to see how many pools we could jump in on the way back to our hotel; we called it the 'The Pool Challenge'.

The first victim was a small hostel opposite the bus station called Marco Polo. We dived into the water fully clothed before being apprehended by security and asked to leave. Security came in the guise of a fifteen-year-old girl, so it wasn't exactly a hostile ejection.

In all we managed six different pools, one almost resulting in us being in the deep end with the law.

We ran through the grand marble reception of a posh hotel soaking wet and headed out towards the pool. As we threw ourselves into the water we heard someone shout from a distance. We surfaced to find two huge security guards standing over the pool in light brown uniforms with batons. Craig tried to reason with them by explaining in the only way he can by shouting,

'It's the pool challenge; our friend has offered us both $100 pesos to do this! So you see guys, we had no choice!'

They were not interested and threatened to call the police. We climbed out of the pool and were escorted off the premise by the guards with the disapproving faces of hostel guests watching on. Thankfully they let us off with a warning. It was a stupid way to spend an afternoon but it was good for me and Craig. I could tell he was still sorry about the email that he sent Mark as he brought it up whenever we were having fun.

'Sorry geez,' he sighed.

'Forget it wee man, it's gone,' I assured him.

We arrived back at the hotel soaking wet and smiling. Mark's face was the polar opposite. I asked him what had happened but he said nothing. Maria was sat in the room, the tension in there was unbearable so we left her and went into town to find an internet cafe.

I felt sorry for Maria but there was nothing that I could do. She had come out to see Mark and even the blind could see that things were not working between them. She had come along way looking for love and Mark was totally uninterested.

It was clear he had tried but I could tell that he resented her coming out to see him. He was still very much in love with his ex-girlfriend from back home and no one could fill that void, not even a beautiful French woman.

We returned to the hotel a few hours later to find that Maria had gone. She had taken her stuff with her so it was clear she was not coming back. We each felt guilty but at the same time it was a relief that she had gone. We lay in the room each on our own single bed, drinking the bottles of wine we had taken from the bus. We talked and caught up properly for the first time since going our separate ways in Mexico.

The whole trip should have been this way. The three of us taking on whatever this continent had to throw at us and laughing back at it. Perhaps for the last few months of the trip that would happen, there was no reason to think otherwise.

Mark finally buckled under the constant pressure Craig and I exerted on him and finally revealed what had happened in the bedroom with Maria. Before he did so Craig read out the list we had drawn up on the bus. He wanted to see if he had guessed correctly; it was the most excited I had seen him all trip. All fourteen of our scenarios were wrong.

Mark explained in graphic detail that during an anal session she had farted and covered both him and the sheets in shit. He told us the scene looked like someone had filled a whoopee cushion with brown sauce and jumped on it. Anal sex wasn't for pussies and he had to deal with it.

'Cost of a candle-lit dinner for two: $80 pesos.'

'Cost for theatre tickets: $100 pesos.'

'Cab fare home: $30 pesos.'

'The look on Mark's face as he explains heavily soiled sheets to reception: priceless.'

'There are some things money can't buy. For everything else there is Mark.'

The next morning we arsed around the hotel before finally getting a bus from town to Iguassu National Park.

Iguassu Falls were breathtaking. The powerful water cut through a calm tropical valley, it was a surreal sight. To me it resembled something from Jurassic Park; it was so beautiful it couldn't have been real, not in this world anyway. Despite the crowds of people it felt like I had discovered something new and wonderful. It was an untouched paradise in a world that had been robbed of its natural beauty.

The spray from the water cast a rainbow over the valley in the crisp blue summer sky. Around the waterfall everything was deep green, lush and full of life. I was for once lost for words and didn't know what to think.

At the start of my trip I had visited Niagara Falls and was impressed by what I had seen. I stood in front of Iguassu and felt sorry for it. Niagara was the girl next door, Iguassu was the exotic temptress.

Mark wouldn't speak to me for most of the day as I chose to wear the Argentina top that I had bought with Priscilla. He was deeply patriotic about England, threatening to throw me and the shirt to a watery grave through Craig - his interpreter.

The more time we spent in the national park the more likely it was that we would start messing around; it came in the form of a three way photo. I sat my camera on a nearby rock and set the timer as we pulled off a three way 'Mangina' with aplomb. This involved each of us tucking our penises between our legs to create the illusion of a lady's vagina. Luckily nobody saw us.

After an adrenaline-fuelled ride on a speedboat into the mouth of the Falls, we made our way back to the hotel in high spirits after seeing such a breathtaking place.

We met up with Harry, Sam and Jules that night, unlike us they had managed to get into one of the better hostels in the town, Marco Polo. We told them how impressive the waterfall was before informing them we planned to leave the following morning for Brazil.

We proceeded to get plastered as was always the case when we all met up. After drinking a couple of bottles of vodka at their hostel we ended up downtown in a club called Cuba Libra.

A beautiful Argentinean girl joined us who I had been speaking to at an earlier bar. She was apprehensive about going to the club as her ex-boyfriend was working there. I thought nothing of it, which proved to be a mistake.

I danced around in the club with her and Harry when I suddenly felt a fist crash into the back of my head. As I fell to the ground I caught site of the girl running for the exit, her white dress lit up in the florescent glare of the lights in the club.

As I stumbled in a confused drunken state to my feet I felt a large pair of arms wrap around my neck. I was dragged across the dance floor by my throat and thrown out of the club onto the street like a ragged doll. I sat on a curb outside nursing my head as muffled music escaped through the double doors.

Harry had reacted to what he had seen and within minutes was sat on the curb with me confused but laughing,

'You looked like Jesus man, cruelly ejected with your arms in the air. Sorry mate but it was fucking funny.'

I woke the next morning with wet hair, half naked in bed with Jules. Mark was next to us lying on the floor in the foetal position. Once again I was scratching my head as to what had happened.

I looked at my watch and jumped from my confused slumber. It was 10:00am and our bus was leaving for Brazil in an hour.

'Mark you tit, we need to get going or we are going to miss our fucking bus!' I yelled.

'Urgh,' was his drawn out response.

The commotion woke Harry and Sam who just lay on their beds laughing at us. Sam sat up and looked at both of us with his glazed eyes,

'Do you guys remember walking past the bus station naked last night?'

We both stared blankly at him saying nothing.

'We will catch up with you guys in Brazil. Top night as always.'

We left their room and ran back up the hill to our hotel where Craig was waiting. We were still steaming drunk from the night out that had not ended until 7:00am. None of us could be bothered to pay the bill so we packed our bags and just walked away from the hotel to the bus station.

Waiting for us at the station was the owner of the hotel, he did not look pleased,

'You have not paid for your final night's stay at the hotel seniors!' he barked.

I ignored the man and looked at Mark,

'I thought you had paid it mate?'

Mark looked at Craig,

'You got it didn't you?'

Craig looked at the irate hotel owner and said,

'I thought Gaz had sorted it, sorry mate our mistake.'

He handed the man $60 pesos and apologised for the mix up. We got onto the bus just as it was about to leave the platform.

The Bus to Brazil

We left Iguassu at 11:00am safe in the knowledge that the bus was to be our home for the next twenty hours. However, it didn't fill me with any excitement. I still felt like I was out in Iguassu as my head was drowning in alcohol. I remembered why I had woken up with wet hair as the memory of hurling my naked body into the hostel's swimming pool flashed through my mind.

Mark, Craig and I sat at the back of the bus like three naughty school children and we were joined by two Australian girls that had got onboard. They had more friends near the front of the bus.

Bus journeys form a big part of any trip to South America. The continent's size was huge so it took a long time to get around. Mark and I frequently discussed that on one journey we should get absolutely hammered. As we were already halfway there, this was to be that journey.

'Mate let's beat the hangover and get fucked,' he said.

'I'm game if Craig is in. Not sure he could drink again though,' I replied.

'Fuck off, I'll drink double what you do you northern monkey,' he contested.

I looked across the aisle and introduced myself to the Australian girls.

'Hi girls I'm Gaz, where are you going to?' I asked.

'Florianopolis, where the bus is going,' was the sarcastic response.

'It so happens that we are going there too. We should celebrate?' I suggested.

'With what exactly?'

They had a good point, regardless I continued,

'At the next stop we shall go buy some wine, you fancy getting pissed?

'Yeah why not, nothing else to do.'

'Hey girls come back here these guys are getting some wine,' they shouted down the aisle towards their friends.

One of the girls, Katy, joined me on my seat as she apparently wanted to listen to my iPod. I used her shoulder as a pillow and had an hour's sleep until the first stop. I was sure that she liked me as she had a perfectly good iPod of her own. Katy had dark features and beautifully soft skin; I hoped my instincts were correct as I liked her and her iPod too.

We pulled up at a small station in a little town and were told we had thirty minutes until the bus was due to leave for Brazil.

I was now in two minds about drinking as, despite being in a stupid mood, the hangover was taking hold. Mark and Craig felt exactly the same. Had the girls not been on the bus and keen to drink we would not have bothered. Mark echoed this thought,

'We have a chance here boys, they are all well up for it.'

We scoured the town looking for booze but around each corner, down each street were rows of closed stores as it was Sunday, the day of rest. We began thinking that this wasn't going to be our day. We sat on a metal bench in the village square running out of ideas and time.

Craig spotted a restaurant in the top corner of the square and suggested that we go in and ask if anything was open. The restaurant was empty apart from an old Italian looking man that sat on a wooden stool by the door.

'Ola Amigo, comme estas?' screamed Craig.

'Bien, bien,' he replied.

'Donestas el Vino?' quizzed Mark.

'Aqui,' was the gentleman's response.

The man lowered himself from his stool and took us inside the restaurant. We had hit the jackpot; a bottle of wine cost $5 pesos. Unsure how many to get, we decided to put in $20 pesos each and buy two cases, equating to twelve bottles.

We arrived back at the bus station with the boxes of wine, sweating like three men in leather trousers. The girls looked on in horror when they saw just how much alcohol we had bought. It was going to be a good trip.

Katy was joined by Siobhan, Claire and Caffa, who seemed almost as crazy as us. As the bus drove towards the Brazilian border we made inroads into the wine.

Mark got out the iPod speakers and as we continued drinking the bus turned from the conventional to the unconventional; it had become our very own party bus.

Mark and Craig sat enjoying themselves absolutely steaming and covered in red wine that had spilled onto their clothes, as I sat letting Katy cover my face in make-up. I caught people looking up the bus towards the commotion we were all creating. For some of them it must have been a nightmare, I walked down the aisle insisting that everyone should join us.

We stopped briefly at a service station a few miles from the border and the party spilled from the bus onto the road. Mark, Craig and I were out of control and the girls were not far behind. We handed out plastic cups of wine to other passengers and ran around like we had just escaped from a lunatic asylum. I wore a selection of clothes supplied by the girls, totally forgetting that were about to cross an international border. The state I was in I had no chance of entering Brazil.

The bus stopped suddenly two miles down the road from the services where we had had all that fun. Everyone looked out the side windows to see what the holdup was but nobody could see a thing. There was no traffic and it didn't feel like we had broken down, it was a total mystery. We sat by the side of the motorway for a few minutes in silence until we saw the driver opening the luggage hatches under the bus.

I noticed that he was now joined by several armed police officers, something was clearly amiss. I looked at the girls laughing and said,

'You better not have anything in your bags, the police are here!'

Another couple of minutes passed before two police officers climbed onto the bus and into the aisle. They scanned up and the down the coach before calling out the following seat numbers.

'155 and 153.'

My broad drunken smile evaporated in an instant as they continued,

'Jones and O'Conner.'

I looked at Craig in shock but as I was drunk I didn't realise how serious it could be, surely there had just been a mix-up. I rocked onto my now unstable feet and waved to the passengers on the bus as I fell down the aisle,

'See you all later, it's been emotional, remember to write me in prison.'

I stood outside on a grass verge as one of the policemen pointed towards my bag and motioned for me to open it. Luckily for Craig it was my bag they were interested in so he was very much in the clear. Deep down I wished it had been the other way around.

I stood covered in eyeliner and girls mascara wearing some black pyjama bottoms and a tight blue vest with 'Tenerife' across the front as a uniformed police officer began to tug at the red zip on my bag.

I saw everyone on the bus clambering over one another to see what was going on. Had they weighed more the bus would have fell on its side and crushed us on the side of the road. As the officer went through my bag I was genuinely concerned as I did not remember packing my bag that morning, and had not checked through it since Buenos Aires.

I hid the sinking feeling that engulfed my stomach by performing to the watching crowd. As the officer bent down to rifle through my things I foolishly stood behind him and pretended I was riding him like a pony while he was concentrating on the contents of my luggage.

I stood back and as the time passed I became less and less concerned, if there had of been anything in my bag they would have found it.

The officer took a bottle of talc powder from my bag and emptied the content onto the concrete floor. A small pile rested on his finger which he lent down to sniff. I was in the clear.

Satisfied that they had thrown all my clothes onto the road and grass verge they then instructed me to pack my things and get back onto the bus.

I returned up the stairs onto the bus in my mind a hero, inside my heart was racing. I was a maverick; I had come face to face with the law and won.

We crossed the border into Brazil without incident and at around midnight we stopped for dinner. As everyone got off the bus and faded into the darkness, Katy and I stayed onboard.

We kissed each other properly for the first time and couldn't keep our hands off each other. She must have thought I was a wild rogue who acted and did as he pleased; I wasn't going to tell her the truth.

Things got heated quickly but then out of the corner of her eye she spotted that one other person had chose to stay on the bus. I looked over and saw that a disabled girl with a wheel chair was craning her head and looking in our direction. I told Katy to ignore her but knew that it was impossible to do so. It wasn't like we could have asked her to leave. I don't know about you, but I'm sick of seeing disabled people being pushed around.

Katy climbed off me and we sat waiting for the guys to return from the service station. They returned with a bottle of peach schnapps and vodka. The rest of the journey ebbed away with sleep, memory loss and the comfort of a beautiful Australian pillow.

Mark lay passed out in the aisle while Craig spent the night snuggling up to a six foot Israeli man called Italie.

We arrived in Florianopolis six hours later than scheduled; it had been an eventful twenty-six-hour bus ride that was for sure.

BRAZIL

Florianopolis

Tired and hungover, we went with the girls to a hostel in Florianopolis they had booked, assuming we could join them. It turned out the hostel was full so the three of us were unable to stay. I looked and Craig and said,

'Never assume because it makes an **ass** out of **u** and **me.**'

'Shut up you mug,' he shouted with a playful grin across his face.

'I feel like an ass,' grumbled Mark as we walked aimlessly up the street.

We eventually found a hostel a few hours and pints of sweat later that sat above the rest of the town up a large hill.

The hostel clung to a cliff face overlooking the natural lagoon of Lagoa da Conceição; the views were breathtaking. Florianopolis was clearly an affluent place; the pretty receptionist confirmed this by telling us the cost of the dorm per person, per night was $60rls.

'What a robbery, that is about £20 in my money,' shouted Craig.

'Let's just book a few nights. Look at the place, it's well nice,' suggested Mark.

We dropped our bags in the room and decided to head straight for Praia Mole, which was the nearest beach to the hostel. The beach was a place I had dreamt about for months. I remembered being stuck in a cold van on the mountains surrounding Machu Picchu for thirty long hard hours; I deserved a beach and I couldn't wait to get there.

I had an image set in my mind about the beaches in Brazil; scores of hot, sexy women straddled the coast line as groups of men played football on the scorching hot sand. For the first time this trip I was not to be disappointed, as we stepped onto the sand at Praia Mole it was everything I had imagined.

I walked down the beach with Craig and Mark and saw the postcard image of four girls lying on beach towels in thongs several times. Everywhere I looked scantily clad women were smiling and having a good time. Men played football by the surf where the sand was firmer, they rolled around like children laughing. It was a vibrant place bursting with colour and oiled with life.

We settled down outside one of several bars that sat at the back of the beach and had a much needed rest. Brazil was going to be an expensive destination but I knew it was going to be the best. It was country that felt so alive.

We bumped into Katy and the girls who joined us for the afternoon. I sat happily people watching for most of the afternoon and appreciated every second.

The next morning I woke up looking like the elephant man. Something had bit my left eye in the night, resulting in some major swelling. I went up for breakfast clutching my face where I was greeted by Harry, Sam and Jules, newly arrived from Iguassu.

It was the first time I had seen Jules since mysteriously waking up next to her in Iguassu, I could only guess what she must have been thinking.

After breakfast I went down to the beach, filling the three of them with lofty expectations about how busy and good it really was,

'Harry it's amazing, like Bondi beach on steroids!' I boasted.

'What loads of muscle men walking about is there? Bet you like that.'

'Fuck off, it's just class mate, you will see.'

We cut through a narrow path onto the beach and it was practically deserted. It was as if moments earlier the sea had come ashore and eaten everyone in sight. I stood at the far end of the beach puzzled. Harry and Sam were not bothered, being from Sydney they had grown up by the coast so to them it was not a big deal.

'A beach is a beach Gazza,' Sam summarised.

Despite his words I was gutted. The atmosphere and buzz from the previous day had been swept away; the beach was an empty stadium. We were joined on Praia Mole by other people from the hostel including an Australian called Lee, who had taken a shine to me after I completed another of Mark's now infamous bets.

Lee took great pleasure in seeing me run towards the hostile water at full speed before throwing myself into a series of powerful waves. Florianopolis is an annual site for the World Surfing Championships and without a surf board I was thrown about like cheap meat. Several times the water churned me up before spitting me back out onto the beach.

Disorientated after several attempts in the water I gave up. As I managed to get to my feet a huge wave smashed against the back of my head and sent me down onto the sandy sea bed. As the current tried to pull me away from the coast I got up and made a dash for the shore. I was glad to get back to my towel in one piece and felt I deserved the modest applause.

'That was fucking horrible,' I lamented as I coughed up more sea water.

The waves really were ferocious and there was no way I was going back in. Maybe they had eaten everyone just before we arrived? Stranger things have happened.

On the evening we went to a local Sushi restaurant that sat close to the hostel. They were offering an all you can eat buffet so we rounded up people from the hostel and went down.

Mark for the second time that day announced in front of everyone that I was to undertake a challenge,

'Mate I implore you to eat as much wasabi as you possibly can,' he said as he called over the waiter.

'Can you get my friend a big piece of wasabi please?' He continued.

I had no option but to accept the challenge as earlier in the day I had stated that wasabi was not hot and would not be a problem. The waiter came back with a green lump the size of a golf ball. I stared at it and laughed,

'Why do I get myself into these situations?'

The waiter looked at me in amazement as I took the soft ball from his hand. He agreed to give me a free beer if I could do it and he also wanted to film it on his camera to show his friends. There was no backing out and I had to succeed.

The first piece I broke off hit the back of my throat and went down without a problem, but the more I ate the thicker and hotter it became. By the halfway point my mouth was plastered with what felt like a concrete mix and looked like a year's worth of snot. Spurred on by the partisan crowd now banging their cutlery on the marble table and chanting, I took a big breath and rushed the final few mouthfuls. I completed the challenge in less than two minutes and could now sit back and accept the plaudits.

I sat with a burning green flame in my stomach so was unable to eat as much sushi as I had planned; the challenge had been a bad idea. In Palenque I drank some hot sauce, more to bond with Mark than anything else. I was troubled that he still had this power to make me do things. Maybe it was time he did something?

After the meal I went to bed as I was unable to shake off the burning sensation in my stomach. During the night I found it impossible to sleep as I wasn't drunk and it was far too hot. I lay sweating with fever-like symptoms as my mind raced around in frustration.

Mark, who had gone out with the Australian lads, came in and broke the silence at 5:00am yelling,

'I love you, you are a legend sir, come here!'

He grabbed my face and tried to kiss me before he collapsed onto his bed and fell to sleep instantly. I sat up in the darkness of the room wondering what I could do.

I woke up at 8:00am and could not hear anything as my ears closed shut. I walked into town to a pharmacist and, after some baffling dialogue, acquired some ear drops.

With Priscilla's help I had got to grips with the Spanish language and now in Brazil, I learned that everyone spoke Portuguese. I thought that the two languages were similar, I was unfortunately wrong. With only another month of my trip to go it seemed stupid to attempt to learn another language; the little Spanish I now knew had taken long enough.

I walked along the lagoon staring out at the numerous boats before making my way back over the hill past the hostel to the beach. I had my iPod on full volume but I could barely hear the music. It felt like I was wearing ear muffs instead of headphones and I was deeply concerned.

I sat at the beach with Lee from the hostel cursing my luck and hoping that my ears were going to be ok. I stared out to the ocean trying to relax as Lee stared at me like a lost dog. I could tell he was waiting for me to do something entertaining but I wasn't in the mood. I threw him a stick but he didn't move; he wanted to play football.

I liked Lee as he was a kind lad who had done a lot of travelling and was at ease talking to anyone. It was clear to everyone except me that he had developed a man crush. I had known him for two days and he already referred to me as 'The Legend', despite the fact I had done nothing to deserve such an accolade.

I felt uncomfortable at him referring to me as 'The anything'. It was something that should be reserved for people of importance like 'The King' or 'The Queen.' I was sure that he wasn't the latter of the two. Lee was just a nice harmless bloke and the lads had him all wrong. It was like thinking of a dolphin as a gay shark.

The weather turned nasty so by mid-afternoon I was back at the hostel. I returned to the sight of Mark and Harry in the pool smoking cigarettes and drinking. They had been smoking and drinking all day, I decided to join them.

They were joined by a guy called Woody who we had met the previous evening at the hostel bar; he was from Adelaide in Southern Australia. Woody looked like a polar bear in sunglasses, he was the whitest Australian I had ever seen, his pale skin matched by his white blonde hair. He reminded me of my first rabbit, Snowy.

Craig had jokingly asked him,

'Are you wearing glasses to cover up your red eyes?'

We were slightly disappointed that his eyes were hazel in colour. Woody wasn't an albino but he could have passed for one. We all sat in the small pool that overlooked the huge lagoon and got blind drunk on cheap vodka as rain thrashed down from above.

After three bottles of vodka and a shower we all rolled down the hill and into town. It was my first proper night out since Iguassu. The first bar resembled an American themed saloon. We sat at a table where I was propositioned by a couple of girls for kisses. I was tempted but something told me that they both looked a bit young. I found out they were aged twelve and fourteen. Together they were twenty-six but whatever way I looked at it, it was wrong, so I politely declined and wished them well.

All the bars were expensive; Florianopolis was a popular tourist spot not just for travellers but for Brazilians. We realised after a few drinks at the bar that you were able to drink out on the street. I looked out onto the road and saw a series of poor street sellers with white cool boxes full of small beer cans. The street was as busy as the bars so it made sense to go outside.

We stood around drinking and talking complete rhubarb to locals. I found just like in Argentina I had a famous look-a-like in Brazil; Internacional footballer Fernandao. The night failed to take off. We drank more and more in the hope something would happen but it didn't, we all just got really drunk for the sake of being drunk.

The three of us missed the bus stop outside the hostel as we chatted with some amorous Argentinean women. Harry realised a few minutes later as the bus sped down the hill that we had passed the hostel and asked the driver to stop the bus. We had to walk up to the hostel and were all battered.

Woody and Harry chose to walk back to the hostel naked while playing chicken with oncoming cars. I could only imagine what the locals must have thought, as out of nowhere their headlights centred on a thirteen-stone human polar bear running towards them with blue boxer shorts over his head. I could already tell that Woody was going to fit in well, like the rest of us he just wanted to have fun.

Whilst a beautiful place there wasn't an awful lot to do in Floripa (Florianopolis) apart from sunbathe due to our tight budget. The next day I spent around the hostel as it did nothing but rain. It stopped by early evening so a few of us went out to alleviate the boredom.

Mark and Craig decided to stay in so I was joined by Harry, Sam and Woody. We sat down by the edge of lagoon at the bottom of the hill and drank a bottle of Jagermeister between the four of us. After a few days drinking we needed something strong as each of us were convinced that we would be unable to get pissed.

Half an hour later we were all staggering along the promenade that ran alongside the lagoon into town.

I woke the next morning in a green room with a roaring headache and no memory of the night that had landed me in such a situation. I peered out of the bedroom window like a prisoner of war and tried to logically piece together where it was I could be. I couldn't think of anything.

Out of the small window all I could see was a drive. On the drive sat two motorbikes; one green the other black. Past the drive was a narrow dirt track that ran to the right and left and was bordered by a wooden fence and further housing. I was clearly lost in suburbia.

I edged towards the sliding door of the bedroom and pressed my infected ear against the wood; I could make out two female voices. I decided that I had no option but to go out and see who I was dealing with. I slid the door along its rickety metal spindle and stared a few metres along the hall and into the kitchen. I stood in sheer bewilderment as I recognised the people in front of me and instantly felt at ease. It was Tahlia and Mimi.

I had bumped into them on the way into town and after a similar night of drinking on the street I was unable to walk home. It all made perfect sense. I wasn't sure if anything had happened with Tahlia and I didn't ask. I grabbed my clothes and headed straight to the doctors as my ears had gotten worse.

I sat in the doctor's surgery for over an hour before I was greeted by an English speaking doctor. I was growing inpatient as, unlike the previous few days, there were beautiful blue skies over the town. The doctor had the clear efficient look of a killer. She asked me to follow her down the hall.

I walked into the consultation room and explained to the doctor what had happened to my ears,

'I was surfing and a wave crashed against my head,' I said.

'You need to take ear drops for three days and it should clear up. There will be water in there,' she told me in an informative matter.

'Yeah I already have those drops. They haven't worked, can't you syringe my ears?' I enquired.

'That would mean hospital and very expensive, maybe try antibiotics?'

'Ok yes, I would like antibiotics,' I agreed.

'You buy them from the pharmacy,' she told me.

She passed me a piece of paper that simply read: Antibioticos.

It was the second Portuguese word I learnt after 'obrigardo', meaning thank you.

The doctor wore a white lab coat and looked to be in her mid thirties. She was lightly tanned with dark eyes and jet black hair that was tied tightly back in a ponytail. Her eyes narrowed as she passed me the instructions for the antibiotics and to my horror the bill,

'Senor here is the instructions for your treatment and the bill for my time.'

I gazed at the receipt as the figure of $190rls stabbed me in the heart,

I looked up with a smile and quizzed the doctor,

'What is the reason for the charge? $190rls is a lot of money!'

She looked calm as if there was nothing wrong with the figure and assured me,

'It is for my years of study in medicine.'

I resisted the urge to tell her to 'Fuck off' and instead continued,

'That is fine; my insurance actually covers such incidents, would I be able to make a call to them to check?'

'Yes, there is a payphone in the reception,' she informed.

'I will be back shortly, obrigardo.'

I rose from the cheap plastic seat I had been sitting on and casually opened the large white door of the office, making my way back to the reception area. I looked over my shoulder to check that the doctor had not followed me and made my way past the phone and through the exit. I got onto the street outside the practice and ran up the dirt track and onto the main shopping square. There would be no money changing hands.

I got back to the hostel and spent the day recovering while thinking about the end of my trip. I played with the idea of going back to Buenos Aires to see Priscilla, we had stayed in touch through the internet and seemed to be getting on great. I was confused about my feelings towards her and the prospect of going back to my life in England. I wasn't sure what I wanted and being hungover made it all the worse.

That afternoon Mark and Craig suggested we took Tahlia and Mimi up on their kind offer of a place to stay. They had told me that we could stay for a few nights free of charge in their spare room. I was against the idea but reluctantly agreed.

That night but I chose to stay in and have some time to myself. I sat in the girls' kitchen writing my diary and taking stock of everything that had happened so far on the trip.

I was woken up at 3:00am by Craig who had returned to the flat and was screaming 'Hold me', right into my ear.

He then questioned whether or not I loved him, before scuttling out the small green room and sliding the door shut. He went into the kitchen as I drifted off into an awkward, sweaty sleep.

Florianopolis had trapped us into the routine of a beach holiday. The days, weather permitting, were spent on the beach recovering from a night of heavy drinking and it was proving a tough cycle to break.

Craig spent most of the next day worrying that he had contracted a life-threatening sexual disease as he had slept with Mimi after leaving me in the green room the previous night. The reason for the drama was that Mimi had slept with Mark in Mexico. Craig knew better than most about Mark's sexual escapades and I did little to dilute his worry,

'You probably have something Craig but at least you are now custard cousins. It could be worse, who knows who she has slept with?'

'Leave it out mate, I am seriously going under,' he quietly replied.

I bumped into Katy and Caffa on the beach, who I had not seen since arriving in Florianopolis at the start of the week. I arranged to meet up with them that evening on another part of the Island called Barra Da Lagoa, about fifteen minutes past Praia Mole by bus.

Mark and Craig felt rough from the previous night so I got a bus up to Sunset Backpackers to meet up with Woody, who had become a firm friend. We had a few beers at the hostel as the sun set over the lagoon before making our way down to Barra.

We got off the bus by the side of a small beach soccer pitch laid behind a high wire fence, where two local teams were playing in front of a couple of hundred spectators. The floodlights shone onto the pitch, lighting up the sand and casting large moving shadows.

The atmosphere was great, I wasn't sure what was at stake but it felt like a final. For the last ten minutes of the game I could feel the spirit and passion for football in Brazil. The overenthusiastic commentator screamed over the speaker system throughout the match, neither Woody nor I had any idea what he was saying but it was entertaining.

With only a minute left on the clock one of the players in yellow picked up on a loose ball. He flicked it into the air with his right foot before crashing a volley into the bottom left corner of the net from twenty yards. The crowd went wild as the commentator shrieked one word for a solid thirty seconds without taking a breath,

'Goooooaaaalllll!'

That was the winning goal, the match ended 6-5 to the team in yellow. As the crowd dispersed into the night Woody and I stayed in the temporary stand drinking a bottle of vodka we had picked up earlier from the supermarket.

I went onto the pitch and played football with some young Argentineans who were in Florianopolis on holiday. It was extremely hard to play because I was drunk. While I represented Queen and country on the pitch, Woody ran off to get some cocaine from a local dealer he had heard about.

Woody returned smiling so I knew that he had got some drugs. He suggested that we should meet some of his friends that were staying close to the beach. His friends were staying in a small holiday shed a few minutes from where we were so I agreed.

Though it was only a few minutes walk, it took us half an hour to reach the house. I had started chatting to a couple of Argentinean gypsies who were selling bracelets by the side of the road. As I spoke with them I handed them the vodka which they poured into their mouths like it was water.

Gypsies travelled around South America on an even tighter budget than mine. They effectively travelled and survived on nothing. Every day they set up on street corners, by the beach and outside bars selling handmade bracelets and bangles.

Unable to afford accommodation, they had no choice but to sleep outside. They could only eat or move to another place when their finances dictated they could. They had no grand plans; their aim was to travel as much and for as long as they could. It was an approach to life that I admired. Each of them had such a free spirit and as they explained their belief systems to me they enjoyed drinking mine.

What I didn't admire about these gypsies was their hygiene. On reflection giving gypsies with black teeth vodka wasn't the best of ideas. I didn't resent them wrapping their mouths over the bottle but knew that I would no longer be doing the same. I air-poured afterwards just to be safe as the last thing I needed was another ailment. I imagined it was similar to sharing dinner with a prostitute. I joked with Woody about the time I took a hooker for dinner,

'I gave her my peas and she gave me herpes.'

We arrived at the rented wooden green house laughing and ready to start some serious drinking.

We walked up to the holiday shack and were greeted by a large Australian bloke who called himself Pringle. He showed us into the flat and offered both of us a large line of cocaine, which I felt I had to accept. The lines were racked up on a small coffee table in the back room and there were a lot of them, it looked like a miniature race track.

Pringle had numerous tattoos on his body, one of which was the moustached Pringle character. He was talking about getting more; 'Once you pop, you can't stop' I thought. I wished that he had a different name like Richard and imagined him showing us a dick that he'd had tattooed on his arm.

We sat around talking nonsense drinking and taking drugs. The house sat at the start of a narrow walkway that went all the way down to Barra beach. The advantage was that we could see everyone walking past and thus engage with people that looked interesting. It was good to be around new people for a change, without Mark and Craig.

I decided to take a walk down to the beach, and so left Woody at the flat. I had heard that there were always parties down there and was eager to see for myself. On route I heard someone shouting from a balcony up the rocky headland,

'Gazza you gay.'

I looked up and saw Harry smiling down at me. He was drinking with the three Australian girls from Buenos Aires, Nikki, Louise and Claire. I joined them on the balcony for a couple of drinks. They were joined by Gemma who I had not seen since Buenos Aires. I couldn't help but feel sorry for Gemma.

Gemma seemed a determined girl who was at ease in her own company. At the start of the trip I found her dominating and rude. I still did but I had softened to her. Gemma was a kind girl but when she got drunk she changed. It was her drunken alter ego that had managed to ostracise her gradually from everyone that she met. She was impossible to travel with.

Harry and I went to the beach that sat in a tight rocky cove. On the beach sat a mix of travellers and hippies smoking marijuana and staring up at the clear night sky. Muffled conversations gave way to crashing waves and peaceful benevolence.

Harry and I sat and had a few beers before deciding to go back up to the house. As we climbed the steep path I bumped into Katy and Caffa. They had been to a big club in town and had just come back looking for a party.

I still had a soft spot for Katy. I knew that she had a boyfriend back home but still felt I was in with a chance. I walked the two of them back to their apartment that fell further in land away from the beach and overlooked the huge bay. Caffa was hilarious, climbing into bins and flying around the streets, but Katy was strangely subdued and quiet.

I sat with the girls on their balcony talking about anything that happened to spill into my mind as the sun rose over the island. Darkness gave way to a hue of orange as the mist over the ocean began to clear. The air felt fresh and the oxygen invaded my lungs, making me feel wide awake and alert.

Despite the air, physically I was dog tired and asked the girls if I could stay at theirs. Caffa jumped excitedly off her plastic chair and said,

'Yes, of course you can funny man.'

While Katy grumbled,

'I guess but I'm off to bed and you can't come with me.'

Caffa kindly offered me her bed, consisting of a small mattress on the floor in the kitchen. It looked like a human dog basket. While I curled up for the night she elected to stay outside on the balcony but not for too long.

I couldn't sleep due to the drugs and felt bad knowing Caffa had given up her bed. I was physically exhausted so could not be bothered to walk home and doubted the buses would run so early in the morning. I went outside and told her to come in,

'Caffa you dick come inside, you have the mattress and I'll just sleep on the floor honestly it's cool.'

After slight resistance she responded,

'Yeah, ok cool,' and giggled.

Caffa was a tiny girl who I had gotten on really well with as I liked people with a good energy. She was the type that could make you smile in even the worst of situations just by being herself.

Caffa was dressed in a small French maid's outfit with black tights and tiny shoes. She had long blonde dreadlocks and while not my type, dressed how she was, I couldn't help but think something would happen. I was right.

We ended up having sex in the dog basket. I lay there as she took control of everything. I couldn't help but think about Katy in the other room but she had a boyfriend and Caffa was a lot of fun.

Afterwards I lay on the floor sweating as she fell asleep on my chest. The inevitable hangover and comedown began to take hold and I needed to leave; I needed to get back to my friends.

I got back to the girls' flat in town for 11:00am. I was mindful that we had been asked to leave after the neighbours had complained to the landlord about the noise. Mark stood in the front garden with his bags and looked at me in shock.

'Fucking hell mate where have you been, we've got to do that move you know. Where did you end up last night, we couldn't find you anywhere?' he quizzed.

He had asked too many questions so I just mumbled incomprehensively at him and grabbed my bags. Tahlia had kindly arranged another place for us to stay as she was sleeping with the Brazilian landlord. He was only too pleased to assist us.

We had decided to stay in Florianopolis for two more nights before heading to Rio. In truth I had wanted to leave for Rio days before but not strongly enough to say anything about it. We still had loads of time to get to Salvador so there was no need to rush.

We checked into some doting old woman's house about a quarter of a mile from the girls' apartment in a residential area. Craig decided that he wanted to leave and announced that he was going to Sao Paulo,

'Lads I can't afford Rio or Carnival in Salvador so I am going to a moody little gaff near Sao Paulo to stay with a girl I met in Guatemala.'

'Don't Craig, it will be shit and she probably won't sleep with you,' said Mark.

'At least come to Rio with us mate. Football on the Copacabana, the Christ statue, don't be a tit mate you will regret it,' I stated.

It was no use, he had made up his mind and there was no changing it. I offered little resistance in trying to get him to stay.

Craig was selective over who he liked and who he wished to spend time with. He did what he liked and despite his faults I respected him for that. Mark and I had arranged to meet up with Kash and Nash for Carnival and I knew this was a major reason behind his decision. Craig simply did not like either of them.

He left Mark and I on the beach that day with a loose promise of perhaps seeing us in Rio before our planned flights home on the 9th March. The reality of that happening was small.

As the afternoon went on I couldn't help but worry about my journey coming to an end. I was sat on a warm sandy beach leering at ladies and drinking beer without a care in the world. In just four weeks I was going to be sat back at my parents' house watching Ant and Dec on TV as the rain fell outside. I wondered if anything had changed or if everything would just be how it was before.

I felt my mind reattaching to the thought of home like a tractor beam and my natural instinct was to fight against the pull. I still had four weeks to enjoy, I still had Carnival to experience and I still had Rio de Janeiro.

The old lady that rented out her flat had kindly asked us to look after her home for the next few days and unfortunately we didn't.

We had asked Harry, Sam and Jules if they wanted to move in for a few nights in order to spread the cost. I cooked us all beef chilli for dinner to celebrate our new abode. Mark and I were temporarily housemates.

A nice dinner turned into an unorganised party as Sam came back from the shop with three bottles of Natasha Vodka. We were joined by six travellers from the hostel, one that looked and acted exactly like Hollywood movie star Will Ferrell, he was a genius. Will was so enthusiastic about the smallest of things you couldn't help but smile.

'Shall we all have a shot?' I suggested.

'Yeah good shout,' replied Harry.

'YEAH too fucking right, awesome idea man!' bellowed Will.

This routine continued throughout the night. At some point I decided it was a good idea to cool off so tried to climb into the fridge. After removing the trays and successfully carrying out this stunt I thought that Will was going to have a heart attack; it was funny but he really needed to cool his boots.

'That is the best fucking thing I have ever seen in my life,' he bellowed across the room.

By 1:00am the old lady's flat was covered in booze and broken glass. We gave it a temporary rest by going into town but as the heavens opened outside we found ourselves flooding back there in a flash.

All of us were hammered. My head was in pieces as nonsense just slurred from my open mouth and my eyes narrowed and began to wander. I decided to sit down and fall back into the inviting couch.

Just as I decided to throw in the towel and go to bed I was lucky enough to witness what was the funniest moment of an already hilarious trip. It had taken over four months to happen.

The flat had a small spiral staircase that was almost impossible to climb given its size. At the top lay an attic with three beds. These were the three we had kindly offered to Harry, Sam and Jules. Mark decided that he wanted to go up to have a look at their room.

'I'm going up there to have a look at your manor,' he garbled.

I had only seen him crouch this much during the mine experience in Potosi. Mark, like me, had a tendency to take off his clothes when he was drunk. He ascended the small staircase wearing only his unfeasibly large boxer shorts. As he climbed he hit his head on the metal stairs circling above his six and a half foot frame. He yelped,

'Fuck off you stupid fucking stairs.'

'Watch your head Mark,' Harry joked.

We were all sat on the couch just watching him scale the stairs like some inquisitive Neanderthal. Mark turned and said,

'You what you silly cunt?'

As he did this he slid his legs between two of the staircases spindles and was now sat down on one of the wooden steps looking through the bars at us. He was about five feet off the ground and looked like a giant baby in a high chair. We were all in stitches of laughter.

Mark smiled down at us waving his legs in the air in drunken delight. He tried to move to come back down and then the realisation hit him. He was stuck.

'I can't move. I'm stuck, I'm fucking stuck,' he shouted.

He wasn't getting any sympathy from us. Rather than help I decided to get out my camera and film what was surely a once in a lifetime event. Putting on the voice of the legendary David Attenborough, the documentary 'Stuck in a staircase' began,

'Here we are deep in Southern Brazil in one of many suburban homes to witness an oversized man attempt to escape from the clutches of a deceptively small spiral staircase. We must be careful not to antagonise the beast or upset him, in this, his most trying of times. It will be interesting to see...'

'Turn that fucking camera off you dickhead, this is serious,' interrupted Mark.

'As you can see viewers, the man is wary of our presence, the crew could now be in very real danger.'

I turned the camera to Harry, Sam and Jules who were all by now rolling around on the alcohol soaked floor laughing.

'We will against our better judgement try and insert a bottle of beer up the man's bottom in a bid to free him from his temporary imprisonment. It is not normal for me as a wildlife reporter to interrupt the workings of nature, but at this point it would be remiss not to act.'

'Fuck off mate, call the fire brigade, I can't stay here all night, call the bombardier!' Mark pleaded.

Harry then put a bottle of Brahma beer up his arse and took a photograph. At that point we all decided we had had enough fun and would try and help Mark out of the predicament he found himself in.

Mark was fuming, he was clearly anxious and annoyed that we were taking advantage of him,

'I can't believe you just did that Harry, it's tantamount to rape.'

'Tantamount,' I repeated before bursting into laughter.

Thankfully I was able to get behind Mark and pull him back up onto the steps. Rather than be annoyed at us he was just thankful to be free. He stumbled back down to the main room and grabbed an open bottle of beer from the kitchen table. As Harry and Mark continued to drink I decided to call it a night and went to bed.

The next day I sat by the beautiful lagoon thoroughly ashamed of myself. The weather had been overcast for most of the day and I had once again been bored. For some reason while walking through the town I decided to go into a Texaco petrol station and have a wank in the toilet.

A pull in a petrol station was an all time low. I came out of the bathroom and nervously bought a bottle of coke worrying the attendant would know what I had just been up to.

The shame I felt reminded me of the time I came home from school to find a sock I used to wank with on my bed with googly eyes and a mouth drawn on it. There was a note attached which read:

'Because you can't find a real girl, I made your current one prettier, Love Mum.'

That evening we all stayed in and managed to clean up the flat. Mark lay on the sofa groaning. I knew the next few days were going to be a write-off and told him that the following day I would arrange our bus to Rio; I'd had enough of Florianopolis, we had been there too long.

The next morning I got a taxi to the station to sort things out for the two of us. The Australians were leaving so I got a cab with them. I arranged tickets for Mark and I to leave the following morning at 10:00am. I said my farewells to the guys and flagged down a taxi to take me back to the flat.

The taxi driver's name was Rodrigo and he was recognisable to me. It turned out that I had met him on our first night out in Florianopolis. He was excited to see me.

'Fernandao it is good to see you my friend. Is it ok if I smoke?' he asked.

'Of course amigo, it is your car,' I replied.

Rodrigo reached into his pocket and pulled out a huge joint, he looked at me grinning like a five-year-old child that had stolen some sweets.

As he meandered through the traffic of downtown Florianopolis he puffed on his joint, kindly asking for me to smoke with him. I wasn't sure it was the best idea but nor did I want to insult him by refusing.

I looked out of the window as he drove and realised that I had only seen a small fraction of the island. I was slightly annoyed at my lack of effort and adventure, but given my lack of money I hadn't many options.

We both inhaled and exhaled the fumes from the joint as conversation flowed freely between us. Rodrigo told me about his family and the mother to his child, who sounded like a complete maniac. He then steered the conversation towards himself and his grandiose plans for the future,

'Gareth, in the future I aim to overthrow the Government of my country through military force and rid Brazil of the corruption that plagues its society. I know people that can help me to achieve this and it is only a matter of time. For now I like to be a taxi driver as I get to meet many good people like you, but you must understand this is not forever.'

I found myself agreeing with everything he had to say; the weed was obviously good. Maybe I should join him and become part of the surely inevitably military coup? All great leaders had to start somewhere, though at twenty-eight Rodrigo needed to get his political skates on.

He dropped me in town soon after and we swapped email addresses so he could keep in touch. I went back to the flat and back to sleep.

The next morning we boarded the bus to Rio, a city that I was sure would be the highlight of my trip. It was an iconic place and I couldn't wait to get there.

The bus was full and for the first time Mark and I were unable to sit together. While he was lumbered with a fat old Brazilian man, I had the pleasure of sitting next to what I guessed was a sixteen-year-old girl.

The pleasure didn't last all that long as for the first hour she leant forward and looked to be playing Rock, Scissors, Paper with what I guessed was her father behind me. I thought about challenging her to a game with the rule that if I won she would stop fucking playing it.

There was something that just annoyed me about the rules of Rock, Scissors, Paper. Now, I could understand how rock beats scissors, and how scissors beat paper, but how the fuck does paper beat rock? What does it do? Wrap itself around the rock and leave it immobile? Why can't it do that to scissors?

I started to think beyond the game and at paper in general. Why can't paper do that to people? Why aren't students being suffocated by their books as they take notes during a class? I'll tell you why, because paper can't beat anything. A rock would tear paper up in two seconds.

When I next played Rock, Scissors, Paper I decided I would always pick rock, then when somebody claims to have beaten me with paper, I'll use my already clenched fist to punch them in the face and say,

'Oh sorry, I thought your paper would protect you.'

Thankfully they eventually stopped playing and I tried to get some sleep as the bus journey to Rio was a long one and my iPod was dead.

Rio De Janeiro

The bus pulled into Rio at 9:00am in glorious sunshine. We got straight into a yellow taxi outside the station and drove to a pre-arranged hostel called Mellow Yellow. The hostel was located close to the famed Copacabana beach; I was tired and couldn't wait to see it.

The people at the hostel reception were rude on arrival, the place felt more like a tatty hotel than a hostel. They instructed us to leave our bags and return in the afternoon when our room would be ready.

Mark and I put on our shorts and dumped our bags. We made our way through the shaded city streets flanked by hotels and large office blocks towards the beach.

The beach was huge in both length and depth. It was around 200 metres to the water and must have been at least a few miles long. I stood looking curiously down the coast as the beach was mostly empty.

There was no denying that it was spectacular. The city landscape grew in and around the green mountains that towered above them, forming a fantastic backdrop from the water's edge. It was beautiful but I couldn't help the feeling of disappointment. Where were all the people?

Undeterred, we did what all experts in the field of sunbathing did and pitched up, challenging the hot midday sun to do its best.

'Go on; do your best, burn me,' I shouted up at the hot yellow berk in the sky.

After an hour Mark's face looked, not for the first time this trip, like a hot jacket potato, the temperature outside was baking. As the beach was quiet we decided to take a walk along the promenade that ran along the back of the beach next to the road. We had heard about another beach called Ipanema and wanted to see if it was any better.

We both walked with our shirts off in the glowing sunshine, staring at absolutely everything. I wished England had places and weather like this. Numerous sand sculptures clung to the side of the walkway; they were all architecturally stunning and varied across a range of subjects.

I stared at a fine sculpture of three women lying on their fronts on deckchairs; their sandy arses were perfectly carved, giving way to three pairs of long sandy legs. Mark had his eye on one of them; she was wearing a cleverly painted orange thong, and it looked like she was topless. She was Sandy; I looked in his direction as he pulled his camera from his left pocket. I could tell he had chills and they were multiplying but thankfully he didn't lose control, he just took a photograph.

We continued walking up the promenade past several small huts emblazoned with the Brahma beer motif, resisting the urge to have to beer; it was too hot and there was so much to see.

Despite being in such stunning surroundings I kept thinking about home, comparing things to home and worrying about going back there.

I spoke to Mark about it as we walked down the bricked road to Ipanema,

'Travelling for me, and this may make you laugh, is sort of like being in prison.'

Mark laughed and asked me to explain.

'After you have been away for a while you detach from your life at home and realise that while away there is nothing you can do to alter things at home. You live for each day, in the now, in what you are experiencing.'

I continued, sensing he was about to interrupt,

'When I was in Canada and Mexico I found it difficult to leave home behind; hence texting friends back home and constantly being on the internet. They couldn't help me or understand what I was experiencing but I still texted them. As time went on and I got comfortable with you and Craig and being away, I detached from home as I would imagine a prisoner does while behind bars.'

I concluded,

'So now that we are due to go home soon, I am finding it hard to re-attach with people and the thought of being back home; look around you, how much better are things here?'

Mark looked at me in bewilderment,

'Mate you do realise you have just compared travelling, that is a sign of freedom, with prison? Get a grip.'

'Ha ha I know I'm talking bollocks, I just don't want this to end.'

'Pretty sure a prisoner can't wait to get out of jail and nail some girls you tit,' he concluded.

The walk to Ipanema was incredible, visually there was too much to take in. The city was alive, exciting and brand new. I felt like a child experiencing a big city for the first time. Everything was wondrous and I could feel myself wanting to touch and experience everything.

I noted people, mostly locals stopping for a rest by advertising boards. The boards were not dissimilar to those at bus stops back home in England. I spotted people leaning really close to the boards and, as they leaned closer, a mist sprayed from the frame of the billboard onto their bodies. I went over to investigate.

The signs had small silver buttons on their frames; off the frame were hundreds of small holes. I tentatively pressed my thumb against the button, curious as to what would happen. I was covered in pellets of water. The advertisements gave off water vapour, I thought it was genius.

I contemplated stealing the idea and implementing it back home. Perhaps I could get the backing of one of the self-made millionaires on Dragon's Den?

My idea was to have a button that gave off heat in the winter; not dissimilar to a hair dryer. I had stood freezing at bus stops on many occasions back home. This invention could have me lauded as a creative genius; it would have to wait till I got home.

We took a much needed break near the end of Copacabana as we were both dehydrated and sweating. We sat down on a bench looking out over the beach and watched four men playing volleyball, only they weren't using their hands. The men were playing with their feet and had amazing technique. The server chipped the ball from the sandy baseline over the net, only for the receiver to volley it with the side of his foot to his team-mate by the net. He then kneed the ball high along the length of the net for the receiver to run onto and spike the ball back over the net with his head. Each rally lasted for minutes; it was an incredible thing to witness as they made it look effortless and I knew from experience it was anything but, especially on sand.

We reached Ipanema and I stood to take a photo from the bottom end of the beach. I was nearly knocked off my feet by a strong runner who was making his way down the promenade. Mark pointed at the bloke and began laughing at the way he ran. He bounced down the concrete path without moving his arms. We then noticed that everyone was running in a similar fashion. Several tanned human chickens clucking up and down the beach; it was unreal.

The beach was equal in length and depth to the Copacabana but a lot busier. In the distance dramatic cliffs scaled upwards towards the sky with scattered shanty settlements at their base, providing the best views Rio had to offer. The way the city had developed was unbelievable.

Ipanema beach had a younger and more electric vibe than the Copacabana, there was far more going on and it suited the both of us better.

We sat by one of the numbered lifeguard towers and soaked up the typically Brazilian atmosphere; everyone was having fun, there wasn't a sad face in sight. As with the first day on Praia Mole in Florianopolis, I was taken aback and loved what I saw.

The beach, though beautiful, was far from relaxing. It was as if we had put towels down in the middle of a busy shopping centre. Vendors, of which there were hundreds, constantly touted for business ranging from drinks, to clothing, to once in a lifetime deals to events and shows playing in the city.

A likeable gentleman approached Mark and I holding a long piece of bamboo over his neck. On either side he had a collection of football shirts that he assured us were 100% authentic. They clearly were not but given his persistent attitude we decided to humour him and have a look. The shirts were all fake, but rather than tell the chap and potentially offend him I just said,

'Amigo I have no money, only credit card I'm sorry.'

This was an easy way to get rid of him, I was proud of myself as I flashed the card in his direction.

'I'm sorry, maybe tomorrow Robinho,' I concluded.

The man's skin was dark, he glistening in the sun like a melting lollipop. I didn't envy him lugging so much merchandise up and down the beach. He looked at me and smiled as he fumbled in the pocket of his oversized shorts with his left hand. He pulled out a plastic block that was attached to a pack on his lower back by a curly black phone cord; I couldn't believe it, he had a card reader.

'MasterCard or Visa?' he chuckled triumphantly.

Smiling and laughing I grabbed the wet lollipop man and kissed him on the head.

'Robinho what is your real name?' I asked.

'Fernando amigo,' he was still laughing.

'I'm Gaz, here have a beer.'

He caught the beer in his right hand, almost losing balance and dropping the shop of football shirts hanging from his back.

'See you tomorrow,' I concluded as I shook his hand.

There was no way I was using my credit card on the beach, especially to acquire a fake football top.

The beach resembled a human zoo; at first it was daunting and felt unsafe but as the afternoon wore on I got used to it and fell in love. If you wanted a drink, you could get whatever you wanted. If you needed food, you could get something to eat and if you wanted to relax and lay in the sun, despite the noisy distractions, you could.

One thing we didn't do was leave our bags for a second. The atmosphere was fun and playful, but behind the smiles I couldn't help but worry. We were in a big city and there were bound to be a number of opportunists, especially in a city with a reputation like Rio de Janeiro.

Laying on the beach it was easy to forget that you were in the middle of a city. It was easy to be seduced by the alluring water of the Atlantic Ocean and because of this the beach was a notorious hunting ground for pick pockets and thieves. Mark and I took it in turns to venture into the sea.

Come late afternoon Mark and I made our way back to the hostel. We walked through the downtown area of Ipanema away from the beach and past numerous shops that sold globally recognisable brands.

The city had a real buzz coursing through its veins, I didn't feel safe but I felt alert and alive. My ears became attuned to every little sound that made up the soundtrack of this unique city.

Being in Rio reminded me of my first visit to London; big cities and the sheer volume of people always impressed me. The big difference with Rio was that I was only a street away from a striking beach and the weather, unlike London, was sublime. Both drowned in people and noise.

At the hostel we checked into the Santa Teresa dorm. All the rooms were named after areas of Rio. I was thankful we were not in the Favella, a twenty-bed dorm on the fourth floor of the building. The hostel reminded me of an old school boarding house. My mind drifted off to the numerous residential weeks I had been on at school growing up, they had been a lot of fun. Despite the hostel's drab appearance I knew we would have a good time.

During the evening Mark and I watched the England vs. Spain football match at an English bar in Ipanema called The Lord Jim. The pub looked like an old Tudor house, with black beams and white walls making up the outer shell. It was not in keeping with other buildings in the area and looked typically English.

The proprietor of this fine drinking establishment was a Brazilian called Eduardo and he immediately liked us. I made a bet with him before the match that England would win, but they didn't so I had to pay him $20rls.

The bar was dark. It resembled one of the hundreds of thousands of Irish bars found in every corner on the globe. Maybe Eduardo had made a geographical hiccup? Or maybe England and Ireland meant the same thing to him? I decided not to ask.

We were joined at the bar by several Australian acquaintances Mark and I had met earlier in the trip. Facebook was proving to be an invaluable tool for staying in touch with people.

We were joined by Dommy, Doug, James, Paul and Harley. Mark had done the Road of Death in Bolivia with a few of them; the rest had apparently witnessed both Mark and I in some interesting mental states in Buenos Aires. They were likable lads and all up for a laugh.

After the game we caught a taxi across Ipanema to a small street side bar called Zig Zag. There was an air of excitement in Rio at night. The promenade was lit up like it was hosting the Oscars. Pockets of light lit up the otherwise dark beach, as the crashing waves shimmered in the moon light.

Bars and restaurants were all alive with people enjoying each other's company, enjoying life. I stared out of the taxi window and wondered if anyone in this city was sat at home watching television with a microwave dinner on their lap; I doubted it very much.

The small cafe bar the boys had recommended reeked of garlic and looked uninspiring at best. We sat outside on the corner of a street just off the main road in some yellow Brahma sponsored plastic chairs.

I had planned a steady night on the drink as I was taking medication for my ears. My plan had failed. After several large bottles of lager I was exceptionally drunk; the mix of prescription drugs and alcohol was not a good one.

The bar was tiny. I had seen several similar looking places dotting sidewalks during the day. Inside stood a glass food counter with sandwiches and pies; a fridge by its side was full of ice cold beers. It was simple place and the more I drank, the more I liked it.

Desperate for the toilet, I ran into the bar to the gents and was confused with what lay before me. I pushed through the fragile wooden saloon door that creaked on its rotting axis; in the half darkness of the small cubicle I could not locate the toilet or a urinal, there was only a sink.

It was reminiscent of the room from the movie Saw. Thankfully no one was chained to the pipes on the walls but, like the characters in the film, my eyes scanned the tiled puzzle of a room for clues. Maybe there was a secret room and I had to find a key? I wasn't sure.

I then noticed a few limes in the sink. Maybe they wanted me to piss in the sink? The sink had to be the urinal? There was nowhere else to go so I used it before then washing my hands. This little bar really was no frills.

Bent on alcohol and the excitement of being with a big group of people I wanted to move onto somewhere new; somewhere busy with girls and a dance floor.

Mark was still smarting after England's defeat to Spain and I could tell he was in a mood. He jumped into a taxi and went home after I knocked some newly purchased peanuts out of his hands.

'What is wrong with you sir?' I asked as I hit the cone from his hands.

'What the fuck did you do that for you dick?'

'Easy, I'll get you some more, they are only nuts.'

'Don't bother,' he said as he turned away from me.

At times he really was a moody little child. I looked over in disbelief as he hailed down a taxi and headed off into the distance. Harley passed me a beer and suggested we found a club to go to.

I got into a cab with Harley and a girl called Kath who we had met on the Salt Flats in Bolivia. On the advice of some passing locals we went to an area of the city called Lapa.

Harley had tight curly black hair and looked like the main character from Disney's Boy Meets World. Though I had just met him, he had a good aura about him and we got on really well.

Lapa was an area known for its famous street parties that took place from Thursday though to the early hours of Sunday morning. Lapa was also known to be an extremely dangerous part of the city with some of the highest crime rates. We were going on a Tuesday and didn't know or care what was waiting for us as we got out of the taxi.

The night fell away into some sort of hallucinating dream and I only managed to retain a selection of images. A transvestite in a large blonde wig sold us some off-white cocaine as we danced around the floor of a loud music bar. She warned us to be careful on the surrounding streets and certain bars. We then went to these bars on some sort of fool's errand to find danger. All we found were people smiling and having a good time. I remembered having a good time myself.

I danced stupidly in front of the predominantly black crowd in one of several bars we fell into. The three of us were the only backpackers, the only gringos and we could not have stood out more if we had tried. Because of the alcohol I felt totally safe.

The night ended with me and Harley stumbling around the beach in some sort of surreal reality as the sun began to rise from the ocean. Before it did I made it back to his flat and passed out.

The next morning I woke to Doug hitting me playfully over the head. He was accusing me of pissing myself as the sofa was dripping wet. Apparently I had urinated but curiously there was no indication of this on my shorts so I denied any wrong doing and left soon after.

I walked for what felt like several hundred miles along the beach promenade back to the hostel. I completely forgot that the bus advertisements offered me brief sanctuary from the river of sweat that now ran down my spine. Unlike the previous day the beach was no longer glorious, it was a witch's cauldron. I felt like death and wanted everyone to stop smiling.

I got back to the hostel and climbed into bed where Mark was still fast asleep. He had suggested we do the Favella tour at 1:00pm so I needed to rest for a few hours.

I woke up 4:00pm to the sound of rain splashing against the window, the lights in the room were off and I was alone. The weather seemed to mirror my mood. When I had been happy it was clear blue skies but now in the depths of a comedown, the heavens had opened and all was grey and troublesome.

I sat up and wondered why Mark had not woken me? Surely he hadn't gone on the Favella tour without me? Surely he wasn't still in a mood about the peanut incident? I hoped not, as given my state of mind the last thing I need was another roasting from him.

I did nothing all day. I was completely broken and resolved not to drink for a few days. It was something that was difficult to do, especially when you are in a situation where you are constantly meeting new people every day and don't have any privacy. Alcohol had been the evil temptress for the whole trip; it broke down inhibitions and was the ideal lubricant for travelling. I hadn't fallen out with her as I liked her a lot, but I needed a few days to recover.

That night I sat in the hostel's TV room and watched City of God, a movie about the lives of several people in Rio's notorious Favellas. It turned out Mark had gone that day with Harry and the others who had arrived that morning. The film was likely to be the closest I was going to get to experience the slums, unless I went on my own.

I had mixed views on the Favellas. I was curious to experience it first hand but I didn't feel entirely comfortable with the concept of the tours. The shanty settlements were people's homes and communities; yes they were unique and interesting but they were still homes.

I wondered how I would feel if tours came through the suburban estates that I grew up in and took photographs of my children riding their bikes or playing on their Playstations. They were real people and not animals. While the money raised from the tours did go back into the community there was still a bone of contention in my mind that wouldn't go away. I would have to think about it.

The next morning Mark was still inexplicably annoyed with me; there had to be more to it than the peanuts. I couldn't be bothered trying to get it out of him, if it was just about that then he had finally gone nuts.

I went with Harry, Sam and Jules to the beach as it was their only day in Rio before heading towards Salvador for Carnival. I took on the role of cameraman before it once again began to rain.

Mellow Yellow was a huge hostel and, despite its worn appearance, it was a lot of fun. At the top of a never ending series of stairs lay the hostel bar; it offered what any self respecting traveller was after, cheap drink.

The bar contained a series of long benches, making it really social and a good place to interact with other travellers. Behind a few pillars lay a small dance floor, beyond which was the bar. Like the rest of the hostel it was worn and far from eye-catching, but it worked.

As always happened when in the company of Harry and Sam I ended up drinking a shed load of alcohol. Mark, the ever affectionate drunk that he is, finally made his peace with me, despite me being unable to offer him an answer to the question,

'Why did you punch the peanuts out of my hand?'

Harry and I started getting stupid at the bar. Shots of Sambuca and Tequila gave way to shots of each other's spit and limes being squeezed in our eyes. When we'd had enough we roped others into doing the same. A New Zealander called Rodrigo, along with the ever-reliable Woody, bore the brunt of the action as others looks on in shock.

Happy hour had worked its magic and we were all extremely pleased with ourselves. We left the bar before at around 10:00pm and stumbled onto the streets of Rio trying to find a flat being rented by some of Jules' Australian friends.

We eventually found the flat and tore through a few bottles of vodka within an hour. I could feel the alcohol intoxicating my brain. I stopped caring about what I was doing, knowing tomorrow I would remember nothing.

The flat occupied by the three charming ladies from Sydney was basic but functional. It had no air conditioning system and, being in the centre of an already sweltering city, it felt like we were inside a modern cooker. In a bid to cool myself down I took the only sensible option and removed my clothes. I covered my manhood with a Coke Zero apron I found in the kitchen drawer.

After several complaints about the noise and subsequent threats to call the police by neighbours, we vacated the premises and got a street cab to Lapa. It was Thursday so it promised to be more hectic than my visit with Harley two days earlier.

Lapa is a rundown area of Rio; full of dilapidated architecture and pulsing with character. I could not remember much from my first visit, but knew from what I had read that the area was not as safe as Ipanema or districts closer to the beach.

Mark was speaking with the taxi driver, instructing him to drop us at the steps; these were famous and sat at one end of the long strip of road where the party was well under way.

The steps consisted of a series of different tiles that artists had collected from around the world and decided to cement onto the staircase. As it was dark and we been drinking for hours I thought it was strange Mark wanting to see them, sometimes he was odd like that.

We arrived at Lapa just before midnight and I was in a state, barely able to stand. I looked up at the steps and was unmoved. I was more interested in the menagerie of odd-looking locals that stalked its base like a pack of hungry hyenas.

'Where you from, you want weed? You want marijuana, you want coke? Anything you want?' A dirty looking woman with five decaying teeth hanging from her rotting gums like bats in a cave chuckled.

'Just here to take a look at the steps darling, we are good,' replied Mark sarcastically.

'Maybe it would be best to visit during the day?' suggested Jules.

The main drag was alive with the sound of samba; crowds of people continued to stream onto the already packed street. It had the feel of loosely organised chaos. Thousands of people just floated in and out of bars, drinking beer and going with the flow; we all jumped in.

People from a broad spectrum of backgrounds and classes mingled with one another, tourists were outnumbered by the heavy local influence, from what looked like a range of social backgrounds.

Small boys weaved in and out of the sea of people like sharks tapping at pockets, looking for opportunities to steal from the thousands of drunken party goers.

I hadn't to worry; I was so drunk that I looked poorer than most people there. I was still wearing the black apron and looked mental; no one steals from the unhinged. I was also wearing a pair of skinny jeans so the little thieving sharks had no chance. I had my bases covered; I was the human equivalent to a maximum security bank.

Within five minutes Woody and I had lost everyone. It was impossible to fight against the current of people. We wriggled our way to the side of the road and bought a beer each from one of the several vendors that paced up and down the street with polystyrene cool boxes.

As I stumbled down the street I drifted in and out of consciousness, I could feel my legs buckling under my weight. I was on auto pilot, constantly slurring my words and talking complete and utter nonsense. Woody sat me down on some steps realising it was going to be impossible to find the guys.

Music filtered from the numerous bars, samba and rock 'n' roll muffled into one overriding sound. I woke up outside the hostel at 4:00am, falling out of a taxi like a puppet. Woody helped me to my feet.

My mind had deserted me for the best part of three hours; I was thankful to Woody for looking after me and somehow managed to stumble to my room after saying good night.

I woke up with a small lump on my head; I didn't notice it until I brushed my hair but it was there. The surprises continued as I went in the shower to discover than half my pubes were missing and the surviving strands were covered in what looked like wax.

I had no idea what had happened, it looked like I had been to Madame Tussauds and had my way with my favourite celebrity figure. I went down to breakfast unsure that I wanted to find out. As I ate some cornflakes Jules was only too happy to fill me in,

'How are the pubes Gazza?' she purred.

'How do you know about that?'

'I was there you idiot.'

'What happened, I have no idea?'

'At the girls you were walking around naked and they were winding you up saying you had a small penis.'

I felt my skin turn red with embarrassment as she continued,

'You told them it was because you had not trimmed your pubes since coming away, so they offered to get rid of them. You seriously don't remember lying on the bed as they tried waxing you?'

'Thankfully not, I also remember next to nothing about Lapa after losing you guys,' I admitted.

'Don't talk to me about that place.'

Jules went to pack as Harry told me what had happened. It turned out that Jules' camera had been stolen by a group of local children.

'She got a group of young children together to take their photograph. They played nice and everything seemed fine so she took the snap. As she turned away they quickly converged on her all together and snatched the camera out of her hand. Before I could react and slot the little fucker, another boy had ran off into the crowd, he was well quick as well, like a black road runner, there was no way we were gonna retrieve it!' He explained.

'Annoying but I guess you can't blame them, probably do the same in their position,' I suggested as I stole some of his toast.

'Fuck off,' laughed Harry.

After breakfast we once again said goodbye to Harry, Sam and Jules but were sure we would see them in a week or so up in Salvador.

I sat in the reception of Mellow Yellow with my head in my hands as three ditsy girls came through the main turnstiles of the hostel and looked at me like we had already met.

'Alright Gaz how is the lump on your head?' one of them asked in a scouse accent.

'How do you know about that?'

'You were talking to us in the computer room last night after you got hit,' was the response,

'SHIT, I had completely forgotten about that. Oh lord I do apologise, who are you?'

'I'm Laura, this is Katy and this is Vanessa.'

The girls had arrived in Rio from England a few days ago and were at the start of their trip. They had a charming naivety about them. It was clear that they had no plans and I instantly liked all three of them.

The two short blonde girls, Laura and Katy, were sisters from Liverpool and neither of them could stop speaking. They battled it out for air time, constantly talking over each other.

The other quieter girl was Vanessa, who I instantly liked the look of. She had dark features and was clearly not fully English as her skin resembled that of Mowgli's from The Jungle Book. She wore a polka dot Disney top and I asked if I could wear it,

'Vanessa you fine looking woman you, can I wear your top? You can have mine.'

Mark and Woody arrived from upstairs laughing at the site of me in Vanessa's Mini Mouse shirt. I introduced them to the girls before suggesting to them we should meet later at the bar.

I asked Mark if he remembered me getting hit before going to bed and he did,

'You were shouting a load of shit into one of the rooms as you thought Harry was in there. You weren't being a dick, it was funny. Then this Irish tit came out and accused you of stalking him before hitting you in the side of the head. You fell down and started shouting 'Mark I'm being attacked' it was well funny, you were furious!'

'I can't remember any of that!'

With the lump and pubes explained I left the hostel with no real idea where it was we were going.

Mark, Woody and I felt horrific so rather than go on one of the numerous excursions, we decided to rent some films from a nearby video store. On the way back to the hostel we passed one of the tiled cafes like Zig Zag and noticed that Chelsea were playing and losing to Watford in an English FA Cup match.

I needed to go to bed but Mark and Woody were adamant we should sit down and watch the rest of the match. Woody came back to our plastic table with three glass bottles of beer, I looked at him, shaking my head,

'Don't be soft Gazza, hair of the dog, a few beers and you will feel a lot better.'

I wasn't sure he was right but was willing to give it a go; I owed him after last night.

The first beer took half an hour to drink and was followed by a second and then a third as we completed a full round between us.

The people at the bar took a shine to the three of us. As I was now drunk I began speaking to an aging black man sitting alone next to us; his name was Wayne.

Wayne was a charming old man who lived not far from the bar in the southern section of Rio. He was black with fading grey hair either side of his egg-like head; we all immediately liked him. I bought him a beer and motioned for him to join our table.

Conversation centred on football and Rio; it was primitive at best given that we spoke little of each other's languages. Woody, like most Australians, could not speak a word of Spanish or Portuguese. Australians as a rule made me look like a multi-lingual god and I only knew a handful of words.

Wayne bought us back some beers and before we had realised it, we had begun another full day on the drink. As we drank more we naturally became more animated which resulted in lots of attention.

A street vendor snaked past on the pavement with a selection of panama hats available for a rather modest $5rls. We bought four and gave one to Wayne.

Two young black men sat behind us that I learned lived in the Favella. They joined our table and had a good understanding of English. We bought them a beer each and they relaxed into their chairs. As the minutes turned to hours our number grew, it was not your typical crowd of people.

Mark told the well-groomed waiter that Woody liked men. So from this point every beer Woody received was done so with affection, a rub of the arm and a wink; he had no idea and it was hilarious once Mark had told me what he had done.

Three retired gentlemen from Italy entered the bar as Lazio were now playing football on the television. They had come to watch the game over a bottle of wine. As with everyone else they joined us.

One of the Italian men had a relaxing demeanour; he talked like he had seen and done everything the world had to offer; nothing could surprise or upset him. I liked him a great deal and he seemed to love me.

He constantly kissed me on the cheek saying that I was a kind spirit. It was not until his friend showed up that I realised these kisses were perhaps not as innocent as I had thought.

I had assumed that he had drunk too many glasses of red wine and was just being affectionate. A curly haired man in an open collared zebra printed shirt and leathers turned up to meet him and it made me think otherwise. He was a big gay old man.

Mark stumbled past the plastic furniture that we had set in a row like a beer hall around the outside television. He asked the barman for a black marker pen. We had been sat outside the bar for almost four hours; the manager would have given us anything we asked for.

Wayne was still with us drinking and laughing away. He gave me his address and email on a napkin and asked that we stay in touch. I wrote my email address on his arm with the newly acquired marker pen as I was worried he may lose a soft piece of paper; the arm was the safer option.

Woody was now slouched back in his chair topless with a cheap Panama hat covering his eyes, he was steaming drunk. Mark decided to write 'I eat ten-year-old pussy' across his chest in definite dark blue pen.

This act resulted in the start of 'Slogan wars', a warfare of wit that covered each and everyone at the table in pen. I wrote 'I love men' across Wayne's aging forehead while Mark followed it up by writing 'I love cock' on the chest of the now obviously gay Italian man.

Being off our heads on alcohol, the slogans never got past insinuations of gayness or the drawing of large genitals. But, despite the lack of originality, everyone was happy.

It was a surreal afternoon; the three of us were mixing with locals and entertaining them. They laughed at us and we laughed at them, it was as random and out of control as it was mutually respectful.

We thanked the owner of the bar and embraced the impish gay waiter before stumbling back to hostel. The gang around the table had said they would see us tomorrow; I doubted the possibility without totally ruling it out.

Back at the hostel we met up with the girls and Rodrigo; it was only a matter of time before we were downing shots and squirting limes into our ever reddening eyes.

The girls were clearly taken aback by our stupid behaviour and did their best to catch up and take advantage of our drunken generosity.

By 11:00pm I was stood by the bar ordering shots wearing a neon pink tutu and a full face of makeup. I looked like one of the ladies that work in the cosmetic section of Boots. They had covered me in every bit of make-up they owned, and Vanessa owned a lot.

The bar was teeming with people, all travellers and almost all Australian. I had met more Australian people in South America than I had when living in Sydney; it was ridiculous.

My mind and memory once again gave way to the booze as yet again I didn't know when to stop drinking. I stopped when I passed out.

I woke up the next morning with a monster of a hangover and a severe dead arm. I looked to my left and noticed that my arm was trapped underneath a fleshy stone. It was Laura. I pressed my stubbly chin against my neck and looked down my body. I was still wearing the pink tutu. I lay like a trapped rock climber before deciding to wake Laura.

Laura, my mind recalled, had promised me a 'Blozzer' that I was told was scouse for a blowjob. Nothing had happened so not for the first time someone from Liverpool had lied. To my surprise she did tell me that I had a big willy.

Laura clumsily left the room and slammed the door. I climbed out of my bunk and rocked onto my feet. At eye level on the top bunk laid a Norwegian lad who looked at me with a wry smile across his face. The room began to spin around as my vision temporarily blurred. The long mirror on the room's back wall confirmed that I was still wearing the tutu and half a cosmetics store on my face.

Mark, Woody and I planned on going to a football match at the Maracana Stadium; the clocks had thankfully gone back an hour so I had plenty of time to sort my head out.

We walked to the metro stop all still drunk. Mark had slept with Laura's sister Katy so was in high spirits. It wasn't difficult to find the stadium as an army of fans steadily packed the train as we got nearer to the ground.

The game was between Flamengo and Botafogo. The teams were both based in Rio and shared a hostile rivalry, so despite being a friendly it would only take a small spark to ignite trouble. Because of this there was a strong police presence as we left the metro station and started to walk towards the ground.

We bumped into several recognisable faces from the hostel and as we were a couple of hours early for the match decided to go for some drinks in a nearby bar.

I felt horrible from the previous days and nights on the booze, but decided to give it a shot. The bar was similar to the simple tiled ones we had frequented in Rio, the difference being that it was three times the size and covered in black and white paraphernalia, the colours of Botafogo.

I got talking to two Flamengo fans that looked to be in their forties called Marcello and Fabio. Marcello was trying his hardest to get me to support Flamengo but it was too late, I had already decided on their opponents Botafogo.

As the time ticked down to kick off the bar got busier and notably louder. Passionate fans covered in paint and waving flags congregated outside chanting songs in reference to their teams. It was loud but friendly.

Half an hour before the game we walked to the ground with a young group of Botafogo fans who had promised to sort out our tickets; Mark, Woody and I had forgotten to buy some as we had again got wrapped up in drinking.

We bounced into the ground making up our own chants while being swept towards the pitch with the tide of supporters, it was a carnival of colour and sound.

The atmosphere inside was incredible, everywhere I looked painted faces were shouting and waving flags; not one person was sitting on their seat. The ground bounced up and down as if magically it had come alive for the afternoon and the noise was deafening. I looked around in sheer bewilderment as the game had yet to start.

The stadium itself housed an impressive 80,000 people and by kick-off was around two thirds full. The referee blew his whistle and the game got underway.

Brazilian football has a reputation for being open and attacking; as the game ebbed and flowed it felt more like they just didn't know how to defend. The game was slow and predictable and paled in comparison to the ferocity and power of the English game.

The crowd, undeterred by the underwhelming performances on the pitch, put any fans I had experienced to shame. As half time approached everyone was still standing, still dancing, still chanting and still waving flags above their heads; the energy in the crowd was incredible.

The second half dwindled in the afternoon heat. Botafogo's goalkeeper came seventy yards out of his goal to take a free kick. He ballooned the ball into the stand behind the goal and then frantically raced back down the pitch like he was being chased by a trained police dog.

The game ended in a 1-1 draw after Flamengo cancelled out Botafogo's opener with a scrappy last minute strike that sent half the stadium into raptures while the others finally slumped onto their plastic seats.

The volume of people that spilled onto the streets was phenomenal. Rather than queue for hours to get the metro we elected to go back to the bar for some more alcohol. You were not able to drink in the ground so we were all flagging badly.

Back at the bar I bumped into Marcello and Fabio, who joined our table along with several other fans. We drank and joked with one another as things once more began to get out of hand.

Mark recorded a video on his camera of Marcello imitating giving the invisible man a blowjob. He then found it necessary to stand behind me and perform a fully clothed mock buggery. I took it like man and laughed; Marcello presumably had a job and a family, what had we done to him?

We were once again sat drinking, engaging locals in our foolhardy behaviour and loving every minute of it.

We eventually got back to the hostel where the debaucheries continued. Mark and I sat by the bar when over the tannoy system came the following announcement:

'Could Gareth and Mark please come to the reception, Gareth and Mark to reception, thank you.'

We ignored the message and just continued drinking, safe in the knowledge that we had forgotten to inform the hostel that we wished to stay for another night. We would just stay anyway and we were not going to pay.

I woke up with Laura the next morning barely able to move after a heavy three days of non-stop drinking. I lay in a pool of sweat as I gently peeled off the human backpack attached to my body.

Laura woke up and looked like she had just eaten a lemon. She was disgusted by the situation that she found herself in and suggested that she'd had enough and wanted to go home.

'This is disgusting, I've had enough already I'm going to think seriously about going home,' she squawked.

Her thoughts were compounded when an Australian at the far side of the huge twenty-bed Favella dorm awoke to find that someone had shit on the floor near his bunk. It was time for me to make my exit.

After a shower Mark and I were concerned that the hostel was going to work out we were no longer paying guests. We decided to leave the hostel discreetly and go out for the day. Unfortunately I failed this simple task in spectacular fashion.

As we both didn't have keys we had to negotiate the turnstiles to get out of the hostel. As I ducked to pass under the iron bar I drunkenly stumbled and fell towards the open glass door. My head took the brunt of the impact as I clattered against the glass and spilled onto the road outside. I lay there in agony as the three people at reception stared wondering what had happened. I got to my feet clutching my head and gave them a nod, before casually crossing the road to catch up with Mark who was laughing uncontrollably at my misfortune.

In the afternoon we decided to finally go up to see the Christ Redeemer statue as finally the skies were blue. The statue is the main icon of Brazil and the wonderful continent that is South America.

The views from the statue were phenomenal. You could see how the city had cut itself in and around its natural surroundings; I had never seen a city quite like it.

At the summit of the towering mountain were thousands of tourists. It was the first clear day in Rio for three of four days and people were taking advantage. Tourists stood by the statue as their friends several steps lower took pictures of them imitating the pose adopted by the statue. The statue stood proudly with his arms stretched out to the sky like a child impersonating an aeroplane.

I was still half cut and with the high temperature I was sweating profusely. The amount of people and heat were making me extremely anxious. Despite this feeling I did appreciate where I was and what I was seeing. This was the moment I had dreamt about all trip and I wanted to treasure it, convinced I would never be back.

I have a tendency of speaking to people wearing football tops and by the statue there were several targets to choose from. I chose a heavily set black man that looked like he sold glasses or fake bags on the beach. He was wearing a Beckham LA Galaxy jersey.

'Argh David Beckham, Inglaterra,' I called in an appalling Spanish accent.

I was aware the nation's language was Portuguese but it was the best I could offer.

'I'm from London mate,' was his thick southern response.

'Oops!' I muttered under my breath before engaging in an awkward conversation.

After the statue we ate before heading back to the hostel. Our bus to Salvador had been booked earlier that day for 10:00pm. The three of us got showered before collecting our belongings and leaving the hostel; we were still there illegally but had managed to get away it.

We got into a taxi and headed towards the bus station. We stopped after five minutes as Mark, who decided he didn't want to leave, wanted to get a quick McDonald's.

His ten minute stop along with the sheer volume of traffic meant that we were pushing it for time and were likely to miss our paid bus out of Rio. I sat annoyed in the back seat as we hit a wall of traffic on the motorway.

I knew at this point we had missed our bus, throwing away more money that I didn't have. Mark had not wanted to get the bus in the first place;

he hated the long journeys and so had taken longer than usual to get ready. Woody as always was not bothered either way; I was really annoyed but there was nothing I could do.

We had no option but to go back to Rio and look for a new hostel. We couldn't stay at Mellow Yellow after what we had done. It was late and as the taxi meter continued to climb we had to make a decision. We ended up making a bad one.

We checked into The Girl from Ipanema, a hostel located near to the beach in downtown. The hostel was the worst that we had stayed in all trip, I found myself unable to sleep as beads of sweat poured into my eyes and my ears again blocked up.

I lay sandwiched between Mark and a large Israeli in a three-storey bunk bed that swayed on its thin metal frame with every movement.

I awoke at 6:00am hearing a commotion coming from the reception that was a few hundred yards from the room. Something was happening but I chose to ignore it.

The next morning we were unable to get a refund for the coach to Salvador that had cost $120rls. Rather than rebook the bus we decided to search for a cheap flight as unlike the thirty-hour bus journey, it only took two hours by air.

We booked a flight that cost double the price of the bus but agreed it was a better idea and meant that we would not miss the first day of Carnival.

We spent all day on the beach before returning to the hostel. I learned that the commotion that morning had been serious; the reception had been held at gunpoint and robbed. The receptionist who was clearly shaken by the incident was now revelling in showing guests the CCTV footage of the crime.

It again served to highlight the underbelly in Rio's society. We had been lucky and not seen or experienced anything the likes of this but each and every day you were aware that it happened and you had to be careful.

After another terrible sleep in the sweat box room we woke early and made our way to the airport. None of us chose to pay for the accommodation; to have paid to stay in such was place was daylight robbery.

Salvador and Carnival

The plane played absolute havoc with my ears. I sat thousands of feet from the ground and all I could hear was the ocean sloshing around in my head. Poseidon stabbed his fork continuously into my ear drums and it was agony.

The drinking in Rio had really taken its toll on all three of us; without saying anything we knew it was likely to get far worse before it got any better.

The Carnival in Salvador is regarded as the biggest street party in the world, lasting six days and accommodating around two million people. We would be drinking from start to finish, of that there was no doubt.

We stepped off the plane and into the arrivals hall at the airport. We were greeted by several black women in dazzling bikinis, singing and dancing; I couldn't help but raise a smile. They greeted us warmly, offering ribbon bracelets in blue, yellow and green that read: '2009 Carnival Salvador'.

We had successfully flown to the right place. I looked down at the ribbons and then up at Mark.

'2009, bloody hell,' I exclaimed.

I was genuinely confused as I had forgotten that I had been away over New Year. In my mind until then it was still 2008. I had to laugh.

We left the airport after arranging a hostel for the night from a local kiosk. We had arranged to stay with the boys from Cusco, Kash, Nash and their friend Joel, but had not heard from them. They were not the easiest people to cement plans with; neither were we. I resolved to email them later that evening to let them know we had arrived in Salvador, in the year 2009.

We drove through the grubby streets of Salvador when my pocket began to rumble; my phone had received its first text in months. I had convinced myself that it was broken so rarely bothered to turn the thing on. The battery had swelled in Bolivia due to the altitude where it had doubled in size and snapped the back cover off as a result. The battery had looked like a pregnant woman, but now it was back like a phoenix from the flames; the message read:

'Yo fuck face you landed yet? We need to hook up and get loose!' It was unmistakably Kash.

I replied,

'In a cab now with your mum; can our mate stay for the night? He shagged her?'

Seconds later my phone again vibrated,

'Yeah sweet man he better be pretty though; I want to cum on him! The address is Flat 5 Lucio Bahia sees you soon, can't wait, word to my mother ha ha.'

I relayed the information to Mark and Woody. Mark wanted to go to the hostel as he wanted a quiet night. He knew that if we met Kash and Nash a quiet night was highly unlikely; together we were a toxic mix.

We pulled up outside an aging white tower block of flats and could see Kash hanging from a balcony at the very top of it. He was screaming at us but I couldn't make out what he was saying as the engine of the taxi rumbled on. He was wearing his black bowler hat and looked exactly how I remembered him.

We arrived the day before the start of carnival. Nash and Joel had bought a few pirate DVDs for a lads' night in. The week ahead was going to be hard on all of us. I wasn't sure I was ready, but I had no choice, it was Carnival.

The flat was an old lady's house, similar to the one Mark and I rented in Florianopolis. The old wood front door opened into a large front room with two old sofas against the far wall. To the right were two glass cabinets full of trinkets and family photos. I looked worryingly at the cabinets convinced they were not going to see out the week.

Nash showed us our room; we both had a bed so it was all we could have asked for. Two single beds lay against opposite walls of the ocean blue painted room. In the corner we had our own bathroom that linked to one of two balconies.

The flat was huge, reminding me of a retirement home. This suited Kash who told us that while working in Southampton he actually lived in one for a few months; it was the most unlikely home for someone like him.

Kash was excited to see us, I knew there was little chance we would watch the films. Mark was adamant that he was not going to drink, until Kash told him about some girls he had spoken to on the beach,

'These girls live down the road, all smoking and shit. They said if we wanted we could go round their place by the beach. They have a pool on their roof and shit, I reckon they will put out for sure.'

Mark's eyes widened, but he was still unconvinced,

'Seriously?'

'Scouts honour,' replied Kash as two fingers flashed up above his brow.

That was all it took for Mark to change his tune and we started drinking. After several drinks around the coffee table we all got dressed and ready to make our way down the hill into town. We left the flat without finding out what DVDs Nash and Joel had bought.

We marched down the steep hillside road towards the beach. The road gradually flattened out and ran parallel to the beach. The beach was a lot smaller than the large, brash beaches of Rio. We stood outside one of the tiled cafe bars and bought some beers. There was a sense of expectation in the air, as people prepared for the start of carnival. Signs and billboards were going up everywhere.

I felt a strong pull on my arm as I stood talking to Nash. I looked down to my left and was greeted by a caramel skinned woman in a white dress. Without saying anything she pulled at the neck of her dress to reveal her right breast. She then pulled at the waistband of my jeans wanting to see my penis. She acted and looked like a sex starved zombie, rather than turned on I was scared.

'You want fuck?' she said in broken English while provocatively biting her lower lip.

I was stunned. The rumours about Carnival were true; I was going to get eaten alive. This woman was just the first of many, it was going to be a meat market and I would have to be careful.

I politely declined the lady's kind offer but thanked her all the same,

'Non obrigardo.'

Despite this rejection the woman would not stop pestering me. Nash stepped in and told her to piss off.

She got the message and left me to my drink. We sat around a plastic table catching up as our limited inhibitions gave way to the alcohol.

Kash had not been lying about the girls he had met earlier in the day. Before I could really process where it was we were going I was sat in a beautiful apartment around a swimming pool with a bottle of vodka in my hand.

The top floor flat was being rented by five Brazilians from Rio, who like many came to Salvador for Carnival. I had wanted to be in Rio for Carnival; back home that was the one that everyone dreamt of being part of. As our trip through South America progressed it was clear everyone favoured Salvador. It was more authentic, had less rules and everyone got involved in the show.

The girls at the flat were all extremely accommodating; being from Rio three of them spoke perfect English so conversation was not difficult. I spoke at length to a girl called Adrianna. She had light brown skin, long black hair, and legs that seemed to never end. She had fire in her belly and came across as a passionate woman.

The pool was ten metres in length and sunk into the wooden decking outside some French windows that led into the flat. The water looked inviting but we resisted the urge to push each other in. As we became more boisterous we decided to leave the flat; the girls weren't drinking and it was clear we were beginning to outstay our welcome.

We were too wrapped up in each other to try chatting up women; intoxicated, we spilled onto the streets looking for action.

The six of us stumbled along the road unaware that almost everything was closed, preparing for the next six days of madness. In our own way we were preparing; we had a head start on everyone in the town. As predicted the aim was to be the drunkest people at Carnival.

Restaurants and shops lined the road to our left, looking out to sea. To the right lay the beach now in total darkness, the sea twinkled in the moonlight. The strip was quiet with only a few people walking up and down its concourse. The atmosphere was subdued but with the start of Carnival only hours away there was a touch of magic in the air.

Nash and I walked at the back of our group trying to think up dares for one another to do. Our brains were no longer functioning anywhere near capacity so ideas were thin on the ground. We passed one of several trees planted on the pavement and my eyes fixed on what looked like dog shit. I looked at Nash and joked that he should eat it.

'Nash, I dare you to pick up that poo and eat a bit,' I drunkenly chuckled.

I didn't expect him to say yes, it just entered my mind as I saw it lying there.

'Yeah alright why not, I'm game,' was the enthusiastic reply.

We stopped still on the sidewalk a few metres past the tree and both tentatively looked back in its direction. I could think of hundreds of reasons not to do it but kept those to myself,

'Please do it mate, I'll pay you. There is no way on earth you will do it.'

'Fuck that I don't want money, I'll do it for the attention,' he declared.

I laughed as he began walking back to the base of the tree. The rest of the guys were now a few hundred metres down the road oblivious to what was going on,

'Mate if you do this you are a legend. Let me film it, seriously you have to.'

'Fuck it, let the camera roll.'

I pulled my camera out of my pocket and hit record. Nash brought his smiling face close to the camera and said,

'Watch this you fuckers!'

I burst into uncontrollable fits of laughter as the gravity of the situation took hold. The camera shook as I tried to regain control of my arm and capture this unreal moment on film. Nash marched up to the tree and pointed down towards the faeces.

'You want me to eat that?' he asked.

'Pretty much, why not?' I replied.

I pressed the zoom button on my camera with my right thumb as the true horror of his meal became apparent. Sat on a small patch of dry dusty grass lay two pieces of shit; they had been there for a days, the two together looked like a broken cigar.

I zoomed out and focused the camera back on Nash. His hand reached down without any hesitation and picked the larger of the two pieces from the floor. The camera centred on his face as he quickly bit the brown nugget in half and swiftly swallowed. The surplus dropped to the floor.

I couldn't breathe such was the astonishment at what I had just seen. Nash was clearly out of his mind and buzzing off my twisted excitement.

'No man would do that again,' I provoked.

'You want me to do it again?' he excitedly asked.

Without giving me time to answer he picked the smaller piece off the floor and bit through its dried out centre, before laughing and spitting its chewed carcass onto the middle of the path.

We caught up with the boys as I explained what had just happened. Nash triumphantly marched around while they each watched the unfortunate event on video.

'I ate a poo, I ate a poo,' he repeatedly chanted.

I felt sure he was going to regret it in the morning and hoped that he wasn't going to get ill.

As most places were closed we sat at the end of the beach by a lighthouse having a party of our own party; we didn't need anyone else.

On the walk home we all got distracted and broke up. Nash, Woody and I bumped into the girls from the flat. We stood against the aging white wall of the promenade talking, but I had no idea what about.

Adrianna grabbed me by the back of the neck and kissed me. I had heard that Brazilian women were animalistic when it came to sex; I was left in no doubt as Adrianna bit into my lower lip and I tasted my own blood.

Adrianna had a small baby girl, so I was in no doubt that she would put out; the problem was that I didn't want to as I was intimidated by her. Woody, Nash and I went back to their apartment for drinks.

The apartment was modern and predominantly white in colour. The walls were ghost white as was the tiled floor. We walked into the front room where four men were sat watching MTV on a large black plasma television that was mounted on the wall.

Nash and I sat intoxicated and unable to concentrate on anything anyone was saying. Rather than leave we decided to go onto the balcony and jump into the pool. It was more inviting than it had been earlier and we couldn't resist. It lay out on the deck all calm and innocent smiling in our direction.

Both our bodies hit the surface of the water, ruining its peaceful tranquillity. The pool overflowed as the excess water lapped through the French windows into the apartment. The girls were far from happy.

Adrianna didn't seem to mind. She peered out and smiled before elegantly strutting out onto the wet decking. She took off her tight denim shorts and danced in front of us wearing a tight black thong. We splashed her with water and stared as her perfect arse shone in the night air and swayed rhythmically to the songs that spilled out of the TV.

The men in the flat became animated and forcefully asked us to leave. Nash and I trod through the house in our sodden clothes laughing but apologetic. As we got to the front door the bathroom door swung open and Woody stuck his head out,

'Are we leaving guys?'

'Looks like it mate,' I replied.

As we walked down the tight staircase back to the street we noticed a group of people having a party on a midlevel terrace. We had got the lift earlier so had not known it was there.

The host was a large blonde Scandinavian and he did not look best pleased with us gate-crashing. He stood in the corner mixing a large metal pan that was full of Cacacha and limes. They were drinking Caprinhas, considered Brazil's finest cocktail. It was a simple drink consisting of ice, limes, sugar and Cacacha.

I grabbed a handful of limes from the pan and squeezed them into my eyes, I was so drunk that I didn't care what people thought. I was craving action for action's sake.

It was clear that no one at this gathering was anywhere near the level of drunkenness we had achieved, so they all seemed boring as a result. I dreaded to think what they thought of us, but in all honesty didn't care as we were having more fun.

The booze engulfed my brain and my memory began to lapse as it had too many times this trip. My eyes struggled to focus as the booze and citric acid from the limes overwhelmed me.

Before leaving I kissed one of the girls on the terrace whose name was Elin. She passed me a piece of paper with her name on it and told me to get in touch with her through Facebook.

We stumbled up the hill towards the flat like three broken warriors after a long battle. Woody admitted that while in the bathroom one of the five girls had given him a blow job. She looked no older than sixteen years old.

'Mate she was well young,' I said.

'She was only fifteen. She told me afterwards and I'm screwing,' he admitted.

Woody had by British law committed a sex crime, we wondered if this mattered in Brazil. Carnival had yet to start and already it had gotten ridiculous.

Back at the flat Mark and Kash were sat up the spiral staircase on the roof terrace of our apartment laughing. We sat with them and exchanged stories from the night.

While we had been at the flat they had both been up an alley away from the beach with a prostitute. Kash boasted,

'Yeah it was amazing mate, we both fingered the bitch. I even put my toe in her.'

He pointed to his toe that was caked in blood; thankfully a result of stubbing it on the curb not inside this unfortunate woman. I had seen and heard enough for one night. A quiet night out had descended into anarchy; I trundled down the stairs and passed out in one of the double beds.

I woke up confused as Kash hit me repeatedly around the head.

'Fuck off mate, what are you doing?' I groaned.

'Get up you soft cunt,' he screamed.

'Fuck off,' I replied as I pulled the sheets over my startled head.

I drifted back to sleep as Kash stormed out of the room. He was back minutes later fuming,

'No one tells me to fuck off.'

I moved the sheets from my face as I could hear him pushing something towards the bed. It was something heavy that scraped slowly against the boarded wooden floor.

'Kash don't,' I screamed.

But it was too late.

I covered my head as the large double wardrobe fell towards me like a giant wooden domino. It crashed against the footboard of the bed as one of the high drawers spilled out onto my head. I lay in the aftermath on my bed confused and scared. What was wrong with him?

I had no option but to get up. I walked into the front room and sat on one of tired faded sofas with my head in my hands. On a raised granite table were two bottles of vodka and a two litre bottle of coke. Against my better judgement I poured a large glass.

I scanned the flat and thankfully saw that the glass cabinets were still intact. It was the roof terrace that had bore the brunt of the mayhem.

I clambered up the spiral staircase that was situated in the corner of the living room and up onto the terrace. It looked like a war torn Afghan village, only no troops had passed through, just Kash.

Glass lay strewn across the floor; four glass tables were now wooden frames. A plant pot had fallen and was now scattered in the corner against the low cement wall. I grabbed a brush and swept the shards of glass under one of the wicker sofas that lay against the back wall next to the only survivor, the TV.

I went back down the staircase and into the middle of the chaos.

Kash had completely lost the plot. His eyes were vacant, it was definitely him walking around but no one was driving. He had a cut on his forehead above his right eye. Mark entered the room with his bags ready to leave,

'Gaz he has lost it mate, go have a look up on the terrace. He has put his head through four glass tables and smashed one of the clay pots over my head.'

'So fucking what mate. You're a pussy! I'll smash the whole place up,' slurred Kash in threatening manner.

'Come on mate this isn't funny now, let's just get out of here and go to the beach,' I suggested to Kash.

'Fuck off you pussy, not getting up, I thought you were a man,' was his response.

'I didn't realise you were a dickhead,' I retorted.

I had never seen someone as drunk in all my life; it was a miracle that he was still functioning on any level. His mood showed no sign of abating, with the help of a rested Nash and sober Joel we were able to get him out of the flat, before he broke everything.

Woody had clearly had enough and decided it was best to leave and find his friends. I wanted to go with him but did not have the option.

The apartment sat in a residential area a hundred metres from sea level. The area comprised of several large apartment blocks resembling those built in England in the 1970s. Despite its proximity to the Carnival it was a relaxing area with a safe family atmosphere.

We stood outside on the street at 8:00am trying to control the uncontrollable. Kash could barely walk and was determined to fight anything that he could. He tried on several occasions to punch his own shadow, resulting in him falling to the deck each time,

'I fucking missed. I'll get you. Stop following me you black bitch,' he slurred.

Despite the heat he had chosen to wear his skinny jeans, not that he would have noticed in such a state. We arrived at the beach and despite the time there were thousands of people, but we still stood out.

By 10:00am the four of us were out of control and steaming after drinking several cocktails.

The beach had a vibrant feel to it, similar to Rio but on a much smaller scale. The vendors thankfully didn't have card machines, just bum bags full of change. There wasn't too much room on the beach as it was packed with people that had arrived ready for Carnival. The mix of nationalities on the beach was as incredible as the weather; it was scorching hot without as much as a cloud in the sky.

Behind the beach on the road several large trucks called Trios were preparing for the start of Carnival at 5:00pm.

We were drinking cocktails from a green marquee that pitched against the sea wall by the back of the beach. The three muscular locals that ran the stall stood laughing as the four of us got out of control.

Mark decided to ask if they knew where we could buy some good cocaine. He stumbled back over with a small wrap containing an off-white, almost yellow powder. I was suspicious as they had just handed him the gear,

'Mate I'd be careful with that, it's yellow.'

'Let's try it out, I haven't paid him yet,' Mark declared.

Alarms bells rang in my overly suspicious drunken mind,

'Mate they aren't just going to give you drugs without money.'

'He said we could go get the money,' reassured Mark.

Mark dipped his finger into the bag to taste what he had been given. It wasn't coke but it did tingle on his gum.

'Mate give it here, I'll give them it back!' I declared.

I snatched the small bag from his hand and lumbered over to the stand. I looked the large black man in the eyes as he removed his dark glasses,

'This is not coca,' I complained.

'Relax my friend, it's good,' was the cocky reply.

'We don't want it my friend,' I smiled and put the bag into his large hand.

Before he could reply I walked back to our deckchairs and slumped back into my chair like an inconvenienced alcoholic.

We drank a few more Caprinhas before Kash, who looked as if he was about to die, declared he was going home for an hour. Nash went with him as it was obvious he wouldn't make it back on his own. This left Mark and I on the beach.

We decided to go on a walk along the beach, first having to settle our bill for the drinks and deck chairs bought at the same marquee where we had been offered drugs. After settling up and calling us 'crazy' the largest of the three men, a huge black man with braids, told us to come behind the counter. Reluctantly we did what he said.

We slid past the wooden table out of the sunlight and into the shadows of the tent. The man called Sousa reached into his pocket and pulled out a small, folded piece of card. He unfolded the definite creases before resting the paper on the stack on white cool boxes to the rear of the tent,

'You men, you men crazy, I like you. This stuff is 100% pure, I guarantee.'

I didn't believe him at all nor had I any reason to.

'Sample, taste?' Mark and I both suggested.

'Ok, no problem,' he uttered as he moved sideways to allow us past.

We both licked our index fingers before pressing them on the powder. The white powder covered the tip of our fingers like snow on the peak of a mountain. We rubbed the snow caps onto our gums and immediately it hit us. It was real cocaine.

I felt a rush of euphoria run through my body, immediately feeling alive and giddy. I awoke from my drunken slumber and felt as good as I had all trip, the hangover lifted in an instant giving way to the drug. I looked wide-eyed at Sousa, who was smiling and said,

'Non obrigardo, maybe tomorrow?'

With that we left the tent and skipped joyously towards the inviting ocean. People looked on as Mark and I rugby tackled each other and rolled in the surf in fits of euphoric laughter.

Mark needed to rest and, as we didn't have any towels, he jumped into a seemingly abandoned inflatable blue and yellow dingy. I stood laughing as he grabbed the ores and began to flick sand in an attempt to make it towards the ocean. People looked at him like he was insane but to me it just felt normal.

We spend hours pacing up and down the beach talking to an endless list of people that approached us curious as to what we had taken and why we were so drunk. Carnival had still officially not started.

Vendors approached and handed us beers whenever we finished the ones we were drinking. We both bought some cheap pink sunglasses and were having the time of our lives. My mind was the Carnival; I didn't need music and moving trucks to verify anything.

The Carnival started on cue at 5:00pm as the first of hundreds of Trios fired up and began their precession down Av. Oceânica. Mine and Mark's precession went in the other direction, back up the hill to our flat; we hoped the boys were there and that they were both ok.

I stumbled back into the flat as the sun began to set over Salvador. Kash was passed out on the sofa while Nash was cooking several packets of Super Noodles in a pan. On the table sat two more bottles of vodka; the party was most definitely continuing.

Mark and I poured ourselves generous measures of vodka and collapsed covered in sand onto Kash; it was small retribution for his insane antics that morning.

Mark and I put on some music and went to get ready for the night. I stood in the shower cubicle swaying around but feeling better for getting clean. Being without a towel on the beach meant I was covered in sand, it had gotten everywhere. Just as I began to relax the shower door burst open and Mark bounded in with force singing,

'I would go out tonight,

But I haven't got a stitch to wear.

This man said "It's gruesome that someone so handsome should care" Na, na-na, na-na, na-na, this charming man ...'

He was far from charming and was naked apart from his newly acquired pink sunglasses. I didn't quite know what to do.

Moments later Nash crashed through the cubicle. To an onlooker it looked like three homosexuals showering together but the reality was very different. It felt like being on tour with a rugby team. I had heard many stories of what went on those excursions. I remember a friend at University telling me,

'One of the Rugby lads put his cock up my arse for £50, just for the laugh nowt gay or anything about that, it was just a bet.'

I never understood that story and always thought that they were just gay. What were the boundaries of a bet? Could it go even further? I didn't want to think about it.

As I was drunk the shower was only mildly uncomfortable. Mark started to point and laugh at my penis as he had many times on the trip. He believed firmly that my testicles looked like ravioli and so once more he was chanting,

'You've got balls like ravioli, balls like ravioli.'

As we stood naked with water firing down on us I felt a warm jet of liquid on my leg. I was clean and ready to get out when I realised that Nash had done what most men do when in the shower. He was having a piss, only it was on my leg.

As I stepped out of the shower Mark grabbed my foreskin and pulled on it hard to the point where it hurt. It stretched out before snapping back into place; I looked into his eyes he was barely recognisable, his eyes had gone vacant as he suffocated on booze.

'It's not gay if there's no hard on,' he chanted.

In a perverse way I guessed he was right.

We sat around the flat drinking for another few hours, each trying to do something that outdid the other. I was desperate for the toilet but rather than go I pissed into the pint glass I was drinking from.

It looked like a bitter but unquestionably smelt of urine. I challenged Mark to drink it as he told me he had done something similar in the Student Union at University. Finally I got him back for all the earlier bets,

'Go on then Mark; shouldn't be too hard for a man of your ilk.'

'Urgh give it here you lowie. It's easy mate, easy,' he drunkenly reiterated.

I passed him the glass but he snatched it from my hand, spilling piss all over his shorts. The glass was full to the brim. He brought the glass to his mouth and chugged at it like he was drinking a pint of ice cold water. The reality was he was drinking my urine. I stood with Nash and Kash pointing and laughing at him as Joel stood in the corner of the room sober shaking his head.

Joel knew Kash and Nash from back home and had decided to join them part way through their trip through South America. Joel had been hit by a car years before while backpacking through Europe and it had been serious.

It had taken him over a year to learn to walk again after he thankfully came out of a coma. He told me about the frustrations of his rehabilitation; an example being that he knew how to walk but could just not physically do it. I couldn't relate to his situation, I don't think anyone truly can unless they experience it themselves. I was sympathetic and could tell he was a strong character.

Joel had difficulties breathing due to the series of operations and as a result spoke differently to what you would expect. He was slow so you had to be patient. When we were all together getting drunk it meant he was often ignored. He couldn't drink which made it even harder as we were all so stupid after a few beers. After finishing the vodka we decided to leave the house. It was time to make our mark on the Carnival.

We boisterously took to the streets as Joel pleaded for us to be quiet. You could hear the commotion half a mile ahead. Muffled music filled the air as the streets were covered by a quilt of human bodies moving as one like a giant flag.

Temporary stalls sat outside bars selling cheap cocktails; we stopped at the first one and ordered eight Caprinhas. To the side of this stall stood a young woman with long curly wet hair who sold kebabs. Kash stood complimenting her meat and whispering how he would love to get into her pants.

We made our way to the start of the strip as yet another Trio prepared itself for the two kilometre parade down the street.

The trucks were all dressed differently but performed the same function. Their job was to slowly drive down the packed street as dancers and musicians performed to the crowds. The trucks gave them the platform, the rest was up to them. The selection of mobile concerts started every twenty minutes and continued until 5:00am, offering a range of different music and visuals.

At the rear of each truck people danced wearing designated t-shirts that acted as tickets. They were sectioned off inside a roped area that was attached to the performing vehicle. This zone was typically fifty metres by ten and flanked by stewards. They carried the rope at waist height like bridesmaids carrying a long veil at a wedding.

Kash had been to Carnival before so while my eyes darted about staring at the trucks, the performers and the people he warned us,

'If the police come get out of there way hey, those fucks will just hit you with those batons and break your skull.' He wasn't joking.

He pointed over at one of several officers dressed in green riot gear. They didn't look threatening but given the amount of people, I assumed that they had to be forceful.

'If we lose each other we'll meet up by that lighthouse, get loose up there,' he suggested.

And that is precisely what we did.

The lighthouse marked the halfway point for the Trios and was the first area where there was any space to breathe. The walk to that point was hectic. You had no real say on how fast you walked. Everyone was being channelled down a bottleneck, you had little choice but to go with the flow. It was like feeding a watermelon down a straw.

I swam with the current of people down the narrow footpath, past where Nash had eaten a shit the previous night. To the left were the Trios and trailing 'blocos' playing tune after tune to party goers, while to the right lay the calm of the beach.

Every few seconds I felt pinch after pinch, grab after grab at the pocket of my jeans. The thieves were like piranhas. Salvador is a notoriously poor area of Brazil and Carnival, with the wealth of visitors, acted as a magnet for criminals.

Small lively children ran through the forest of oncoming legs trying to steal anything they could get their grubby hands on. There was no way of catching them given the volume of people. I had left my valuables at the flat and was wearing my trusty skinny jeans so groping at my legs was futile.

I was unbelievably drunk and while my eyes took everything in, it once again felt like an alternative reality. I couldn't imagine being sober in such surroundings, it would be a nightmare. I looked back to see Joel struggling to catch up.

We were all smashed on booze, if there had been a chart on drunkenness the four of us would have occupied the top five. Out of two million that was some achievement, one my parents would be proud of,

'We always knew he could drink and now he has proved it. It's like a dream come true for the two of us. It goes without saying that we are ever so proud.'

We had planned to get with as many girls as possible. Carnival was a week where Brazilians committed their sins for the year; there was no confession or guilt.

Brazil is said to have a large number of births in the month of November, the children are all affectionately termed 'Carnival babies'. I always liked to speculate about conception dates. I was due to be born on the 16th November 1982, but escaped from my mother's ovarian Bastille several weeks early. Without having to be good at maths it was obvious my father got more than just a card on Valentine's Day 1982.

We chose to ignore the thousands of girls out in the streets, preferring to drink and hurt each other as much as we possibly could. The Carnival went by as we sat on the grassy hill by the lighthouse acting like five-year-old school children.

I awoke the next morning in bed still drunk but feeling like I had been run over by a bus. It was nice to wake up naturally without a heavy object flying towards my head. Any other time I would have woke up and said to Mark that we should stop drinking; but this wasn't a normal time, it was Carnival.

Nash came into the front room holding a beer and laughing,

'Which one of you loose cunts has shit in the plant pot on the terrace, fuck!' he exclaimed.

'It wasn't me,' I said, imitating Shaggy.

The blame was Mark's.

'It was you wasn't it?' I asked.

'Guilty as charged sir,' he put his hand up and admitted it.

By midday the five of us sat on the packed beach talking to groups of girls and buying the occasional beer from the countless numbers of vendors that paced up and down in the sandpit.

Mark and I had made friends. We walked down the beach and were motioned over by unrecognisable groups of people who laughed about our performance the previous day and were equally surprised that we were still alive.

'You guys will die this week for sure, you are fucking crazy man,' reassured an unknown Israeli.

Kash was back to his normal self, still obnoxious but a lot of fun. He had an aura about him and was a genuine character with a good heart. His energy allowed him to act how he wanted to without causing too much offence.

As a group of four our energy was incredible, people wanted to join in and be a part of it. While there was a lot going on down at the beach, we stood out without having to do anything. We were the ones having all the fun, making most of the noise and people either laughed with us or at us. There was no doubt that locals took us to their hearts as we personified what Carnival was all about; all our inhibitions died the moment we met at the flat.

We arrived back at the house after another full day of drinking on the beach. We all wore tops we had bought on the beach. We all wore Carnival beads and sat chatting about the people we had spoken to that day and who we wanted to sleep with. Typically we all liked the same person; a girl from Melbourne called Laura.

We had met Laura and her friends on the way to the flat at the beginning of the strip. Kash was immediately all over her. He had such confidence with girls and whatever he said they seemed drawn to him.

'Come here you dirty little slut, I wanna kiss you,' he slurred.

And sure enough she did. Mark and I were puzzled as to how he managed to pull it off. Perhaps I needed to drop the 'Mr Nice Guy' routine and be more of a twat? Laura seemed to like him so that was that, I had to move on.

Back at the flat once again we pushed the boundaries of what was acceptable. While Mark showered, Nash decided he was going to defecate from the balcony onto the residential street below.

His laughter was short-lived as he then bathed his soiled arse and lower body in a plastic basin that Kash and I had pissed in while he wasn't looking. He sat splashing around like a three-year-old child before passing out naked on the sofa.

I sat looking at Nash and laughing as Mark came out of the shower with a worried look across his face.

'Look mate, look what I have fucking done, I look like a tit,' he groaned.

'What's that under your eyes?' I asked, trying not to laugh at his misfortune.

'Bloody burnt my eyes haven't I?' he lamented.

It turned out the cheap pink glasses that had never left his face offered no protection from the sun. For two days he had been wearing a tinted pink greenhouse over his eyes, and now looked like a gay panda. Mark was not happy. It took me back to the terrace in Salta where he refused for a short time to go out as his head had peeled.

Kash came out of the kitchen holding a metal pan and without warning wrapped it across my arse. I writhed around in agony as he laughed and said,

'Get me back if you want soft cunt.'

So I did.

Before I knew it all kinds of instruments were being used to hurt each other. Nash, who had woken up in the all bedlam, hit Mark with a waffle iron as I smacked Kash with a wooden beach ball bat that left large whelps on his already bruised back.

He retaliated minutes later by hitting me across my stomach with a wooden spoon. We had all lost the plot; it was mindless but at the time we all found it hilarious. Our chemistry was similar to that of the guys in Jackass or Dirty Sanchez and we couldn't stop even if we wanted to.

Thankfully the kitchen torture died down and we eventually all relaxed in the front room drinking while Kash cooked us some noodles in the now wrecked kitchen.

After a few minutes I walked into the kitchen to make sure Kash was ok. He had drunk so much booze that I was convinced the gas hob would either burn or set the whole flat on fire.

As I turned the corner into the kitchen I could smell something burning. It smelt like plastic. I called for Nash and Mark to join me.

'Mark get your camera. Nash, you have to see what he is doing,' I whispered.

We looked on in disbelief as Kash stood naked in a black apron by the white stove. He wasn't cooking the noodles as planned; he was there with a wok cooking his passport.

There was nothing we could do to save it; it was in flames and crinkling in on itself while spitting ash into the air.

'Mate what are you doing?' I laughed.

'What does it look like? I'm cooking my passport,' he replied.

Inevitably I had to ask him why.

'I want to be English. I fucking love Mark and Gaz. Fuck Australia! Oh and you guys are eating this by the way! If I need it you have to give me it back,' he instructed.

He served up his black pudding of a passport sprinkling it with pepper like this was nothing out of the ordinary. We all took a piece from the plate and ate it. It was the least we could do as he had taken the trouble to cook.

Kash showed no regret at all in doing this. He wasn't bothered by anything. His toe that he cut on the first night was now clearly infected. Rather than sort it out he took delight in showing us it, then proclaiming that he didn't care,

'I don't care; they can cut my leg off when I get home aye.'

We washed his passport down with the remains of the alcohol before once more making our way down to the Carnival.

Again we stood by the lighthouse, and again we drank a lot of alcohol. Mark picked up a coconut shell that had been broken in half and put it down his jeans and over his crotch like a cricketer's box. We took it in turns to kick him between the legs; Joel, who again was sober, cleverly missed and caught him up the arse. He rolled around in agony as not for the first time we pointed and laughed at his misfortune.

The night passed in yet another intoxicated haze. It began to feel like the days and nights were all just part of one thing. I couldn't with any clarity remember going to sleep. I was either on the beach, at the flat, or by the lighthouse.

The next day I didn't wake up until 1:00pm. Kash sat in the front room and told us that on the way home he had managed to sleep with the Brazilian girl that sold meat at the bottom of the hill,

'I shagged that street meat chick last night you know?'

'You didn't ha really?' Mark asked.

'Too right mate, she is in my room but she gotta go to work in a bit,' he explained.

Mark went off to peek through the door and sure enough she was there under the covers; I went over to take a look. All you could see was a curly mass of black hair that poked above the covers. It was either her or he had stolen a chimney sweep's brush and put it in his bed. I wasn't sure but both outcomes were equally as funny.

'Mate I shagged her on the beach, only in this cave away from the main strip. As I was shagging her I noticed a huge shit on a rock by my head, it was sick!'

I didn't know what to say. Kash really was something else. He toddled off back to the room as I sat staring at the ceiling in the front room.

We were all suffering and decided to have a day and night without any booze. Outside the weather was overcast so we were not missing out on any sun. There were still plenty of nights to party and we didn't want to burn out after three days.

After the sweeping brush left our flat we sat in the largest of the three rooms deciding to watch the films Nash had bought the night before Carnival.

Before watching the copied film, a piracy warning came up saying:

'You wouldn't steal a handbag.'

It got me thinking. No I wouldn't steal a handbag, however if I had a machine that could make a perfect duplicate of one so I could hand the original one back I think I probably would.

The typically fast script of the film was hard to follow. I lay feeling like a retard as my body craved the one thing it needed the least, alcohol. None of us could talk with any real cohesion; it was the worst I had felt for a long time.

As the plot knitted together the film paused and crashed minutes before the end. As we did not have a controller, we had no option but to re-watch the whole film again in the hope that the same fate would not await us the second time. An hour and a half later, it did.

I had watched the film twice but made no sense of it as we had not seen the climax. The film mirrored our time in Salvador, it had become a repetitive mess with no sign of an ending.

.

After the film finished I lay on the floor talking with Kash for hours. We stared at the TV as the manufacturer's emblem darted around the black screen.

As it touched the sides of screen it randomly changed one of six colours. We tried to predict what that next colour would be and kept score.

After tiring of that game an hour or so later I decided make up a story. I had a natural flair for storytelling and so asked him to give me three things to base the story around,

'Give me three random words or things and I'll make up a story.'

He thought for several minutes before deciding,

'Jay-Z, unicorns and raisins.'

'What the fuck?' I asked.

'Hey you said anything and I'm waiting,' he replied.

I lay there for five minutes thinking of a plot. My story centred on Jay-Z and his time at the school of hard knocks. He wasn't a good looking boy and wore blue eye shadow, making him look like a California Raisin. As the Raisins became a TV and merchandising sensation across America, Jay became increasingly popular at school.

This new found popularity earned him the lead role in the school upcoming play. He was to play the part of Charlie the Unicorn. This seemingly happy tale turned sour as The Sugar Hill Gang became jealous of Jay-Z's popularity and set him up.

It ended with Jay-Z being shot by the police. He visited Dr Dre at hospital before facing up to a long stretch in prison. Despite pleading his innocence, the police were convinced he was just Naughty by Nature, another Nigger with Attitude.

As I weaved this elaborate tale Kash sat in silence collecting water from the dripping light fixture above his head. He kindly asked if I would like a drink. I was thirsty but declined.

If someone had entered the room and heard what was coming out of our mouths we could have possibly wound up in hospital under the mental health act. We were so bent on alcohol it was unbelievable. As day turned to night I became more able minded; the things that had already happened scared me.

I went down to the Carnival with Nash on the night but the volume of people now frightened me. I was anxious and needed to go back to the flat.

The next day we met up with Laura, Katy and Vanessa by the beach. They had decided to come up to Carnival on our recommendation; while slightly strange it was cute they had come and they were more than welcome.

Their faces upon spending an hour with Kash and Nash were hilarious; it was clear they had yet to decide whether or not they liked them. It was obvious they found the two of them offensive. For the first day we were all able to sit in one spot and get drunk in relative peace.

I felt rejuvenated after a day's rest but had not learnt any lessons. By late afternoon I was once again blind drunk.

Mark decided on impulse to get a henna tattoo. I came out of the sea to the sight of a small Brazilian man painting a karate figure on his forehead. I knew he would regret getting it, so treasured these hours of drunken happiness. Mark regretted everything he did drunk, but never learned from his mistakes.

It began to rain heavily over Salvador so everyone left the beach. Most people had run off like a Tsunami was imminent, it was only rain so we didn't rush. We walked back along the ocean road past the dormant party trucks with the girls.

I separated from the group and with the torrential rain couldn't spot any of them. As I drunkenly searched for the lads I decided that from behind Mark's head looked like a giant kiwi fruit. So while I searched for the furry fruit I came up with the following chant,

'I thought I was lost, I said oh shoot, and then I saw the kiwi fruit.'

The chant worked as a few minutes after staggering around yelling at the top of my lungs, his furry head was in my sight.

Again an extremely social day on the beach resulted in us further abusing the flat. This time we had guests.

The girls' presence did not change the way that we acted, mixed in a cocktail of music and booze were a number of stupid things. Nash challenged me to eat a can of shaving foam. As I chewed on the froth it kept expanding in my throat, making it almost impossible to breathe yet alone swallow. I spat balls of white perfumed foam onto the wooden floor of the front room.

Kash came back into the old ladies' front room and stood by one of the glass cabinets. He bent over and let Mark spray a whole can of deodorant up his arse,

'It's for the effect people. Chicks are gonna fucking love it.'

It was quite the sight and had everyone laughing. I assumed that when he next farted it would smell like one of those plug-in air fresheners. It didn't, it smelt like flowers and shit.

Mark was now well known for having oversized boxer shorts so it was only a matter of time before we all attempted to get into a pair at the same time. Nash grabbed him in the kitchen as both Kash and I dropped a leg into either side of his shorts.

'Stop it, you are going to rip them you stupid twats,' Mark shouted as we fell.

We hit the tiled kitchen floor hard and lay laughing uncontrollably for minutes.

After each stupid action the humour of it was sometimes punctured by a moment of guilt. I could sense that I was losing control and fought to regain it. I wasn't sure if it was a reaction to Carnival, to being with the lads or just the thought of going home, but something was powering this behaviour and I was teetering on the edge.

Travelling offered an intense freedom, a freedom that amplified during an event like Carnival. Being away from home was a privilege and it was being abused. While we were with Kash and Nash it felt like we could get away with anything; the normal rules of society didn't apply. We were buying stuff with Monopoly money and living on a Monopoly board where all the squares said 'Go'. Nothing was being taken seriously because it felt like nothing was.

Kash came out of the main bedroom wearing some old clothes he had found in one of the wardrobes. He stood before the seven of us holding a stuffed toy from Disney's Dinosaurs while wearing a light blue blazer, pink skirt and linen shorts. His face was plastered in shaving foam, the only way we knew it was him was that his bowler hat was sitting on his head.

The stuffed toy bungee jumped from the window without a chord and we decided to venture once more down to the Carnival. We had become the stars of the Brazilian adaptation of Groundhog Day. Again we went out in an attempt to destroy ourselves, knowing full well we would wake up the next morning in the flat with a hangover and a few hazy memories.

As the days and nights whittled on there were signs that for some people Carnival had ended. People lay on the curb passed out, while others lost that sparkle and cheer that had engulfed the start of the event. People were out not because they wanted to but because they were expected to; it was after all the biggest party on earth. For every single person that looked worse for wear there were hundreds of thousands with wide smiles.

We didn't buy tickets for the blocos but kept running into them and past the bridesmaids carrying the rope. As the music blared from the rear speakers of the Trios I looked to the sky through the branches of arms and limbs in a hedonistic daze. I was with some great friends and it was some party.

Many visitors to the Carnival went to town with their outfits. I had an altercation near the lighthouse with three homosexuals that kept poking me in the face with a large foam penis. One of them danced around wearing a pair of sparkling transparent fairy wings and some bright white pants engulfed in glitter.

I reacted to this by trying to cram the foam penis in my mouth; it proved an impossible task as it had a girth of about a metre. Kash grabbed the fairy boy and pretended to bum him from behind; everyone laughed before being swept up in the vociferous, energetic crowd once again.

Beautiful women in exotic outfits danced down the streets; we had been told that if you gave a woman beads and they accepted, then they had to kiss you. Each of us tried and failed to capture the best looking girls in the crowd. Mark walked over to a vendor and bought himself a lot of necklaces.

Rather than ask girls it was more fun to try and force beads onto people, in the hope they adhered to the Carnival code. I looked over to Mark as we passed the lighthouse; he was acting like a cowboy with a lasso. He was swinging beads above his head and yelling at women, it was incredible.

I bumped into Elin, the Norwegian girl from the first night and though not needing to I threw some beads around her neck. Elin was beautiful and typically Scandinavian. She had a petit frame and striking white blonde hair and blue eyes.

She had a cute unblemished face whose innocence was questioned by numerous piercings including her lip. There was more to this girl than it appeared and I wanted to find out. Unfortunately as the wave of people crashed against us she had to leave, as she didn't want to lose her friends.

I woke the next morning in the flat with a hangover and hazy memories. I was not alone; I had a fleshy human backpack clinging onto my shoulders. It was Laura. I made the obvious assumption that she had come back with me late in the night and that we'd finally had sex. It was either that or I had blown my nose in a condom and thrown it on the floor. I stared at the ocean blue walls and felt horrible.

After a shower I decided to get some breakfast as there were still two more days of Carnival to endure and I needed some food.

By midday Kash, Nash, Mark, Joel and I were sat on the beach close to the lighthouse where we had spent all of our time at Carnival. Five days had passed and none of us had done as well with the ladies as we had anticipated. It left us with only one option:

'No one can leave the beach until you kiss a girl, and I mean properly,' declared Nash.

'Fair enough,' Mark remarked.

We all agreed. Nash hadn't kissed anyone since the first night, so how he thought this situation was going to work I had no idea. The one thing we had in our favour was that we were not yet smashed on vodka.

On the beach we bumped into Katrina, an Australian from Melbourne that had been out with us in Cusco over Christmas. Seeing Katrina reminded me that I had not seen Harry or Sam; they were here at Carnival in the same city and I had forgotten all about them.

As the day passed, each of us struggled to fulfil the criteria of the bet. I sat chatting to Katrina who was a pretty girl and the most viable of the limited options. She told me that she was a kick boxer. Not sure precisely what I was doing I suggested that she show me,

'Ha-ha girls can't kick, tell you what I will let you kick me in the stomach.'

'I will hurt you,' she warned.

'Do your best big shot,' I retaliated.

By this time I was once again drunk as Kash had been filling coconuts up with vodka for most of the afternoon. I looked at the lads and asked if someone could video me being kicked,

'Can someone get this on camera? I'm going to let her kick me.'

As Katrina lined up my mind clicked into gear. While I was convinced she wouldn't kick me that hard, I was worried that I could throw up and at worst crack a rib. I moved the goalposts.

She was warming up a few metres away, building up the tension.

'Kick me in the side of the head instead; I don't want to be sick. Just watch the nose, I don't want to ruin my good looks,' I teased.

So I was stood with the watery surf lapping over my feet, bent the knees and learning forwards. My hands clasped over my nose, protecting my face as the camera began to roll.

For a split second my mind hesitated and I started to think this was a really bad idea. It was too late and I was too involved to pull out now. It would be fine, she wouldn't hit me that hard, and she was a girl after all.

Katrina walked slowly towards me, her eyes fixed on my head. I glanced up at her as she prepared to strike. She jumped a few inches from the floor off her left foot. As she pushed off the sand her right leg snapped back before crashing against the side of my head with force. My mind went blank; it felt like a car had just crashed against my skull. I had hit a brick wall.

I woke a few minutes later on my back staring up at the blue sky. For a moment I could see a bright light and thought that I was dead. Strange people crowded around me, some were smiling while others expressed concern. Katrina had knocked me out.

'Fucking hell you ok mate, that was the best fucking kick I have ever seen,' laughed Nash unsympathetically.

The force of the kick was so strong that I immediately sobered up. Rather than revel in what was the stupidest video we had made to date, I was annoyed at myself. If I continued in this fashion I was going to do myself some real harm.

Katrina sat nursing her swollen foot but seemed unconcerned about the damage she had caused. I guess I had asked for it so there was no reason for her to take things so seriously.

I managed to get a kiss out of sympathy from a Spanish girl sitting several metres away from us. She asked why I let a girl kick me in the head. I was unable to answer because I really didn't know. I had gotten my kiss and so was allowed to leave the beach.

The beach got quiet as people left to get ready for Carnival. We sat talking to a homeless Brazilian man that we had earlier saved from drowning in the surf. He was off his head on something and had passed out face down in the water. Luckily Kash and I had seen him and pulled him out. It was our one good deed of the week, absolving us from all the wrongs we had done. Well, we thought so.

That night the Carnival felt like a funeral march and could have resulted in my death.

I walked down the quiet beach to get away from the swarm of people dancing down ocean drive. My calm walk was interrupted as a girl ran up to me saying that someone had thrown her shoes into the ocean. Before I had chance to respond she was wading out into the darkness in the hope of finding them.

My head was spinning after another night on the strip but something told me I should stay and make sure she was ok. It was dark and no one knew she was down here. I could barely make out her features; all I knew was that she was most definitely Australian.

Moments later I was glad that I had stayed to watch her. She was only ten metres from the shore but looked in trouble as her head bobbed up and down, in and out of view.

I took off my shoes and t-shirt and went in to get her; I wasn't a strong swimmer by any stretch but she wasn't far away so there was no danger.

As the water reached my shoulders I realised I had forgotten to take off my jeans. They now weighed double what they normally did and were growing more and more uncomfortable. They were tight against my damp skin, making it impossible to take them off. My movement in the water was restricted and I could barely swim.

I reached the girl and told her to swim back to shore,

'Your shoes have gone, it's ok you can have mine.'

Out of breath and panting she agreed,

'I loved those shoes, shit what are we doing out here?'

She started swimming back to shore and made it back comfortably. She hadn't been in trouble at all; she was just treading water looking for her shoes.

I followed behind but became more and more disorientated as the current felt stronger. I had swum for what felt like miles but had only gained about five metres. The coast danced tantalisingly in front of me but I couldn't reach it. My jeans felt like cement and I began to struggle before panic set in.

The girl called from the coast,

'Are you ok?'

It was no use, I was unable to respond. I needed the energy I had left for one last push towards the beach. A large wave crashed over my head and my mouth filled with thick salt water. Thankfully the wave pushed me closer to the sandy edge of the coast. I clawed my hand into the sea bed as the water tried to pull me back into its dark wet mouth.

The girl could see me struggling and grabbed hold of my arm, she stood knee deep in the water and pulled me to my feet.

We both sat on the beach in silence as I caught my breath. The dry, welcoming sand caked itself against my tight sodden jeans. The girl apologised for what had happened, but it wasn't her fault, it was mine.

She kissed me on the cheek and thanked me before skipping up the stone steps back onto the road. I lay down on the beach thankful that I hadn't drowned. It could have ended so badly.

I looked around and noticed both my t-shirt and sandals had gone. I didn't know if the girl had taken them or if they had been stolen, but I was angry.

I staggered back to the flat sodden and alone. Several thieves picked away at my pockets like hungry birds as I made my through the crowds. I was past caring and gave way to the undercurrent of crime for the first time. They took whatever money I had. I eventually just turned out my pockets and let the white lining hang out like white flags.

I rocked past the bar where the street meat girl still stood selling kebabs. I looked with no expression at the happy gentleman who had served us Caprinhas most days before we reached the strip. He asked if I was ok and handed me a free drink. As I walked up the road I threw it against a wall, I'd had enough.

I went to bed alone in the flat hoping that when I woke up the Carnival would be over, it had me close to breaking point.

I woke up and could not decide whether I had concussion from the ferocious kick or, like most mornings, was just heavily hungover. Either way I couldn't be bothered to get up.

The last night of Carnival passed me by without incident, following the same pattern as the five or six days that preceded it. Mark paid £70 for a ticket to one of the blocos. Erick Morillo was playing and a lot of people we had met were going to be inside the rope and part of it. I stayed with Kash and Nash as I could not afford it and was becoming increasingly tired.

At the end of booze fuelled night Kash and I passed out on a piece of cardboard outside of Laura and Vanessa's flat. As fate would have it they were passed out inside ours.

As morning approached the five of us came to the decision that we would have to do a runner from the flat. Too many things had been broken in the week that we had stayed there. We were certain to get a huge fine so the only real option was to run.

We crept quietly down the stairs without so much as breathing. We then dashed up the road and out of sight towards the taxi rank at the bottom of the hill.

Carnival was thankfully over; I had survived but only just.

Morro de Sao Paulo

We hurried into two taxis and asked to go to the ferry terminal. I was with Kash who having been to Morro de Sao Paulo before, knew exactly where we were heading.

Kash and I sat at the huge ferry terminal for thirty minutes and still the lads were nowhere to be seen, which was strange as we had set off at the same time. We were both concerned.

'Where have the dumb bastards gone?' asked Kash, knowing I didn't have the answer.

We sat drinking a carton of orange juice unsure as to what we should do. We couldn't go back to the flat and we had no way of contacting them as we were the ones with phones.

'We will just have to wait and hope they arrive, the boat leaves in fifteen minutes,' I said.

Kash finished slurping the sun coloured juice and looked at me,

'You know what dude, I don't think this is the right place.'

'How would you not know? You have been here before,' I replied.

'Yeah but I can't remember mate, I was fried good,' he admitted.

We approached a cab driver and asked him if we were indeed at the wrong terminal. It turned out that we were. The cab driver warned us that we would not make the boat as it was due to leave in fifteen minutes; we decided to take a chance. With a cough of grey smoke the cab shook to life and we were gone.

We flew through the city at frightening speed. It was like we were involved in some high speed car chase as buildings, lights and sound blurred as we hurried across town towards the port.

The cab screeched to a halt by the terminal and the engine breathed a sigh of relief. On the curb stood hundreds of backpackers, we had got there just in time. Mark, Nash and Joel looked at us both with huge smiles across their faces.

'Where have you been you dumb bastards?' Joel asked.

'Don't ask me, ask him,' I muttered.

Morro is an island 60km from the coastline of Salvador. It is a popular spot for people to recover after the excesses of carnival. I lay on the boat looking forward to a relaxing four or five days in paradise.

As we approached the island we all drank a few beers. As I was slightly drunk I set Nash a challenge, knowing full well that he would do it,

'Mate I dare you to jump off the boat.'

'Fucking oath mate no problem,' he roared.

Nash took off his top and dived from the top deck of the boat into the deep blue water. The boat was still a good half a mile from the coastline and it refused to stop. Other passengers looked on in horror as the gravity of his swim registered. We sat laughing as Nash turned from a man, to a boy, to a black spot and then to nothing.

'He'll be fine, he is a good swimmer,' Kash screamed.

'Shit I hope so, that's a long swim, I'd comfortably die,' Mark chuckled in disbelief.

We set foot on the island as the sun began to set and the views around us were spectacular. The small port sat at the bottom of a steep hill. At the top of this hill lay what looked like a huge white stoned mansion set in the centre of thousands of tall palms.

We were greeted at the port by several athletic men that wore yellow t-shirts with their names emblazoned across them. The gentleman I spoke with was called Wellington, he told me that he was a taxi driver. I did not see his car or any evidence of roads.

'What do you mean a taxi you crazy man you?' I joked.

'I can taxi your bags sir. Do you have somewhere to stay?' he asked.

'Wellington I don't but we will be fine, thank you good man,' I offered my hand.

As we walked up the steep gradient away from the port I noticed that these men each had a wheelbarrow. Painted on the side of each in white paint read the word: 'Taxi'.

I could tell I was going to like this island. Scores of travellers walked through the fairy lit streets as the athletic men raced in front of them with a taxi load of luggage. In the midst of a hangover we all walked aimlessly with our heavy bags, sweating and looking for somewhere to stay.

The first night was a quiet one as the alcohol slowly ebbed out of our systems. I was sure that we had poisoned ourselves in Salvador, but given we were all young I was sure our bodies would recover.

Mark left the apartment and spent the evening on his own. I sat around a circular kitchen table with Kash and Nash in our new apartment. We spent an hour sticking black tape onto a kiwi fruit in an attempt to make it look like Mark. Our minds and bodies had a long way to go before they recovered.

The next morning Laura, Katy and Vanessa arrived on the Island so we changed flats in order to accommodate them. We moved to a ground floor flat that lay directly below the one we had stayed in the night before.

We spent the day relaxing on a beautiful beach. The atmosphere was calm as most people were still feeling the effects from the excesses of Carnival. This laid-back mood started to turn sour as by late afternoon Kash had bought a bottle of vodka and several coconuts. The coconuts were expertly sliced at a kiosk and served with long straws leading into their milky centre. Kash had been getting restless and it was clear that a few harmless drinks would turn into several.

Our apartment opened out onto the tight street through two heavy wooden doors. The street had a Caribbean feel to it as the haphazard buildings were painted in different colours and looked handmade. A laundrette sat to the right of our apartment with a corrugated iron roof and a rotten wooden sign hanging above the entrance. The sign read in light blue paint: Wash 'n' Go.

I decided this was a good time to wash my clothes as I couldn't remember the last time they had been cleaned. The people on the island were laid-back and charming, no one seemed to get out of second or maybe even first gear.

Across from our small porch was a hostel with painted green walls and a wooden hatch window. I couldn't help but think it resembled a bar; so Nash had to ask the owner if we could open it.

Within the hour the eight of us sat out on the street on plastic chairs listening to music and ordering drinks from the now open hatch window. Mark worked the first shift as he declared himself the pub landlord. The pub still needed a name.

'The Red Lion?' said Mark.

'The Brazilian?' offered Kash.

'The Boozer?' said Nash.

'The Pig and Whistle?' Laura suggested.

'What about The Flying Paedo?' I asked.

And that was it, the birth and subsequent naming of our first island bar,

'The Flying Paedo, owned and run by people that are uptight cunts,' joked Kash.

'Sure,' the pub landlord replied.

We sat in the street (now a beer garden) with music blaring out of our speaker system drinking bottle after bottle of vodka. The music and good humour attracted people as they walked past. Our flat was on one of the main routes to the beach so the number of people joining us by the bar steadily rose. We told everyone to spread the news,

'The Flying Paedo is open for business and tomorrow night, like every night, is ladies night.'

We spilled onto the beach with a group of travellers and headed to a party at the far end of the beach; there clearly was going to be no let up or recovery just yet.

We larked around in the sand talking to strangers and reminiscing about Carnival in the beautiful surroundings. At the back of the beach sat a series of temporary fruit stalls roaring like bright fires in the darkness, each manned by an innocent looking old lady.

They looked like your typical English fruit stall only with more exotic produce. On closer inspection I realised the women were not selling the fruit, they were selling alcoholic cocktails. You could create your own mix based on the fruit they had available.

Mark and I had lost the others, as with Carnival the volume of people made it inevitable. We stood at the back of the party and finished the second of our fruity drinks. Mark returned with two more but within seconds they both spilled to the floor, being eaten by the dry, thirsty sand.

I lay on the sand with Mark in a headlock, refusing to let him get up as two men plunged their feet into the base of my back,

'Get off you dickheads. I'm helping him,' I screamed as another foot crashed into my back.

Thankfully they stopped kicking me and I managed to stumble to my feet. I fended off Mark to make sure that the already bad situation did not get any worse.

Mark had been hit from behind by a large Israeli man wearing a Juventus football top. He had gone up to the man and drunkenly kissed the badge on his shirt. It was funny watching Mark stoop down to embrace the team's badge.

'Juventus, the old lady beautiful,' he said as he kissed his fingers and raised his arm flamboyantly.

'Me forza Lazio,' he continued.

Within seconds he was on the deck with a mouth full of sand in a chokehold. I stepped in at this point and clawed this huge man from Mark's back. I had then dived onto an infuriated Mark to stop him from getting up. It was obvious that he was going to fight and looking at this man, it was a bad idea.

Israeli men have a reputation for being good at fighting. They are typically all fresh from the army where they have completed a period of mandatory service. In this time they are taught how to fight, giving them a distinct advantage over someone like Mark.

Hordes of people converged on the scene like moths to a flame and a large fight circle had formed. Inside this circle was me on the floor with Mark in a headlock. People thought the two of us were fighting each other and wanted to see how it would end.

As I got to my feet the situation fizzled, out the man in the Juventus shirt had gone. I hoped that would be the end of it.

There was no doubt that the attack on Mark was unprovoked, he hadn't deserved it but in some situations you just have to back down, unfortunately he wasn't prepared to do that.

Mark stormed back to the flat like a steam train and did the one thing I asked him not to do; he told Kash. Kash would do anything for the people he liked; if it meant fighting then he would be on the front line without asking any questions.

Kash went into the kitchen and came back with not one but four knives. It was clear things were going to get out of hand very quickly,

'I'll fucking stab the cunt mate, no one hurts one of my mates, not ever,' Kash barked.

Kash wasn't a big guy and didn't look particularly strong but he had a lot of heart. His face scared me; it was vacant and showed no fear. I had no doubt that had he gone out he would have used one of the four knives he had at his disposal. He was a man of action, looking for thrills for their own sake, indifferent to any long term consequences. Mark stoked the fires,

'I'm gonna fucking kill him. Gaz you should have let me fight him you cock.'

I lay in the corner of the room on my bunk with Laura and chose to ignore him as the night slowly turned to morning.

Kash and Mark didn't make it on the beach; they stayed up drinking and shouting anti-semetic drivel out onto the deserted streets. There were a lot of Israelis on the island who all tended to travel in insular groups. The chanting was not the smartest thing to do, however I was sure the culprit could not hear their screams.

I woke the next morning convinced Mark's temper would have subsided as the alcohol wore off and some perspective took hold. I was wrong.

Mark was still visibly drunk, he stated that he was going down to the beach to kill the man, who by now he had no recollection of.

'I'm going to kill the Jewish cunt,' he said for the umpteenth time.

'Not if I don't first,' called Kash from the back room.

Kash appeared from the back room wearing a small pair of red Speedos and his bowler hat. His eyes were glazed and he was also still off his face on drink. He stood with a small hunting knife in his mouth, looking like he'd just been sacked from Baywatch. I looked at him and laughed,

'What you laughing at? I'm serious, I'm gonna get him.'

'Who are you getting? None of us know who it was, just drop it's gone.'

'I'm just gonna kill all of 'em, the bloody Jews.'

'Hitler would be very proud.'

As they left for the beach, I thought long and hard about leaving the island. I was happy to drink and have fun as there wasn't much else to do on the island but this situation was something far removed from fun; it was out of control and I wasn't sure what to do.

The girls were all clearly shaken by the experience and I couldn't help but think Kash had scared them, which was unfair.

As the day passed tempers gradually subsided as they drank coconut after coconut of vodka on the beach. I decided not to join them for most of the day as I was upset with what had happened and needed time to clear my head.

The seven Australian girls had come to the island so I met with them and talked about Carnival and their plans for the end of their trip. I spoke with Mel as we floated up and down in the calm tropical waters off the beach. Mel and I got on really well; it was shame she had a boyfriend back home in Australia as the more I spoke to her the more I liked her.

Mel was Australian but had Armenian heritage so looked different to the rest of the girls. She had beautiful skin and was blessed with a womanly figure; everyone stared at her chest, it was hard not to. On top of being good looking she was incredibly sweet with an almost childlike demeanour. There was nothing threatening about Mel; I was convinced she was only capable of nice things.

I roped her into joining us that evening at The Flying Paedo. The girls' apartment was only a hundred metres from ours so it wasn't too much to ask. Mel had spoke in the day about wanting to have a break from the girls.

Travelling in a group of seven must have been difficult. I had travelled for most of the trip with just Mark; whenever there were more of us it became more difficult. Seven would have been a personal nightmare. Even at home I liked to go out drinking in small groups, it was easier and always more fun. The same was true with travelling.

The Flying Paedo was becoming more and more popular; we had told people about it on the beach and they flocked to join in on the tight back streets away from the beach.

The island had a couples feel to it. You couldn't help but be seduced by the softly lit streets, the fine restaurants and laid-back atmosphere. It made me want a girlfriend, but that was something I had made impossible. I didn't want to get hurt by another girl and this trip had proved to me that being single was a lot of fun.

Rather than walk around the island and get depressed by all the smiling couples eating at restaurants I took refuge at The Flying Paedo, a brash new bar oozing with masculinity and cheap drinks. In the space of two days we had become revered by the locals of Morro de Sao Paulo, who looked at us in amazement before inevitably joining us and having a good time.

The pockets of lunacy were infrequent, for most of the time we were just a group of lads having fun. We opened our arms to anyone that wished to join us and when they did they had a good time. I was sure not everyone liked us; I bet some people hated us but at the time we just didn't care. Together with the girls we were a hurricane that blew through paradise without causing any damage.

We could not have looked more out of place on the beach if we had tried. Unlike the previous night there was no party and no one seemed to be drinking. Kash and Nash decided to have a fight, clearly craving some sort of action. They were politely asked to leave the beach by a restaurant owner soon after breaking two plastic chairs. It fell on me to get them back to the apartment and it was not easiest of tasks.

Before this I'd had a good night talking with Mel. I couldn't help but feel there was something between us, but I respected that she had a boyfriend. It was pointless thinking that something would happen, but I hoped it would.

Mark had hit a wall and had reached his limit. He sat as the heavens opened collapsed in a large wooden chair that had tipped on its side; he was oblivious to both the rain and the fact he had tipped his chair.

He laid wearing his sodden blue checked shirt and darkening cream golf shorts. His eyes were framed by the pink glasses that he had since forgiven for burning him in Salvador; the left lens of the sunglasses was missing, making him look mental.

Our time in Morro had started peacefully but was developing into a continuation of the Carnival, if anything we were all drinking more. I spoke with a recovering Mark the next day and we decided that after Nash's birthday it was time to leave. Drink was getting the best of both of us. Mark had woken up swimming in his own piss so he had to agree with me.

He tried to pass off the incident by saying that he had spilt beer on himself. The problem for Mark was that beer didn't smelt like urine and the whole flat most certainly did.

Nash's birthday was the next day but we suggested to him that we celebrate it early. He would be turning twenty-six at midnight and there was a big party at a club on the other side of the island. The party was being held at the mansion we saw hidden by all the palm trees when we arrived. Mark, Nash and I walked to the beach as Kash stayed in bed motionless, dead to the world.

We had become notorious on the island because we didn't fit in and were loud. We hurried through the narrow backstreets of Morro past the small shops and cafes at pace, before busting onto the beach with our speakers turned up to the max. This was to be our last hurrah, a celebration of a new friend's birthday and the final nail in the Carnival coffin.

Mel joined us on the beach for the day as the other girls drifted in and out like the coastal tide. Nash, joined by Mark, the girls and I, was having a great time as the cans of beer disappeared. In a bid to enhance his mood I kindly offered to buy him a tattoo for his birthday; it would be something for him to remember the day by.

The condition of the tattoo was that I could pick it, and for me there was only one thing that it could be. I offered him the opportunity to have the pub name inked onto his skin for all of eternity, and Nash being Nash he agreed.

Nash thought it was a great idea to have 'The Flying Paedo' permanently scrawled on his body and no one was going to suggest otherwise.

As the day drifted into evening I realised that Kash had not been down to the beach all day. I went back to the flat but he wasn't there either. Katy and Laura told me that Vanessa had taken him to hospital back on the mainland; there was no other news.

As we were celebrating Nash's birthday I chose not to tell him, and told the girls to do the same. There was nothing he could do and we could worry about it tomorrow, if there was anything to worry about.

Nash, Mel, Laura and I went to the tattoo shop to get his birthday present. After an hour or so deliberating where the tattoo would go we settled on the arch of his foot. The tattoo shop was small, about the size of a disabled toilet, and it looked like one.

The tattooist looked at Nash in disbelief when he wrote down on a piece of paper what he was after:

The Flying Paedo

Smiling, he proceeded and drew the stencil onto his foot in a dark blue pen. I stood by the hatched window looking on as the temporary pen was replaced by permanent ink. Nash sat like a little boy at the doctors with a clenched fist in his mouth. The girls started laughing and taking photos as the tattoo was finished.

The tattoo was a success so Nash was excited to get back to the pub and celebrate. It was his day, he wanted to show everyone and thrive on the attention.

Back at the flat Mark was doing a sterling job as pub landlord. People crowded the streets, a mix of locals and travellers had all been brought together by an idea to start a bar where the drinks were free.

A group of Israeli guys walked up to us as we arrived back and asked,

'Is this the Flying Paedo?'

'It is indeed kind sir, let me pour you a drink,' declared Mark.

By our apartment was a small newsagent that sold liquor and basic provisions. The boy that ran the shop was no older than sixteen; he had white hair and a sparkling earring. He dressed like he was in the NBA and looked like American rapper Sisqo. He revelled in our parties and he was able to get drugs at a relatively cheap price.

Fuelled on alcohol and whatever Sisqo had given us, Nash and I excitedly made our way through the beautiful town, flanked either side by expensive restaurants, wearing neon tutus and vests, bought from vendors on the beach.

Mark did not have the energy to join us at the party. He stayed by the flat drinking and listening to music as The Flying Paedo had its first and last lock-in. He had become attached to the place and it was clear he was proud to be running it.

I was excited about going somewhere different. Although it was dark it was good to finally see more of the island. In the days I had been there all I had seen was the beach, our flat and a few bars. The club rested up on a hill on the other side of the island, it was near to the port where we had arrived days earlier.

The converted mansion cut into the hill and was even more beautiful close up. The dance floor spilled over the edge of the hill, leading to a maze of steps and walkways that led to seating areas and various exits. As midnight came and went the DJ announced that the foam was about to start, everyone on the neon-lit dance floor let out a loud cheer.

The dance floor lit up with a hue of dark blues and greens that illuminated the cloud white bubbles that shot from the sides of the floor. I danced around like a maniac laughing, having the best time standing on a large speaker by the left of the DJ booth.

Amy Winehouse's Rehab gave way to a mixed version of Arctic Monkeys' hit Good On The Dance floor as I ran over to the pit of inviting foam and jumped into its frothy centre. As I sank into the foam I fell over and my head crashed against the floor.

Panic set in as I was unable to get to my feet. Rather than get out I sank further and further as the foam kept rising and rising. I clutched at the increasing cloud of bubbles. I felt a kick to my head as I rocked forward onto my feet. It was like being in a bucket of crabs as people unknowingly blocked my escape. I was in real trouble. The music started to sound distant and unclear as I was now totally engulfed in the white froth.

The lights on the dance floor and sparkling night sky went out of view as I began to choke on the soapy spray. I managed to punch an arm out to the side of the basin in a desperate plea for help. I felt someone grab hold of my arm and pull me out of the sunken death trap.

'Are you ok?' he asked in a calm Australian accent.

'I am now mate,' I slurred.

I sat on the floor looking like a five-year-old that had just got out of the bath. I was lifeless, I was broken.

I had reached my limits and decided it would be best to go back to the flat. I gathered my breath and tried to gather my thoughts as I left the party. I felt strange mentally as thoughts and conversations whizzed through my mind. I was thankful that I had not drowned but wished all the people in my head would go away.

The sun broke in the sky as I walked through the town and onto the beach. Couples walked hand in hand in the surf, despite the voices I felt alone. I was jealous of these people as I wanted what they had. It was something that I wanted back home but was too scared to find.

My bitter thoughts subsided as the alcohol and drugs took hold. I started to play volleyball on my own which was all the more strange as I didn't even have a ball. As the romance of a peaceful sunrise surrounded the front of the beach, I was at the back in the shade watching a twenty-six-year old man in a pink tutu play imaginary volleyball. Something was not right.

I woke up at midday lying next to Nash in one of the bunks in the front room. I jumped up in shock as I didn't know why I was there. I stood up and looked down at what I was wearing. I had on a black boob tube and a pink thong that looked disgusting as my warm relaxed testicles fell either side of the gusset. It resembled the jowls of a cockerel.

Nash woke up laughing and told me what had happened,

'You came in smashed mate asking if I fancied playing volleyball without a ball. I couldn't be arsed and was moaning about the lack of fanny I've had this trip. So minutes later you came in wearing Laura's clothes taking the piss. It was too funny mate. Then you just passed clean out, you dickhead,' he chuckled.

'I was worried for a moment, ha ha good times, is Kash back yet?' I asked.

'They are due back in an hour or so I think? Ask Laura,' he said.

The apartment was a state. There was no damage but it stank like a public toilet. I had to get outside as soon as possible.

By lunchtime Kash returned and he was the calmest I had seen him. He was clearly shaken by whatever it was he had just experienced. I went for a drink with him in the shade as I wanted to know that he was alright. Kash told me that while we had been on the beach he'd had a fit in the room and couldn't stop shaking. It was a blessing that Vanessa had stayed with him.

'If I wasn't for her mate I reckon I'd be dead. She had to get one of those taxis to take us to the port mate. There I am cold as fuck and shaking, speeding through town in a fucking wheel barrow with a black gardener at the helm,' he explained.

'Then what?' I prompted.

'We got a boat and then a taxi to a hospital on the mainland. Mate this hospital was horrible, in the corridors there were loads of people with open wounds just lying around moaning in all sorts of pain. It was like a horror film. The doctor sent us back here coz he doesn't want me getting more infected.'

'What's wrong mate, you going to be ok?'

'Not sure mate it's the fucking toe, got a blood infection and as I didn't get it sorted it's got into my blood stream and fucked with my ticker. Can't drink or shit. I asked him to saw it off but it wasn't an option,' he joked.

'Just take it easy mate, sure it will be fine,' was all I could offer.

It was clear that he was not well, but I liked how he joked about it as it made me feel comfortable. It was clearly not funny and we were all concerned. We had pushed the boundaries to their limits. His illness was a clear sign; it was time for us to take a break from each other.

Mark and I booked to leave the following morning. As it was our last night in Morro, we went for dinner to catch up and to make plans for the last few weeks of the trip. We both agreed that we needed some time without drinking, agreeing that things had got way out of control. No one was to blame and it couldn't be explained. We just had a destructive chemistry when we were all together; it was unlike anything I had ever experienced.

On the way home from our meal I finally broke. As I walked side by side with Mark his voice drifted out of my mind and his words became more distant and dream like. I fell silent and broke into an uncomfortable cold sweat. It felt like an insurmountable amount of time but in reality only a matter of seconds passed. My vision blurred and I fell like a puppet onto the cobbled streets of paradise.

I woke up shaking and confused. Mark stood over me concerned without fully knowing what to do. He sat as I tried to gather my thoughts. I wasn't sure what was wrong and could feel myself begin to cry, not out of pain but out of worry.

It was time to leave.

The following morning we said our goodbyes to the lads, the girls and The Flying Paedo. We all joked about opening fictitious franchises across Brazil before boarding a boat back to the mainland.

A weary Kash carried my bags onto the boat and waved us off. As he went from man, to boy, to black spot and then to nothing I looked forward, it had been a mad couple of weeks.

Itacare

Mark and I arrived in Itacare by mid afternoon. It took only six hours to reach the town, which suited me as I sat on the bus in a state of recovery. We checked into a hostel and got a private room. The hostel was a short distance from the main strip that ran through the middle of this small town.

Itacare had a warm little town feel. While it was not as striking as Morro, it felt safe and a good place to finally relax. The wide main street that ran up a small gradient was awash with internet cafes, shops and a variety of different restaurants. The buildings were all low-lying and run by local people, it was a charming place with an unmistakable surf culture.

The town catered for all your typical tourist whims. There were numerous tour operators offering all type of adventures. I had found my happy place, a place where we could do absolutely nothing. After wandering aimlessly around town, Mark suggested we get our heads down and sleep. I could think of nothing better, so we did.

The next morning we visited a series of beautiful, small cove beaches that lay just out of town. We spent the day relaxing and reflecting on the events of the past two weeks.

There was no denying that we had had a lot of fun. At the time it was unbelievable but as I lay there on the beach I was thankful it was all over. Carnival had pushed things to the limit. It had taken me to my peak and sunk me to my depths. It had been a real rollercoaster both mentally and physically for all of us.

Mark had adopted a tone of perpetual dissatisfaction and annoyance about everything that happened at Carnival. He pointed the finger of blame at everyone but himself.

'So were we mate, they didn't exactly hold guns against our heads,' I said.

I had learned to accept the flaws in my character but he was still denying his. It was no one else's fault but our own and it was now time to recuperate. Itacare was our rehab centre.

The next four days we did very little. The highlight was a trek to one of the most beautiful beaches that I had ever seen in my life. The walk took us through the edges of the national park leading to a gateway to the rainforest, and it was worth it.

We arrived at the beach sweating and out of breath, but as we looked across the bay we noticed that on the vast expanse of lightly coloured sand sat only a handful of people. The beach was as beautiful as it was wild.

Palm trees clung to the back of the beach offering shade from the midday sun whilst the rocks on both sides of the bay glistened as ferocious waves crashed against them. Small crabs danced across the hot sand, scurrying into small holes when they sensed imminent danger.

To the far right of the beach a group of Brazilians played football, using small brown branches that stuck out of the sand like royal guards as goal posts. Their muffled cries and celebrations were drowned out by the rumble of the untamed ocean current.

It was the most peaceful place on earth and I was glad we had found it.

I had a joint with Katy and the girls who had arrived on the beach an hour or so after us. They had arrived in Itacare the day after us and it was the first time we had seen them since Morro.

I sat alone on the rocks to the left of the beach contemplating my future and looking back over my trip. I was due to go home in nine days' time and I wasn't sure how it made me feel.

I sat as the soft waves broke against the hard rocks and felt a great feeling of peacefulness, you couldn't help but feel that way in such surroundings. For those moments I felt at ease and the clouds of trouble lifted and began to clear in my mind.

My mind drifted from the serenity of the beach to the grey listlessness of the life I left back home. Why couldn't I just stay here? Why did I feel I had no other option but to go home?

I resolved from this moment to do what I wanted to do instead of what I was expected to do; there was a difference. If it meant hurting people or letting them down then that was a sacrifice I had to make.

I started to wonder if this was the reason for me coming away. I had got trapped into the routine and perceived normality of society back home, and I had tried to kid myself I was happy; I knew that deep down I wasn't.

The beach and my experiences on this trip made me realise that I could strive for better; be whoever and do whatever I wanted. I just had to be positive and set myself tangible goals.

I stood up, took a deep breath of sea air and realised that I was stoned, really stoned.

The next morning I put back the dates of my flight home. There were still a lot of new places on the coast that I wanted to see, and I was in no rush to return to the familiarity of home. I gave myself an extra two weeks.

We didn't drink during our time in Itacare. As the dry nights chalked up Mark was growing restless. The realisation hit him that unless he was drinking, he never picked up girls. It was a sobering fact for both of us.

I had taken the drastic measure of having a wank in an Internet cafe. It had been as exciting as it was uncomfortable. The cafe sat next to our apartment and had several computers that sat in wooden cabins with saloon-style, swinging doors. Each of the doors had a number.

I nervously sat behind door number seven that sat against the far wall. Before loading up a suitable website I peeked out from my cabin to check that the coast was clear. I had to be careful. It took me twenty minutes to find a suitable video; I was always picky when it came to choosing what to watch.

I sat with my shorts at half mast pressing one of the headphones against my ear. The other ear listened out for people, while my left hand went to work. Juggling the volume of the movie with the sounds of the cafe was a difficult task; why did porn stars have to moan so much during sex?

After an awkward few minutes I completed the mission without being caught, but I had been shot. I looked at my shorts and they were covered in fresh stains. I felt my skin burning as I was overcome with embarrassment; I had missed the tissue.

I left the cafe in a sheepish manner. I brushed past a twelve-year-old boy who was sat on a plastic seat innocently playing Crash Bandicoot on one of several Playstations. I hurried back onto the street outside with my head hung in shame.

On our last night in Itacare we sat in one of the several bars that dotted the main strip chatting with a group of Australians we had seen on and off during our time in Brazil. It was nice to be sober and just sit and listen to people, I found it relaxing.

The bar had a Jamaican theme and was built around a wooden shack. The seating sat on a wooden decking that was surrounded by thin trees and lit with fairy lights. A series of speakers played soft reggae music that drifted along with the streams of conversations.

Bobby, who I spoken with briefly in Morro, lit a joint and we all sat around having a smoke. As the smoke snaked up into the air a local Brazilian man stumbled over to our table and asked if he could have a smoke with us.

'Sure man not a problem,' Bobby said as he passed over the joint.

The man's long black fingers reached over and snatched the joint from Bobby's hand. This strange man refused to give us back the smoke. Two minutes had passed and he was still holding it while trying to touch up one of the girls. We had to do something.

He sat with a wide grin on his face, managing somehow to look threatening. He was clearly poor as his clothes were covered in dirt and he smelt like gone off sausages. I began to get annoyed,

'Give it back you fucking clown,' I yelled as I grabbed his arm.

He beat me off with his other hand. It smelt like someone had just opened a bin.

'Stop being a dick you smelly twat, why are you being such a tit?' asked Mark.

The man clearly didn't understand.

He shouted at us in Portuguese before shaping his right hand into a gun like a five-year-old cowboy. He pointed his right finger at each of us and shouted, 'Bang, bang, bang,' laughing manically as he shot each of us in the head.

We decided to just let him have the joint and ignore him. He soon grew tired of us ignoring him and left with the joint still in his hand. If he had tried to steal my iPod speakers I could have said it was stereotypical, some people rich or poor I could just never understand.

Mark and I got on a night bus soon after. We were both fully rested and ready for the next stop that we would reach by early morning.

Arrial de Ajuda

We arrived in Arrial early the next morning. The town had a similar feel to Playa Del Carmen in Mexico though it was smaller in size, it was unquestionably an upmarket seaside town geared towards tourism.

Rather than hostels, the majority of the accommodation came in the form of small apartments called Posadas. This was perfect for Mark and I as we had grown tired of dormitories; we were approaching the end of our trip so it was nice to have our own private space.

The first day Mark and I walked around the town to get our bearings and a general feel for the place. There seemed to be a lot of people in this town that had in Mark's words, 'Lost it'.

The coast of Brazil seemed to be a breeding ground for the insane. Back in England seaside resorts were typically full of pleasant old people in the twilight of their lives eating fish and chips and talking about the war. In Arrial the old people were all schizophrenic; talking to themselves and taking drugs.

I sat in an Internet cafe checking my emails when a curious looking gentleman sat down on the machine next to me.

The man was in his late sixties and, despite the warm weather, was in full leathers. The staff seemed to know him. He was unable to log onto the computer, so the attendant came over to help.

The man looked like a dead frog; he had a long drawn out smile and huge bug-like eyes. His face was framed by long withered grey hair that looked like smoke. He mumbled incoherently at the employee tapping the screen in front of him. He then stared directly at me and pointed. I started into his vacant eyes and smiled.

'How are you sir?' I asked.

Another series of mumbles followed before he shouted in full voice,

'It's rock 'n' roll but that's how I like it,' grinning wildly in my direction.

I wasn't sure how to reply or what to say, so I said nothing. This man was something else. I wondered how long he had been in the town and at what point he had, as Mark put it, 'Lost it'.

I left the cafe and went to a different property than the one we had chosen to stay in because it had a pool.

Laura, Katy and Vanessa had joined us in Arrial but were staying in a beautiful resort five minutes from our more humble abode. We spent the day illegally in their pool listening to music and fooling around in the midday sun. We had finally recovered from the Carnival; it had taken a week but it was nice to feel like some semblance of a human being again.

Mark and me stayed at an apartment called Manga Rosa that sat behind the town's main square. It was owned by an old Brazilian couple that lived in the main house. They had fashioned a small reception area in the porch of their home. Leading from the house sat a series of small apartments, eight in total that lay adjacent to the drive. It was a simple place but more than adequate for the two of us.

Our location was ideal; it was at the throat of the main strip of bars and restaurants that led down to the beach called Broadway. We planned to give our regards to the road and the beach over the coming days.

On our first evening we planned to have a few beers near the apartment at a relaxed bar called the Chopperia. We left the girl's resort and went home to have a shower and get ready.

As Mark was getting into the shower there was a loud knock at our door. I looked out and saw that it was one of the German girls who had checked in at the same time as us that morning. The two of them were a sight for sore eyes, so we hadn't made any effort to talk to them. Mark looked at me and said,

'Is it the German girl?'

'Yeah how did you know that?' I asked.

'She knocked earlier asking if she could borrow some money as her card isn't working. I told her you may be able to help her out,' he replied.

'Why would you do that you nipple? I asked.

'Banter mainly. Here, watch this,' Mark's face lit up, I knew that he had an idea.

He took two large steps across the room to the door and dropped his towel. I lay on my single bed against the far wall laughing as he opened the door wearing nothing.

'Hallo aus Berlin? Sorry I am a naturalist, it's rock 'n' roll and I like it,' he explained.

The girl was not fazed by Mark's nakedness. She stood emotionless in the door and simply replied,

'Good for you, can your friend lend me money or not?'

I began to laugh and Mark replied,

'When you suck my willy.'

He then shook his manhood in her direction and smiled at her. She rolled her eyes and sighed before leaving,

'Stupid English boys.'

Mark closed the door to a chorus of laughter. The noise of us laughing bounced off the walls as she stomped away from the porch and back under the rock that she had crawled out of.

This girl had been unfriendly since we had met her. She sat in a hammock by her room chain smoking with a stony face; I doubted that she had ever had a day of fun in her whole life. She had long dry, tangled black hair and her skin looked like rice cakes. She had asked us for money, two complete strangers, like it was expected and not a big deal. I didn't like her at all and hoped she would not bother us again.

We walked down to the Chopperia where we met up with the far more attractive threesome of Vanessa, Laura and Katy. We sat on stools at a tall table that lay over a large wooden beer keg.

The bar was simple; all the seating was outside on the square under a huge red canopy. It had a relaxed ambience; people sat and enjoyed drinks breathing in the night air. People stood around on the street dancing and drinking in a peaceful cosy manner.

Mark was a little bored by the calm so again drunkenly decided to get a henna tattoo. The one he got at Carnival on his forehead had taken days to disappear and he had moaned about it constantly. I reminded him of this in a bid to deter him from doing it again, until I saw the image he had picked from the man's book.

The tattooist grabbed Mark by the upper arm and began to draw out a stencil on his arm. The stencil was of Nickelodeon's Sponge Bob. Mark thought it was hilarious and again suggested that I should get one,

'Mate it's banter, look at him, it's Sponge Bob.'

'Mate it's not even funny, it just looks ridiculous,' I replied.

'Does it?' Mark asked as we both looked down at his arm.

'I'm not getting one,' I told him firmly.

The tattooist was making a real mess of his work. I looked and noticed that his hands were both shaking. He was sweating like a blind poof in a sausage factory, I couldn't work out if he was nervous or on drugs. I guessed it was the latter.

The little Brazilian eventually completed his artwork. It looked like a five-year-old had attacked Mark's arm with a blunt crayon. Had it been on paper I would have taken it home and put it on the fridge next to my three-year-old nephew's scribbles.

I looked down at Mark's arm and finally had to admit that it was indeed funny,

'Mate, I apologise that tattoo is genius.'

'It is a good one indeed,' confirmed Katy.

My eyes fixed on the wobbly square outline; the two tentacle arms and the mismatched eyes, in no way did the tattoo look like Sponge Bob. I knew that Mark would regret getting this latest piece of work, but at least it wasn't in the middle of his head this time. He had learnt that lesson the hard way.

We sat with the girls and decided to get blind drunk on the fruit cocktails that were being sold on the street. By the Chopperia there was a selection of temporary fruit stalls and, as in Morro, they were cheap and delicious.

We befriended an old Brazilian lady who kept making our drinks exceptionally strong. She handed them to us laughing. The fruit disguised the amount of alcohol we were drinking which meant we got really drunk, really quickly.

I sat looking around the bar for something to do. When I get drunk I hate sitting still and talking to the people I already know. I was getting bored and was in need of some action.

I looked across the bar at a small group of Israelis sat below us on one of the lower metal tables. Two of them were kissing, which left one of the girls sat looking awkwardly into the starry night sky. Fuelled with alcohol my confidence had finally returned so I went over to the table and asked,

'Shall we kiss too?

To my surprise the girl said,

'Ok, why not,' in a cute, carefree fashion.

Mark returned from the toilet and looked over at me in shock. I could tell that he was wondering what had happened in such a short space of time. Laura, who I had a history with in Rio and once in Salvador, did not look best pleased. We were now friends so while I didn't want to hurt her feelings, it was time for both of us to move on.

Alcohol pumped through my system and began to take over as it had at Carnival. It was a relaxed bar but my mind was working over time. The direct approach I used with this girl was not in keeping with my usual character. Something had changed inside of me; it felt like a weight had been lifted.

I felt free and realised that I could do and say what I thought. Ideas started to race through my head as I looked to explore avenues that would lead to fun.

Vanessa had been ill since Carnival and Morro and decided to leave the bar; mentally she never arrived. She had sat on our elevated keg table without talking for over two hours, it was clear she needed to rest.

Mark went back to our apartment to defile Katy, who he had slept on a handful of occasions since Carnival. That left Laura and I at the bar. I didn't fancy Laura and began to think that she clung onto me too much. She was a nice girl and a good friend so I didn't want to hurt her feelings.

Vanessa had suggested in Morro that the only reason they had come to Salvador was to see Mark and I; Laura had been the driving force behind the decision. I was glad they had come but the girls had on occasion stifled opportunities with other girls; leading to one big argument on the beach in Morro. I knew that I had to tread carefully.

I stepped straight onto a land mine. Laura and I argued instantly outside the bar. She denied liking me, so I had no idea why we were arguing at all? I was drunk and ultimately confused by the situation. The result of our heated exchange was that Laura stormed off into the darkness leaving me at the bar. I stayed and joined the Israeli girl and her friends on the smaller table.

I walked the Israeli, who I learned was called Mayan back to her Posada; coincidentally she was staying at the same place as the three girls, where we had been the whole day. The hostel had a security guard so as we walked up to the main gate I had to think of something to do. I decided to pretend I was from Israel.

I was able to sneak past the security guard by impersonating Kazakhstan's most famous export Borat. I was pretty good at his voice and in my mind it was similar to those from Israel,

'I like-a very much this hostel it's-a nice,' I said.

That was all that was needed, somehow it worked and he let us both through the gate.

Mayan started to look around the large resort for somewhere to go. I thought I can follow her and maybe make a sexy time with her? My mind, like my voice, was still in character.

She looked into her room but it was out of bounds as all her friends were sleeping. It was clear that she did want to have sexy time with me, it was just a case of where. Our options were limited and neither of us could think, so we stopped thinking. We had sex in the corner of the corridor near her room.

I stood intoxicated as she took control of everything, including the use of a condom. She looked up at me saying,

'I have not seen one of these before,' in a Middle Eastern tone.

I looked down at her confused.

'What-a penis? Are you a virgeen?' realising I was still speaking like Borat.

'No the foreskin, it's strange,' she laughed.

For the second time in a day I wasn't sure how to respond,

'It's rock 'n' roll and I like it.'

We had sex as a catalogue of old jokes raced around my inebriated brain. After a few minutes of fumbling around on the floor my drought was over. I had collected the flag of a notoriously tough country.

'Wawaweewa that was nice,' I told her as I got to my feet.

I skipped through the now deserted main square in drunken delirium talking to myself, proud of the situation I had got myself into. Had my new Kash-like arrogance made me irresistible to women? Or had I just met a slut? I wasn't really sure but I was happy.

If Mark had been sat at a bar watching me skip past he would have remarked,

'Look at him sir, that boy has lost it.'

I would have agreed.

As I rounded the corner to Manga Rosa a thin black shadow approached me from the darkness before standing by one of several street lights. The light revealed the figure of a malnourished black woman.

'Good price, you want me to come to your room?' she squawked.

I brushed passed her without the dignity of an answer and firmly snapped the metal gate to our apartment shut. I passed out in the room on my single bed next to Mark and Katy who shared the double.

The next morning two Australian lads joined us at Manga Rosa. I had spoken to them in Morro but being with Kash and Nash made it impossible to have other friends, especially men. We had mentioned to them both that we would be in Arrial and had since arranged through Facebook to meet up. Their names were Sam and Bobby.

Sam and Bobby were both from Sydney and had kicked off their trip with Carnival. So while my adventure was coming to an end, theirs was just beginning. I was jealous of them, but was happy to pass on as much information as I could. They had a lot to see.

Sam and Bobby didn't like sitting around and were keen to do and see as much as possible. While we were weary and winding down, they were like two children high on caffeine.

We decided to rent out a beach buggy and go for a drive around the coast. Arrial was a small island close to the tourism hotspot of Porto Seguro; there was a lot to places to visit around the area.

We rented a buggy for the minimum amount of time allowed, three days. Bobby and I sat on the back of the Jeep with our arms over the black roll bars as Sam fired up the engine and brought the thing to life. Mark sat in the front with our speakers; he was in control of the music.

The buggy was no more than four foot in height and looked like a toy. It only had three gears but was capable of reaching about 50mph. Being so close to the ground it felt a hell of a lot faster so we were all satisfied.

After fuelling the engine we drove away from the town and headed south towards Tradesco. We had been told there was a dirt road you could take there that was a lot of fun to drive on. The engine roared like a lawnmower on steroids, as we darted round narrow country roads. It was going to be a good day.

As we bumped off the tarmac and onto the sandy back road, Sam asked if anyone else would like to drive.

'Give me the reins son, I drive for a living back home,' boasted Mark.

'You're a field sales agent you tit, hardly Michael Schumacher,' I giggled.

'I'm the one and only Lewis Hamilton,' he replied.

'What black?'

'Sure,' he nodded as he theatrically revved the engine with his gangly right leg.

Mark set off at speed along the bumpy red soil; plumes of red dust filled the air as Bobby and I winced to protect our eyes. To the sides of the road, banks of red earth rose several feet into the air before flattening out to jungle forest. The road cut through the natural landscape, snaking through the wilderness like a river.

Air raced past my face as I stood up on the back of the Jeep to lessen the impact of all the bumps Mark was hitting. The cars brakes and suspension were questionable and sitting on a plastic bonnet you could feel every part of the road.

It was like the three of us were taking part in a rally, reminding me of the tracks on Colin McRae's Playstation game. As we rounded the next series of bends it could have so easily been game over for all of us.

Mark was driving too fast for the road and as we flew down the steady gradient at another blind corner he completely lost control of the buggy. The red Jeep bounced off the crumbling road and the steering locked, failing to respond to anything.

The next few seconds felt like hours as I experienced an extreme slowing down of time. I had all the time in the world to make a decision as we careered around the sharp bend. Should I jump or just sit tight and hope we somehow survive? As the seconds past and the bend opened up I worried that we were all going to die.

The toy Jeep slid across the road from right to left at speed towards the hard face of the embankment. I quickly began to evaluate the safety of the buggy. The roll bars wouldn't help me or Bobby in the back as we both sat above them. We were using the bars as hand grips; if the vehicle flipped I was in no doubt that we were dead.

Sam and Mark would slam into the hard dashboard or through the windshield as I realised the buggy had no seatbelts. It still felt like I had a vast amount of time to decide my own fate. The Jeep was out of control but I felt at total ease.

The car edged closer and closer to the cliff face and with every inch Mark's grip tightened around the large black wheel. He had decided to stay and fight against the inevitable, our lives were in his hands; the three of us were helpless, there was nothing we could do.

The cliff face got nearer and as it bore down upon us I decided to jump. I looked at Bobby and was sure he had decided to do the same. The wind blew against our powerless faces and we knew we had to do something.

It was then I realised that I couldn't. I had all this time and all these options but my body wouldn't move. I looked down at my hands as my knuckles turned white against the black of the roll bars. I was frozen still and my life was Mark's to take.

Like Machu Picchu images flashed through my head, too quickly for me to make any sense of them. I gave up and time stood still as everything fell deafly silent. This was it, the end.

Just as the wheels hit the side of the ditch they caught the road and miraculously started to respond. Mark had hold of the unresponsive wheel as it came back to life. Millimetres from the mound of red earth the Jeep pulled itself back onto the road.

Mark pressed down on the weak breaks as we spun to a standstill. We sat in a shroud of red dust in total silence. The gravity of the situation hit each of us as the adrenaline pumped through our veins. I looked up into the dusty red sky and smiled.

Mark looked at each of us like he had just seen a ghost,

'Lads fucking hell, I'm so sorry I thought we were gone, the thing just wouldn't respond.'

'Yeah what a fucking rush that was, shit it was close,' said Sam.

'I was seconds away from jumping off this thing, me and Gaz would have got mangled,' Bobby contemplated.

'Would have been a Jeep way to go Lewis you idiot!' I joked with Mark.

Mark and Sam swapped seats with Bobby and I and went to the back of the buggy. Bobby calmly drove the rest of the way to Tradesco. We talked non-stop about what had just happened and how lucky we all were to be alive.

We sat on a near deserted stretch of beach with a slab of beers and celebrated still being alive. While the situation was far from funny we gradually began to joke about it; it was our way of dealing with what could have been a disaster.

Tradesco was a total blur. We could have been anywhere as none of us could concentrate on where we were or what we were doing. The event brought the four of us closer together than any amount of time could. We had shared something that we would never forget. We agreed that when we returned to Arrial we were going to hit the booze hard.

We arrived back in Arrial by late afternoon and parked up by the supermarket that sat in the corner of the large square. Bobby and Sam went in to pick up some alcohol while I sat outside with Mark who began beeping the Jeep's pathetic horn at any young ladies that passed.

We got talking to some girls from Israel who had just come out of the supermarket loaded with shopping. There were four of them, two of which were attractive. Mark showed off our motor before kindly offering them a lift home,

'I'll run you home if you like; I'm a master of the roads in these parts.'

The girls gratefully accepted his request. I got out of the car as they got in and watched as Mark ran a red light and sped off out of the square and out of sight.

'That boy has completely lost it,' I said to myself.

Mark met us back at the apartment where we sat outside on the porch drinking and talking rubbish. Mark seemed rushed and it was clear that he had something he wanted to tell us.

'Those girls are well up for it lads. I took them home, well close to their home as I got lost, and they said we can all go round. I'm not sure where it is, but when I see it I will know. We have to go, I'll regret it otherwise,' he said.

'You don't know where they live though mate, I'm sure we will see them out,' I said.

'Mate it's nailed on, please I don't ask for much.'

'Ok sir, why not?' I agreed.

We walked through the dark residential area of the town, away from the lights and crowds of the bars on Broadway looking for a house that Mark had never seen but was convinced was nearby. It was mission impossible.

The town wasn't that big and after an hour of frustration we bumped into one of the girls outside a local mini-mart. We had gone past their house five times; I couldn't help but laugh.

The girls had rented a house for five days; it had several bedrooms over two floors and its own private pool. Sat around the TV in a large living space were all seven of the girls. They were watching MTV while chatting and smoking a shiesha.

The girls were all fairly sober; I wish the same could have been said for us. I sat down and asked for the shiesha before telling them about what had happened to us earlier that day. We had taken round a few bottles of vodka but only a couple of the girls seemed interested in drinking any of it.

Israeli people were difficult to talk to. I wasn't sure if it was simply because of cultural differences or something else. When I met a talkative person from Israel it came as a surprise and was not expected. Kfir, who we met in Playa Del Carmen, was an example of this. He had told me that many people in Israel feel they are hated by the rest of the world, hence why they all stick together when they travel abroad.

After an hour conversation in the house dried up and began to feel awkward. When I'm drunk and feel awkward I tend to overcompensate to mask my feelings. In the girls house that is exactly what I ended up doing.

The shiesha made its way back to me and I sucked on the pipe for almost three minutes. I blew the smoke out fiercely looking like a human smoke machine, as everyone started to laugh. Sam was clearly not enjoying himself as he didn't like Israeli people and had nothing to say to them. He set me a dare, knowing there was a high possibility I would do it,

'Mate I dare you to go for a piss and come back out starkers.'

I felt like a performing monkey at a zoo but thrived in the attention. After necking the rest of my vodka I let it be known to everyone that I was going to the toilet.

I locked the door and quickly removed my clothes, before looking in the mirror to confirm to myself that I was going to do this.

'Are you ready?' I asked.

'Yes I'm ready, are you?' asked my reflection.

'Yes, let's do this!' I said.

We both nodded at each other in agreement. I turned the silver lock, the door clicked and the door swung open. I stood in the girl's front room with my penis tucked between my legs; they looked on in bewilderment. A chorus of laughter was followed by the flashing of cameras and for reasons unknown to myself, I started to finger my fake vagina.

As the seconds passed I felt a wave of embarrassment; Sam and Bobby sat on a sofa that rested against a large open window in hysterics. Rather than shyly return to the bathroom, the idea to finish in style drowned my drunken brain - I was going to run and jump through the open window.

I pranced across the hard slate floor like an astronaut before hopping over Sam's head and through the frame of the window. As I fell towards the bone hard grass I got entangled in a hammock that was resting low down between two trees.

I rested on my back looking up and the sky and laughing. I knew that once again I was being an idiot, but I didn't care as everyone seemed happy.

I got to my feet and asked Mark to throw my clothes out of the window. To my surprise he did. I stumbled back into the house and theatrically bowed to my audience before pouring myself another tall glass of vodka.

I found it hard to make eye contact with anyone for a few moments as I realised what had just happened. My eyes scanned the room for something to look at or involve myself in. I picked up one of the girl's novels from the kitchen unit that was written in Hebrew.

I had never seen a Hebrew book and it made no sense to me whatsoever. I stared blankly at the pages and realised that the book read from back to front and the writing looked like it was upside down. Rather than put it down I decided to draw attention to this fact as more drunken ideas flashed like beacons in my mind. I stood up excitedly and started chanting while pointing at the book,

'Upside down and back to front Hebrew, Hebrew

Upside down and back to front Hebrew, Hebrew hey

Hebrew, Hebrew hey, Hebrew, Hebrew Hey

I can't read this fucking book

It makes no sense, it is gay'

I was marching around their house out of control on alcohol and the sheer joy of being alive. Nothing could bring me down. I was euphoric and didn't care what anyone thought of me.

The best looking of the girls was called Mor; she was the reason that Mark had offered to give the girls a lift in the first place. She was small with olive skin and thick curly hair. She was shy but had a look that suggested that maybe she wasn't. I liked her.

I pulled some change from my pocket and asked if she would give me a kiss. She snatched the money from my hand and pulled me towards her. She pressed her lips against mine and kissed me passionately in front of everyone. It was worth the money and I wanted Mor.

Mark looked annoyed; his face said everything I needed to know. I knew that he wanted to kiss her, but knew that he would not begrudge the fact that I had. I sat with him as it dawned on both of us that the best way to get with girls was to act like complete wankers.

'Kash was bloody right mate, we just need to act like twats,' Mark said.

'Strange isn't it, I think it is just about making an instant impression,' I said.

The girls all began to loosen up as they all began drinking as we became more comfortable with one another. Bobby went to the bathroom hand in hand with one of the girls as Sam sat on the sofa refusing to talk to anyone that wasn't me, Mark or Bobby. Mark sat sucking back beers, bemoaning the fact that not one of the girls seemed interested in him.

Before leaving the house for the Chopperia I allowed Mor to cover my face in make-up. She told me I was the craziest person she had ever met. I was unsure whether that was a good thing, but at least I had made an impression.

I woke up in bed next to Sam who had passed out in my room; Mark was nowhere to be seen. I stared at the cream walls and towards the bathroom trying to gather my thoughts. My camera lay on the floor on a pile of my clothes; I reached for it hoping it would provide some answers.

I scrawled though countless photos of me standing naked in the girls' house and the memories came flooding back, what had I been doing? We had met Laura, Katy and Vanessa at the Chopperia, the photos proved this but I could not recall anything past leaving the flat.

Sam's eyes opened and he smiled,

'Mate that was a fucking awesome night, you were absolutely hilarious.'

'I don't feel all that hilarious now mate, where is Mark?' I asked.

'No idea mate I think he is with that Katy girl, he has the Jeep too,' he grumbled.

I stepped out into the morning sun bleary-eyed and confused. I felt like a vampire, convinced that the sun was going to melt me. It was either that or overnight I had contracted meningitis and was now light sensitive. I wasn't sure which of the two scenarios was worse? An immortal vampire or a soon to be dead human being, I couldn't decide so just got on with my day.

On the way back from the shop I heard the sound of a spluttering machine behind me. I knew before arching my head it was Mark and our red Jeep. I ran back to the room to give Sam his water before jumping into the buggy with Mark.

'Good morning sir,' he gleamed playfully.

'Hi mate, you are absolutely steaming, I'm driving,' I ordered.

He shuffled into the passenger side of the red plastic death trap.

'What happened to you last night you weapon?' I asked.

His tone went serious,

'Mate I should have been locked up! I took the Jeep out last night and crashed it into a tree, a tree!'

He had spoken to a man outside the bar that could get hold of some good cocaine. Rather than walk he followed the man with Katy in the Jeep. The man's friend was not at home so the trip had been unsuccessful. On the way back into town he foolishly gone off road and had crashed into a tree. It was fortunate that we were on an island with little to no police presence. There was no way I was letting him drive again.

Both of us were still drunk as we aimlessly meandered around the town. The town was beautiful, all low-lying and white-walled. The sun just bounced off everywhere. The town was so laid-back that most shops didn't open until late afternoon when everyone returned from one of the surrounding beaches.

Behind the main square, above a huge drop into a tropical valley, was an old church that was in immaculate condition. To the left was a small version of The Christ Redeemer statue. Arrial was a calm, charmed place and we stood out because we were the opposite.

I picked some beers up from the supermarket as we decided to keep drinking rather than surrender to the effects of a hangover. As I bought beers Mark took a large Pringle umbrella from the table of an unopened restaurant; it was hot and he sought the shade. The umbrella locked under the back seats and covered the backs of our shoulders.

Outside the off-licence we bumped into Julio, the gentleman that had rented us the Jeep. He asked if we were having a good time, the answer to anyone with eyes was clear,

'Yes Julio, the Jeep is amazing.'

Mark asked Julio if he knew where we could get any drugs,

'Julio amigo, coca?'

'Si, follow me my friends.'

It was as easy as that. Before we knew it we were tailing Julio in the Jeep. Julio was a dark-skinned lanky local who was riding on a large dark blue dirt bike. We followed him through the town's narrow backstreets into the heart of the local community.

I drove along in the small red Jeep with the stolen Pringle umbrella spilling out and a beer in my hand. It felt like an early mission on Grand Theft Auto; this town had no rules and we had no boundaries, so it was the perfect match.

We pulled up outside a decaying house on the outskirts of town. Julio motioned to us that he was going inside and that we should wait. We sat with the engine purring for ten minutes and still there was no sign of him. As the seconds ticked by I began to get suspicious. Mark and I sat fully aware of the ridiculous situation we were in and revelled in it.

'Mate this is hilarious. We are in a toy car driving around on an island in Brazil with the sun beating down on us,' he said as he threw back his ice-cold beer.

'I know mate, imagine been sat in an office back home staring out of the window into the rain, waiting to go home. Sitting there watching TV and lamenting the fact that tomorrow will be exactly the same. Horrible sir,' I said.

'If I could travel till the point of losing it I would,' stated Mark.

'I think we are close to that already, look what we are doing.'

'Shall we jog this and get Sam and Bobby?'

'Sure.'

With that I spun the micro machine around and we swiftly made our way back to the apartment to get the boys.

Bobby looked like a massive bear; built like a wardrobe but not fat. He had short light brown hair, and a well-kept ginger beard. He was an extremely laid-back, honest individual who didn't seem to have a care in the world.

Sam in comparison was well groomed and, despite having short hair, he took longer to get ready that either me or Mark. He was a good looking, friendly guy and both Mark and I were happy to have met both of them.

I jumped into the back of the Jeep and let Bobby drive us over to see the girls by their pool across town.

The pool was full of Israelis. Given the amount of men it looked like a massive homosexual hangout. We entered the complex drunk and drawing attention to ourselves with all the noise. I looked at the pool and started singing,

'All of Israel in the pool do-dah, do-dah,' repeatedly over and over.

At Mark's request I then ran and did a huge belly flop into the water; as if we had not created enough of a scene already.

Mark sat on a sun lounger laughing as the pool community looked on in horror. I swam around chatting to everyone and after a few minutes the majority had warmed to me. I tended to follow up offensive stunts by being nice to people, subconsciously I still knew where to draw the line. The problem was it was my line, not theirs.

We loaded the four-person Jeep with some drink and seven people and headed off towards one of the nearby beaches. We drove down Broadway past the rental office playing tunes and singing like we were on our way to a car rally; some looked on smiling while others were clearly displeased.

Bobby pulled up at the base of the steep hill in a car park by the beach. As we got off the Jeep a fat local in a Hawaiian shirt pulled up and aggressively snatched the keys from his grasp. He then opened the back of the Jeep and pulled at the engine.

'What the fuck are you doing?' Mark asked.

The man hit Mark across the chest and before we could react he had driven off in a cloud of smoke with the keys to our Jeep. We had no idea who he was, or what we had done. He had achieved nothing as we knew the Jeep started with any key. Sam used his room key to move the Jeep to another car park as we were convinced this man would be back. I was scared about what may happen and I didn't want to get involved with the police.

We spent the day on the beach talking to locals and drinking. The day turned to night as we witnessed a beautiful sunset over the ocean while finishing the last of our vodka.

A young couple sat on beach towels twenty metres from us entwined in each other's arms, enjoying the beautifully calm evening. We were all smashed, sat at a table and talking about the night ahead. I had an idea and acted on it accordingly.

I grabbed the iPod speakers and slowly crept up behind the couple that were now lying down on the sandy surface. I placed the speakers by their heads and pressed play before looking back at them and insisting that they enjoy.

As I walked back towards my table of friends they looked on wondering what I was doing. The calm lapping of the waves gave way to Elton John's classic Don't Let the Sun Go Down on Me. The couple looked back over at our table and gave us the thumbs up.

Sam came running over from darkness of the car park telling us that someone had covered our buggy in palm leaves; we decided it was time to leave.

We got to the car park and our little red machine had been covered in palm leaves; someone had tried to hide it but they had been unsuccessful. We cleared the vegetation from the car and tried to start the engine. It wouldn't work, someone had tampered with it and it didn't take a genius to work out it was the man in the Hawaiian shirt.

As Bobby stared into the engine using my iPod as a torch, we heard the sound of a motorbike racing down the hill. I looked up and saw the headlights flicker through the trees like a searchlight. It was definitely coming for us and I was petrified.

The sound of the bike was deafening against the now deserted tranquil beach. The lights got closer as what now looked like a train headed at us at speed. The bike broke hard metres from our Jeep and slid to a stop, covering us in dust. It was Julio and he was joined by the man in the Hawaiian shirt; it was clear we were in trouble.

The atmosphere was hostile as they began shouting at us in Portuguese, a thankless task as we had no idea what they were saying. I looked at Laura, Katy and Vanessa and suggested that they leave; it had nothing to do with them and they were not to blame.

We stood in the darkness of the car park as Julio then said a word that we all understood: Policia.

My face dropped to the floor. Bobby and Mark argued with Julio as Sam and I cowered behind them. The amount of drink we had consumed was only going to count against us; arguing was futile.

As tensions ran high Julio asked us to drive the Jeep back to the rental office. We were to return the car and were not entitled to a refund. It came out that they had seen us drive past with seven people in the car, it was a breach of the rules and considered dangerous. The fact we had been drinking seemed of little concern to them.

We drove the Jeep back to the office in convoy like four school children that had been ordered to visit the school head.

'At least the police haven't been called, if indeed this place has any?' I said.

Much like the near fatal accident on the road to Tradesco, this situation tightened the bond between the four of us. We sat outside our Posada in hammocks drinking and joking about what had happened the last few days.

Mark and I had started to keep tabs on the girls that we had slept with on the trip. He was currently winning 10-9. It was not something I had concerned myself with early on as I had not felt it was important. I had slept with more people in the last four months than in the twenty-five years that preceded it. I had Mark's influence to dubiously thank. He had helped open me up on this trip. I think it was something that I needed to get out of my system. I had taken sex too seriously but I now saw it as something different, it was a bit of fun.

Mark worried that I was going to beat him in this game. He convinced himself that Mor would have sex with me. The competition really mattered to him, so I goaded him that the scores would be equal by the end of the night,

'I will draw level Mark. Mor well wants it!'

'He will beat you by the end of the trip mate, it's nailed on,' joked Bobby.

'No chance,' Mark slurred defiantly.

Out of drunken desperation he got to his feet, downed a large glass of vodka and said,

'You're not drawing level mate, not on my watch.'

We all looked at him smiling as he ducked under my hammock and, rather than leave the complex, he walked to the left and banged on the

German girls' door. I looked at Bobby and Sam, before we collectively said,

'No fucking way!'

Mark entered the girls' room. I caught a glimpse of the stone-faced German lying on her bed in black underwear smoking. I turned to Bobby, now concerned,

'He couldn't could he?'

Her slightly less attractive friend came out of the room smiling as the three of us descended onto their porch like hyenas.

'Leave them alone, give them some privacy,' she said.

The smiles on each of our faces must have scared her. Bobby looked like a crazed cat about to pounce on an unsuspecting mouse. This situation was unbelievable.

We decided to return to our hammocks and just wait for the aftermath. We each sat wondering if he was actually doing what we thought he was.

'He couldn't could he? Her face looked like cold porridge and she's German,' I said.

'I don't know, he seemed pretty serious,' said Sam.

'I hope he fucking has,' laughed Bobby.

Five minutes later Mark stormed out of her room, slamming the door behind him. We all sat laughing as he marched past us without uttering a word and into our room. Something had gone very wrong.

'Shit what has he gone and done now?' I asked Bobby.

'Who knows let's find out though ha-ha.'

I leant over the white wall separating the two porches. As her friend opened the wooden door I saw the dark haired monster half naked on the bed smoking a cigarette. She was so ugly I bet her pillow cried at night. I lent round and looked at Sam and Bobby,

'Mark has stooped to a new low boys.'

I walked cautiously into our room drunk and trying my best not to laugh. Mark was not in the main room, I could hear him groaning in the bathroom; he was having a shower. I walked into the bathroom and looked down; he was cowering on the floor as water fired down at his naked body.

'Mate what have I just done? That was horrible.'

He was visibly shaken.

'You didn't mate did you?' I asked, already knowing the answer.

'I did mate and it was a deplorable act, she stank,' he shuddered.

'Did she taste like Cig-a-rettes?' I replied, impersonating Forest Gump.

Mark sat in the shower in a state of shock for an age. I decided to leave him to come to terms with his inner demons. The only positive to take from the situation was that he had now opened up a clear two point advantage in a game that only he cared about.

Mark eventually recovered from his ordeal as the water washed his sins down the plug hole. He came outside to modest applause and poured himself another large glass of vodka.

A few hours later he was dancing outside the Chopperia with a random biker's crash helmet moulded around his head. It was Friday so the square was alive. People danced on the streets, drinking at cocktail stands and having a good time.

Mark and I got chatting to two lads from London called Teddy and James. They had flown out to Brazil just after Carnival and were making their way from Rio up to Salvador. We found the two of them hilarious, and they took an immediate shine to both of us.

Teddy looked like Phil Mitchell from East Enders. He was short with a shaved head and a deluded sense of strength and importance. As with our friend Craig, he communicated by shouting.

James had shaggy brown hair and piercing blue eyes. He looked very much like the former Libertines front man and habitual drug taker Pete Doherty.

As the night descended into drunken chaos, the Israeli girl from the first night approached me at the bar and told me that she was horny.

'I want you English boy,' she said.

The problem was that I really didn't want her. I had decided the morning after the incident that she bore a striking resemblance to Batman's nemesis The Penguin. Any chance of a repeat performance subsequently died with that image. I looked at her and said,

'I can't sorry, it's my friend's birthday, have a good night though.'

She waddled off with her short arms slumped either side of her body and sat back in the corner of the bar with her friends.

The Chopperia was heaving with people so I grabbed Mor and asked if I could walk her home.

I walked her home away from the crowd of people. We arrived at the gate to her home and stood for a moment. I realised she was not going to let me into the house. After a long kiss she confirmed what I was thinking,

'You can't come in, the girls are all inside.'

'I can leave then it's not a problem. Or you can come to mine?' I suggested.

She grabbed my arm and took me to the pool that sat to the right of the main house. The water was lit up and gave off an orb of blue light. We sat by the water's edge together, it was silent and no one else was around. We kissed again and within a few minutes I was in at the deep end.

I woke up momentarily confused with a sore neck on the sofa of Mor's house. She brought me some food from the kitchen and said good morning.

I heard someone coming down the stairs and could instantly recognise the voice, without looking I knew it was Mark. He pointed at me with a big friendly smile painted across his face. I knew exactly what he was thinking,

'The two point lead is still intact.'

We walked back to Manga Rosa sweating in the morning sun like two homeless dogs. After being quizzed by Bobby and Sam we all went around the corner for breakfast. I decided to get some Acai as I felt awful. I always ate Acai when I felt ill.

Acai is a berry that apparently is a super food. In Brazil it is served ice cold in a small tub or as a thick purple drink. It is typically covered with granola and banana and always made me feel better.

We bumped into Katy, Laura and Vanessa who told us that it was their last day in Arrial before they moved on.

The last thing that I wanted to do was spend another day on the drink but that is exactly what happened. There was no fighting it.

The day on the beach once again descended into night as our drunkenness clouded time. Days and nights, as at Carnival, were slowly merging into one big mess and there was no Kash or Nash for us to blame.

On the night we had people round to our Posada, including an American couple we met on the beach called Alice and Mike. Alice was a lot of fun and looked gorgeous; she looked like a Californian sorority girl. Mike was far more conventional looking and far more uptight.

Our party spilled out into town and we were all off our heads. Mike had given each of us a small line of cocaine. Sam, Bobby and I declared that we did love each other,

'It's not the drink or anything, I fucking love you guys.'

'I love you too, I love everyone,' Sam shouted enthusiastically.

'You are both my brothers,' stated Bobby as his huge arms clawed around us both.

Hallucinating on the coloured lights of the dance floor, I jumped around the bar until the early hours of the morning. No one could touch me, I felt free without a care in the world.

As dawn broke Mark, the girls and I stumbled through the streets of Arrial with Ted and James. We were stopped by an old man with a steel drum around his neck and a set of Maracas in his hands. He had lost his mind,

'I play you all a song, a good song, a good song.'

We sat at the front of a supermarket drinking while listening to this crazy old man bang his steel drum with the end of his maracas. The girls stole bags of crisps from a stand at the front of the store but no one seemed to care - until the police showed up.

'They do exist after all,' Mark said.

I walked away from the supermarket back to room as the police asked us all to leave. I passed out instantly in our room as Mark kept the party going on the porch.

I woke up four hours later and looked across at Mark's double bed. He was fast asleep on the double bed with Katy and the two lads from London. They looked rotten and the room stank. I looked on the bedside table and saw that two of my antibiotic capsules had been split in half. The white powder sat next to the empty shells in a series of lines. Had they snorted my antibiotics? I had to get out of the room, so I went for a walk.

The room sounded like an abattoir full of retarded children as the four of them awoke in unison a few hours later. I sat outside on the porch reading as they crawled out of the dark room and into the sun.

Doherty had pissed on the bed and they were all dripping wet. Rather than apologise he danced around the room naked singing Can't Stand Me Now by the Libertines.

'An ending fitting for the start,' I said to Sam who was sat with me.

'He has completely lost the plot, what is it with this place?' Sam replied.

It was time for us to go somewhere new. The girls left later that day. Mark and I only had a week of our trip to go. We booked a bus with Bobby and Sam for Rio, but had to wait a few days as all the buses were full.

We spent the next two days relaxing in Arrial without drinking any alcohol whatsoever. We did the sort of things that most people would do: ate at nice restaurants, sunbathed and we even managed a day trip to the neighbouring town of Porto Seguro - a tourism hotspot wildly considered the Blackpool of Brazil.

Paraty

We arrived at Rio bus terminal at midday and decided that we would travel down the coast to Paraty. I had seven days of my trip left and wanted to see some new places before going home.

We found out that Radiohead were playing an open air concert in Rio a few days before we planned on leaving for home. Their name was all over large billboards on the way into the city and we couldn't believe our luck.

So with a few hours to spare at the station we got a yellow taxi across town to the venue, hoping to buy some tickets.

I told the old man at the kiosk that both Mark and I were students, using my UK driving licence as an international student card. It worked and drove the price of a ticket down by 50%.

With tickets safe in hand we arrived back at the bus station and boarded a bus to Paraty in good spirits. We would be back in Rio in a few days for the concert and the penultimate few days of the trip.

Paraty is a historical colonial town located four hours south of Rio on the Costa Verde. We got off the bus in torrential rain at 10:00pm, checking into a Posada a few hundred meters from the town centre. The receptionist sat watching a TV that hung in the corner of the entrance. I looked up and saw the images on the screen; Sao Paulo had flooded and cars were floating like bars of soap in a dirty bath tub.

'That looks serious fucking hell, never seen a city like that,' I said.

'Look at the weather, we are going to lose our tans if it doesn't stop,' Mark moaned.

As the weather was so bad we just decided to have an early night.

The next morning we walked through the cobbled streets of Paraty, staring at the aged whitewashed buildings that looked like they hadn't changed for hundreds of years. The low-lying buildings contrasted to the steep mountains and lush green vegetation that drowned the area; my eyes darted in every direction to take in as much of this town as possible.

Sunshine filled the quiet streets as old men in brimmed hats ambled down the wide roads with horses and carts. The clip clop of horse hooves vibrated off the cobbled streets; it felt like I was on the set of a period drama.

I expected to turn the next corner to see knights arresting a local store owner for witchcraft, before marching him to the town centre to be hung in front of the honest town folk. It was a unique town; you could tell that things had happened, battles had been won and lost.

We walked through the streets towards the ocean that lay to the back of the town, and stood proudly by the side of the huge bay was a quaint old church.

The church, the Capela de Santa Rita, was the oldest church in Paraty. According to the plaque outside, it had been there since 1722. This town was quite unlike anywhere else we had visited and I wasn't sure whether that was a good or bad thing.

After lunch we hopped onto a bus to a neighbouring village called Trinidade. We had heard it was home to a beautiful beach and we wanted to take full advantage of the good weather.

I stared out of the window of the bus listening to The Enemy on my iPod. My ears listened to the lyrics that moaned about the limp reality of life in England. I couldn't help but think about having to live my life once more by the alarm and waking every day at eight.

Surrounded by a sublime tropical coastline, I changed the music and resolved not to worry as I knew that every little thing was going to be alright. I was appreciative of where I was and wanted to savour every moment, taking as many photographs in my mind as I could.

The beach was spectacular. It cut into the bay that was surrounded by dark cliff faces and elaborate rock formations; it looked like a water park. We relaxed for the afternoon in the sun before returning to Paraty by late afternoon.

Our room was huge; one of twelve rooms set around a low-lying courtyard. The thick wooden door split in half, much like what you would find in a stable. The walls inside were yellow, we had two large wooden beds and it was comfortable.

Mark decided that we should try and get some weed as it was clear that the town offered little in the way of nightlife.

We left the room planning to buy some weed and sit by the old church by the water with a couple of beers. Mark asked Luis on reception if he could help. Luis had told us on arrival that if there was anything we needed, we only had to ask.

'Luis, Amigo, is it possible for you to get us some weed?' he asked cautiously.

Luis looked around reception to check that no one could hear him. Satisfied he looked at us both and grinned,

'For you guys no problems, give me a few hours.'

Two hours later there was a loud knock on our stable door; it was Luis and he was on time. He walked into the room with a very serious look across his face and asked that we lock the door. I slammed the door shut and bolted it across the middle with the clumsy black lock.

'Did you get us some weed?' Mark asked.

'I got something better for you,' replied Luis who started to relax. 'But you cannot tell anyone.'

'What is it?' I asked inquisitively.

Luis reached into his black rucksack and pulled out a white plastic bag. He unravelled the bag and emptied the contents onto our small wooden dining table. It looked like cocaine and there was a lot of it.

'Is that what I think it is?' I asked.

Luis just smiled. He was confident that we would prefer what was on the table,

'This is the best that Brazil has to offer. I like you guys.'

I wasn't too keen on the idea. Mark suggested that we should buy a few grams to take back to Rio for the Radiohead gig at the end of the week.

Luis could sense that we were not sure. As Mark and I discussed what we should or shouldn't do he racked up six huge lines, using his card that he scraped against the wooden table by the far wall. He snorted two large lines, one up each nostril without hesitation.

'It is the best, I take it all the time, please my friends try before you buy,' he joked.

In Brazil our experiences with drugs had not been positive, so we had stopped buying them; his offer for a sample was a good one.

Still not convinced, I asked Mark to go first. He arched his back over the table as the lines disappeared up his nostrils with the help of a rolled up bank note. He rocked back upright and started at me like a rabbit caught in headlights,

'Mate this is really good, please you have to try it.'

So I did.

We bought two of the twenty grams that Luis had brought to our room. He said that if we wanted more we only had to ask. He hugged us both like brothers and said he would see us later on.

Luis was a friendly man of average height and build, with a bald black head. He was a part-time receptionist and the town's full-time drug dealer. I joked with Mark as we both started to come up from the hit of cocaine,

'Chocolate and the Charlie factory!'

'Ha-ha that's class, he is a quality little chocolate man.'

Paraty was not the best of places to be high on coke and 6:00pm was not the best time. We walked aimlessly around the beautiful old town for hours. We toyed with the idea of eating at restaurants before admitting we were not hungry. We went onto the Internet but couldn't focus on the screen. There was nothing for us to do; we were in complete limbo.

Hours passed before we ended up back where we started, in the room. I hadn't blinked for a few hours and the sea air had started to hurt my eyes. We lay listening to music and talking.

We tried to plan the last few days of the trip; it was clear neither of us wanted to go home. We decided that we would try to get jobs at a hostel in Rio.

'There has to be some way of delaying the inevitable, imagine working at a hostel - it would be genius,' I said.

The next morning we walked down to the harbour after deciding to spend the day touring the neighbouring islands aboard a pirate ship. The crew aboard our vessel were far from the fearsome bunch I had pictured. Mark and I sat at the front of the boat and realised we were the only single people on board.

'Have you noticed that everyone is with someone sir?' I asked Mark.

'And you are with me my dear boy. Least we have banter,' he replied.

Our sea captain was a likeable black man in dark sunglasses and a vest. He looked like an American rapper. I looked at Mark and joked,

'What do you get if you cross a pirate with a paedophile?'

'I don't know, you? Why do you know so many jokes you nipple?' he asked.

'Arrrrrrrrr Kelly,' I replied, ignoring his question.

The ship was huge and wooden, with large white sails. The colonial church and streets of Paraty drifted into the distance and we set sail out onto the big blue watery road of the Atlantic Ocean.

I hung from the large white sails as they flapped in the wind. I was pretending to be Jack Sparrow as Mark sat listening to his iPod and going under about a range of trivial matters. He was worried about his back, his suspected broken toe, his bank balance and the henna tattoo he had got in Arrial.

Unlike the tattoo he had got on his forehead, Sponge Bob had refused to wash away. The ink had gone but it had given way to red spots and seared skin. He was the proud owner of a pink scar of a square with wonky eyes and deformed limbs.

'Mate it's fucking horrible, imagine if it had been on my head? I would never be able to have sex with anyone ever again. My life would literally be over,' he moaned.

I thought for a moment about that situation and laughed before responding,

'It's not though mate, it's on your arm. No one will see it and at least it's a story. It's something to remember the trip by so calm down.'

'Mate you would go under about it as well. Look at the pink wanker, it doesn't even look like Sponge Bob, it's a mess,' whined Mark.

'Like your toe and your back?'

'Exactly mate, when or if I go home I need patched up big time.'

Things were back to normal once again, Mark was just being Mark so I laughed and chose to climb back onto the sail and let the sea air brush over my body. I felt like a pirate and wished that I was.

At the first stop I dived off the boat and crashed into the cool waters. This place was another world to the one that I knew and I loved it. As the day progressed, the boat anchored next to different islands and floated in the clear blue waters that matched the pristine skies.

Come late afternoon the sky turned grey, clouds assembled overhead like a well-drilled Roman army ready to attack. As we pulled into the harbour the heavens opened and the first deluge of rain burst down from above.

That night Mark and I booked our tickets back to Rio de Janeiro. We chose to leave at 8:00am the following morning; so decided to pack our bags and have an early night.

We argued in the room for hours on what we were going to do with the cocaine we had bought from Luis.

'You can take it mate it was your idea,' I said.

'No way mate, we should just leave it here,' Mark said.

'You are a tit, what was the point then?'

Both of us were paranoid at the best of times. I always thought that the worst was likely to happen. The chance of being caught with drugs on one of thousands of local buses to Rio was minimal, I knew that but I argued with Mark like it was inevitable.

'If I take it and get caught then you are going down with me,' I said.

I lay on my bed trying to think of elaborate way to transport the small amount of narcotics. I suggested to Mark that we bought a dog and placed the bag up his or her arse.

'Why would we buy a dog you weirdo?' he asked.

'If a sniffer dog suspects anything, the police will just assume that their law abiding dog is frisky. We will have to buy a good looking pooch just in case sir.'

'Stop talking bollocks.'

I chose to ignore him and continued,

'I haven't seen any dogs in Paraty, only horses. Maybe we should get a horse and shove the drugs up its arse? Though I reckon taking a horse onto the bus may rouse more suspicion than a dog. We need a simple idea mate.'

'I will sort it if you agree to take in onboard,' Mark told me.

The next morning I nervously boarded the bus with my bags. We had put the drugs in my empty camera case. Mark had put the small sealable bag into my camera case, using two plastic carrier bags as gloves. As I laughed he explained,

'I don't want to get my finger prints on the evidence.'

It was hilarious watching him carry out the procedure; it was the most delicate and concentrated I had seen him all trip. I imagined him painting eggs at Easter and couldn't stop laughing.

The bus was not a laughing matter for either of us; we were living dangerously. We sat down near the back of the bus leaving the camera case in the overhead storage near to the front. We had thought it through; we were two modern day pirates setting sail for the big city aboard a bus.

Every time the bus stopped so did my heart. I was convinced that the bus was going to be overrun with undercover police. Nothing would surprise me. Two hours into the journey back to Rio my fears were realised.

Four armed police officers climbed up the stairs onto the bus and into the middle aisle. They looked down the coach and slowly but purposely made their way towards us at the back of the bus. I sat motionless as the next five years of my life flashed through my head. I wasn't going home after all, I was going to a Brazilian jail.

As the men got closer they started to slow and each removed their hats before stopping a few rows in front of us. They looked at the passengers on the bus and smiled before sitting down in a row of empty seats. They just needed a lift back to Rio. I breathed a sign of relief, we were going to be fine.

Rio De Janeiro

For the final time we arrived in Rio, feeling more comfortable than on our first visit. We ignored the scores of yellow taxis and got a local bus to the Copacabana. We heard that a hostel there was looking for two barmen; we thought we were the perfect candidates.

The hostel sat half a mile from the beach in a downtown residential area of the city. It was a hundred metres from one of the busy roads that cut through the huge urban landscape.

Che Lagarto was a beautiful hostel, much larger than it looked from the street. We spoke with the manager at reception who informed us that there was only one job available. She also told us,

'The hostel is full tonight but I can book you in for tomorrow. You should try Hostel Bamboo around the corner.'

We checked into a shared room at Bamboo. The beds slotted into the room like Jenga blocks. From a bird's eye view, the plan of the room resembled that of an old slave ship; thankfully we were not chained to the floor - but the beds were.

The staff at Bamboo did not like us. The receptionist looked like the actor Vin Diesel with his waxed head and muscles, and through his body language and attitude it was clear that did not like Mark. Unable to move or breathe in the room, we decided to sit outside in the courtyard and get drunk.

The courtyard was small; it was more of a back garden with a small bar decorated with Christmas lights to the rear. It was flanked at each end by high rise housing.

We were joined outside by four girls who were staying on the slave ship with us; they were all from York in England, and were just starting their trip through South America. I told them about some of our experiences while we worked our way though a bottle of Natasha vodka.

It started to get late so the neighbours began complaining about the noise in the yard. I looked at my watch, it was only 11:30pm so we ignored the grumbles and continued to have a good time.

At midnight a man in the neighbouring building threw a bucket of cold water out of his third floor window in our direction but missed his target. We decided to take the party to a nearby bar as he was clearly annoyed.

The bar we chose was unremarkable at best; it was really quiet. The problem in Rio was the same in any large city; you needed to know where to go between the six of us we had no idea.

Armed with a fresh bottle of vodka we returned to the hostel and sat around a table in the garden trying to be quiet. Mark and Jessica went up the stairs giggling towards the room. I sat outside in a drunken daze staring up at the clear night sky.

The silence was broken as I heard a loud voice screaming from the first floor of the hostel. It was a man's voice and someone was clearly in trouble.

'What was that?' one of the girls asked nervously.

'We're about to find out,' I replied as I sucked back on my cigarette.

Footsteps bundled down the stairs beating like a drum and increasing in noise as they drew nearer. Seconds later Mark appeared at the door with his bags, behind him stood Vin Diesel. He looked furious so Mark left fast.

Mark had been caught by Vin in a XXX situation with Jessica, resulting in him being forcefully removed from the hostel. We had only been there for a few hours but it was useless as he had made up his mind. Despite being caught sucking on Mark's penis like a pacifier, Jessica was allowed to stay. It wasn't right and Mark was rightly fuming.

'Why are you kicking me out, are you not allowed to have fun here?' he barked.

'No, not in public places and not here,' replied Vin.

'What about Jessica then?' Mark asked.

'I will deal with it,' he said.

Mark stormed off and away from the hostel; the chronicles of his dick had once again landed us in trouble. I decided to leave with him so went upstairs and grabbed my still unopened bags. Rio was not the sort of place to be wandering around at 4:00am on your own; Mark needed me, I was his knock around guy.

We stumbled over to Che Lagarto where thankfully the current barman Josh was clearing up; we had talked to him earlier that day. He let us through the security door and into the hostel where several travellers sat around tables worn out after a night on the drink.

As I sat talking to Josh at the bar, Mark made a beeline for a heavily set Canadian girl with curly blonde hair. He had been caught halfway through the act at Bamboo and could seemingly only think about one thing.

Moments later he was walking hand in hand with this lumberjack of a lady to her room, leaving me on my own. I had left the other hostel to make sure he was ok and now it was me that needed some help.

Josh was staying across town and couldn't offer me a place to stay; I wasn't sure what to do but by this point was too tired to really care.

I wandered down to the beach and sat on an empty bench watching the sun appear from under the ocean as I drifted in and out of consciousness. I began to worry about getting robbed. I was sat with all my belongings alone on the deserted beach at 5:00am in a city known for its crime rate. I was dog tired but knew I had to get up and walk.

I decided to swallow my pride and return to Hostel Bamboo as it was my only option. I stumbled into the reception and asked the bald wanker if I could have my bed back,

'Can I just go to my old bed please?'

'Yes but you will need to pay,' he replied.

'Can I just pay half? Check out time is in four hours,' I asked.

'The bed is full price,' he smiled.

I reluctantly handed over the money that I had previously been refunded and went up to sleep on one of the chained bunk beds. I was annoyed at Vin Diesel, but more so at Mark for being so selfish. At least he hadn't knocked peanuts out of my hand I thought as I drifted off to sleep.

The next morning I woke up as Mark hit me around the head with a pillow,

'There you are you nipple, how random was last night. That guy downstairs is a right idiot. Anyways get up I've checked us into Che Lagarto, let's drop off your bags and get on that beach.'

I grumbled back at him as my head was spinning and I was shattered.

As we left the hostel Mark threatened the manager when she refused to refund him for his night's stay.

'You broke the rules. We will not refund you, I am sorry,' she said.

'Fuck you then, I'm going to write bad reviews on this place. I don't care if I have to create fifty profiles, I bloody will. It's a fucking joke I didn't do anything wrong. I'm going to say you have bed bugs, the lot,' he threatened.

'Please calm down sir, there is nothing I can do,' she replied.

Seeing Mark angry always made me laugh. His threat towards the manager was hilarious; I told him such as we walked to Che Lagarto and he was not best pleased.

'Mate you sounded like a right geek. You have just told the manager you are going to log onto a computer and start a hate campaign. Why don't you email her friends and tell them she is horrible and smells of farts you nob?' I joked.

'Fuck off, it's not right and you know it,' he moaned.

Mark was too nice a guy to be angry; it was obvious that he wasn't going to do anything. He just needed time to calm down.

I checked into Che Lagarto with Mark and spoke with the manager who said that she would do her best to find us both work. As it had been Mark's idea to get jobs I told him that he could take the job at Che Lagarto and I would look elsewhere. I had four days to find something or I would catch my flight back home. My plans were where they always were; up in the air.

Josh showed us both around the small bar at Che Lagarto. Essentially the job involved getting cans of Heineken from a fridge and passing them to people; it was something I was confident both of us could do. The bar was only three metres in length, but open on both sides. One part opened out onto the small courtyard while the other opened into a small room with a pool table. I was jealous that Mark had this job as it was the easiest in the world.

The manager of the hostel was a young woman called Nati. She was an extremely warm character with tied back mousy brown hair and a beautiful large smile that was temporarily ruined by metallic green braces. Nati offered to ring around hostels in Rio on my behalf telling me to go and enjoy the beach.

Mark and I promised ourselves that we had to have an all day drinking session on the beach in Rio. It was so busy and there was so much going on that it couldn't help but be fun. Mark suggested that we should spend the day fulfilling this promise,

'Mate, what is wrong? Today is the perfect opportunity, the pre-gig drinking times. It will be amazing sir, of that there is little doubt.'

I resisted his constant pleas, still shattered from my lack of sleep and annoyed about the previous night. He had still not apologised. I finally buckled under his persistent pressure at 2:00pm,

'Ok, get me a Caprinha you nob sack.'

'It is about time my good man, about time,' he replied.

The eagerly anticipated day of heavy drinking had begun.

Ipanema was alive with people from different backgrounds enjoying different aspects of the beach. Local people played football by the sea, no doubt dreaming of one day playing at the Maracana for Brazil. Holiday makers lay on sun loungers, enjoying the weather and reading. Scores of backpackers lay on towels listening to iPods and drinking. Wherever I looked something was happening.

The loud vendors called up and down the beach offering drinks to those that were thirsty, food to those that were hungry, and lotion to those out of sun cream. The beach was a melting pot of culture and activity; blessed with colour, noise and an exciting atmosphere.

Mark and I sat on deckchairs by the ninth lifeguard tower on Ipanema. We sat drinking ourselves into a stupor and drawing attention to ourselves. The beach in Ipanema is segregated into different numbered zones; it was something Kash had made us aware of in Salvador. He told us,

'You two should go to section seven, it's where all the cool people hang out.'

I didn't trust Kash so I had asked at the hostel. It turned out rather predictably that tower seven was the gay friendly area of the beach; Kash had tried but failed to trick us. Section nine was the 'cool alternative space' and it was in that bracket we classified ourselves.

The vendors kept swarming around us and seemed to feed off our energy and stupidity. We shouted at several of them and asked for them to come over. Rather than buy a drink or some cheese on a stick we wanted to buy their uniforms,

'Name your prices my friend.'

'Ice tea is $3rls one cup,' he replied.

'Not the tea my friend, the jacket,' I asked as I stumbled to my feet.

The bright orange Matte Lao Ice Tea waistcoat and matching orange cap cost me $50rls, which I felt was money well spent. The man sat down with Mark and laughed as I walked off down the beach with his small metallic kegs of ice tea and cup dispenser.

'Matte,' I screamed as I stumbled like an old drunk in front of a sea of people who all looked up and smiled but bought nothing.

As the day wore on people drifted from the sandy beach back behind the large buildings and into the concrete maze of the city. Mark and I remained on the beach drinking. We were joined by several locals whom we bought beers, it was good to be around local people.

I loved how friendly all the vendors on the beach in Rio were, and I appreciated how hard they worked for such little reward. I didn't know how the government worked in this country but I guessed that the poor got no help whatsoever.

I liked the city's scams and the people's enterprise. Rather than simply begging, most of them were industrious. The motivation for these people to work was to provide for their families and simply survive. Competition was fierce and if some could make money by walking up and down the beach day after day selling drinks to lazy tourists then I applauded them.

I wondered why the homeless back in England didn't have this drive or initiative to make money. I sat on the beach drinking with society's have nots and I couldn't help but think that people back home should use their initiative more. These men, despite their struggles, seemed happy and I was happy to buy them beers.

We arrived back at the hostel by late afternoon in high spirits. This contrasted sharply to the mood of everyone at the hostel. It was tense and everyone was quiet; it was clear that something had happened.

Josh filled us in as we sat at the bar and opened a couple of cans of Heineken,

'We aren't allowed to leave the hostel lads. An hour or so ago there was a shoot-out. Apparently it was drugs related. The police had managed to catch two guys that came off a motorbike on the corner of the road just up there. The sound of gun fire was incredible, I was shitting myself.'

'I keep forgetting how dangerous this city is,' I said.

This event served as a reminder of the dangers of a city like Rio. The wild location with the mountains, the jungle and the beach were matched by the wild nature of the city's inhabitants. The divide between the rich and the poor were massive; Rio was a city of extremes, physically and socially.

Undeterred by an undercurrent of fear, Mark and I showered before coaxing a group of people to come with us to the Radiohead gig. It promised to be incredible.

Outside the tube station we met up with Bobby and Sam. Given the volume of people packing the streets leading up to the venue we were lucky to find each other. Crowds of people marched off the decaying streets and dispersed into the arena.

I began to get nervous as we approached the entrance. Mark had made me carry the drugs and I had turned into a Paranoid Android, convinced that the Karma Police would find them and have me arrested.

I took a deep breath and sandwiched myself between Bobby and Sam before pushing myself through security and into the arena. I felt a wave of relief wash over me and gained a second wind; I felt awake and I was excited about the night ahead.

It was a clear evening, as the numbers in the crowd grew there was a huge cloud of expectation over the main stage. Radiohead were known the world over, but this was the first time that they had played in South America.

The stage was awash with colourful lights and lasers. As their set began a series of flashes blinded my vision as the roar from the crowd drowned out the music. I sat on Mark's shoulders above the crowds, surveying the now packed arena. We were part of a blanket of bodies rocking in Rio to music that reminded us of home. It felt like a lucid dream and we were captivated by it.

I danced around, rambling to myself incoherently as the alcohol once again took hold of my body and my mind. I was enjoying losing my inhibitions and control. I was with friends and felt completely safe.

Mark was being the creep and I was being a weirdo as the two-hour set reached its conclusion. We each grabbed hold of the girls that danced by us and kissed them. Mark then kissed me as he always did after a few drinks,

'I love you mate this trip has been incredible. Let's stay and live in Rio as rogue barmen.'

I woke up half naked in the wrong bed at the wrong hostel covered in shaving foam. I looked around the room wondering what had happened after the gig.

I stumbled out of bed and rested my hands against the post of the bunk. Above me Sam was fast asleep and in the far corner Mark was passed out, like me he was covered in shaving foam.

I wandered into the hall of this foreign hostel and bumped into Bobby.

'Mate what the fuck happened last night, why the hell am I covered in cream?' I asked,

'Sorry mate, I'll take the bullet for that. We got back here at like 5:00am and you and Mark were lying in that room. It is a total coincidence, you came back with two of the Swedish girls I think,' he said.

The jumbled images began to piece together in my tattered mind. Bobby was right, we had come back with two girls from the gig.

'Ha ha shit of course. Mark fell out with one of them so they fucked off for food as soon as we got back here. We must have passed out in their beds; pretty glad to be honest as I'm pretty sure they were both pigs in wigs,' I joked.

'I rooted one of them the other day,' admitted Bobby.

'Definitely ugly then,' I replied.

I was still drunk from what had been a special night; rather than go back to bed I went with Bobby into his dorm next door. Lying on the middle of three bunks was Elsa, who I had vague recollections of meeting at the concert.

Elsa was French and had huge breasts; one had to assume that they were not her natural pair. She was older than us, I guessed in her early thirties? There was something that I found intriguing about her. I asked if I could lie down with her. She didn't seem to object to the idea nor was she overly enthusiastic. I climbed in and as she rolled to face the wall I gently put my right arm around her.

I began to relax and drifted off to sleep with my arm around someone who was essentially a stranger. I woke up soon after and lazily began stroking her back, she moaned and it was clear she enjoyed it.

I reached down into her pants and before I knew it she had turned round and we were kissing. As things heated up Bobby crashed through the door and into the room. He looked at us in shock before instinctively leaving. As the door closed he peered through the tight gap and winked at me.

'This is the life of the dorms,' purred Elsa.

I got up several minutes later as I heard Mark stirring next door. I left Elsa lying in her bed, slightly confused at what had happened, but happy with the result. I must have been at my drunken best at the gig as it took little effort to get into her bed and I wasn't that good looking.

Mark and I left the hostel and made our way back to Che Lagarto. We spent the day pottering around the hostel, and eating loads of food from the surrounding street stalls.

We had both fallen in love with these small balls of meat that looked like kiwi fruits. They were called Kibes and were delicious with hot sauce. The best thing was that they were cheap.

While walking through the streets of Copacabana we came across a shop called The Miami Peep House. Within seconds Mark had vanished inside and up the stairs.

He bought tokens for a private show as I stood in the lobby feeling uncomfortable and unable to meet anyone in the eye. The last thing I wanted to do was stand behind a screen in a dark room watching a naked woman revolve around a stage, but I did.

I stood uncomfortably looking through a piece of glass no bigger than an A4 piece of paper at the woman on stage. I looked around and saw nine or ten other pieces of glass; four with men's faces pressed against them. Worried that they could see me, I took two steps back into the darkness of my small cabin and peered through the window at the stage.

The stage revolved at a steady pace as this woman snaked up and down a silver pole peeling off her clothes. I felt uncomfortable watching her from behind glass, it felt dirty and as two of her fingers slipped into her hairy pussy, my two minutes' viewing was up.

Back at the hostel I asked Nati if she had managed to find any jobs at hostels in Rio. I had been to meet the staff at Stone on the Beach earlier that day but their response had been lukewarm at best. Nati had no news so it looked like being my last Saturday in Rio.

We sat the hostel still recovering from the night out and watched Snatch on DVD. One again there was gunfire outside of the streets. At first I thought it was coming from the TV. We were instructed by staff to stay inside and the green iron door of the hostel was slammed shut.

The atmosphere once again was tense and I started to feel nervous. We could all hear bullets flying through the sky as panic hit this action-packed part of the city. Half of me wanted to climb over the fence and see what was going on while the other wanted to get as far away as possible. I decided to stay inside and concentrate on the film.

In the few days at Che Lagarto Mark and I had made friends with everyone that worked there, including the kitchen staff who had kindly made us both a free staff meal.

Che Lagarto was a new hostel replacing an older development a few streets away in Copacabana. To celebrate they were having a big party at the old place. It promised, according Bruno who was working at the hostel, to be something special.

Despite still feeling special myself, I decided to have a shower and go to the party. Mark was settled at the hostel safe in the knowledge that he would be staying so did not feel the need to go out.

'Mate if you are going home on Monday you should go,' he said.

I left the hostel with Bruno. Bruno was from the northern state of Bahia and was down for a few weeks to see how the hostel was run. He was going to manage a Che Lagarto hostel in Salvador and was learning the trade from Nati here in Rio.

Bruno was a nice man; the same height as me at 5ft 11 but clearly a lot fitter. Most people in Brazil were toned; they had the advantage of good weather and beautiful beaches. Most of their free time was spent outside on the beach or playing sport, I envied the lifestyle.

Too much time in England is spent inside, mostly because of the climate. The majority of people at home work inside, drive to and from work inside a car, before sitting and watching television night after night in the comfort of their homes. It was a lifestyle that I had detached from and no longer wanted to be part of. Far from being normal I thought of it as insane.

One of the things I loved about travelling was being outside and interacting with real people. Rather than watching a soap opera on television you are constantly part of one; involved in your own plot twists and turns on a daily basis. It was what living should be about.

Armed with a bottle of vodka Bruno and I joined the party along with some other people from the hostel. The party was a honey pot of men, mostly Israelis. Had I been a woman or gay it would have been special, but it wasn't and I missed Mark.

I bumped into Caffa who I had not seen since Florianopolis. As I chatted to her I noticed that she was grinding her teeth and speaking at a thousand miles an hour.

She told me that her friends had all gone back to Australia and she was now on her own.

'I'm keeping the dream alive buddy continuing my trip,' she said.

'I can see that my love, just be careful though,' I warned.

'It's all cool, under control my brother,' she replied.

I liked Caffa, she was unique but now she was alien and barely the same person I had met six weeks earlier. She was bent on drugs and I just hoped that she was going to be ok.

She reminded me of James, who had lost control because of the availability and low cost of drugs on this continent. I wondered if he was still in La Paz wandering the streets, re-running the same day over and over again in his head. I wondered if he still carried the crayon-covered postcards. Was he even still alive? Caffa needed to be careful.

Bruno came over and suggested that we leave the party and go to a bar in Ipanema called Emporio. There was sure to be girls and a more varied crowd so I agreed. It was my last big night in this enchanting city and I didn't want it to end in a decaying hostel full of men.

As we stood trying to flag down a taxi, Bruno smiled and asked if I would like a tab,

'Would you like one of these tabs? I have had three.'

'It depends, what it is?' I asked.

'Acid.'

'What does it do? I have heard of it but have no idea.'

'It just makes you happy, look at me and best of all, unlike coke, there is no side effects.'

He placed a small white paper tab in my drunken hand and continued,

'It will put us in the same mind, it will be ok.'

I trusted Bruno, but was still unsure as in the back of my mind I knew that this was a drug that shouldn't be taken lightly. Had Mark been there I was convinced I would have said no; but he wasn't, he was at the hostel in bed.

I gave in to the gentle pressure that Bruno exerted on me. The devil on my shoulder won the battle, it was my last night and he wanted me to dance with him.

Emporio was a well-known gringo bar sitting a few blocks back from the beach in Ipanema. It was a popular hangout for tourists, drug sellers, prostitutes and Brazilian fortune hunters wanting to meet travellers.

The taxi pulled up at the top of the street as people spilled from the bar and onto the streets dancing and drinking. The cab ride had taken ten minutes and thankfully I was not feeling any ill effects from the acid. I was convinced it was a bad idea and so couldn't completely relax.

Bruno went to the bar and got us both a pint of lager. We stood in the middle of the noisy crowd of people unable to talk. I realised that we didn't have anything in common and began to feel increasingly conscious of that fact. Anxiety pumped through my veins and into every corner of my body. The palms of my hands began to sweat.

I felt my mind start to drift, it was leaving my empty body that stood motionless by the dance floor of a lively bar. Bruno suggested that we go outside. His voice sounded muffled and far away; it didn't even sound like him. I was unsure what was happening but remained relatively calm. I made my way outside without thinking, just following Bruno.

A girl with dark hair came over and started speaking to me, but I couldn't concentrate on anything that she was saying. Instead my eyes fixed on her mouth as it moved up and down, up and down. I looked blankly straight through her, I wasn't there, and I wasn't sure where I was going. Time, sounds and movement were all speeding up and slowing down, I was confused and felt dizzy.

Bruno had also started to struggle; neither of us had said a word to anyone for what felt like a few hours. I was stood outside on the street looking through the houses and high rise blocks towards the beach, still clutching a full pint of beer in my hand. The glass was fixed in my hand and I was convinced that it had somehow got stuck.

Failing to talk to any girls, we walked to the beach and sat on the edge of the promenade looking out at the dark ocean. My mind was flipping out and falling up and down, up and down as my inner voice kept trying to reassure me that it was just the acid, that it would pass and that I should just relax. I had bought the ticket and it was time to enjoy the ride.

I couldn't relax or enjoy anything. I was in the middle of a dangerous city at 3:00am with a stranger. I needed to get back to the hostel before things got worse and reality distorted even more than it was.

'Bruno I need to get back to the hostel, I feel strange,' I muttered.

Bruno agreed and paid for us to get back to Che Lagarto. He told me outside on the street that I was going to be fine,

'You will be ok my friend. Do not tell anyone about this and I see you in the morning at breakfast.'

With that he disappeared up the stairs of the hostel to his private room. I was left with the prospect of laying down in a twenty-bed dorm and was scared to go up to bed.

Rather than wear off, the drugs pulled harder at my mind and dug their nails in. There was no end in sight as I eventually plucked up the courage and climbed into bed. I was surrounded by darkness and covered in a thick uncomfortable layer of sweat.

I lay down on the bed trying to close my eyes, hoping that I would just fall asleep but I couldn't as my eyes flickered. Flashes of light and obscure images sloshed through my mind like a potion in a witch's cauldron. Colours, sounds and objects started to distort, to swirl around my mind and the room.

I didn't know what to do. An army of dancing prawns appeared from a vivid image of the ocean by the bottom of my bunk and marched uncontrollably up the sheets towards my face. I opened my eyes and they were gone. It was just me lying under some thin white sheets.

I looked to my left as the row of undefined bunk beds blurred and flashed, sucking towards me like a vortex in a tunnel. I felt like I was at a rave as strobes of light hit my eyes at awkward angles before vanishing into nothingness.

I turned onto my front to hide my face in my pillow but then began to sink into my bed as it tried to devour me. My arms pressed against my chest and moulded together as I clutched them under my paralysed chin. For a second I felt like I was turning into the world cup trophy but there was no sense of victory or cause of celebration. I was terrified but the voice in my head kept telling me to stay calm. I was safe and it would eventually wear off. My mind was just trying to trick me, but I was too smart to fall for it.

My ears started tuning into conversations as I again slipped into the trip. I sat talking to some Argentinean gypsies, my favourite being a man called Rodrigo. I liked Rodrigo and wanted Mark to meet him, so I climbed out of bed. As I went to hit Mark, who was sleeping above me, I realised that Rodrigo had gone, and then realised that he was never actually there. I began to think that I was going insane and would never get better; panic began to set in as my body poured with sweat and my skin felt loose.

I walked to the bathroom to get some water. I was nervous that there was going to be someone in there but thankfully there wasn't. I stood looking at my reflection in the mirror; telling myself that it was ok as my ego battled against the hallucinogenic effects of the acid.

Part of me wanted to give in, to relax and just see where it was going to take me. The other half of me was scared and worried that if I did let go then there would be no return. I had to fight it, I couldn't let the drug win.

I timidly slid back into bed and under my now soaked sheets. I was dripping with thick sweat but was as cold as I was hot. The air conditioning unit rattled overhead, blowing more cold air into the room; I was convinced that it had also blown in a ghost.

I pulled the thin white sheets over my head trying to remain silent, hoping the ghost would not find me. It whistled and swirled around the room whispering my name; I held my breath and wished that it would stop. I heard a storm outside, there was nothing I could do, eventually it would get me. The room suddenly went quiet. Unsure if it was a trick, I removed the covers shaking wildly.

I sat up in bed, jumping at every little noise like a boy lost in the woods. If Mark rolled over I was convinced it was an earthquake and took cover. This routine continued until morning as gradually the hallucinations faded and the drug began to subside.

I went down the stairs and looked acid up on the Internet. I was shocked to learn that it was the street name for LSD, something I had promised myself I would never take. I was worried about mental psychosis already and I didn't need a drug to tip the balance in its favour.

The site told me a trip could last up to twelve hours, but there were no long term effects from the drug; it was good news and what I wanted to hear so I was able to relax.

I spent my penultimate day in Rio sweating in bed, waiting for the storm of insanity to blow over. I had planned on visiting the Favellas or going up Sugar Loaf Mountain. Unfortunately they both now had to be missed. I lay motionless staring at the uninteresting four walls of the room.

I woke at 4:00pm with a thick layer of slime over my body, so got a shower. I thankfully felt a lot better, but felt nervous and didn't want to leave the hostel.

Mark wanted me to go to a night match at the Maracana between Flamengo and Vasco de Gama. The thought of 70,000 people in a hostile football stadium was terrifying but so was staying in on my own.

I mustered all of my remaining energy and courage and went to the game. I wore my black beanie that acted like a comfort blanket over my head. It shielded me from the thousands of eyes and faces on the way to the ground.

The stadium was full; awash with noise, flags and painted faces, lit up in a huge bowl under floodlights. The atmosphere was magical and the colourful crowd lifted my spirits. I looked around the ground at all the smiling faces. I listened and felt as the stadium came alive and bounced up and down with the fans; it was remarkable feeling, the game felt like a major final.

The game itself ebbed and flowed with Vasco coming out 2-0 winners on the night. The referee gave out an astonishing five red cards; only one of which would have been considered a foul back in England. Neither team defended, it was attack versus attack as the shots rained in on both goalkeepers. I felt like I was watching an arcade game.

After the game we all got into a cab and headed to Emporio in town. It was the same place I had visited with Bruno the previous night.

The bar looked like a converted house. Three large windows opened, allowing fresh air to circle around the tight bar. Inside was a small dance floor no larger than a disabled toilet. Two small bars linked the two main rooms together, as rock 'n' roll music reverberated around the bar.

Bobby and Sam were sat on two chairs around a table by one of the large windows. They had also been to the game and it was good to see them.

Unlike the rest of the group I was not drinking, so after an hour of standing outside on the road I decided to walk back to the hostel and have an early night. I needed the rest.

I arranged to meet Bobby and Sam on what was looking like being my last full day in Rio.

I walked to Ipanema beach the next morning, finally accepting that all good things have to come to an end. I had fallen in love with this city but, as much as I wanted to stay, I knew that it was finally time to accept that I was going home.

I sat on the beach with Bobby and Elsa as Mark lay in the dorm in a world of hurt after a big night on the booze. We were going our different ways; I had become nostalgic and sought conclusions while he was coming to terms with the idea of staying in this mad city on his own.

I drank several beers as morning turned to afternoon, and afternoon turned to night. I sat appreciating everything that had happened, everything that I had seen, and most of all where I was.

Rio was so vibrant, so full of colour and life.

I sat talking to Elsa about life and the decisions that I had to make when I got home. I had put off what many people would call 'real life' for six months; I wondered what people thought real life was? For me this was it.

Elsa had a beautiful energy about her. She was extremely spiritual and believed that if you wanted something enough you could get it.

I had to work out what I wanted from life. I had been negative for too long. This trip had made me realised how easy my life was; my troubles were trivial and my goals were achievable.

My last hour amidst the beauty of Ipanema was a period of great calm and reflection.

I washed the sand from my feet for the last time and got a cab back to the hostel. My head had cleared and I was ready for one last night in Rio.

I returned from the beach to a sea of police and news reporters at the bottom of the road. The ongoing shootings of the past few days had come to a devastating climax. Seven young criminals had been shot dead in cold blood in the sweltering urban backstreets of the Copacabana by our hostel.

People from restaurants, shops and neighbouring apartments flooded the streets as the police patrolled the area with semi-automatic machine guns. As I crossed the road to the locked hostel I saw two black figures collapsed on the curb in a pool of thick, deep red blood. They were both dead.

The sight of the bodies did not shock me as much as I thought it would. Rio was as dangerous as it was glamorous and that was part of its charm. The city was never boring; something was always happening whether it was good or bad.

Had the shooting been in my hometown of Leeds then I would have been more shocked. I looked at the figures as if I had expected it to happen. It was part of life here.

I had sat on the beach seriously looking at my life and where I wanted it to go but maybe that was the problem. Life is short and can end at any moment; the best thing to do is just enjoy yourself and be as happy as you can.

As I knocked on the door of the hostel I began to feel sick. I looked back at the bodies and saw the pain in both their faces that were now caked in blood. Josh opened the iron door and I left the scene.

I walked into the hostel where the atmosphere again was tense. In a bid to calm the situation Josh was giving out beers for free. I sat drinking with Mark who was finally up and about after a day in bed.

After a couple of beers Mark suggested that we go back to the Miami Peep House,

'Mate let's get out of here, the atmosphere is terrible. We should get some food and then go for a little peep. It is your last night sir.'

'I'm going to meet Bobby and Sam later; think that Elsa is out as well,' I said.

'You want to shag her don't you?'

'I'd like to try mate, it is my last night.'

'Come on, let's go,' instructed Mark.

Mark and I left through the front gate of the hostel and onto the street where a few hours' earlier seven young men had been murdered by the police. The killings had been gang and drug related; it was all over the local news.

I wondered if the men that died were bad people. I guessed that they had got into crime out of necessity after struggling in the unsavoury parts of Rio all their lives. I felt sorry for them, it wasn't right but there was nothing that I could do to change it.

I had heard that employers in Rio refused to give jobs to people that came from the Favellas. They were not trusted and it was assumed they would steal. It left many with no option but to steal, not out of choice, but through lack of other options.

The bodies had now gone but the streets were still stained with blood. We walked past a five star hotel at the bottom of the road, having to cross the road as the pavement outside was crimson; stained by the life of someone that never had a chance.

I needed to clear my head and Mark suggested,

'Come on, let's both go have a wank.'

'Yeah ok then,' I agreed.

We walked up the narrow staircase and into the main room of the peep house. Stood at the counter was an elderly black man in a flat cap. To the left on a bright wall was a series of photographs, fifteen in all. It gave punters a look at the girls that were on show. Above each of the tattered pictures was a small red light. The red light for girl number eleven was lit, but the others remained dark.

I scanned the photos as Mark went straight to the counter and asked the man behind it for some tokens.

'Mate you have to get a private dance this time, trust me it is phenomenal,' he shouted.

I was unconvinced by the fifteen pictures on the wall and replied,

'I'm not sure mate the girl the other day was disgusting. She was so hairy it looked like she'd got Bob Marley in a headlock.'

'Ha ha you are a dick, just do it,' he ordered.

With that Mark disappeared around the curved booths and into one of three private rooms against the far wall. I stood looking at the wall, unsure what to do. Ideally I wanted to go find Elsa but I was here now and she could wait.

I decided to take the plunge. It was no different from a lap dance back home and they were deemed as socially acceptable so this was fine. I stood there weighing it up before realising that it didn't matter. Mark was right, why not? I wasn't going to die and if nothing else it would be funny.

As the soft 1970s' music played in the foyer I studied the list of women, this time with more purpose. They were all black and I didn't fancy any of them so I decided to pick the darkest of the lot, number five.

I approached the man at the counter and bought a token for two minutes. I felt awkward and didn't want to be in there for any great amount of time. If it was good I could always buy more.

I opened the thin wooden door and locked it behind me. The room was dark like the public booths but with a wooden stool. I sat down on the stool as my breathing began to shudder, I was nervous.

I sat looking at the large clear screen directly in front of me. In the relative darkness I could see a red velvet curtain hanging at the back of a small stage. In the middle sat a plastic backed metal chair. I took a deep breath and dropped my single gold token into the metre on the right hand wall and pressed the number five.

The light inside the plastic cube flicked on, it was a single bulb. The curtain rustled as the woman's hands pulled them open; she looked at me and smiled. She had a pretty face and was wearing a small black bikini and tiny thong. She looked better than she did on the photograph. She gazed through the glass at me and said,

'Chico muy lindo.'

I knew that she thought I was attractive and it made me felt more at ease. I glanced to the right and saw that the digital clock was ticking down from **2:00**.

1:59 I sat on the stool as she stared in my direction, biting her finger and swaying from side to side like a snake. I waited for her to do something and felt awkward.

1:40 She motioned with her finger for me to stand up as she removed her bikini top. Her breasts were pert but her nipples looked like flying saucers.

1:30 She pointed towards my stool and started to speak through the glass in Portuguese. More confused than ever, I sat back down as instructed.

1:25 She again motioned with her finger for me to stand as her other hand started to play with her now exposed pussy. Again I did as I was told.

1:20 She pointed towards my stool and again spoke in Portuguese. I stood explaining that I did not speak Portuguese. I was really confused but slightly turned on as she started to lick her wet fingers. I sat down again.

1:00 I ignored her request to stand as I was sick of playing musical chairs with this woman. I pointed for her to touch herself. She lay on her chair removing her tiny thong and placing her shiny black heels against the glass. I glanced at the clock realising I had less than a minute left.

0:50 The girl aggressively fingered herself while licking the saucers on her chest. She stared directly at me through the glass. Her eyes moved between my legs and she pointed at my crotch, demanding to see what was under my jeans. I thought for a second as Mark's voice gently prompted me to do it.

0:40 I pulled out my cock that was already fully erect. I felt embarrassed as she could see me but knew that we would never see each other again. It was a guilty pleasure and I had the glass to protect me.

0:20 The woman stood against the glass with a wild glint in her eye. She playfully rolled her index finger and asked me to stand as she turned and pressed her arse against the glass and started to gently rub against it. I stood as close as possible to the glass now wishing it wasn't there.

0:10 She looked at my penis and again pointed towards the stool. Her eyes were transfixed on my cock as she rolled her tongue around her wet mouth. She enticed me forward but once again I was confused. She pulled her chair to the glass and stood on it; her pussy now staring me in the face a few centimetres and a thin piece of glass away.

0:05 Her right arm reached over the glass and finally I realised what she had wanted. Without a moment's hesitation I stood on the stool as her hand met my cock for the first time. I was unsure how I would feel afterwards but I blocked that out and just tried to enjoy the moment.

0:00 The light went out and my two minutes were up. I could make out the girls' figure but it was dark. Her hand, to my surprise, was still running up and down my cock as I clung to the glass worried about losing my balance.

+0:20 Excited by the situation and the intensity of it I finally climaxed. I stood on a small three-legged stool with my jeans around my ankles as my knees trembled and I shot a load of cum all over the glass screen.

+0:30 The girl blew me a kiss before skipping behind the filthy velvet curtain, leaving me alone in the dark. I stood wondering if I should clean up the mess but decided that it would be best to leave it. I quickly fastened my jeans and left.

The acrobatic hand job had cost me just $3rls; the smile across my face was priceless. I walked slightly sweaty around the corner where Mark was stood waiting by the wall of photographs,

'What are you so happy about?'

'I'll tell you outside mate,' I replied.

I breathed in the night air and nervously told Mark what had happened to me in the booth. He refused to believe me at first,

'Ha ha you nipple there is no way that happened.'

'It felt good but now I feel guilty,' I said.

As I explained further he was captivated, wanting to know all the small details. Happy he then proudly declared that I had been with a prostitute,

'Mate you realise that counts as a brass? I have made you like me, brilliant.'

'It's not the same at all mate, she was behind a screen and I didn't shag her,' I replied.

'Did you or did you not get a tug?'

'Yes,' I replied.

'And did you pay her to do it?' he asked.

'Well not really, I dropped a token into a machine, no silver crossed her palm,' I argued.

'Still counts,' he told me.

I continued to protest my innocence but knew he was right. In Mexico City there was no way I was even going into a peep house. Six months later I was stood outside of one arguing with Mark about what classed as prostitution; a lot had changed.

We ate at a sushi restaurant close to the hostel where you paid for food based on the weight of the plate. On the TV reports were still coming in about the shootings close to the hostel. A wave of panic washed over me as I saw the young man's bloodied face pressed against the curb.

After a few beers Mark and I left the restaurant and took a taxi to Bobby and Sam's Hostel Ipanema Beach as it started to rain.

The heavens opened over Rio de Janeiro as a heavy shower of rain blasted the streets, absolving the city for its earlier sins. The blood of seven men washed away down drains and everyone could just forget about what had happened.

We caught a cab down to Emporio as the rain switched itself off, the city was clean.

Mark disappeared home as he was still feeling rough and was devoid of banter. I was annoyed he left without saying goodbye; I was leaving at 9:00am the next morning and knew that I would not see him before I left.

I drank with the boys while keeping one eye on Elsa. I was convinced as I left the beach earlier that there was something there. Whether it was mental or physical I wasn't sure but I knew I had to at least try; there is no room for regrets in life.

As it got later the group of people we were with dwindled. I took this opportunity to ask Elsa if she would like me to walk her home.

'Would you like me to walk you' I asked.

'Oui,' she smiled.

We walked slowly past bars in Ipanema as they closed for the night and then onto the residential streets away from the beach. As we walked away from the glare of the main roads Elsa turned and kissed me passionately on the lips.

I rocked back as she pushed me against an iron fence that was protecting one of several apartment blocks from thieves. She dropped down to her knees as I looked down the deserted street then up the night sky.

We arrived back at her hostel and went out into the back garden through the communal kitchen and sat by the pool. We lay on a sofa lit only by the pool and the night sky as I pulled one point back on Mark. He had won the competition 14-12 but to me it didn't matter, it was the perfect end to my trip.

I arrived back at Che Lagarto just before 6:00am. The taxi sped through the deserted streets of this busy city as it slept. I sat looking out of the window soaking up as much as my narrow eyes could take in. I wondered if I would ever return to this city and I wondered what was next for me.

I checked out of the hostel at 9:00am saying my goodbyes to the staff, and Nati the hostel manager. She said that I did not have to pay for my week's stay. I thanked her and promised that one day I would.

Before this trip I lacked self belief. As I left Rio and made my way to Sao Paulo I knew that I was now a stronger person.

As the wheels of the plane touched down on the runway of Heathrow airport I made a promise to myself; it was one I planned on keeping,

'I am not going to let my life pass working in an office and hiding behind a computer.'

I didn't want that life, my life didn't have to be serious, all I wanted was to be happy.

I walked into the arrivals hall at Heathrow with my backpack on my tired shoulders. A hundred or more people stood by the barriers waiting to be reunited with loved ones, or meeting business associates for the first time. I looked at all of them.

In the crowd I spotted a young man holding a bunch of flowers near the back. He had a nervous expectant look across his face; I walked slowly across the hall. As I got nearer his nervousness disappeared giving way to a full smile. I opened my arms and gave him a huge hug,

'I told you not to buy me flowers, you really shouldn't have,' I said.

He was unable to speak as his skin turned red. He looked me in the eyes the way you look at a complete stranger.

As I stepped away from him I bumped into a small Chinese girl in a yellow coat. She stood behind me looking equally as awkward as he did. She was his girlfriend and I had ruined their reunion.

'Sorry guys,' I said.

I walked out of the airport into the night air alone with a huge smile across my face.